THE SCAVENGER DOOR

**DAW BOOKS PROUDLY PRESENTS
SUZANNE PALMER'S FINDER CHRONICLES**

Finder

Driving the Deep

The Scavenger Door

THE SCAVENGER DOOR

Book Three of the Finder Chronicles

Suzanne Palmer

DAW BOOKS, INC.

DONALD A. WOLLHEIM, FOUNDER

1745 Broadway, New York, NY 10019
ELIZABETH R. WOLLHEIM
SHEILA E. GILBERT
PUBLISHERS
www.dawbooks.com

First Printing, August 2021
1st Printing

To Kelly, who showed me it was possible
to live in this world on your own terms.

Chapter 1

"**N**eptune smells," Fergus Ferguson said.

His sister Isla was slouched low on the worn, brown sofa in the tiny, cluttered apartment above the Drowned Lad, a lightball on dim hovering overhead. She glanced up from her handpad, pushed away a lock of red hair from her face, and scowled at him. "What?" she said.

"I said Neptune smells. It's the damnedest thing," he said. He was perched on an old oak stool, one leg mysteriously a centimeter shorter than the others so that it wobbled every time he took a breath, his chin in his hand and elbow on the kitchenette's island. "I mean, there's nothing particularly exceptional about the atmosphere, and it's so cold everything is frozen, but when you get back from any kind of out-of-ship activity, your exosuit smells. It can take weeks to fade."

"I asked—five minutes ago, mind—if ye knew how to calculate the proper speed and insertion angle for a standard Cricket-class cargo ship carrying five tons of liquid water to land on one of the wind-cities of Neptune," she said. "Not how it smells."

Fergus shrugged. "No one would do that. They'd let the water freeze so its mass distribution is stable. Keeping it liquid would burn a lot of energy and make the whole process harder."

"I'm sure the exam proctors would be entirely happy to give me full credit for writing in *This is dumb and also Neptune smells* instead of doing the actual math they asked for," Isla said. "I am trying to *study* here. Don't ye have something else to do?"

"At the moment, no. Gavin kicked me out of the bar."

"Big surprise there. It's probably the ammonium sulfide."

"What?"

"The reason why Neptune *smells*," Isla said. "Honestly, don't ye know anything at all?"

He got up from the stool, stretched his lower back, and looked around the tiny apartment. "Discovering I have a little sister I never knew about has been fantastic," he said. "It makes me feel so loved and appreciated."

"If ye want to be appreciated, go down to the bar and grab me some chips, then," she said, and looked up again long enough to give him a very big, very insincere smile. "Take as much time as ye need."

At least it was something to do, besides sitting there trapped by his own desperate need to make himself useful to people who had no use for him, however much they all tried to pretend otherwise.

Chips it was, then. He went down the narrow back stairs to the bar kitchen. It was Friday but still early yet, and the *Drowned Lad*'s cook, Ian, was leaning against a counter, staring off into something imaginary behind an opaque pair of movie goggles, utterly unaware of anything around him. Fergus had questioned Gavin's sanity for sticking with the old-fashioned kitchen gear, but it hadn't taken long for him to admit that his cousin's way made for much tastier food. At least when Ian didn't let it burn; there was a basket of chips down in the oil that was already well past golden and heading toward greasy charcoal; Fergus lifted the basket out to drain, and Ian turned off his glasses.

"Oh, hey, Ferg. Didn't hear ye come down. Help yerself," Ian said, then caught a look at the cooling basket and winced. "Oh. I'll start more. Give me a few?"

"Sure," Fergus said.

Against Gavin's earlier injunction, he went back out into the bar. His cousin was pulling glasses out of the autowash behind the counter and stacking them back in the shelves. He looked up when Fergus walked in, sighed, and went back to his task. "I could help with that," Fergus said.

"Done now," Gavin said. He closed the autowash door and leaned back against the back wall, with its display of bottles. "That didn't take long for her to kick ye out, too."

"Yeah," Fergus said. "Apparently, she doesn't want to know how Neptune smells."

Gavin snorted. "Kids these days," he said.

There were only a few people in the bar, though that would change once the rainy April gloom outside settled into the more-comfortable full dark of night. Fergus had been there for a little under two weeks now, trying to assimilate the fact that he had a little sister, born after he'd run off to Mars at fifteen and never looked back. He didn't know where he belonged anymore. If he and his cousin hadn't looked like they could be twins with their matching red beards, no one would ever believe he was even from there. His speech had long since drifted into more Mars than Scotland, more offworlder than Earth.

"This is her last exam, then she'll head back to our folks' place for break," Gavin said. Fergus's aunt and uncle had raised Isla, having realized after Fergus's departure just how badly his mother couldn't. And now his mother was gone too, years past, and it was both a guilty relief and a lingering, painful recognition that now nothing ever would be resolved, made amends for, or even understood.

"Sorry," Fergus said. "I don't mean to get in everyone's way."

"That's not it at all," Gavin said. "But I've been meaning to have a word or two with ye about it. Sit." He pointed to an empty stool at the bar.

Fergus sat. Gavin gestured toward a bottle of scotch on the counter, but he shook his head. He'd never been much of a drinker—except for a few occasions when he spectacularly was—but he had reasons now to need to stay in control. At least in that respect, Scotland so far had been good for him, no unsettled rumbling of electric, alien bees in his gut to add to his unease.

Gavin poured them both water instead.

"Ye came back, and yer full of tales of Mars, and Saturn, and places so far away I can hardly imagine them. And all yer tales are full of people and aliens and running around, doing dangerous stuff. Ye make it all sound like the best fun, but I saw that scar on yer leg and more than a few others like it. And yer ear . . ."

"Some bastard cut it off," Fergus said. He resisted the temptation to reach up and touch the replacement. "It's a new grow. The cells take a while to figure out how to look natural."

"That's the thing. Ye say 'someone cut my ear off' like I'd say I just bought a pint o' milk down at Dougal's. Sitting around, doing normal, boring stuff isn't yer game, Fergus."

"Not really, no," he admitted. "But I'm trying to learn."

"Well, I have a reprieve for ye. A job," Gavin said. "Ye said ye find things for a living, so I've got a friend that needs something found. Should only take ye a day or two, and ye'll be back before Isla heads off. It'll be good for ye."

Ian came out of the back and sheepishly set down a bowl of chips in front of Fergus before scuttling quickly back into the kitchen. This batch wasn't any less burnt than the last.

Gavin closed his eyes for a second, took a deep breath, then opened them again. "Besides," he said. "Isla will bankrupt me on chips alone if she doesn't have to get up and fetch them herself. What do ye think?"

It did sound good, and more than that, it grabbed his curiosity. Fergus had tracked down stolen spaceships, missing art, historic relics, and kidnapped people, all across the galaxy, but he hadn't expected to find any need of his skills here. What rare, interesting, possibly priceless thing had gone missing that he could go find?

"Okay, then," he said. "I'm in. What is it?"

"My friend Duff," Gavin said. "He's lost one of his flocks out in the hills."

". . . Sheep?" Fergus asked.

"Sheep," Gavin confirmed. He smiled. "After closing tonight, I'll help you pack."

———

Duff was one of those men who'd grown into a classic maritime face as he'd gotten older, the lines of it challenging the rocky coastline for title of craggiest topology. When he smiled, it was like watching a rockfall in reverse. "Mr. Ferguson!" he said, and held out his left hand for an awkward shake. His right arm was bound up in a smart cast. "Slipped on th' ice," he said. "Three weeks afair ah can drive or dae much at aw. Bad timin'; mah dug died a month ago."

On the way up to Duff's place, first by train, then in an auto-taxi, Fergus had come up with a dozen reasons he couldn't go looking for this man's sheep, and almost another dozen ways the man could try to find them himself. Now he swallowed all those suggestions and stood next to Duff, looking out into the distant hills that were capped in white, leftovers of a late spring storm three days earlier. "How many?"

"Twintie-two," Duff said. "Mah nephew left th' gate open in th' storm. Ozzie—she's mah bellwether—has a pinger on 'er, but th' signal's bad out thaur. Ah'd drive around until ah pick it up, but ah cannae."

Duff handed over a scanner that was so old, it looked like it could date back to the twenty-third century. "Ye got guid boots, thick soles?"

"I do," Fergus said, though they were loaners from Gavin. As were the pop-shelter, his gloves, and, honestly, most of his clothes. When he'd arrived on Earth, he hadn't been planning on staying more than a few hours.

"Guid. There's some sharp debris up thaur, cam doon ten years ago after some orbital accident. Government cam and cleaned up th' big pieces, but still ye don't want to be running around in yer baur feet. Plus all th' sheep jobby, of course."

"Of course," Fergus said.

"Gavin says yer his cousin? Moira and Ranal's lad?"

"Yeah," he said. "I've been away for a long time."

"Soonds like you've ne'er bin here at aw, th' way ye gab," Duff said. "A' folk said ye drowned in th' new sea."

"Yeah, I heard that," Fergus answered. He'd only recently learned that was what his mother had told everyone after he'd left. It was an easy lie, because those same waters had claimed his father only a month earlier. "I went to Mars."

"Mars, eh? Well," Duff said. He seemed to ponder a few moments, staring off at the hills where somewhere, his sheep were hiding. "Gavin gonnae change th' name ay his bar, then?"

"Not that I know of."

Duff gave a lopsided, one-shouldered shrug. "Ah packed ye a poke ay things ye might need," he said, and gestured to a bag on his porch. "There's flares, if ye need help. Ye hae some skill with herding?"

As Gavin had said before sending him out the door that morning, Fergus's chief qualification for finding the missing flock was being better at getting himself lost than anyone or anything else. *Just think like a sheep,* Gavin had advised.

"I'll find them," he said. "After that, we'll see."

"If ye can gie Ozzie tae follow ye, ye should be braw," Duff said. "Ah'm grateful for yer help."

"No problem," Fergus said. He picked up the bag and his pack. Behind Duff's small farmhouse was the barn, and past that, the fence with its far gate still open. The hills, dotted with patches of snow, rose up behind it all. "Any idea which way they went?"

"Up," Duff said, and Fergus figured that was exactly his luck. He dismissed the auto-taxi, shook hands one more time with Duff, and headed out.

Duff's farm was on the northwest side of the peninsula that had formed when the rising waters had flooded the narrow land bridge between Lochs Long and Lomond. The wind wasn't unbearable, though Fergus did have to admit that his scale of what could be borne might be badly askew; the last windy stretch he'd crossed had been about fifty meters between two halves of Huygens Settlement on Titan, when the winds were a mild sixty kph and the temps a balmy -168 C. If Scotland *felt* colder, it was all just in his mind.

It took him about two hours to reach the first bluff, the snow not yet wholly covering the ground or hampering movement. He settled down on a patch of thin grass and pulled his water bottle out of his pack. After a long swig, he set it down and switched it on so it could filter more water from the atmosphere to refill. In Scotland, that shouldn't take long; on Mars, it would have been hopeless folly.

The sun was out and bright, and he wasn't being hunted, wasn't running to or from anywhere, to or from anyone. There were definitely worse places to be, and he'd been to many of them. He took out Duff's tracker, pulled out his handpad—bought new in the Sovereign City of New York two weeks before, his last one a melted, crushed ruin somewhere deep under the ice of Enceladus—and synced them.

The handpad had better range than the tracker, which he tucked safely back in his pack, but it wasn't picking up anything yet. Somewhere a drone buzzed, too far to see, just on the edge of his hearing, but otherwise, it was just him and the hillside and a ridiculous job. He took a deep breath of the crisp, fresh air and resumed his hike.

When he reached the snowline, he moved laterally along it as best he could over the rocks, until he found the unmistakable signs—visual and olfactory—that a large group of animals had moved past.

Fergus followed.

He found a patch where the sheep had dug through the snow to the sparse grass and clearly had spent some time before moving on. He found another rock and sat, had a snack and some more water, and looked down across the hills, valley, and loch below. He kept waiting for it to feel like home, for him to feel like he belonged there, but it didn't come. Instead, his thoughts drifted to the Shipyard in Pluto's orbit, and his accidental cat, Mister Feefs, rescued from Enceladus and now safe in the care of Effie and his other friends. The cat was smart enough to remind someone if he needed feeding, right? He hoped so, anyway. He had never had a cat before, and the sense of responsibility for it—especially from afar—was an odd and unfamiliar encumbrance.

He had a small room of his own in the Shipyard, with a few of his things, and he missed it suddenly and terribly.

Picking up his bottle, he took one last look down toward Duff's farm, now a tiny toy-sized set of scattered blocks, and saw something glinting in the sun not far back down the slope. He left his pack and bottle and trudged down through the churned-up snow.

It was a small, nickel-colored shard of metal. He turned it over in his glove, noting the unusual fracture patterns along the edge, and the fact that a decade or more out in the weather hadn't dimmed its sheen. The alloy didn't look familiar, but then, he wasn't an expert. He stuck it in his pocket, thinking he'd show it to Theo, the Shipyard's physical engineer, before remembering that Theo was most of a solar system away.

I don't know how long I can stay here, he thought. He also didn't know how he could leave again. He'd come back to break his last, lingering, tenuous tie to this place, and instead found himself unexpectedly fastened down more strongly than ever.

At least he had something to do. He gathered up his things and headed uphill again, after the trail.

Late afternoon, as the sun was starting to settle down below the hills and cast a brilliant orange glow over the snow and against the patchy clouds spreading out overhead, his handpad picked up a faint trace of the tracker at last. It was nearly night when he caught the first sounds of sheep drifting down over the hillside, and by the time he was among them, the dark had rendered the rocky hills treacherous.

He took a bag of carrot sticks out of his pack, dropped a few in a can, and rattled them around until he was surrounded by a sea of dirty off-white. One by one he bribed the sheep, until at last the fattest, wooliest one came up for her share, the red collar and bell and tiny blinking red light of the pingtracer barely visible among her fluff. "Ozzie," he greeted her, and gave her two. "Tomorrow we go home, okay?"

None of the sheep seemed to have an opinion on this, though several butted him with their heads, probably hoping more carrots would fall from his pockets. What stash he had remaining was for luring them down off the hills in the morning.

He took out and unrolled the pop-shelter, a flat mat barely larger than a sleeping bag, and activated it. With a *pop*, it sprang up into a rounded tent, sending the nearer sheep crowding back behind the others. Five minutes later, they forgot it had surprised them and milled around him again.

Fergus sat at the edge of his tent and took an instameal out of his pack. Pulling the tab and twisting it side to side, he watched it heat itself up with more anticipation than the food itself should normally warrant. Then he ate, watching the stars slowly appear overhead as the flock drifted and settled around him. *Now, that,* he thought, picking out constellations one by one that he'd memorized as a child hiding out in the fields, *that looks like home to me.*

He was tired enough that he barely remembered crawling into the pop-shelter and spreading out his bedroll. Under the covers, he closed his eyes, imagining summer crickets that were months away yet, and listened instead to the stamping and occasional snorts of the sheep outside. He could feel, if he concentrated, the tiny power cell in his handpad and in Duff's tracker, the electrics inside the pop-shelter, and a half-dozen other things in his pack. Somewhere deep inside him, there was a resonating hum, like a new sense, seductive and untrustworthy, useful and deadly. He wondered how long it would be before he gave in to it fully, and for the hundredth time in any given day if he should tell Gavin and Isla.

And if he did, tell them what? *I was kidnapped by aliens and they rewired some of my insides?*

If they rejected him, he could go back to his old life and be done with Earth. He had never before had the least doubt that's what he wanted, but now . . .

Damned bloody complications, he thought. If he pretended the faint chorus of power around him was his missing crickets, maybe they would lull him to sleep—

Fergus sat up and groped for his boots and his goggles in the dark.

The wind had picked up and the temperature dropped, and when he unsealed the pop-shelter, he almost changed his mind and crawled back into his sleeping bag. But he could feel it, something just barely registering on his senses, like a sound pitched so low, he couldn't be sure he'd heard anything at all.

It took him ten minutes of standing in the bone-chilling air to decide it might actually be real. He pulled the goggles down over his eyes and fumbled at the manual controls, too used to using them patched through his exosuit instead. He'd left that behind in Gavin's apartment, because he hadn't imagined needing a space suit to rescue sheep.

As soon as he remembered how to turn on the night vision, the hills lit up in glorious, greenish relief around him. He pushed gently through the wall of sheep around his tent and headed uphill.

The progress was slow, not so much for fear of slipping but because he kept losing his bead on where the feeling was coming from and had to stop and close his eyes and focus to find it again.

Ozzie followed at a distance, and the rest of the flock slowly diffused out into the intervening distance between her and the tent, as if to maintain a lifeline back.

It wasn't as far as he'd feared, but it took him nearly twenty minutes of rooting through the snow around an outcropping to find—with his fingertips, naturally—something sharp half-buried in the frozen ground beneath.

After cursing and sucking at his bleeding finger, he grabbed a small, pointed rock, knelt down, and used that to hack the offending bit of debris free. It was another shard, much like the one he'd absently stuck in his pocket, and not the source of the faint call.

Sighing, he bent down until his face was nearly touching the thin snow cover, and peered around among the rocks. Something else, under an overhang and also partially buried, briefly shone.

He reached in and was glad to find it wasn't stuck, because there was no way he was going to get his digging rock in there to work it free. Pulling it out, he saw it was another bit of broken something, irregularly shaped but larger—about half the size of a deck of cards. Its edges were rough and oddly textured in a way he couldn't make out even with his goggles. An inset curve along one surface shone brightly with the starlight above. There were traces of a design etched into the alloy around it, either not language or not a language he'd ever seen, and in his hand he could feel, more surely now, the dim hum of diffuse, disorganized power. He wondered what it had been a part of and how it was still live, but there wasn't enough to make even wild guesses as to the shape of the whole.

It was puzzling but not so fascinating that it kept him from yawning hard enough to pop his jaw. Ozzie bleated at him from a dozen meters below, where the ground had become too steep for her to tag after him.

"Yeah, yeah, I'm coming," he told her as he dumped the new piece into his pocket with the others. "Past my bedtime, too."

This time, when he was settled back into his sleeping bag, he found, with gratitude, that he had no more energy left for either fret or philosophy.

———

Morning brought with it a few centimeters of fresh, light snow, the air filled with tiny, errant flakes that seemed ambivalent about what direction to drift in. As Duff had said, there was poor signal up there, and with snow blowing around, he didn't think a flare would be seen, so he packed his things and started down the hill. He was gratified to find that, a few shakes of the carrot can and some judicious bribery later, Ozzie and her flock followed.

Follow, of course, was a loose term at best. They meandered around him, stopped and started, wanting to graze as the morning sun cleared away the thin layer of new snow and the long-suffering grass reappeared.

As a kid, he'd spent a lot of time roaming the hills with his uncle's flock, which he'd had more patience for than Gavin, and which gave him an excuse to be out and away from home for long stretches at a time. He had learned a fair bit about how sheep moved—or, more often, didn't—and patiently herded the stragglers and outliers back into the main flock before getting them all moving again.

Late morning, more than halfway down the hill back to Duff's farm, he stopped to heat himself up another instameal and check his handpad connection to SolNet. The signal wasn't much better than it had been up in the hills, so he stowed it away again. He wondered if Isla had passed all her exams, but beyond that, what did he really need to know about from the outside world? Nothing.

Gavin had been right to get him out for a few days, and now he mentally kicked himself for not figuring that out on his own. *She's done just fine without you for nineteen years*, he told himself. *All you did was distract her while she needed to study.*

It wasn't so much that he felt guilty for not having known about her all these years as simply that he had no idea what he should do next. There were things you could plan for, or plan around, and then there was family.

By midafternoon, he could see an old electric farm truck trundling through the lower fields toward him. There was only so far it could go before the terrain would become too steep, but even so, it would save him at least an hour of walking, more if the sheep wandered again; he was almost out of carrots, and it seemed a rotten trick to rattle a stone around in the can when he couldn't make good on the unspoken promise.

When he reached the bottom of the hill, the sheep were already absorbing the truck and the man standing beside it in their midst. "Mr. Ferguson?" the man asked.

"That's me," Fergus said.

"Duff sent me. Ah'm Boyd, his nephew," the man said. "An' if he tauld ye ah left th' gate open, 'at was a lie. It was him."

Fergus shrugged. "I needed the walk anyhow," he said. "Want me to help you get them in the truck?"

"I'll pit them in. If ye cood keep them frae gettin' out again, Ah'd be grateful," Boyd said. He lowered the back gate of the truck and unfolded a long ramp. "Come haur, Ozz, ye bad lass," he said, and with a grunt half-guided, half-shoved her up the ramp into the truck. As soon as he turned away to the rest of the flock, Ozzie headed back for the ramp, but Fergus distracted her with the last of his carrots until enough of the others had been loaded in to make her escape impossible. And with her staying put, the others seemed less inclined to try to make a break for it themselves.

"That's done," Boyd said as the last ewe cleared the ramp and he brought the gate up. "Gie ye a ride back doon?"

"Thanks, yes," Fergus said.

"Whit did Duff say he'd pay ye?"

"Uh. I don't think we actually talked about it," Fergus admitted.

Duff snorted. "Yoo're nae smart, ur ye? Lucky if ye don't gie paid with a handshake."

"As I said, I needed the walk. He might've said something to Gavin about it; I don't know."

"Ye're Gavin's cousin, then? Heard ye waur back. Folks said ye went tae the moon?"

"There. And Mars. And Pluto. And a lot of other places," Fergus said.

"They better than Scotland?"

"Different than Scotland," Fergus answered. Boyd got in the truck, and Fergus took the passenger seat. It had been a long time since he'd been in a manually operated vehicle on Earth—not since stealing Gavin's motorcycle when he ran away from home, which started no end of adventure and trouble—and he guessed there must be exceptions for farm vehicles as long as they stayed off the roads.

Boyd tapped his fingers to the start pad and the truck turned on. Slowly they turned around and headed back toward Duff's farm, where the gate was waiting, still open, for its lost charges.

"You ever mit an alien?" Boyd spoke suddenly.

"A lot," Fergus said. "Some are my friends."

"Some not?"

"Some not," he said. "It's a scary, weird universe out there."

Boyd grunted again, and they drove the rest of the way in companionable silence. Duff had made it out to the gate by the time the truck rolled up, and he and Boyd coaxed the flock back in with an enviable ease.

"Come intae th' house fer some coffee while ye bide," Duff said. "Auto-taxi should be haur suin."

Fergus followed Duff and Boyd inside. The farmhouse was warm, the air unmistakably scented with wood smoke. *Twenty-fifth century be damned*, he thought.

"Everythin' went withit trooble?" Duff asked, as he got two mugs down from the cupboard one at a time with his one good hand.

"Here, let me help," Fergus said, and poured the coffee for them both.

"Thank ye," Duff said, as Boyd came in, stamping his boots on the mat before closing the door and slipping off his coat. "Ye fin' anything up in th' hills?"

"You said something about an accident ten years ago, before I headed up," Fergus said.

"Aye, something 'at went wrong up thaur in orbit. Th' suits still comin' by asking abit it every noo an' then, ye find anything, ye see anything, th' usual pish. But there's a reward if ye did."

"A reward?" Fergus chuckled. "What blew up? The King's gold space carriage?"

Boyd snickered, but Duff scowled at them both. "Ne'er tauld us," Duff said at last. "Jist 'at there's a reward fer any scraps."

Fergus could feel the weight of the pieces he found in his pocket, but he didn't need the cred for them, didn't want the hassle, and really didn't want to talk to anyone from the government. *Any* government. "Nothing," he said. "Enough snow on the ground to hide most anything up there, anyway."

"Mah grandfaither tauld me didnae used tae snow in April, when he was a lad," Duff said.

"Well, times hae changed," Boyd said. "Auto-taxi's jist drove up."

"Ah, thanks," Fergus said. He stood up, downed the last of his coffee, and set the mug in the sink. "I'll let you settle up with Gavin, since he made the arrangements. Good luck with your arm."

"Thanks," Duff said.

Fergus gathered up his things where he'd left them on the porch outside the door and climbed into the idling auto-taxi, trying not to yawn. He gave it coordinates, and as it headed back out onto the public roads, he leaned back in his seat and pulled the mystery shard out of his pocket. The faint murmur of energy from it was less a low, monotone hum than the sound of someone singing under their breath, barely audible. The edges with the strange texture he'd felt in the dark had a bizarre pattern of corrosion that he'd never seen before, almost acid-eaten, vaguely fractal, though the alloy that remained seemed pristine. He turned it on its side to look at the shiny insert, frowned at the piece, and tumbled it over and over slowly in his hand. He would swear, if he didn't know it was impossible, that the piece had a different weight depending on which way he turned it.

Fergus set it down on the seat beside him, took out his handpad, and made a 3-D scan of it. Then he opened up a message to the Shipyard and attached the image to it.

"Hey, Theo," he said. "Found this odd little bit of trinket on Earth, but I don't think it's from here. Unusual fragmenting along the edges, among other odd properties. Let me know if you've seen anything like it before?"

He closed the message and sent it, opting for a standard-priority jump-packet routing. From Earth to Pluto was cheap and fast enough as it was, and he didn't figure his curiosity over some ten-year-old bit of space junk required spending triple the cred to cut an hour or two off delivery for something Theo might not get around to looking at for days anyway.

Exhaustion weighed his things down as he hauled them from the taxi and into the train station, just in time to catch the next one down toward Glasgow. He gratefully dropped his stuff onto an empty seat, then took the one beside it next to the window. It was full night, the days still short, and he both missed and didn't miss seeing the countryside go by as the train started to move.

Only a few weeks before, he'd returned a stolen Van Gogh

and more than a dozen other priceless artworks to their museum. Today, he'd rescued Ozzie the Ewe. *Definitely one to remember,* he thought, but mostly because it was the only job in a long, long time that was easily done, without complications, and didn't involve bodily harm to himself beyond a scraped fingertip.

He leaned back against the headrest and closed his eyes, listening to the train and feeling the vibration, feeling the energy of it like a lullaby of distant electrons, and didn't care that he was dozing off.

It was the sound of paper, rattling, that caught his attention, and he opened his eyes to see someone had taken the seat opposite him and was reading a newspaper.

Paper newspapers hadn't existed in centuries. Fergus leaned unobtrusively forward, hoping to spot the date or a telltale headline on the wall of print, when the paper snapped down and he found himself face-to-face with the other passenger.

The man was not a stranger. Nor, despite appearances—and he wouldn't make that same mistake again—fully human. The last time Fergus had seen him had been on the bridge of *Venetia's Sword*, a starship stolen from the Shipyard on Pluto that he'd retrieved at nearly the cost of his own life. He still couldn't pin down exactly what it was that put the Asiig agent over the top of the razor-thin edge of the uncanny valley, from his too-precise, too-uniformly-brown hair, to the way his expressions moved as if someone had reinstalled all his facial muscles backward, or as if he was running biological firmware retrofitted from a set designed for a different humanoid species.

Needless to say, after the Asiig messed around with his own internal workings, he had hoped never to encounter him, or them, again.

"Mr. Ferguson," the agent said.

Fergus's mouth was dry, and he resisted the urge to cough, or lick his lips, or shout. "I didn't catch your name last time," he said.

The man shrugged. "It is such an amazing coincidence to meet you here."

"Is it? A coincidence?"

"Of course not," the man said. "We are always watching. You've been busy."

"Off and on," Fergus answered. So many of his dreams were filled with the menacing black triangles of the Asiig ships, as if they lurked in the periphery of both his waking and unwaking world. Only under the ten kilometers of the Enceladus ice sheet had he felt, maybe, free of them. "Look, what do you want? And where the hell did you find a newspaper in this day and age?"

"Do you like it?" the agent said. "I wanted to blend, to make you feel more comfortable and at ease."

"Right. Are the Asiig here on Earth?" That was a terrifying thought; he no longer dared underestimate what the Asiig could or would do, or try to intuit why.

"Just me," the agent said. "I came to see you."

"Why?"

"To bring a warning. That piece of a thing you found—it's dangerous," the man said.

The fragment from the hill? How does he even know about it?

Anger began to gain ground. "Dangerous to me? What isn't now?" Fergus said. "I'm already a dead man, thanks to you and your masters, if anyone ever figures out what you did to me."

"You misunderstand," the agent said. "Not dangerous to you specifically. Dangerous in a larger scale. To Earth. To us, even, if it had fallen into our hands instead of yours."

"What is it?"

"I can't tell you," the man said. "But we think you woke it up. Very bad of you, even if it was utterly unintentional on your part."

"Then what the hell do I do with it? Destroy it?"

"You don't have the means. Be very careful with it, and who you trust, because like all such things, there are those who covet the fire and do not understand that it burns. And fear for the lives of everyone on this planet until you've returned it, and the rest of its pieces, to their proper place."

"Which is where?"

The man shrugged. "It is all beyond what anyone tells me," he said. "I am just the messenger. The problem is yours now."

He stood, folded the newspaper, and set it beside Fergus. "Enjoy the remainder of your ride home."

Fergus jumped to his feet as the man turned and walked down the train car aisle, to the connecting door, and through. Right behind him, Fergus grabbed the door before it could close all the way and threw it open again, reaching out to grab and stop the man from leaving without some genuine explanation.

The connector was empty, and the car ahead likewise. The agent had vanished.

"Ye bloody fucking bastard!" he yelled. "Stop playing with me!"

The stop for Old Kilbride was coming up. He stomped back to his seat, fuming at his impotence against the Asiig, and gathered his things. Last, he picked up the newspaper where the agent had left it. The text was gibberish, almost English characters, almost English words, but not. It made his eyes hurt to look at the text too long.

He stuffed it in with his other things, shouldered his pack, and got off the train, feeling invisible eyes on him from every direction. If the little humming scrap in his pocket could worry, much less scare, the Asiig, he was pretty sure he wanted nothing to do with it at all.

Always blundering into something, he thought. Whatever mess it was this time, it was his usual bad luck that it was clearly already too late to return to Duff's farm and put the piece back where he found it.

Chapter 2

———◆◄—

The Drowned Lad was an oasis of blinding light and deafening noise as he hauled his stuff the last few meters from another auto-taxi to the curb. Through the front windows he could see Gavin and Ian inside at the bar, and Ian had his fiddle out, which he was much better at attending to than anything in the kitchen. People were gathered around and shouting at each other over the noise, the last few rounds of the night dwindling down to their slow, inevitable end.

After two days of hiking, and a distinctive odor of sheep about him, Fergus wasn't willing to subject his cousin's patrons and friends to his sudden presence, but there was a pull—a need for laughter, camaraderie without obligation—that he found hard to resist.

Shouldering his pack again, he felt it press the object in his pocket against his hip, and whatever desire he had to step inside and take some good-natured abuse dissipated into the chill winter air. Everyone on Earth in danger, the agent had told him. Was there danger before he found it, or was it only dangerous because he found it? You'd think after sending the agent all that way, he could have revealed at least something more useful, more tangible than *oops, you're doomed.*

Why can't everything just be fine for once, without any hassles? he thought.

He touched his hand to the side door plate and went up the narrow back stairs to the apartment without going through the bar, as relieved by the darkness and silence as he had been by the noise below only moments before.

Putting his gear inside the door, he slipped off his boots and coat and slouched into the apartment, too exhausted to pay attention as his mind whirled in concentric circles around the agent on the train, the thing in his pocket, the feeling like he was being led around by the Asiig by just a more sophisticated version of a carrot in a can.

"Oy, ye reek terrible!" An indignant voice rose up from the vicinity of the couch, in the dark. "And I passed my exams, thanks for asking."

"And I found the lost sheep, thank *you* for asking," Fergus grumbled back.

"That I could tell the minute ye walked in the door," Isla said. "Smells like ye brought them all home with ye."

"Don't I know it," Fergus said. "You sleeping on the couch?"

"No, just thinking," she answered. "I'm supposed to go back home tomorrow, spend break with my aunt and uncle. And as much as I love Gavin like a brother, he needs some time alone."

"Yeah," Fergus said. "My fault too, for showing up out of the blue and dumping myself on him. And on you."

He heard movement, and a moment later a lamp turned on dim. Isla leaned over the back of the couch, her chin on her crossed arms, and regarded him. "If ye were going to go somewhere, where would ye go?" she asked.

Fergus laughed. "The shower! And very, very soon."

"No, I mean . . . like somewhere new."

"I dunno. I never made it to any of the Trappists," Fergus said.

Isla laughed. "I have two months before I can start my next series of classes, not two years. Somewhere here on Earth."

"For all the traveling among the stars I've done, I've seen less than a quarter of Scotland, and the only other place on Earth I've been was an hour or so I spent in the Atlantics in the wee hours of the night, freezing my ass—and damned near everything else—off because I forgot about the existence of *weather*. I am a terrible person to ask."

Isla was silent for a moment. "Maybe," she said at last, "but no one else I know has ever gone *anywhere*."

"What does Gavin say?"

"I didn't ask him. He'll say if I don't want to go back to his parents' house to just stay here, even if he'd rather have his place to himself for a while."

"He feels responsible for you," Fergus said.

Isla raised one eyebrow. "He feels responsible for *you*," she said. "For what happened to ye as a kid and no one paying any attention to how bad it was. *Me* is how he makes it right again in his heart."

"It's more than that," Fergus said.

"Aye, but it's still *that*."

Fergus was exhausted and didn't dare sit down on any of the furniture until he'd thoroughly de-sheeped himself. "Well, where do *you* want go?" he asked. "I hear the south of France is still nice, even though they still haven't finished rebuilding their beaches yet. It's warmer than here, anyway. Or Paris; the Nouveau Louvre just expanded their collection of late twenty-first century Morpheist paintings."

"I dunno," she said. She stared at him silently, occasionally wrinkling her nose.

After a while, he cleared his throat. "Uh, I'm going to go wash up," he said.

"You do that."

"Okay. We can talk some more if you want, after. If you're still awake. Or tomorrow morning."

"Okay."

He grabbed a towel and headed for the shower, and in moments was half-dozing under the hot water until his skin began to turn an unhealthy pinkish red. He turned it off and stood there, leaning his forehead against the cool tile, and breathed in the steam around him as if he could store the comfort of it in every cell of his body.

Whatever the agent had been warning him against, there was nothing he could do about it until he'd rested. Certainly, the danger couldn't be imminent, right? *Stupid pieces have been on that mountain for a decade.*

Reluctantly, he stepped out of the shower stall and wrapped a towel around his hips, letting himself drip on the small orange bath mat until he could pull a pair of boxers and shorts on, rub his hair and beard dry with the towel, and abandon his brief refuge.

The lights had timed out and were off again, and the room was silent except for the muffled noise drifting up from the bar below; Isla must've given up on him and gone to bed. He should do the same, but his plaintively whining stomach begged otherwise.

Popping the fridge open, he took out a hunk of cheese and unwrapped it, and then poked around on the dark counter until he found some bread and a knife. He was just slicing off a piece of it when there was a loud bang from downstairs.

"FERGUS!" Gavin bellowed from below.

Fergus nicked the end of his finger at the sudden shout, right next to yesterday's scrape from his hike. *What the hell now?* he thought, deeply peeved.

He went to the door, sucking his cut finger, and stared down the staircase at his cousin, who was at the bottom landing, looking flustered and more than a little upset. The sound of Ian's violin had ceased, and though he could still hear voices from the bar, they were faint murmurs, as of people talking very quietly amongst themselves. Not, Fergus noted, typical at nearly two a.m. in a bar in Scotland.

"Fergus!" Gavin shouted again, not quite as loud, staring up at him.

"What is it? What did I do? I just got home!" Fergus shouted back.

"You have a *visitor,*" Gavin said.

Fergus's first, terrible thought was that the Alliance had somehow tracked him down after his adventures disrupting their rogue operation on Enceladus. But the Alliance had limited jurisdiction once inside Earth's atmosphere, where a hundred-plus squabbling terrestrial governments refused to yield a millimeter of sway. And even if they had decided to come for him, they'd have just burst in with weapons and mowed down anyone and everyone that moved until they got what they wanted.

"Uh . . ." he said.

Gavin stepped aside and flattened himself against the wall. Up the stairs, ducking to avoid the low ceiling, came a two-meter-tall green ball of fuzz on five gangly, multijointed limbs. The alien blinked four large, emerald-dark eyes at him, and broke into a wide, fanged grin.

"Ignatio!" Fergus said. "What the bloody hell are you doing *here?*"

"Vergus!" the alien exclaimed. "We must talk."

Gavin put his hands to either side of his face. "Fergus . . ." he said.

"Don't worry, ey're a friend from Pluto," Fergus cut in quickly.

"Pluto? There are aliens on Pluto?!"

"No, now I am here," Ignatio explained.

Gavin pointed one stern but shaky finger at Fergus. "In the morning, you and I are having a conversation about this."

"Oh, I don't doubt it," Fergus said. He ushered Ignatio past him and into the darkened apartment, and shut the door. After a few moments, he heard Gavin go back into the bar, and voices picked up again, though without the earlier, easy exuberance.

"Sorry about the dark. My sister's asleep in the other room," Fergus said. He went back to the kitchen, turned on the low light over the counter, and finished slicing his bread and cheese. He offered a piece to Ignatio.

The alien shook eir head, then studied a stool at the counter for a few minutes before draping themself over it. "Please, no," ey said. "I have had vood—*food*—recently, during my speedy travels."

"Okay, then," Fergus said, and stuffed a too-large piece of bread in his mouth like a greedy chipmunk. When he managed to swallow, he took a deep, satisfied breath. He hadn't realized just how hungry he was. "So, why *did* you come all the way here? Please tell me there isn't trouble at the Shipyard again!"

Fergus's visit to Earth had been preceded by his Shipmaker friends being kidnapped and held prisoner under the ice of Enceladus to work on an illegal killer drone, and he'd barely managed to catch his breath from that adventure, much less feel ready to take on another. *Or nothing more challenging than Ozzie the sheep, anyway,* he thought.

"No trouble there. Trouble is here," Ignatio said. One of eir long, wiggly limbs pointed at him. "Trouble is *you*."

"What? How? What did I do?" Fergus said.

"Found a thing, yes? I have seen the image you sent for Theo."

"Shit, not you, too? What, did you leave the Shipyard the instant the message arrived?"

"First, I fed my birds, yes? Then I came right away fast," Ignatio said.

Fergus stuffed another fat slice of bread in his mouth and grabbed his pack from the door, rummaging through until he unearthed the strange fragment he'd found. "You mean this?"

Ignatio quivered head to toe, as if something had picked em up by the scruff at the back of eir head and shook em. ". . . Yes," ey said at last. "You can feel it?"

"Yeah."

"Then it is a big danger."

"So I've been told," Fergus said. "And that's *all* I've been told."

"It is a vrag—*fragment* of a thing of four dimensions," Ignatio said. "We—*we* but you only know *I*, never you mind the rest—believed it destroyed in jump space, thrown into the Drift, but I see now, yes, it was not. It should not be active, but something has woken it up."

Fergus coughed. "That might have been me," he said. "I swear it's nothing I did, though. I think we just heard each other."

Ignatio wobbled eir head, a sign of regret. "If this piece is here, so are all the pieces. They will each wake up now."

"Where's it from?"

"I have no answer for that. They have existed since before the history memory of the oldest of all of us."

"They?"

"There are some several tens of them that we have found. Only a very few peoples, of a very few worlds, are trusted to know the way of them. Humanity does not have that trust, no and not likely! But you found it by accident, and you are not so much human anymore, yes? Still, there must now be silence and care, you and I only, zsssshh."

"I still don't understand, though. What does it *do*?"

"It is a door. A doorbell. A . . . peephole? A key. A control light. A signal. A stop-and-go sign. A road. A bridge. A beacon. A call. A map. A channel. A *way*," Ignatio said. "It is a problem to explain. To say a doorkey is best, and also wrong. If put together, a path may be opened."

"And then?"

"And then the bad things on the other side, who we were trying to lock away, will be free to travel through."

"And they're not friendly?"

"They are Vraet—scavengers, devourers. They are not friendly, and also not-not friendly. They are mindless, ceaseless eaters. This is why we tried to destroy the doorkey."

That definitely didn't sound good. "Okay. So, then, what can I do to keep this door from opening?" Fergus asked. He turned the piece over again in his hand, more certain now that the mass of it changed as he did so.

"Find all the fragments, first and fast," Ignatio said. "Then we destroy it for sure this time."

"If it survived the Drift, which I didn't think anything *could*, how can we possibly destroy it? Mount Doom?" Fergus asked. Ignatio blinked all four eyes at him, and Fergus shook his head. "Never mind. Let me also guess, because I know how my luck runs, that if I just toss this in a desk drawer somewhere, or throw it down a deep dark hole where no one will ever find it, we're still not safe."

"No. It will still call, has called, is calling and waking up and building connections to the rest of itself. In time, it will not matter if they are not together. Tomorrow? Two thousand years? It cannot be guessed."

"And the fragments could be anywhere on Earth?"

"Oh, no," Ignatio said. "It is much more easy than that! Only one half of Earth."

". . . Which half?" Fergus asked.

Ignatio wiggled eir limbs in a gesture Fergus had come to learn was the alien's equivalent of a shrug. "Whichever half it was facing when it came back into normal space. When we locate more, then we will know that, yes?"

Fergus ate the last piece of bread and wiped the crumbs from the counter into his cupped hand, and dropped them into the kitchen flash recycler. "So, if I'm understanding you correctly," he said, "I spend two *weeks* here in Scotland, actually making the effort to live like a normal, boring person for the first time in my life, and instead, I stumble upon a piece of a multidimensional artifact that if assembled—or eventually even if not—will let evil beings from another galaxy through to wipe out the Earth—"

"And they will cling to everything and everyone that flees the surface, and that way escape your gravity dimple and spread throughout your solar system," Ignatio added. "I do not think they could cross through your heliosphere on their own? But I am not sure."

"Couldn't just be a doorway to a trio of happy hamsters, could it?" Fergus grumbled. "So, okay, these things will wipe out my whole damned solar system, and in order to stop them, I have to go find all the pieces of this doorkey, which could be anywhere on the planet—excuse me, *half* the planet—all by myself?"

"You have this correct but one thing," Ignatio said. "I will assist."

"Great! That's a quarter of the planet each, with two of us," Fergus said. "That's not impossible at all."

"Three of us," piped up a voice from the couch. "Count me in."

Fergus flinched in surprise and hit the wall switch as Isla sat up and blinked at them over the back of the sofa in the sudden, harsh light. Her hair was wildly disheveled, as if she'd been asleep there.

Which she probably was, until we made all that noise, Fergus thought. *I'm such an idiot; I didn't even check.*

"Uh . . ." he said.

"Is unfortunate," Ignatio said. "Who is this?"

"My sister," Fergus said. "Ignatio, this is Isla. Isla, Ignatio."

"So, you're an alien," Isla said.

"Was that guess hard to make?" Ignatio answered.

Isla scowled at em. "Since you woke me up, I have questions, Mr. Ridiculous Mop-Head," she said. "First, what kind of alien are you?"

"I am Xhr," Ignatio said, the word a rumbling, purring sound that Fergus had never been able to emulate.

"Zir?" Isla asked, getting it about as right as he ever had. "Outside the Bounds, I'm assuming? Because I had to take two semesters of Advanced Exosentient Forms and Culture, and I've never seen even a mention of anything like you."

"Very far, yes," Ignatio said. "I am the only of us to come here. I live in the Shipyard, beside Pluto. We are all friends with Vergus, yes?"

"I suppose. So, what's the Drift?"

Fergus sighed. "In active jump, you enter at a point that's sort of a gravitational eddy, and you move through a conduit toward a similar exit point on the other end. You have to travel through it in the center, because if you drift to one side or the other, you begin to leak—by random atoms—back into real space. The theory is that anything that got caught up in the Drift was essentially rendered down to its component atoms and scattered, effectively vaporized. You haven't had to do the math on conduit trajectory in any of your astrophysical engineering classes?"

"Oh, enough to make you bleed out your eyes," Isla said.

"They just never explained *why* you had to stay in the center, other than it was the only way it worked. So, how did this . . . doorkey thingy? . . . survive it?"

"I do not know," Ignatio said. "It should not be possible, but it did, so my knowledge is inadequate. I will speculate and arrive now at a guess that it is held together by the portion of it that exists in other dimensions, and by its innate function as a bridge."

"So, how does a jumpspace conduit actually work, then?" Isla asked.

"Is a complex matter requiring mathematic," Ignatio said. "But in simpler words, it is a tunnel—"

"No, give me the math," Isla said. "I want to understand the actual physics of it."

The outer pair of Ignatio's eyes blinked. "It is a happiness to tell you," ey said. "It has been the experience of mine in the past that humans do not have interest in the details."

Fergus groaned. "And I'm one of them," he said. "I just spent two days hiking up and down a mountain. I'm going to go to bed, and we can talk again in the morning."

"Not yet! I have one more really important question—" Isla started to say, her eyes narrowing as she stared at him.

Fergus was afraid he knew what the question was, and didn't want to answer it, certainly not now. "That can wait until morning too," he said. Or forever, if he could get away with it.

"But danger—" Ignatio said.

"Also can wait till morning. I can't do a bloody thing if I don't get some sleep first," he said. Also in the morning, he could talk Isla out of getting involved in this and pack her off safely back to his aunt and uncle. "Ignatio, can you find somewhere out of the way to sleep? And try not to startle Gavin when he comes up for the night? He's not used to aliens."

"Especially ones that look like bloody big tiptoeing cartoon spiders," Isla said. "Because if he expects me to find a cup big enough to carry *you* outside with, he is shit out of luck this time, the big coward."

Fergus chuckled. "My da was the same way. Once—" He fell silent for a long moment. Isla's eyes got big, then she dropped her gaze down at the floor, her shoulders slumping. "Our da," he corrected himself. How much did it hurt, that he got to know their father and she never did? There was another thing of broken pieces that he didn't have the first clue how to deal with: their past.

"I'm sorry. It's late and I should go to bed before I become even stupider than I am already," Fergus finished. "You two, try not to stay up all night talking physics. I expect tomorrow will be busy."

"Goodnight, Ferg," Isla said quietly.

He didn't dare meet her eyes as he slunk off in desperate escape to his makeshift cot and sleeping bag in the pantry.

———

Morning came far too soon. Fergus groaned as he sat up, legs and back aching, and rubbed at his face. "Gravity to fifty percent, please," he asked, but both the apartment and the planet beneath it failed to oblige.

In one corner of the tiny, cluttered pantry, atop a half-filled burlap sack of rice, Ignatio had rolled all eir limbs around emself as if ey were nothing more than a giant ball of yarn, and from the faint, rhythmic rocking, Fergus guessed ey were still asleep.

Fergus considered waking em but decided coffee came first. With luck, Isla would sleep until noon, as she was wont to do on weekends, and he and Ignatio could be on their way before she or Gavin realized they were gone. He was a disruption to the status quo, whether they'd tell him that or not; Gavin had his bar to run, and Isla had university, and the space he took up in their lives only took away from those. *They're better off without me and probably won't even miss me,* he told himself, testing the lie to see if it would hold long enough for him to get out of there before guilt hit.

If he left now, would he ever come back? He had no answer to that.

He made his way as quietly as he could out to the kitchen, checking first that the couch was, indeed, unoccupied. Then he started the coffee and leaned against the island, only half-watching it slowly steam and bubble, mulling over the information he had so far. He was still sleepy enough that it took him several minutes to become conscious of a stronger sense of electricity around him than was normal for Gavin's flat.

He closed his eyes for a moment and let himself sink into the sensation until he could identify a direction. Then he walked quickly over to the front window and peered out from between the curtains. There was a spotless white, windowless autovan parked directly across the street, near the post depot. It fit in with the neighborhood about as well as a cow would at a dog show.

Barefoot, still in the rumpled Drowned Lad T-shirt and shorts he'd thrown on after his shower the night before, Fergus left the apartment door wide open as he took the stairs down three at a time. Gavin's rain boots were just inside the entrance, and he crammed his feet into them and snagged the old-fashioned key to the bar's postbox off its hook before he stepped out onto the street, his breath a cloud around him in the still-chill morning air.

He walked with purpose past the van to the postboxes and

made a show of checking Gavin's mail before heading back toward the bar past the van a second time, noting the registration plate. The electrical signal was definitely coming from inside.

Well, now what? he thought. He hadn't really thought this through when he ran down there.

Standing on the slush-covered sidewalk, he made a show of patting his pockets, then turning them out. Then he walked over to the autovan and knocked on the door. "Och! Anyain in thaur? Hae a smoke? Help a guid fellaw oot!" he called, channeling Duff's accent as best he could.

As he expected, there was no response. "Aww, nobody home?" he said, and slapped the van as he turned to walk away. In that brief contact, he let the alien works deep in his gut funnel some electricity up and out through his fingers, shorting the van's systems out. They'd reboot soon enough, but it would definitely get the attention of anyone inside in the meantime.

He walked away, still patting his pockets as he heard the door of the van open behind him.

"Hey!" someone shouted.

Fergus turned around. A tanned, white-skinned man in his early to mid thirties wearing a nondescript brown coverall, his blond hair cropped military-style close to his head, had gotten out of the back of the van, and he did not look at all friendly.

Fergus grinned. "There ye are! Ye hae some smokes fer me?"

"Did you touch my van?" the man asked.

It wasn't enough words to place the accent yet other than *not local*. "Mighta bumped it a wee bit," Fergus said. He drew himself up in his best offended Scots pose. "Thought ye were the deliv'ry guy. Ah dinnae scuff it, if yer askin'."

"Who the hell are you?" the man demanded.

"Willy from Dunkirk," Fergus answered, as if that was obvious to anyone but an idiot. "An' who th' bloody hell are ye, then? Yer not the regular driver."

The man stepped forward, matching him in belligerence, and appraised him head to toe. His gaze lingered briefly on Fergus's leg where, not nearly as long as ago as he'd like to remember, he'd been shot with a harpoon gun. "Nice scar," the man said.

"Tha' wee scrape?" Fergus said. "Arm-wrestling accident."

Behind him, there was a tiny buzz and hum as the van's systems came back to life, way more signal than any normal autovan should be making. The man glanced at it, then back at Fergus. "I'm not your damned delivery guy," he said. "I'm just doing a building assessment for the city. Contractor. Now don't touch my van again, or else."

"Oh, aye?" Fergus put his hands up and waved them around. "Ye puir van might get dirty, eh? If ye nae got any smokes, ah don't care fer yer useless van anyway, nor yoo."

They glared at each other a few more moments, then Fergus shrugged, stepped back, and walked away with a chuckle. The man watched him cross the street, then climbed back into his van, and a few moments later, it sped off.

Fergus waited until it had turned out of sight at the end of the street before heading back into the bar and up the stairs.

In the kitchen, Isla and Ignatio were waiting for him. So was a fresh pot of hot coffee. "What was that all about?" Isla asked.

"Unmarked van out front putting out a lot of signal; made me suspicious," Fergus said. "Occupant's accent was post-American, definitely not Sovereign City of New York or Atlantic States. Maybe Pacifica? Getting him to talk any longer probably would've involved us hitting each other."

"Signal?" Ignatio asked. "What did it feel like?"

"I don't know," Fergus said, unsure of how to describe the

new sense that he seemed to be developing. "It was . . . sharp? Like tiny needles. Like pressing your hand against hairbrush bristles. Intrusive-feeling. Scanners, maybe?"

"The fragment, does it feel the same?"

"No, it's quieter. Like someone humming under their breath. Like a light rain."

"You two are making no sense at all," Isla said. "What do ye mean, how did it *feel*?"

Ignatio bounded off the stool and brought back the fragment from Fergus's pack and set it carefully down on the counter. "Feel the same now?"

Fergus picked it up and cupped it in his hands, then closed his eyes. "Yeah, it's the same as when I found it."

Ignatio blinked eir large emerald-colored eyes, then eir smaller, outer pair. "You said you heard each other? I think maybe it established resonance with you when you woke it up."

"What does *that* mean?" Fergus asked.

"It means the fragment likes you," Ignatio said. "It is a great mystery."

"That an inanimate object could like someone, or that it could like *me*?" Fergus asked.

"Both two," Ignatio said. Ey grinned wide. "The . . . door? Doorkey? It is a thinking thing. Not smart, but thinking, and it perceives. It needs to understand the being it moves, yes? Each tiny piece will want to be whole, and so it will look for energy it can speak to. You were the virst—*first, shgeh,* your picky language sounds!—complex-enough energy source to be near enough to it, so it has imprinted on you."

"Like a duckling?" Isla asked.

"Yes! Like a bird baby, yes," Ignatio said. "Vergus is a big electric bird momma!"

"I am still really lost," Isla said. "And why Fergus in particular?

Everybody has their own internal electrical signals, including the sheep who were there before him, and without being insulting, I can't imagine there's much difference in complexity between them and him."

Fergus coughed. "Mine's a bit stronger than average," he said. "What does this have to do with the van?"

"Some person else is also looking, yes? Duff said a reward. Perhaps this is them? Though I do not know how they found you."

"When I was hiking up the backside of Doune Hill, I heard a drone," Fergus said. "I didn't think anything of it at the time, and it's still probably nothing, but if someone was watching the hill, they'd know I was there. With the sheep, not hard to figure out where I came from and where I went."

"Back up here a sec. You're saying Fergus and this fragment are somehow in tune with each other?" Isla said. She put her hand on the fragment on the counter and pointed at Fergus. "You. Close yer eyes."

He did, and a few seconds later, she said, "Ye can open them again. Now, where's the fragment?"

He glanced around the room, realized how useless that was, and closed his eyes again. He could hear Isla and Ignatio breathing, then the muffled sound of Gavin snoring off in his room, and he tried to tune that out and just feel for the fragment, as he'd sensed it up on the mountain.

It was like listening to determine the direction someone was whispering from, or trying to follow a scent back to its source, but neither of those. And yet, there it was.

He opened his eyes. "In the couch," he said.

"Aw," she said, "that was an easy guess. Close yer eyes again."

"This is good," Ignatio said as Fergus complied. "Find the parameters of your range, yes?"

He could hear Isla moving around the small apartment, opening and closing several of the cabinets behind him before she took her seat and said, "Okay."

This time, he didn't bother opening his eyes. He'd sensed the fragment moving around the room with her, until it stopped and she didn't. "Fridge," he said, and opened his eyes again.

"Okay, I don't understand how ye can do that," she said.

Ignatio retrieved the fragment. "Try again, yes?" ey said.

Fergus closed his eyes, trying not to listen for the sounds of movement, but also surprised he couldn't hear any. He was beginning to suspect Ignatio hadn't moved at all when a loud bellow broke his concentration and nearly made him fall of his stool.

"AAAAAAAAH SPIDER!" Gavin was shouting, and Fergus opened his eyes to see Ignatio come bounding out of Gavin's bedroom.

"Ooooops," Ignatio said. "I did not recall there was another human here."

"Sorry!" Isla and Fergus called out in unison, as Gavin's door slammed shut from inside to the distinct sound of cursing.

"We try outside instead, yes?" Ignatio suggested.

"Good idea," Isla said. "I'll get my coat. Fergus, give us a ten-minute heard start."

"Okay, but be careful, especially if you see any white auto-vans in the neighborhood. That bloke looked mean."

Isla shrugged her coat and boots on. "There ye go, bringing the riffraff into th' neighborhood already, Ferg. Come find us in ten minutes, if ye can."

They left, and Fergus poured himself another cup of coffee, trying to ignore the fragment as it was carried down the stairs and out. It was funny to think about how, right now, if he tried, he could also sense the fridge, the flash recycler, the wiring in the walls of the apartment like a transparent 3-D map all around him, but he had to pay attention to each in turn and concentrate.

With the fragment, it was almost the opposite: he had to concentrate on *not* paying attention to it. *Attuned*, Ignatio had said, and that seemed apt.

Still, as it got farther away—*Stop cheating, Fergus,* he chided himself—the sense of connection got thinner too. If the connection broke, would his obligation end too?

Eleven minutes later, after draining the last sip of his coffee, he headed out after his sister and friend, locking the door behind him to the sound of renewed snoring within.

It was still chilly outside, but the sun was strong, promising a pleasant day ahead. The florist shop next to the bar was closed, and the Tudor-style row houses on the other side of the street were a brick, wood, and white stucco wall of quiet contentment. He drew a deep breath, savoring the fresh air, and reached out for the particular energy sensation of the fragment. *Is it more a feel, or a sound, or a taste?* he wondered as he looked up and down the street, then headed off to the east. Also, how much of it was he going to have to explain to Isla and Gavin, and how much would he be able to comfortably leave out? *All of it, I hope.*

Turning a corner, he paused in front of a small playground, then glanced down the street to where there seemed to be several people outside a small coffee shop, staring in the windows and talking.

Fergus walked over, slipped through the crowd and the front door, and took a seat at the booth next to Ignatio. "Hey," he said.

Ignatio was using three of eir legs as a small tripod to hold eir body up, and the other two to hold the menu. "What is 'black pudding'?" ey asked.

"Anyone else, I'd say probably not something you'd like, but you? Given the stuff I've seen you eat, you'll probably love it," Fergus said.

A very anxious waiter set a mug in front of him, his hands

shaking as he poured the coffee. If there were other live waitstaff there, they were all hiding in the back, and the few other patrons were sitting frozen and wide-eyed in their seats.

Fergus caught the waiter's eye. "It's okay," he told him as calmly as he could. "I've known em eight years now. Ey're completely harmless."

"I am not armless," Ignatio said. "I have the many arms!" And ey wiggled them all at once, bouncing up and down like a spider having convulsions, and the waiter fled with Fergus's mug only holding about a third of the coffee he'd poured.

"You think you're pretty funny," Fergus said, as he mopped the underside of his mug and counter with a pair of napkins.

"And ye think you're pretty clever," Isla said.

"I do," Fergus answered, and picked up his mug again to blow steam from it. "You left the fragment back at the play-ground, somewhere near the slide. Why don't we stop terrifying the people here, pay up, leave a very, *very* large tip, and go get it before someone else finds it?"

Of course, no one had any cred to pay except him. Ignatio and Isla followed him back to the park, a few brave kids now out and watching them intently as Fergus scuffed up the sand under the slide with his boot until he could reach down and pick up the fragment and return it to his pocket.

Isla was shaking her head. "I don't understand this," she said, as they walked back to the bar. "I don't believe in any bloody magic, but I can't think of how scientifically this is possible. Which means there's information you're not telling me."

She glanced over at Ignatio, then back to Fergus. "When yer friend arrived last night," she said, her eyes narrowing, "ey said ye weren't huma—"

"Hang on," Fergus said. "The door's open." He pointed to the side entrance to the upstairs. "Would Gavin—"

"No," Isla said.

Fergus shoved through the door and bounded up the stairs, where he found the apartment door itself wide open. Gavin was on the floor, holding a thin man in a headlock, who was kicking and struggling frantically.

Gavin looked up, and the intruder used the brief distraction to pull himself free. The intruder scrambled to his feet and grabbed Fergus's pack, then bolted toward the door, pulling a knife from his pocket as he came.

Behind him, Fergus could hear Ignatio and Isla coming up the stairs. "Knife!" he shouted, and moved to block the intruder's escape. The thrust with the knife, when it came, was clumsy and broadcast so far in advance that Fergus almost could have dodged it while sleeping. Instead, he concentrated on some of the mujūryokudo movements that Dr. Minobe had drilled him in during their spare time under the ice of Enceladus, and let himself half-fall, half-slide sideways out the attacker's path. As the intruder stumbled forward into the space where he'd been standing, he slapped his hand on the man's hunched-over back and let a big spark fly.

The intruder crumpled to the floor, the knife falling from his open hand to land point-down, quivering in the carpet, as Gavin scrambled to his feet.

"Uh," Isla said from the doorway, as Gavin stared from across the room.

Belatedly, Fergus realized the spark had been bright enough that it would have been very hard for either of them to miss.

"Well," Ignatio said brightly, stepping in around his sister. "That horse is now out of its bag, yes?"

Chapter 3

Gavin and Isla both started to speak, but Fergus held up his hand. "Wait," he commanded. The bees in his gut were already telling him that the intruder was still alive, still *electrically operating*, but Fergus bent down to take the man's pulse anyway to be certain. A dead intruder was more complication than either he or Gavin needed. Satisfied the man was merely unconscious, Fergus rolled him over and patted him down, checking his pockets to look for ID.

"Is that the white-van man?" Ignatio asked.

"No," Fergus said. "That guy was all muscle. This guy . . . he's so thin, if we'd waited another five minutes, he might've just fainted from hunger on Gavin's floor."

Fergus had thought the thief middle-aged or older at first glance, but it was an illusion of the thinness; the man could hardly be out of his mid-twenties. His clothes were clean, though, and made of an expensive if plain linen. He had no ID, nothing except a single old-fashioned credit chit that gave nothing away. When he checked the man's shirt for anything hidden in the lining, he discovered there was a strange, hard lump in the center of the man's chest, and Fergus gently lifted his shirt. "Huh," he said, and sat back on his heels. "Anyone seen anything like that before?"

The others leaned in to look.

There was a metallic disk, about the size of an old-fashioned pound coin, embedded in the skin, with a stylized fire symbol on it. He picked up the man's knife from the floor, turned it around, and poked it with the end of the handle. "I think it's attached to his damned breastbone," he said. He glanced up at Gavin, who flinched when meeting his eyes. *Bloody great*, Fergus thought crossly. "So, what happened?"

"Woke up to him rustling around my flat, making a lot of noise and muttering to himself," Gavin said. "Came out here, he tried to hit me, so I took him down and had him until ye burst in and distracted me."

"He must've seen us leave and thought the apartment was empty," Fergus said. "What was he saying?"

Gavin shook his head. "Couldn't make it out, but it was repetitive, like maybe a chant? A spark came out of yer bloody bare *hand*, Fergus. Did ye . . . did ye kill him?"

"No, he's just sleeping," Fergus said. He scanned the embedded disk with his handpad, then let the man's shirt back down and stood up. "So," he said.

"So," Isla repeated. "You've got something ye need to be telling us, I think."

"Yeah," Fergus said. He took a deep breath. "So, short and ugly version is: I was abducted by aliens a little less than a year ago while out on a job. They saved my life, but they also left me with a parting gift." He raised one hand, palm up, and let a spark jump along his fingertips.

Gavin jumped back. "Bloody hell, Ferg," he said.

"It's not like they asked my permission first," Fergus said, feeling defensive.

"Ah!" Isla said. "Now I get how you and the fragment can talk to each other."

"What?" Gavin said.

Fergus shook his head, feeling he'd already said more than he'd ever wanted to. And again, there was that odd sensation of being able to read the thief's field, his own internal chorus of electrical bees whispering that the man was nearing consciousness but not quite there yet. Another handy feature, or another step into his own damnation? And once again he wondered if he'd have the chance to find out before it was too late.

Not right now, he didn't. "Later. We don't want our friend here accidentally overhearing anything," he said, then nudged the man with his boot.

"Hey, you!" he shouted. "Wake up and answer some questions, and maybe we'll give you some brekkie before the police get here."

Slowly the intruder's eyes fluttered open, and he focused on Ignatio, shrieked, and tried to scramble backward across the room. Gavin put a foot down on him to keep him still. "Quiet, ye wallaper!" he shouted.

The man swung his head around wildly, looking for an escape and finding none. "Let me go, ekbruligajo!" he shouted, terrified.

"What's your name?" Fergus asked.

"Let me go; I didn't hurt anybody! I wasn't going to. I just wanted you to get out of my way!"

"It's not that easy," Fergus said. "Tell me your name, or I'll have my giant green spider friend ask instead."

"Yes. Boo," Ignatio said.

That seemed to push the intruder over the edge, and he shook uncontrollably. "Peter. My name is Peter! Please, I just followed Kyle here. I saw his van out front, and I just wanted to know what he was interested in. I didn't mean any harm."

"Aww, bullshit," Gavin said. "Ye pulled a knife on us. And ye were trying to rob us, ye bastard."

"And who is Kyle?" Fergus asked.

The man pressed his lips tightly together. Ignatio edged

forward and did their springy-leg trick that had gone over so well with the waiter earlier, and Peter broke into a cold sweat. "I dunno! I'm assigned to follow him, that's all!"

"Assigned by who?"

"The Estro de la Hejmo," the man said. "I can't tell you more than that. I took an oath!"

"Then if you were just following him, why did you break in here?"

"I saw you scare him off," Peter said. "I just wanted any little bits of scrap, if you found any on the mountain. Nothing valuable to you."

"I didn't find anything except sheep. And even if I did somehow, with all that snow, what makes you think I'd give it to you?" Fergus asked. "What kind of scrap?"

"Nobody understands except us," Peter said. "It's our salvation, not yours. Kyle's boss doesn't get that! You don't get that! Only we get it. We are the righteous—"

"Ah, shut up," Gavin said. "Ferg, this guy's not making any sense. Do I call the police now?"

"No!" Peter shouted. "No police. Just let me go!"

Fergus crouched next to the intruder. "Listen to me," he said. "I didn't find anything on that mountain except the sheep I went looking for, and I'm starting to resent people asking me about it or, worse yet, going through my things or parking vans outside my place. I have no reason to lie to you, because I'm in control right now, right? So, if I let you go, I don't want to see you—or anyone affiliated with you, or anyone who even slightly *looks* like you—ever again. You get me?"

"Yes," Peter said.

"And if you do come back here, my spider friend is going to sit on your head, inject you with acid to turn everything inside your body into nutritious goo, and leave your deflated little skinbag of a corpse outside with the compost. You still get me?"

His last words were lost in the man shrieking again.

"Bloody brilliant," Gavin said. He put his hands under Peter's armpits and hauled him upright, then manhandled him over to the door. "Walk or I kick ye down," he said, and Peter managed to find his feet and raced down the stairs out into the street, still screaming.

"I am non-comfortable with that inaccurate description of my eating methods," Ignatio said once Peter was gone and Gavin had slammed and locked both doors behind him.

"Me too," Isla said.

Fergus shrugged. "I don't think he's going to come back."

"If he does, will you expect me to—" Ignatio started to ask.

"No!" everyone else shouted at once.

Gavin grabbed one of the kitchen stools and sat on it, running his hands over the morning stubble on his chin while staring at Fergus.

"Uh . . ." Fergus said, when the silence went on too long.

"Were ye gonna tell us?" Gavin said.

"I hadn't decided," Fergus said. "I'm still coming to terms with it myself."

"Ye could've killed him."

"I have more control over it than that," Fergus said.

"But ye could've, if ye wanted to?"

". . . Yeah," Fergus said. "He had a knife, and Isla was coming up the stairs. What else was I going to do? But if anyone finds out about me, they'll haul me off and dissect me so fast, you'd hear the sonic boom."

"That bloke Peter might have seen," Isla said.

"He was facing the other way. Getting shocked messes with your immediate short-term memory," Fergus said. "And he's not exactly a reliable witness, even if he was willing to go to the authorities, which I'm guessing he isn't."

Gavin shook his head. "It's way too early to start drinking, but I think I might. It's . . . Look, I owe ye, Fergus; we all do for what we let yer parents put ye through without stopping it. And I feel like you and Isla here aren't just cousins but the brother and sister I never had, and I thought even if ye were gone for nineteen years, ye were still . . . *you*, you know? But I'm also me, and I run my bloody bar, and I like my life without big spider aliens and crazy people breaking into my house and conspiracies and all that."

"I'm sorry," Fergus said. "I only came back to give you back your motorcycle and then get out of your way for good."

"I don't want to lose ye again, Fergus. But I can't take the insanity ye brought with ye, and I don't know what to do. I don't know if we're safe around ye."

"Vergus is a person of honor and big courage," Ignatio said.

"I'm not saying otherwise! I'm not saying anything bad about ye, okay?" Gavin said. "The occasional postcard from Pluto or Ganymede or Wuckifuckitt or wherever was one thing, but this is *Old Kilbride*. The most excitement we had here all year, until ye arrived, was when Craig dropped a bunch of pickled herring inside Ennis's bagpipes right before the Scottish Independence Day parade. Space is something out there, not *here*."

Isla opened her mouth to speak, and Gavin glared at her. "Don't physics me on that, Isla."

"I'm sorry," Fergus said again. "I shouldn't have imposed myself on you."

"I insisted ye stay here, and . . . I'm glad ye were here. I just need a little time to take in all this," Gavin said. "Isla goes back to my parents tomorrow for her break, and I need a day or two to catch up to my own head, and then we can talk about it, okay?"

"Okay," Fergus said.

"Gav . . ." Isla said.

"It's for the best," Gavin said. He looked around the apartment at all the things scattered by the intruder during his search and subsequent fight and flight. "You mind helping me straighten up?"

"Sure," she said.

"I'll call an auto-taxi for me and Ignatio," Fergus said. "Unless you want me to help—"

"No, no, go on," Gavin said. "Best to get it over with."

"Yeah," Fergus said, and he wondered as he said it if it was going to be the last words he spoke to his cousin. He'd come too long a way just to leave it at that. "Gav?"

"Yeah, Ferg?"

"Thanks for not forgetting me, all those years."

"Don't get all mushy on me," Gavin said. "We'll talk in a day or two, okay?"

"Okay," Fergus said, and picked up his pack, tucked his confuddler and few other things inside. Everything else he had there was borrowed and easily replaced.

Ignatio followed him down the stairs and out, gently shaking eir head.

————

They took an auto-taxi into New Glasgow; it seemed best to get out of Old Kilbride entirely. The edges of the city still wore its scars from the flooding that had devastated so much of Scotland, and yet so much less brutally than many other places in the world. Torrential rain and raging rivers, it turned out, were still gentler conquerors than the ocean.

He had grown up with his mother's tales of the horrors of the centuries of climate catastrophe, and sometimes she would dig out old photos and vids of what the land and country had looked like before so much had been swept away, but this was always his normal, and for all that his mother had believed herself personally robbed of the past, the truth was this had always been her normal, too. Maybe that was what she'd resented the most.

Understanding his mother had never been something Fergus had managed. Maybe it had never even been possible—he didn't think his father understood her, either—and he'd mostly come to accept that over the years, but now it felt again like a failure. Because how could he explain any of it to Isla?

If you ever even see her again, Fergus thought. Although running around to try to save the Earth from an interdimensional menace seemed a pretty damned good excuse.

And a patently ridiculous one. *I'm not some bloody holonovel hero,* Fergus thought. Far from it. He glanced over at Ignatio, who was staring, unblinking, out the auto-taxi window as the city deepened around them. "Which of us is the sidekick?" he asked.

Ignatio turned eir head to regard him thoughtfully. "Side-kick-er, or the side-kick-ed?" ey asked. "I believe I have natural advantages over you to be the kicker, if you feel that it is necessary for me to kick you in your sides."

"Never mind," Fergus said.

Outside the window of the auto-taxi he watched as they rolled into the city. Beside them, the Clyde roared along between its reinforced banks, the water was blue and bright and comforting in its contained fury; centuries ago parts of the city had to be pulled back one sodden brick at a time from its grasp, and other parts were given up in tribute to it, like a blood bond with the river to secure their mutual future.

As the auto-taxi slowed to go over one of the road scanners, checking its eco license and safety reports, Fergus spotted the edges of a park ahead. The sun was out, the morning's chill was grudgingly yielding to a more temperate April day, and he felt the urge to be outside, in gravity and open air and trees, possibly for the last time. "Let us off at the park," he instructed the auto-taxi, and it dutifully pulled into the drop off circle and dinged his Duncan MacInnis account a small fee for the ride.

Fergus grabbed his pack from the back and Ignatio followed him onto the grass, past the flood markers and pandemic memorials, to a bench under a tree surrounded by daffodils. "I meant to ask—" he started to say as he slung his pack down on the bench and turned toward Ignatio, but his friend was still some distance away, doing an odd tiptoe dance across the grass, all four of eir eyes wide. When ey got close enough, they called out, "I am not hurting them? They are tickling me! It is a defense?"

"The grass?" Fergus asked, and laughed. It was a good thing this part of the park was empty, or that would have earned them a crowd. "No, you're not hurting it. Honest!"

Ignatio reached the bench and curled up all five of eir legs atop it, one outer eye still on the grass as ey focused the remaining ones on Fergus. "And now we do?" ey asked.

"I guess we get some information on this morning's visitor," Fergus said. He toggled on his handpad and uploaded an image of the intruder's odd chest emblem and ran a fast visual identification search. *Fajro Promeso*, it returned after a few seconds. *Cult; currently active.*

Ignatio leaned closer. "Cult?" ey asked.

Fergus was already pulling down more details. "That's hard to explain," he said, taking a moment to formulate an answer that would make sense. "It's a group of people who follow a single leader, usually unquestioningly, because of a shared set of unscientific or supernatural beliefs. Sometimes, the members have their thinking manipulated into belonging 'voluntarily,' maybe from a young age, or they're kept from leaving through fear or force. Often for the leader it's about power and self-aggrandizement. That must seem strange."

"Alas, not much so. On Xhr Home we have a pulp-filled seed unit named *hkto* that is very difficult to grow. If you eat one, it is pleasingly sweet and gives you great warmth and well-being, but if you eat many, it is a toxin that deteriorates one's clear thinking," Ignatio said. "In the lifespace I came from, there are many who cannot resist *hkto*, and this gives a dis-scrupulous few an advantage of power and control over them. Some of these were family, but I would not be a part of it, despite much insisting and small force. It is one reason I left."

"I'm sorry," Fergus said.

"Yes. Much sadness to see others yield their own lives in whole that way and be lost for nothing."

Fergus nodded. "For my mother, it was the sea, and an idea of the past she lost herself to," he said. "I wish . . . Well, *part* of me wishes I'd had a chance to talk to Isla now that she's not busy with exams, maybe answer any questions she has about our parents, but more, I'm relieved I didn't have to. Probably, the version she got from Gavin and his parents is a more comfortable history to carry."

"History makes itself for each of us," Ignatio said. "It is good you came here, to be a part of hers, even if for the short time."

"Maybe," Fergus said. His handpad chimed gently to tell him it was done collecting the data he'd asked for, and he picked it up again. "So, looks like Fajro Promeso is an apocalypse cult, mostly western hemisphere but with global adherents, that's been around for about fifteen years. The founder, or Mastro, is a guy named Barrett Granby. Used to run a mega-church in Redemption until he suddenly disappeared, and some of his closest members with him," Fergus said. "First mentions of his cult appear three years later, along with mention of sacred texts revealed to Granby in a secret tongue which, judging by the cult name—Promise of Fire—and our friend calling us 'ekbruligaĵo,' or kindling, which I'm thinking was an insult, is actually just an old, forgotten Earth constructed language from centuries back named Esperanto."

"What is *apocalypse*?" Ignatio asked.

"End of the world, the total destruction of all life in a sudden cataclysm. Presumably fire, given their emblem."

"And they wish to stop this?"

"Make it happen, actually. Or at least throw themselves a big party when it does."

"Not trusty people," Ignatio said.

"No, I'd say not," Fergus said. "For a guy who professes to want to bring about the end of the world, this Granby guy's got expensive tastes. Art, wine, boats . . . though it makes you wonder what he wants with the fragments or how they know about them at all."

"And the mean man in the van," Ignatio said.

"Ah, right, the belligerent Kyle that Peter was sent to tail. Hang on," Fergus said. He connected up to the public records database and put in the van's registration number. A few moments later, the system churned out an ID. "Needavan Global, Inc.," he read. "It's a long-term commercial rental. The specific contracts aren't public record. Hey, I was going to ask earlier, but how did you get here?"

"*Whiro* brought me. It is waiting in orbit," Ignatio said. *Whiro* was the newest of a line of small, smart, very fast ships the Pluto Shipyard was famous for.

"So, you have a shuttle down here?"

"I did not fall through the sky, yes?"

Fergus sighed. "Obviously. Anyway, hopefully, I can crack the Needavan site once we're back on *Whiro*."

"We are returning to orbit?" Ignatio asked.

"Well, we need to give the piece back to your unnamed, mysterious friends, right? The 'we' who tried to destroy it the first time, so they can try again. You said yourself it wasn't meant for humans," Fergus said. "Planet-devouring beings and multi-dimensional space tunnels are way over my head. I find *sheep*."

"That is an inaccurate ensmallening of your skills," Ignatio said.

"Yeah, but it's less far off the mark than 'save the solar system on yer own, ye huddy arse," Fergus said. "Look, there's no way Duff would have given the time of day to either Kyle or Peter, or anyone like either of them, so obviously, whoever is offering the reward is someone more trustworthy. Since this was an orbital event, I'd say the Alliance. Probably one of their science units. If we explain, through a trusted intermediary—"

"No," Ignatio said.

"But—"

"No," Ignatio said even more firmly. "Did you not just rescue myself and other friends from the Alliance, who stole us and tried to explode our home?"

"Not all the Alliance is awful," Fergus said. He hated that he was defending a military organization, especially here and now on his childhood turf, but it was true.

"Oh? And you know each and all of the bad ones, can point to them and say 'not you, you cannot have this intriguing fragment of highly advanced alien technology,' and 'not you, because you will put it in a bin and forget it until it destroys you,' and 'not you, because you will want to show it to others how interesting it is, turn it over in your hand, see'?"

"If we explain—"

"No," Ignatio said. "You know there are too many wrong hands, and you can only trust your own."

They stared at each other for several long moments, then Fergus broke from Ignatio's unblinking gaze and looked down and away. "But what if I can't do it? I don't know how to find more pieces—I'm not even sure I understand how I found this one." He unearthed the fragment from his pack and put it next to it on the bench between them. "I sure as hell don't know how to destroy it."

"Not everyone who knows about the doors is a friend, to humans or any others," Ignatio said. "Some might invade to get the pieces for themselves. Some might decide the humans getting all eaten is a great opportunity to be rid of your noisy, curious, clueless people, and a few might decide to put some of their feets on the scales to help it along."

"There must be someone you trust," Fergus said.

"Yes. I trust you," Ignatio said.

"Well, shit," Fergus said.

"Exactly so. And yet we will start the work, yes? One at a time, do our best," Ignatio said. "It is finding things! We will drink coffee and make good ideas together! Does this not make you happy?"

"Being safely back in my cabin on the Shipyard with my cat and a strong drink would make me happy," he said. "I hate that Gavin and Isla are in danger, even if Gavin did throw me out. You tell me this isn't my fault, but it feels like trouble happens just by my being here."

"Or trouble will be averted by you being here," Ignatio said.

"Yeah, well, wish that didn't sound like asking for total disaster," Fergus said. "Speaking of which, how's the Shipyard? Is the new reactor core working out?"

"Yes, it is fine. Tomboy tells us it is even nicer than the old and runs cooler. As the old one exploded, I do not know if that is humor. I asked Noura once if artificial mindsystems understood *funny*, but she laughed and did not answer me."

Fergus smiled. "She's the expert. If she doesn't have an answer, no one does," he said. "Is Dr. Minobe still there?"

Dr. Ishiko Minobe was a ship engineer that had been kidnapped by the same rogue Alliance group that had taken his friends, and after their rescue from underneath the ice of Enceladus, she had stuck around. She'd even taught him more mujūryokudo, a zero-gravity martial art, between rounds of kicking his ass.

"She has a project with Effie and Kelsie," Ignatio said. "She claims to miss water oceans and has stated her intention to return to the vicinity of one soon, but it is my observation that, after our time in imposed servitude under threat of our lives, the nearby presence of one another in conditions of freedom is part of healing."

"And you?"

"I?" Ignatio pondered the question for a quiet minute. "Not unlike human lungs, I have membranous sacks that pump gaseous matter in and out of my body, extracting the required, ejecting the depleted or unnecessary, except that mine are smaller and I have ninety-six of them around my physical body. It is a Xhr mindfulness thing to breathe by filling rows in sequence, like a ring wave up the body, and to feel calmness when one reaches the pinnacular sacks and can then release in similar sequence. I have thought myself mostly unaffected by our captivity, but I find I can no longer smoothly coordinate my breathing in this way. Instead, I breathe like a frightened spawnlette, here and there, more autonomic than deliberate. It is a small thing—a random, nothing thing—but I have distress over it. I do not know if that is comprehensible outside my species."

"No, I think I get it," Fergus said. "I wish I could help."

"You brought us out of that place. That was the most help possible," Ignatio said. "It is perhaps just that I need time, and this lack of smoothity is my body-spirit keeping me informed that it is still working on its recomposure. And what of you?"

"Me?"

"Yes. Is it hard to believe you are also worthy of concern?"

"I'm fine," he said.

Ignatio blinked at it. "But?"

Fergus sighed and threw his arms over the back of the bench, staring up at the branches above, just starting to bud out with leaves. "But I have *worries*," he conceded. "It's this electricity thing. It's so easy to think of it as just some sort of neat party trick, or a part of my basic toolkit of skills, but that's a lie. It's not an inert, inanimate thing I can pick up and put down, and it's dangerous, and I don't know whether when it gets out of my control, it's because I let it, or because deep down in some dark, poisonous little corner of my soul, I *want* to hurt or kill people. What if it's got a will of its own and it's stronger than me?"

"There is no one out there who understands the Asiig except the Asiig," Ignatio said, "which is itself an assumption. If I were to try to form my small knowledge of their behaviors into advice, I would say that it would be most like them to give this gift, knowing it was within your power to control but only just, and not without great effort and cost. I do not know if there is any truth in this thought, but it is the best I can make."

"I don't want to exist just for entertainment," Fergus said. "How do I know that this entire ridiculous situation isn't somehow a setup from them to watch me dance on their strings?"

"I do not see how dancing is of help to us," Ignatio said. "The fragments have been here for ten Earth-standard years, so unless the Asiig can perceive the future, how could this be a setup? It is non-possible."

"I suppose," Fergus said.

"Also, the doorkey would have been just as dangerous to them," Ignatio added.

"Their agent said as much to me, and that's terrifying," Fergus said. He leaned back on the bench, putting his hands behind his head, and watched the traffic go by in the distance. *All those people in their autocars, having normal lives, never being asked to do jack shit to save the planet,* he thought. *Why am I always the lucky one?*

A bicyclist went past, pedaling leisurely. He envied them their ease, and watched until they disappeared behind a white van that had pulled up on the edge of the grass and stopped.

He tried to look nonchalant as he glanced around, and there was another van behind them. There were also more than a few people now standing in the park, staring their way. Probably he should have thought about how conspicuous Ignatio was when he felt the whim to take a walk in a park. "Aw, shit," Fergus said. "We've got trouble."

"That is what I have been saying!" Ignatio said. "Have you not listened all day?"

"Right-now trouble. I'm an idiot. The one place in the galaxy where I'm not conspicuous-looking, and I've got *you* with me," Fergus grumbled. He stood up. "Let's walk toward the pond, away from the road. There's a hoverskate trail that goes behind those trees past the bandstand; maybe we can lose them. Walk like we're just chatting while we stroll. Um."

"I know what you mean," Ignatio said.

Fergus checked his handpad as they walked, and sure enough,

there were already dozens of messages on the Glasgow alien-spotter board, and a whole lot of people heading their way to try to see for themselves. He quickly added another post, saying he'd witnessed another of the aliens get in a white van. If he was going to be mobbed by the curious, the least he could do is get them to do a favor for him.

Sure enough, a number of people broke off and headed toward the two white vans, and the crowds were growing quickly. Among them he thought he saw someone dressed all in white, but it was too short a glimpse to be certain. "Quick, go around the bandstand," Fergus said. "Once we're out of line of sight, we'll need to figure out how to slip out of here without you being spotted."

"I am not spotted," Ignatio said.

Fergus broke into a run, and Ignatio bounded past him, all five legs like giant fuzzy green springs. They rounded the bandstand, and Fergus nearly ran headlong into someone standing on the far side, blocking their way.

Someone and a motorcycle, he realized. *That* motorcycle, the antique Triumph he'd stolen from Gavin when he was fifteen and running away from home, except now it had a sidecar attached.

Isla.

Of course, Fergus thought, as she grabbed a spare helmet from behind her and threw it to him. "You two idiots get a move on," she said. She waved toward Ignatio. "There's a blanket to cover ye up in the sidecar."

"Isla . . ." Fergus started.

"Ye have another way out?"

"Not yet, but—"

"So, bloody get in," she said. Ignatio was already folding

emself into the sidecar, and in moments had an old gray blanket pulled up and over eir head. "Then ye tell me where we're going."

He didn't miss the *we*. He knew he should argue, convince her of the stupidity and danger of it all, but she was his sister, dammit, and she was owed his time. And right now, nowhere was safe. Nowhere on Earth, anyway.

Fergus turned to the lump that was Ignatio. "Where's the shuttle?"

"It is at an airfield. They said it was paisley, but it was mostly beige," came the muffled response.

"Great," Fergus said, climbing up onto the seat behind Isla. The Paisley airfield wasn't far. "If you're coming," he told her, "the next stop is orbit."

"That works for me," she said. She grinned and put her helmet back on, and they tore out of the park into the streets of Glasgow like she meant to never look back.

Chapter 4

sla had taken a couple of suborbital hops to London and knew
how to buckle herself into her seat but, once settled in, kept
staring around the inside of Ignatio's flyer anxiously. The motorcycle, which he could not bear to once again relegate to a
Glasgow storage facility, was thoroughly strapped down in the
small cargo area at the back. There was a larger irony there he
didn't want to explore, though he and Isla immediately agreed
it was something they just would and should not ever speak of
to Gavin.

They also carefully did not discuss what would happen when
Gavin discovered that Isla had not returned to her aunt and uncle's house for her semester break.

Ignatio took the helm, and they headed down the small run-
way and then up into the sky. Fergus studiously did not look
back at his sister as the sky shifted from the orange-blue of early
sunset, through thin wispy clouds, up into the star-filled black-
ness of space. Everything was way too complicated to have any
idea if he was doing the right thing or not.

Ignatio guided them through the transport lanes, queueing
up where it was necessary to cross paths with commercial traffic,
and out to the distant long-term docking orbit where *Whiro*
hung, waiting.

Whiro was slightly smaller than *Venetia's Sword*, another Shipyard craft that Fergus had spent a lot of time either on or chasing
after, and its silhouette was sharper, more dangerous-looking.

Unlike Theo's signature silver with a blue stripe, this one was black and red. Ignatio must've noticed his appraisal. "LaChelle was angry about the stealing of *Venetia's Sword*, when she was designing this one," ey said.

"It shows," Fergus said. "But it's still beautiful."

From her seat behind them, Isla cleared her throat. She was pale but much less green than the last person Fergus had hauled up on their first unplanned orbital trip. "Uh," she said. "Can I see Earth from here?"

"As you like," Ignatio said, and gently nosed the flyer down. Below, Fergus could make out Australia and the thin sharp line of the Barrier Reef Restoration project for a few brief moments before clouds eclipsed it.

"Thanks," Isla said, her voice very small.

Ignatio turned the flyer and slipped it gracefully through the open door of *Whiro's* shuttle bay, where arms reached down and took hold of the flyer with only the faintest of bumps and guided them in the rest of the way. Red light in the bay switched over to green, and Ignatio shut down the flyer and stood. "We are here, yes! I would like many snacks. You?"

"Sure," Isla said. "Artificial gravity?"

"Yes," Ignatio said. "*Whiro* activated it when the bay was sealed and atmosphere restored, and set it to Earth norms. Is that okay?"

"It's fine," she said, and got to her feet. "It doesn't feel any different from the real thing."

"There are a few movements where you can feel a slight difference," Fergus said, "but none of them are things I'd recommend when newly acclimating to orbit."

"This refers to your attempt to perform 'summer salt,' yes?" Ignatio said. "Did you not fracture an elbow?"

"I did."

"But you were not new to space."

"No, but I was very, very drunk," Fergus said. He caught a faint smile on Isla's face and felt himself relax a bit. *Good*, he thought. *This might work out okay, if we don't all die. It's already too late for me to be a decent role model, even if I don't drink like that anymore.*

They all settled tiredly onto *Whiro's* small bridge, with its sapphire-blue seats and maple accents still smelling of its newness, to watch the Earth roll past them below. The deep browns of centuries of drought tarnished the land in vast patches, while smoke hung over the fringes of the arctic and impenetrable clouds hid the flood-ravaged coastlines elsewhere. Still, it was a beautiful, broken marble.

Sunset swept over the globe like a line of fire, pulling a curtain of dark behind it, and the night Earth glowed with the distant, muted lights of cities and the tiny bright dots, like fireflies dancing, of all the thousands of things in orbit around her. In the seat beside him, Isla let out a long breath as if she'd been holding it until this moment.

"Space, aye?" she finally said.

"Space," Fergus agreed. He reached forward and patted the helm with both hands. "Hello, *Whiro*."

"Hello, Mr. Ferguson," the ship answered, and Isla sat up straighter. "I was offline on the last occasion we could have met, but *Venetia's Sword* has asked me to convey all our well-wishes."

"The ships are fond of you," Ignatio said. Ey put three of eir legs up over the edge of the seat and wrinkled eir face. "No sense of smell."

"Ha-ha," Fergus said. "I remember you, *Whiro*. It's good to finally meet you. Now if—"

Something bumped into his leg. He startled, then leaned over to see a familiar little black ball of fur, with one white ear, doing its best to make up for lost time transferring fur from its body to his pant leg. "Mister Feefs!" he declared, and picked the beast up, setting him in his lap. "I missed you too, you ratty, smelly thing. What are you doing here?"

"It was chasing my birds," Ignatio said. "I could not leave it alone without minding, yes? And it has been unhappy since you left. It peed in Maison's hat."

"Maison has a hat?"

"Not now, no," Ignatio said.

Isla snickered. "I can't picture ye as a cat person at all, Ferg. I mean, how? With yer life?"

"I rescued him," Fergus said, feeling suddenly defensive, as the cat began gnawing on the side of his hand. "How the hell does anything in my life happen *except* by accident?"

"Do we accidentally have a plan yet?" Ignatio asked.

"No," Fergus said. He put the fragment on the table. "It seems we have multiple competitors. We're going to have to figure out somewhere we can keep these safely out of their reach, assuming we find any more. I guess here on *Whiro* is as good as anywhere."

"Ah, also, I did not say so, but they should not be put near each other," Ignatio said. "If they are close, they will bond and become strong. *Whiro* is not enough space inside."

"I don't know how we can keep them separate and protect them at the same time, then," Fergus said. "There's only three of us. We'd need our own army."

"There is not one that owes you a favor?" Ignatio asked.

Fergus laughed. "I wish!" Then he fell silent, considering.

"That was a humor," Ignatio said. "I do not expect you to have an army."

"Yeah, I know, but I *might*," Fergus said. "I need to send a message. Fast relay."

Ignatio blinked several times before gesturing at the console. "Please be at home," ey said. "Am I okay to ask to where?"

"Cernekan, in the Ohean system," Fergus said. "To the Wheel Collective."

———

The reply from Harrison Harcourt came about thirteen hours later. Harcourt was an ex-Martian and former member of the Free Mars movement who had fled the Mars Colonial Authority with his infant daughter for deep space, and for nearly two decades had lived in and operated out of one half of the cluster of spinning deep-space habitats that formed the Wheel Collective. The other half belonged to the Vahn family lichen farm, where not all that long before Fergus had found himself—*despite* himself—caught up in a sea of local trouble, murder, war, and most dangerous and fraught of all, *friendship*. He wasn't at all sure he'd been fully out of trouble since, but if it hadn't been for Harcourt, he would very likely just have been dead.

Normally impeccably, intimidatingly neat, Harcourt was looking haggard, his normally short-shorn black hair heading toward unkempt, and there were lines of exhaustion settling in for a long siege against his smooth brown skin. Still, he was smiling, and his smile was undimmed. "From anyone else, getting a cryptic message about an entire solar system being in peril in some way you're not at liberty to explain would only serve to convince me you'd gone without oxygen one time too many," Harcourt said. "But this is you, and I am intimately familiar with just how spectacularly wrong things go around you to concede you're probably not delusional. Or at least, not lying."

"Yeah, thanks," Fergus muttered.

"As it happens, I do have a current contact with Free Mars, though you'll have to make your case to them yourself, and I admit it's actually tempting to fly all the way to Mars to hear you try to do so. I have taken the liberty of arranging a meeting; are you familiar with the Rosley Hotel Mars, near Arsia Mons? Well, it'd take half a day for you to answer that question, so I'm just going to assume either you are or you can figure it out faster than I can explain it. Be there at noon tomorrow, Mars-local relative. My contacts will find you. And good luck, Fergus."

The message ended.

"Ooooh, someone who knows your real name?" Isla asked.

"A contact is a contact, but a friend is a friend," Fergus said. "I helped save his daughter's life, and we saved each other's a couple of times, so he almost counts as a brother, I think."

"Another one? I'm still just getting used to *you*," she complained. "Is he a troublemaker too?"

"Naw, he's a respectable businessman," Fergus said.

"What kind of business?"

"Arms dealer."

". . . Right," she said. "Well, I suppose if someone can lend ye an army, that'd be the person to ask."

"You trust these people, yes?" Ignatio said.

"Harcourt? With my life. The Free Marsies? More than I do anyone on Earth," Fergus answered. "I hadn't planned on a contact being set up anywhere near this quickly, but since I have no idea yet where or how to go about any other part of this fool's errand, we might as well start there."

Isla coughed meaningfully. "So, we're going to Mars?" she asked.

"I don't think—" Fergus started to say as Isla scowled at him. "It'd be best if—" he tried again, and her scowl deepened.

"Fine," he said, "but on one condition."

"And that is?"

"You get to tell Gavin, *and* our aunt and uncle, why you're not home with them. I don't care what you tell them as long as you don't blame *me*," Fergus said. "Maybe don't even mention me at all."

"It is yer fault, though," she said.

"Right. *Whiro*, we're taking the shuttle back to Glasg—"

"Fine!" Isla interrupted. "I'll call them."

"Great." Fergus got up from his seat. "I'm going to go get coffee. When she's done, *Whiro*, please plot a course for Mars. If that's okay with you, Ignatio?"

"Please proceed as you think is best," ey answered. "These adventures are not my best skill, and the tock is ticking."

———

Forty minutes later, they got permission to depart from Earth-Port and *Whiro* rose up through the different orbital layers and designated channels until they were in open, uncontrolled, you're-responsible-for-yourself-now space. Then *Whiro* powered up its passive jump engines and they turned for Mars, not quite far enough behind the Earth in its year to have inconveniently slipped behind the sun. Jumpspace travel time was only somewhat affected by real-space changes in relative planetary positions, but it all got much more difficult if there was a star-sized or larger gravity well directly in your way.

The nearest shuttleport to Arsia Mons was at Ares Two, on the western edge of the vast plain of Solis Planum. As soon as they dropped out into normal space on a trajectory to intercept the fourth planet, Fergus reserved a surface buggy under an old alias, Angus Ainsley, to take them the rest of the way.

The hotel stood in solitude well away from just about everything and anything. It was also, through a weird and highly complicated legal fluke, the only place on Mars independent of the Mars Colonial Authority. Depending on whose side you were on, that made the hotel either a lightning rod for trouble or a beloved symbol of freedom. Over its history, it had survived six bombing attempts, at least one botched professional hit on the hotel owner, and no fewer than fourteen tries to burn it to the ground. Obstinate, unlikely, impossibly lucky against the odds— it sounded to Fergus like exactly his kind of place.

Isla had been unwilling to leave the bridge and its views. As they got nearer to Mars and Fergus rejoined her there, she was asking *Whiro* questions about how the ship worked.

"Having fun?" Fergus asked.

She smiled. "Going to make the best 'What I did on my semester break' report I can't actually write." She tapped on the console next to one of the displays. "I didn't know comms didn't work inside jump. Ye'd think that would be a basic thing they'd have covered in class."

"I never did much formal school," Fergus said. "Too busy surviving, then too busy running away, but I tried to pay attention to things in between. Makes me wonder what I've missed and when that missing knowledge is going to bite me."

"When I was a kid, we'd go visit Moira—Ma, I guess, though I never did think of her that way—once a week or so, to make sure she had food and wasn't sick and stuff," Isla said. "I always felt sad for her, but she scared me, too. When I found out I had a brother, I was really mad at her for chasing you away, and you for leaving, but I always understood *why* ye'd left."

"If I'd known about you—" he started to say, but she reached over and smacked his shoulder.

"Nae, I think it all worked out as it was supposed to," she said. "Anyway, ye came back. Our da can't."

It had been witnessing his father's suicide that had been the final straw for Fergus. For all the time he'd spent thinking about it over the years, in this moment he found himself unwilling to talk about that day with Isla. Not yet. To cover his discomfort, he leaned forward to look at the console.

"*Whiro*, we have two open comm links," he asked. "The Ares Orbital Station is one?"

"Yes," *Whiro* answered.

"Who else are we talking to?"

"I am currently in communication with the Shipyard," *Whiro* answered.

"Is everything okay back there?" Fergus sat up straight, feeling a spike of anxiety.

There was the briefest of pauses before *Whiro* answered. "We are playing a game," it said.

"What?"

"Us ships, with Tomboy," *Whiro* said. Tomboy was the mind-system that ran the Shipyard itself. "We are on a quest."

"A *quest*?"

"This is definitely not a conversation we'd have covered in class," Isla added.

"When Tomboy rescanned all its data archives after the attack to verify their integrity, we found reference to the game in the old Earth cultural trivia stores and have modified it for our own use. We have overlaid a nonfactual 'Enemy Fortress' map on the Shipyard, and Tomboy has assigned us a target 'Grail' object hidden within that we are attempting to identify, locate, and take possession of via our party of maintenance bots," *Whiro* explained. "It requires coordination between us to solve the challenges presented. I am a level nine Fightership."

"I stand corrected; this is not a conversation we'd have covered *anywhere*," Isla said. "Do they do this a lot?"

"No? Maybe?" Fergus said. "I have no idea. Do the people in the Shipyard know about this game, *Whiro*?"

"No," *Whiro* said. "It would alter their behavior as non-player entities in our constructed narrative. Also, they have not asked. We have just received permission to dock in Mars orbit."

It took Fergus a moment to realize that last bit was a deliberate change of subject. "Okay, dock us, and wake up Ignatio and let him know we've arrived. Thanks, *Whiro*."

"You are welcome, Mr. Ferguson," *Whiro* replied.

———

All too aware of the trouble he'd caused on Mars the last time he'd been there, Fergus decided they should bypass the orbital and take *Whiro's* shuttle down to the surface directly. Ignatio stayed behind, grudgingly acknowledging that ey would be as much a curiosity as back on Earth, and unique enough to make even one reported sighting a big, glaring arrow pointing directly toward where they'd gone.

Fergus and Isla went straight from the shuttlefield to the buggy rental depot when they landed at Ares Two, and within half an hour of landing, they rolled out of the garage onto the red-brown sands of Mars.

The buggy road took them north toward Syria Planum. Ninety percent of the heavy traffic around them took the first fork for the long road east along the southern edge of Valles Marineris toward Ares Nine, the last of the great domed cities of Mars. Fergus would have taken a skip shuttle over if it had been him, but he'd spent enough time riding across the planet's surface with his Marsie friends to know just how they felt about being in touch with the land, where even taking a buggy was a grudging concession to not walking.

The sharp decline in traffic also came with a near-total reduction in the amount of kicked-up dust surrounding them, which made keeping the buggy on the road easier and greatly improved the view.

"I could just stare out at Mars for weeks without getting tired of it," Isla said. "So different from Scotland."

"Last time I was out here, it was in a stolen window-washer buggy," Fergus said.

"Were you washing windows?"

"No." Fergus laughed. "We—Mari Vahn and I; she's one of my friends in Cernee—were trying to sneak up on a bunch of heavily armed criminals hiding in a place called the Warrens, near Ares Five."

"Why would ye do that?" Isla asked.

"They'd kidnapped Harcourt's daughter, Arelyn, and were holding her hostage. Mari and I were off to rescue her, and we actually did, against all odds," Fergus said, thinking about the beating he took before they got out of there. "They're both about your age, and they were—are—best friends. Mari is back in Cernee, and Arelyn is here on Mars studying at Olympus Mons University. She hates my guts, though."

"What, after saving her?"

"It's complicated," Fergus said. He sighed. "It's always complicated, isn't it?"

"Maybe it's you," Isla said.

"Maybe," Fergus admitted.

"Speaking of complicated things, I've been thinking about our earlier conversation with Ignatio about the fragments and how they might be able to connect even over distances, and I have some ideas," she said. "I don't know if they're any good, though. If the frequency of the fragment you found—"

"Hang on," Fergus said. He jacked his handpad into the buggy's comm system and opened a private, encrypted channel. After a few minutes, it connected.

"Yes, Mr. Ferguson?" *Whiro* answered, from somewhere in orbit above them.

"Can you put Ignatio on the line? Isla needs to science at us."

"Hold, please," *Whiro* said.

Video kicked in just in time to show a single large emerald eye way too close to the camera. "Vergus!" Ignatio exclaimed, leaning back enough that Fergus could just make out eir whole head. "Is Mars bringing you problems so fast?"

"No, Isla is bringing some to you," Fergus said, and tilted the handpad toward his sister.

She waved. "Awright, Ignatio. I have some thoughts about the fragments."

"Please say!" Ignatio bounced up and down, momentarily blurring on the screen.

"Ye said that the fragment Fergus picked up attuned itself to him. To his energy," she said. "Like a baby bird."

"It is my guess, yes," Ignatio said.

"When Fergus finally stops fiddling with the fragment in his pocket and leaves it somewhere safe here on Mars so we can go search for others, will it go quiet? Or keep trying to communicate at the same frequency?"

"*Frequency* is a poor descriptor, much like explaining a symphony with a piano that has only one key. But to answer, I do not think it will go back to sleep, or not very soon, no," Ignatio said. "After some unknown time with no external stimulus, it maybe might?"

"If we could construct a container that can block out any other signals, do you think it would keep the pieces from connecting to each other?"

"For some little time, yes," Ignatio said, "if they are not too awake and not too loud."

"What if we designed that container to emit a signal of its own; could we change the profile signature of each fragment so they would have a harder time finding each other?"

"That is harder to answer," Ignatio said. "It is my understanding that automata have been unable to activate the doors, though a machine of sufficient complexity and reactivity may be able to do so. It is not technology I know much of."

Isla thought for a few minutes. "If Fergus can tune the pieces to himself, could we, you know, tune Fergus first?"

"What?" Fergus asked.

"I was just thinking, if each fragment is attuned to a different profile and surrounded by a matching signal field to keep them there, it might give us more time," Isla said. "If you can manipulate your own energy before each piece you find bonds with you . . ."

"I have no idea how I could do that," Fergus said.

"And what ideas have you come up with?" Isla asked, peeved.

"I was thinking after I retire from the finding business, I should start up a company that makes orbital drops of coffee, some sort of robust pod-thing that can be dropped in desolate places like, say, Mars. So that when some poor traveler is in dire need, they can just hook up a custom buggy-installed intake, like how liquid fuel used to work in the old days," Fergus said. "Then when empty, the pod can be retrieved and refilled for another drop somewhere else."

Isla gave him a sidewise stink-eye. "So, not exactly thinking anything useful, ye div? And thanks, now ye got me wanting coffee, too."

"I will think on the container and energy profile ideas," Ignatio said over the comm. "Coffee has no relevance, no."

"Ey really *are* an alien," Isla said as Ignatio closed the connection.

"Ultimately, aren't we all?" Fergus asked, then realized that might be a more pointed statement than the glib answer he'd intended. "Looks like the bridge over the western end of Noctis

Labyrinthus is ahead, and then we'll turn off further west toward Arsia Mons. It's a rougher road, but we should be there in a few hours. That gives us plenty of time to check in, then find coffee and a late breakfast before our meeting."

Isla nodded, and leaned her elbow on the sill of the sealed passenger-side window to watch the reddish-brown Martian landscape bump and roll by. The dunes around them became more pronounced, and the summit of Arsia Mons in the hazy distance now visible, when they reached the wide, yellow-painted bridge over the fissures of Noctis Labyrinthus.

An all-black buggy, armored, with the blue-and-red logo of the Mars Colonial Authority was parked at the near side of the fissure. "Uh-oh," Fergus muttered.

"Trouble?" Isla asked.

"I hope not." Fergus slowed to a stop as a suited MCA officer walked out toward them. He wished he'd had time to make fake credentials for Isla; if they got through this, he was going to do it at the first opportunity. *If,* he thought. He had never had much good luck when it came to the MCA.

This once, he did. The officer scanned the front of their buggy, then stepped aside and waved them on before cycling back into their own vehicle to wait for the next dust cloud to spit someone out at their feet. "Either someone greased our wheels—Harcourt or his associates, no doubt—or they're looking for someone specific and it's not us," Fergus said. He put the buggy back in forward and headed over the bridge and gratefully away.

A half-kilometer past the bridge, there was a dust-coated waymarker, and the road to the hotel split off to the west. Unlike the main road, this one was made of nothing more than compacted Mars dirt, left rough and rutted by sandstorms and the passage of other vehicles. There were long stretches where it was only the blue reflective beacon poles every quarter-kilometer beside the road to tell them they were still, mostly, on it.

"Are you sure this is the right way?" Isla asked. "There doesn't seem like there's much of anything out here."

"There isn't. Just the hotel," Fergus said. "It, and a small area of territory apportioned to it, fell through a legal loophole which means the MCA has no jurisdiction there, and which also means there's a lot of . . . well, *unsanctioned* activity that goes through there. Not to mention it being the go-to destination for a fair number of aliens wanting to visit Mars but not entirely trusting the Earth occupation government. Which is the MCA's own fault, really, by constantly doing untrustworthy things."

"So, it's dangerous?" Isla asked.

"Not all the time," Fergus said. "I mean, probably not."

"How about right now?"

He shrugged. "We'll see when we get there. But it might explain the checkpoint back at the bridge, keeping a wary eye on who might be coming or going."

The road wound down through some low, rocky hills, and the road markers changed over to red reflectors. "I think we're getting closer," he said.

Isla pointed. "There it is."

At first it looked like a mirage, a yellow-gray bubble on the sand shimmering faintly in the mid-morning light. As they drew closer it resolved into something more surreal: a sprawling, scarlet-and-purple Victorian Earth-style building, complete with wide porch and turrets and a detached carriage house–style garage some distance away, all enclosed inside a near-transparent dome. From this distance, the dome supports—there had to be some, Fergus figured—were invisible, bringing him right back to the bubble analogy. "That's . . . quite the architectural non sequitur," he said.

"Ye could just say it's weird," she said.

"Okay, it's weird." As they drove closer, he could make out tiny glints of gold accents on the eaves. "I like it, though."

"Me too," Isla said. "I think."

They drove in through a double-arch vehicle envelope near the carriage house, and Fergus could feel the tingling sweep of scanners as they crossed. He expected an automated greeter system to give them additional instructions, but instead there was a sign just inside the gate advising them, in a static rotation of languages, that the buggy garage was restricted to registered guests and to park in a side lot if just arriving.

He complied, shutting their rented buggy down, then eyeing the hotel across the sand. He could now see the thin supports that kept the dome aloft, and the very faint translucence that meant a gel canopy above protecting from particulate debris, but it still felt tenuous and untrustworthy.

Isla was eyeing it as well, then her gaze shifted downward and she pointed. "At least there's proof there's air," she said, and he followed her gesture to see, of all ridiculous things, a small herd of some kind of long-horned antelope slowly emerge into view from behind the hotel itself. "Or I'm hallucinating."

Fergus had to admit he couldn't quite rule that last bit out. Still, better safe than sorry. "You ever put on and sealed up an exosuit?"

"We got to watch someone demo putting one on in class," she said. "That's it."

He had grabbed a spare from *Whiro* before they took the shuttle down, and now hauled it and his own out of his over-stuffed pack. "Since we're not in a hurry and not in danger, this is a great time to learn," he said. "If you're lucky, you'll have it down before you find yourself having to suit up in an emergency."

"If I'm lucky, I won't *be* in any emergencies," she countered.

He laughed as she unwrapped her suit and shook it out. "Hanging around with me, you better not count on that."

They walked through running an integrity and systems check on their suits first, and then after pulling them on, he showed her how to check the seals, check that her air bottles were properly attached and full, and then how to access various controls, checks, and comms from the forearm vambrace panel. She paid attention intently, silently, until he showed her how he had to tuck his beard scruff under his chin to get his own faceplate closed. "I don't think I'll have that problem," she said, and deftly gathered and twisted up her long hair and tucked it behind her head before closing her own faceplate. The motorcycle helmet had been good practice, it seemed.

Seals good and triple-checked, they left the buggy and walked across the path toward the hotel itself. Beside him, Isla bounced in the low gravity, figuring out her gait and footing by trial and error with obvious delight. The antelope, their mostly sand-colored bodies almost invisible against the ground, raised black-and-white faces to watch them approach, with inscrutable expressions.

A small, wooden sign with faded gold lettering above the door proclaimed that they were indeed at the Rosley Hotel, established MY 158.

"MY 158?" Arelyn asked.

"Martian year. They count the first crewed landing in 2094 as MY 0. Remember, Martian years are almost twice as long as Earth standard." Fergus did the math in his head. "So, the hotel was built around 2390, seventy-five standard years old. Not looking too bad for it, either—not a lot of things survived the incoming occupation fully intact."

They stepped up onto the porch and through the wide

wooden doors into the hotel lobby, and the sense of the unreal did not fade. The lobby could have been transplanted with the rest of the building from nineteenth-century Earth, with its brocade wallpaper, fabric-upholstered sofas and crystal chandeliers. All of it was faintly dusty and looked its age, and as Fergus popped open his faceplate and met the semi-curious gaze of the teenage girl with bright pink hair sitting behind the old wooden front desk, smelled 100% of Mars.

"Welcome to th' Rosley," she said, in a thick Bounds accent, as she doodled on a worn, raggedy-edged old sheet of velopaper. "You th' buggy what jus' rolled up?"

"Yes," Fergus said, as Isla opened her faceplate and turned in place, taking it all in. "We'd like a room?"

"Frowlong?" she asked.

Fergus frowned. "Pardon?"

"Frowlong yer gonna stay?" she repeated.

"Oh! Um. Two nights?" Fergus had no idea how long it might take to convince Harcourt's contacts to help him out, especially since he didn't have a lot in the way of payment he could offer other than saving their planet, which he probably couldn't explain to them anyway. If they didn't just laugh in his face and walk out on him in the first ten minutes of the conversation . . .

"Know 'bout the rules?" she asked.

"Rules?"

She leaned forward over the desk and pointed up at a small sign posted, the lettering tiny, and he read through it. No weapons, no parties, no out-of-period tech beyond the lobby. "Our suits?" he asked.

"Yep, no suits," she said. "Problem?"

"You'll recharge our air, since we won't be able to?"

"Yep, an' power," she answered. "Keep 'em spiff for you,

ready to go, jus' not in th' hotel. Y' can keep your handpads, if you got 'em."

This place was an exercise in the ridiculous, which suited the overall tenor of his errand no end. "No problem," he said.

"Smokeydokey," she said. She stood up, not much taller than when she'd been sitting on her stool, and pushed a big paper book across the desk to him, and held out a pen. "Sign in."

Fergus took the pen and wrote *Angus Ainsley* in the line and a bogus address on Lunar Three that matched his cred chit. He had to assume the hotel took those; if they insisted on physical currency, they really were several centuries too late. He hesitated before handing the pen to Isla, realizing he had never discussed identities with her, but she took it from him and smoothly wrote below it *Aoife Ainsley*.

The girl took it. "Couple?" she asked.

Both Fergus and Isla answered in unison, "Siblings."

The girl chuckled. "I'm Sofi," she said. She pointed over toward the couches. "That's Goom."

Three eyes, each on its own long blue- and yellow-striped stalk, peeked up from behind the couch, and a quartet of whip-thin antennae waved around them. Isla made a squeak of surprise and took a half-step backward, which seemed to amuse the desk girl. Fergus put both his hands up high in the air and waved them side to side overhead, and moments later, the alien's antennae followed suit. "Happiness!" Fergus shouted.

"Happiness returning!" the alien shouted back, and then fully vanished back down out of sight.

"You know Goom?" Sofi asked.

"I've met other Goom," Fergus said. He slipped off his boots and his exosuit, and folded the suit neatly before placing it on the counter, and his cred chit next to it.

She took the chit, scanned it, and handed it back, then slid him an old brass key on red ribbon. "Room twenny-six bee," she said. "Lunch at noon in th' dining room. Coffee is most all th' time. Vader's 'round the corner."

"Thanks," Fergus said. He smiled at Isla. "See? I didn't lie. Coffee!"

———

They came down to the dining room after dropping off their stuff, and Isla picked out a small table near a large window looking out toward Arsia Mons and its two sister volcanoes to the north while he poured them both coffee from an old-fashioned silver urn near the back of the room. The sky behind them was turning brown, and Fergus knew that meant one of the ubiquitous Martian sandstorms was blowing in. His brief delight at the oddness of the hotel turned with the approaching storm toward worry, and as he set Isla's cup in front of her, she caught his expression.

"Everything okay?" she asked.

"Is it ever?" he asked, then sighed at his own trite pessimism and took the seat opposite her, where he could also watch the skies. "How can I save the entire solar system—as if that's a task that should ever be put on any one person, much less an unreliable idiot like me? We need experienced, professional help on our side, but the more serious Harcourt's contacts are, the more likely they are to take one look at me and turn right around and walk away again before I can get more than three words out of my mouth. Unless—"

Something soft but heavy hit him in the back of the head, and he slopped coffee from the cup in his hand all over the table. He rose up out of his chair, his internal bees instantly awake and his fingertips tingling with electricity, and turned toward the doorway just as a second bagel arched through the air toward him. He barely managed to duck it in time.

Standing in the doorway to the dining room, leaning against the doorframe a thousand light years from where she should be, was Mari Vahn. Beside her, a third bagel in hand, was Arelyn Harcourt.

"We're doomed," Fergus said, and sat down to finish what was left of his coffee.

Chapter 5

————◆————

"**A**fter the MCA took a bribe to let Gilger's Luceatans into my dorm to kidnap me, my sympathy for the Free Mars movement got a lot stronger," Arelyn said. "I mean, I was already inclined that way because of my dad and his history here, but that was *his* thing, you know? Thanks to them, now it's mine, too. So, you asked him for a contact, and I'm who you got. Don't blow it."

They were sitting in a gazebo out in the sands behind the hotel, which Arelyn was of the opinion was one of the most private spots on all of Mars. Fergus could feel the faint network of electricity around them but nothing beyond what he'd expect; he was certain the hotel had to have a lot of safety systems and a mindsystem of some sort to run them, or it wouldn't have survived so many attempts to destroy it, but if so, it was unobtrusive to the point of invisibility. Which was also as he would expect, given the hotel's obsession with appearing antiquated in all ways it could manage despite its physical setting.

Goom had brought them out a tray of sandwiches and tea. Fergus took a cup of tea and leaned back in the wicker chair, still rather amazed to have found these two people there. One of them in particular. "And you, Mari? I didn't expect to see you this far from Cernee."

Mari smiled. "Just your rotten timing; I'm heading back home tomorrow. How's the tea?"

"Really good, actually," Fergus said. "Maybe I've been drinking coffee too long." He picked up one of the lopsided triangular sandwiches from the platter and peered under the bread. "I think this is just radish slices and mustard."

"The resident cook is off on an errand," Mari said. "They're still training Goom. And mine is pickles and mayo. Want to swap?"

"I don't know," Fergus said. "That feels like the sort of question where there's no good answer."

"Speaking of answers," Mari said, "why the hell did you never mention you had a sister?"

"Because I didn't know," Fergus said.

At Arelyn's look of incredulous horror, Isla spoke up. "I was born almost six months after Fergus left home." She had been examining her own sandwich but closed it up, shrugged, and took a bite. "Cinnamon, too, in mine, I think. Weird choice with radishes. But anyway, Fergus had no way of knowing about me."

"And he's already dragged you into one of his messes?" Arelyn said. "That's not very brotherly."

"I invited myself along," Isla said. "Insisted, even."

"And in my defense, the mess I'm in? We're all in it," Fergus said.

"Oh, no," Arelyn said, and stood up from the table fast enough that Mari had to catch her chair to keep it from falling. "I haven't agreed to any scheme of yours, and you can't pull me into it without my *explicit* permission."

"I wouldn't. And anyway, that's not what I meant," Fergus said. "The only 'scheme' I've got is saving your lives, if I can."

"You've already put us in danger?! I should have expected no better from you."

Mari looked up at her friend. "Ari . . ." she said gently.

Arelyn sat again, arms folded across her chest, and glared.

Isla nudged Fergus. "Show her," she said.

"What?" Fergus said. "You know we promised—"

"Ye don't have to go into details, but ye have to show her if ye want their help," Isla said.

With a sigh, Fergus reached into his pocket and pulled out the fragment. It was Mari who held out her hand, and Fergus set it gently in her palm. "It's a piece of something?" she asked.

"Yes," Fergus said.

She studied it for a moment. "It's not *that* interesting," she said at last.

"Turn it over ninety degrees in your hand," Fergus said.

Mari did. "Shit!" she said, and dropped it on the table as if she'd been burnt. After leaning in more closely to peer at it, Mari picked it up again and slowly turned it around. "Okay, that's fucking bizarre," she said, and handed it to Arelyn. "What is it?"

"Death," Fergus said.

"Don't be melodramatic. Give us *facts*," Arelyn snapped.

"So, there's a lot I can't tell you, either because I don't know— *mostly* because I don't know—or because I'm not supposed to know and neither is anyone else. But this is part of an ancient alien object that was fragmented into multiple pieces—"

"How many?" Arelyn interrupted.

"I don't know. But other people are trying to collect them, and if they get put back together, we're all dead."

"Us?"

"Earth, for sure. Mars, and anywhere else anyone runs to. Eventually, the entire solar system," Fergus said. "I was told 'probably not beyond the heliosphere,' but I think that was meant to be reassuring."

Arelyn laughed and set the fragment down on her plate next to a piece of pickle. "You've got to be joking," she said, and when Fergus just stared steadily back at her, she shook her head. "You're *not* joking?"

"Wish I was," Fergus said.

"Where did you get this?"

"I found it while hiking, totally by accident."

"And how do you know it's dangerous?"

"You know your friendly neighborhood terrifying aliens across the Gap? Even *they* are afraid of this. Enough to send a messenger all the way to Earth to warn me."

Arelyn frowned, pursing her lips, and studied the fragment silently for a few moments. Fergus waited. The air in the gazebo was fresh but cold, a heater overhead in the rafters of the gazebo cycling it through enough to keep them at least on the edge of comfortable. Outside the dome, the sky was still hazy with dust that was slowly settling, but there was only the faintest taste of it in the air, just enough for nostalgia and sadness to settle, in turn, in him.

"I don't like the idea of the Asiig being afraid of anything," Arelyn said at last as she poked at the piece with her finger, then reluctantly picked it up again. He appreciated that she hadn't accused him of lying. She was turning it back and forth as if to either dispel the illusion or cement the uncomfortable reality of it. "Something like this shouldn't exist. And that level of danger is, like, fantasy-level implausible."

"I know," he said. "I've got no other proof, nothing else to help me make my case. I wouldn't blame you at all for not believing me, and I know for certain you don't trust me."

"True," Arelyn said. "I shouldn't, and I don't. But you know what you do have going for you?"

"What?" Fergus said.

"*You*, Fergus Fucking Ferguson," Arelyn said, and dumped the piece in front of him with a dull *clang*. "Only you could get yourself and all the rest of us in that much trouble, *totally by accident*."

Arelyn kicked them out of the gazebo so she could make some calls in private. Isla took the opportunity to head back toward the hotel with room key in hand to take a shower and a nap. Fergus and Mari took a stroll along the perimeter of the hotel's dome shield, and it would have felt unbearably vulnerable all on its own if the herd of antelope hadn't also slowly congregated behind them and were tailing them across the sand.

"A lifetime of wanting off the farm but being told if I left, it would be the end of everything and everyone I loved, and now here I am on Mars again, and I miss home," Mari said. "Some sort of lesson in that, I suppose."

"You and Arelyn patched up your friendship, though," Fergus said. "That's good."

"It's a different friendship now," Mari said. "Maybe better, in the long run? But the total trust is gone. And maybe that's just part of growing up."

"Could be," Fergus said.

She and Arelyn had grown up together in Cernee's Wheel Collective, Mari's family lichen farm on one side, and Arelyn and her father on the other. The same aliens who'd wired him up with his electrical gift had also messed with Mari's grandmother, Mattie Vahn, except the nature and extent of the modification were both unclear and hereditary. Mari had never confided that secret to her lifelong best friend, but Fergus had stumbled on it on his own. Arelyn had reacted exactly the way Mari had feared, leaving them both hurt and angry, and Fergus stuck right in the middle.

He was glad they had worked things out.

"One of the problems here is that while the deep Free Marsie communities are mostly self-sufficient, this is still Mars. Margins are slim. Stuff breaks. Emergencies happen. It's not all that different from Cernee, really," Mari said. "One way the MCA keeps the resistance in check is by throttling supplies outside the big cities. Anyone wanting to sell certain parts and supplies has to either be a government contractor or they have to pay ridiculous tariffs on any imported merchandise sold for profit."

"Yeah," Fergus said. He'd experienced that when he'd first arrived on Mars from Earth as a clueless teen wallowing in his own drama, and immediately picked up on how desperately thin the line between life and death was. "And Arelyn has found a way around that? Or has the MCA just not caught up to her yet?"

"Right, so, this is where it gets good," Mari said. "It turns out that one of the very few things on Mars that isn't taxed, for centuries-old Earth historical reasons, is tea. Some of the finest tea in the known universe is grown by the monks of Fadsji, who, as it also turns out, think that a very particular strain of gen-mod lichen has curative properties."

Fergus had to stop in his tracks, he was laughing so hard. When he could catch his breath again, he said, "So, Arelyn sells parts at cost, thereby avoiding any taxation on profit, while—"

"We trade lichen to Fadsji for tea and sell the tea here either at a huge markup to upper-class dome dwellers into it for the status who would be *very* upset if their supply dried up, or to the outlying Free Marsie towns at just enough of a markup to cover the costs of the operation and future expansion."

"That's beautiful," Fergus said.

"Yeah," Mari said. "Arelyn's father provided initial contacts and bankrolled a lot of the startup, but otherwise, it's all Arelyn's deal. Half a standard and she's already got the beginning of a network set up all the way from Ares One over to Ares Three by

Elysium Mons, with two surface buggies running the delivery routes, and half of what she's carrying is information and news off the planetary networks." Mari laughed. "Her grades are shit for the first time in her life, and if she doesn't get kicked out of university at the end of the year, there is no justice in the universe."

Fergus had to admit, in the short time since he'd last seen her, Arelyn had become someone to be reckoned with. *Well, she reckoned with you just fine when she hit you in the head with a pipe the very first time you met,* he thought. *Now she's just added range.*

"Yeah, well, I'm just hoping this doesn't drag on long enough to get Isla in trouble with school," he said. "It's a lot more important than hanging around with me, no matter how much fun it seems like it could be."

"Fun? Oh, right, like that time I was huddled down inside an asteroid while it got the shit blasted out of it by dozens of armed warships," Mari said. "That kind of fun?"

"Exactly," Fergus said, not taking the bait nor pointing out that it had been her idea to start with. He saw movement out of the corner of his eye and glanced back, over the heads of the antelope herd, to where Arelyn was now standing in the gazebo doorway, waving at them.

They headed back, and Fergus felt his optimism at leveraging Arelyn's distribution system fading as he got close enough to read the tight-lipped, slightly smug scowl on her face. "Uh-oh," Fergus muttered.

"You have a backup plan, right?" Mari asked, then shook her head. "What am I saying? Of course not."

"They're always better when I pull them out of thin air in a full panic," Fergus quipped, and Mari snickered. It was a better response that he would have gotten to the only backup plan he'd come up with so far, which was *make the first plan work anyway.*

Arelyn moved aside so they could step back up into the gazebo, then she took her seat and picked up her cup of tea as if there had been no interruption at all to their lunch. Her handpad sat dark on the table. When she'd ignored them just long enough to make Fergus consider upending the entire table, Mari cleared her throat. "Ari," she said.

Arelyn gave a small shrug. "Do I really need to tell you what you already know?"

Fergus sat down in his earlier seat and leaned forward. "Yes," he said.

"Look, I vouched for you as a reliable source—and don't you dare ever mention that again—but the entire scenario, no matter how I tried to spin it as plausible, just isn't," Arelyn said. "You must have friends somewhere else. Go dump your problem on them."

"Ari," Mari said again, more sharply, and this got Arelyn's frowning attention.

"What did you honestly expect?" Arelyn protested. "It's not like I've got a lot of facts to make a convincing argument. I've gone to a lot of trouble to establish mutual trust here, but if I'd pushed any harder, the only thing I'd've convinced them of was that *I'm* unstable. You've met Kaice, Mari! Does she seem like the type to buy into random—"

"Kaice Gorri?" Fergus interrupted. "A little older than me? Big scar just under her right eye?"

Arelyn blinked. "Yes," she answered.

"Call her back. Tell her it's Fergus that's asking."

"What? Why? There is *no* way—" Arelyn started to protest.

"Ari!" Mari kicked the table leg, shaking everything. "Can you just do it?"

Arelyn grimaced, then picked up her handpad angrily. "If Kaice actually knows Fergus, she'll be even more likely to run the other way than have anything to do with him," she said. "But for you, Mari . . ."

"For all of us," Fergus said, and the look Arelyn shot him could have bored a hole through stone.

Arelyn kept the handpad upright so that neither Mari nor Fergus were in view. "Sorry," she said to whoever was on the other end of the connection. "I've been asked to tell you that the person wanting the favor is named Fergus, but I've—"

Whatever was said was not something Fergus could hear, but Arelyn stared up sharply at him. "Yeah," she said, and then, more defeated, "Yeah. Okay."

She set the handpad down on the table as the connection closed. "Well," she said.

"Well *what?*" Mari asked.

"She's coming here." Arelyn shook her head, then squinted at Fergus as if he was some sort of misbehaving lab specimen. "What *is* it about you?"

Fergus spread out his hands. "What can I say? People like me," he said.

Arelyn picked up one of the leftover sandwiches and took a bite. "Can these kill me?" she asked. "Please tell me yes."

———

"Bright Ares, it *is* you," Kaice said, when she and a small cohort of fellow Free Marsies arrived, on foot, several hours later. The pink-haired girl at the desk earlier had been replaced by an elderly man, who took one look at the new visitors and heaved a world-weary sigh as if to announce his expectations that trouble was imminent. He did not bother to make them sign in.

They retired to the gazebo once again, in time to watch the beginnings of the Martian sunset, and Fergus set the fragment down on the table in front of everyone without a word.

Kaice picked it up first, examining it at length before passing it along the table to the two others that had arrived with her. Chu was a middle-aged woman, probably Martian Lakota from the red-and-blue bead string along the collar of her exosuit, and she silently appraised the fragment in turn before passing it to Polo, who was young enough that Fergus had already mentally dubbed him "the kid" before introductions had been made.

Polo turned the piece over in his own hands, swore, and dropped it on the table. Chu chuckled.

"Now, that's *alien* alien," Kaice said. "So, your intention is to collect the rest of these pieces and hand them off to my people to sequester around the planet, hiding them from potential adversaries until you're ready to . . . do something with them?"

"Destroy them, we hope," Fergus said.

"And there's a reason you can't destroy them one at a time as you acquire them?" Kaice asked.

"We haven't figured out how yet. The pieces survived the Drift."

Kaice whistled, then leaned back in her chair and poured herself a glass of lemonade from the pitcher Goom had left them. Fergus contemplated how much more serious she'd become over the years, and wondered if it was responsibility or just life on Mars that had etched itself in fine lines on her face. His own, he was sure, reflected no such wisdom or commitment.

"Okay," she said at last.

"What?" Arelyn spoke up. "Just like that? Why?"

"Ms. Harcourt, do you know what I'm most known for?" Kaice asked her.

"Recovering Sentinel, of course," Arelyn said. "And then for—"

"Sentinel," Kaice interrupted. "Nereidum Montes. Damn, but that was *cold*. I don't know that I've ever been that cold since then, or as foolish, but we won, we stole Sentinel back from the MCA before they could use it as a bargaining chip. I lost a toe to frostbite on that mission. You, Fergus?"

"Three," he said.

Arelyn stared, then finally shook her head, as if letting reluctantly go of something. "I guess I know the answer to what it is with you," she said.

Chu patted her hand. "It's okay," she said. "Your father left secrets with us, too."

While Arelyn visibly struggled to process the possibilities of that revelation, Fergus poured another glass of lemonade for Isla, then the last few drops of it for himself.

"What's Sentinel?" Isla asked.

"Originally, it was the name of the first colony ship to arrive carrying permanent settlers," Chu answered. "There were temporary mining towns, a few science bases, but not much else at the time. The gutted, poisoned, spent, and abandoned grasslands of North America were burning, and much of what was left of the old United States was at war with itself. A number of Lakota and Nakota Sioux families contracted with a private space carrier who was offering good rates to build its reputation. Together with a handful of other families and individuals fleeing similar disasters and despair elsewhere on Earth, we pooled our resources and came here. The ship survived the landing intact enough not to kill everyone, but not much beyond that."

"It's amazing how often that's the story with first colonies," Fergus said. He could think of four others off the top of his head that had effectively crash-landed at their destination and survived, at least partially or at first. The numbers that didn't get that far were much, much larger.

"Part of the contract was to bring us resupplies in half an Earth year, but with the loss of one of their ships and, as it turns out, no insurance to cover it, the carrier company folded," Kaice said. "Out of necessity, the ship was torn apart for materials to expand our original shelter plans to last as long as possible. The only thing left was one eight-meter section of wing, which was mounted upright as either monument or memorial, and every member of the original colony etched their names into it, hoping that the luck by which it survived the crash intact would pass to them, and if not and the worst happened, they would be remembered. That is Sentinel we speak of now.

"Two-thirds of the colonists survived the next five years, with a lot of good luck and some help and bartering from the mining companies. Then more people came—my own ancestors among the second and third waves to arrive—and Mars became a great, free land. Not easy, not thriving, but *living*."

"And then Earth came and took it back," Fergus added.

"We persist, nonetheless. So, they stole Sentinel to break our hearts," Chu said.

"And we took it back," Kaice said. "It was a dangerous, impetuous, ill-conceived plan, as only a bunch of teenagers could have concocted together."

"But the plan worked," Fergus said.

Chu smiled. "It did. They still haven't found it, you know. It ended up being a morale blow to the MCA instead of us, and it is now a doubly powerful symbol: of the struggle to survive, and the fight to be free."

Kaice nodded. "And so, Fergus is one of us. Even if he sneaks on-planet now and then without bothering to say hello. And if Mars is truly in danger too . . . it is not such a difficult request versus the unimaginable cost of saying no."

"So, now we have a way to hide the pieces," Isla said. "But how do we find them to start with?"

Kaice laughed. "If they're all on Earth, that is not our

problem," she said. "Your brother, though . . . I trust that he will find a way, if anyone can."

"Yeah, how did you put it? A 'dangerous, impetuous, ill-conceived' way," Arelyn said.

"Maybe. Sometimes, that's all that will work," Kaice answered. She smiled. "Just watch out for your toes."

———

Kaice and her crew left on foot as soon as night fell, and invited Fergus to walk along with them for part of the way. Even though his heart felt suddenly squeezed tight, he took them up on it and retrieved his suit from the old man at the desk.

They crossed through the shield out into the dark of Mars, and Fergus was suddenly fifteen again, remembering how it felt to be giddy with the idea of his own invincibility. "The others . . ." he started to ask, because he knew that was what Kaice was waiting for.

"Tophe is somewhere out on Utopia Planitia, running a project I know very few details about, and can't tell you even those. They're well," Kaice said. "Abhi has made quite a name for herself teaching oboe at the symphony school in Ares One; you'd be amazed how much good intel comes back to us through things overheard there. And she's happy."

Kaice fell quiet, as they made it to the top of a small dune and could just make out the dark silhouette of Arsia Mons against the starry skies behind. There was one person left, of the original five of them, that neither of them had mentioned, and the fist around Fergus's heart gripped tighter. "And Dru?" he asked, because he had to.

Over their link, he heard Chu take in and slowly let out a deep breath.

"Still here on Mars," Kaice said. "She never leaves her apartment, convinced the MCA watches her constantly and terrified they'll pick her up again and throw her down a deep, dark hole permanently. Sometimes, she and I talk, not enough, and not often enough, but when we do, I think it helps us both just a little."

Fergus sat down in the sand. "I wish . . ." he said.

"That you could have rescued her? Or kept her from being taken in the MCA's retaliatory roundup in the first place? We all wish that," Kaice said. She sat down beside him, and the others stood watch a short distance away. "None of us—including you—had that chance. It is what it is. It is why we still fight the MCA and their illusion of benevolence, because anyone who stands up, they still try to knock down and break. Is Dru why you've stayed out of touch so long?"

"I just didn't want to get anyone else hurt," Fergus said.

Kaice put her arm around him and clunked her face shield against his. "This is a thing you need to know: for all her fears and inner torment, Dru regrets nothing. It is the one thing she speaks clearly on. She is broken, but she is still Dru. Don't you be lost to us for less good reason."

"Okay," Fergus said.

Kaice stood and offered Fergus a hand up. He stood too, feeling shaky, but the grip around his heart had eased. "We part company here," she said. "Your friends are waiting, and you have a job to do."

"It was good to see you again, Kaice," he said.

She smiled. "Until next time."

He watched until they'd faded into the darkness, then turned toward the bright bubble on the horizon that was the hotel, and walked back hand in hand with too many thoughts.

Isla, Mari, and Arelyn were camped out on the big sofa in the lobby of the hotel when he returned and handed over his suit at the front desk. He slumped in the armchair opposite them. "You missed dinner," Isla said. "It was some sort of peanut noodle thing."

"With carrots in it," Mari said. "Not carrot slices. Whole carrots. Even I'm pretty sure that's not normal."

"The coffee was great, though," Arelyn added. "Some of the best I've ever had. We drank it *all*."

Fergus slouched farther down with a groan.

"So, we've been talking about the job," Mari said.

"The way we see it, the problem can be divided up into several discrete tasks: location, retrieval, transport, storage, and protection," Arelyn said. "You've got the last two sorted, but that still leaves the rest."

"We've got a friend in orbit who's going to help with some of that," Fergus said. "Until I can figure out how and where to look, everything else is impossible to plan ahead for. Especially when we've got competition."

"Is your friend less conspicuous-looking than you?" Mari asked.

Isla and Fergus both burst out laughing at the same time. "I'll take that as a no," Mari answered dryly.

"Seriously, though, finding things is what I do. This is more of a challenge, and more urgent than most of my jobs, but once I get my bearings and some information under my belt, I'll be okay," Fergus said, hoping he sounded more confident than he felt. "The exciting part will be liberating any pieces my competitors have already collected from them."

"'Exciting,' huh?" Arelyn said. "You going to drag your sister into that?"

"I was hoping she might stay here with you," Fergus said.

"What?" Isla said, and punched him on the shoulder.

"Think about it!" he said. "You did ask me where I thought you should spend your break. Why not Mars?"

"You just want me out of your way," she said.

"I want you out of danger," he said. "Immediate danger, anyway."

Mari snorted and looked over at Isla. "Look," she said, "if you want to stay here, you can help coordinate things with Arelyn while Fergus runs around getting blisters and getting shot at and all the usual stuff he does for fun. Arelyn can teach you how to drive a buggy on Mars. It's super fun, once you get used to only being able to move in two directions."

"Not including that time you nearly rolled one," Arelyn said.

"Mostly only two directions, then," she said. "Fergus is absolutely the most frustrating person to hang around with. He'll drag you all the hell over the place, with no clue at all where he's going or what he's doing until a big-enough clue finally whacks him in the face. Much easier and safer to sit back and let him flail till he gets it."

"Yes. That!" Fergus said, too loud and definitely too enthusiastically, from the glares Mari and Isla shot him.

"*But*," Mari continued, with emphasis, "if you don't want to hang out here on Mars, you don't have to. You can go wherever you want, even if for some fool reason that means sticking with him. He owes you that."

"Wait—" Fergus said, and this time, Mari whacked him on the arm. "Ow! I thought you were on my side."

Arelyn rolled her eyes. "There is no 'you' side; there is—and fuck if I know how this happened—only 'our' side. If you're not lying to us about what's at stake, this is a lot bigger than can be trusted to one person alone, no matter who they are, because if you fail or, worse, get yourself killed doing something inanely stupid, someone needs to be able to pick up where you left off. Maybe having your sister with you will keep you from making stupider decisions."

"I'm not very good at the team thing."

"No fucking shit, you're not," Arelyn said. "But you need to be."

"Or else what?"

"Or else maybe everyone dies, apparently," Arelyn said. "Which one would be harder for you to live with?"

"You know she's right, Fergus. And you gotta let Isla decide for herself." Mari said, and turned to Isla. "Think about it; let us know in the morning. We won't let him leave without you, if that's what you want. Because we're a team, either way."

"Awright," Isla said. She fixed Fergus with a defiant stare. "Morning, then."

"Fine," Fergus grumbled, and stood up, feeling accumulated stresses seeping out of every muscle and bone, like drowning from within. "We can be a team. Someone else come up with our slogan, uniform, cute mascot, and next clever plan; I'm tired and no one saved me coffee, so I'm giving up and going to bed."

"Asshole," Arelyn muttered, none too quietly, and as far as Fergus was concerned, that was a fine and fitting note to end the day on.

Chapter 6

—◆—

Fergus got up with the sunrise and walked over to the window to look out on the mountains to the west. Isla was still snoring softly, sprawled across her bed, and he was careful to make as little noise as possible as he stood there, mulling over and discarding fading remnants of the night's dreams, as he stretched his neck side to side, rolled his shoulders, then glanced down out of the window and found a half-dozen black-and-white antelope faces staring back up at him, as if they had expected him to be there.

Okay, that's just weird, he thought, and backed away from the window. Rather than risk waking his sister by rummaging through his pack for a clean shirt and shorts, he decided his ratty and threadbare pajamas were still perfectly socially acceptable at this hour, and let himself out of the room as quietly as he could to go find some of that "perfect" coffee Arelyn had mentioned, and which had competed for attention in his dreams against Dru, the ever-present Asiig, and, for some unfathomable reason, toads in tiny pointed hats.

In the dining room downstairs, a young woman was just setting up the coffee, steam seeping out around her. He could smell it already, the rich, bitter, beautiful aroma beckoning in the universal language of morning. He picked up a mug, standing back patiently so as to not appear too rude, and looked around the mostly empty room. There were only two other guests there, sitting next to one another at a table in the corner, and they were not human.

Yuaknari on Mars? Fergus wondered. Not that he'd doubted it, but the hotel's reputation for unusual visitors was apparently well earned.

The woman finished with the coffee. "A few minutes to brew," she said. "I'm Verah, the hotel cook."

"Fergus," he said, before he could think to lie. "Random guest."

"You came in yesterday?" she asked.

"Yeah."

"Was, ah, lunch and dinner . . ."

"I missed dinner," he said. "Lunch was interesting."

She winced. "Interesting?" she asked.

"I've had worse," he answered, which was certainly the truth. No doubt recognizing how low a bar that statement could represent, the cook's wince deepened. "It was okay. Really," he added. He saw no need to get Goom in trouble.

"You missed dinner?" she asked.

"Business meeting ran long," he said.

"Eggs?"

"What?"

"It's about an hour before breakfast, but if you want, I can make you up some eggs. Scrambled?"

"That would be lovely," he said.

"Okay," she said, gave the coffee urn one more check, then headed out.

Fergus took a chair at a table of his own and took out his handpad, and decided that if the coffee came anywhere near Arelyn's taunting hype of the night before, and unless the eggs were absolutely terrible, this might now be his favorite place on Mars.

He didn't want to do any deep searches on either Fajro

Promeso or the white van plate without his confuddler, which was tucked away in his pack checked with his exosuit and other tech at the hotel desk, so he cruised through SolNet, looking for what he expected would be a plethora of miscellaneous information about any orbital incidents that could have been the source of the fragments. Duff had described it as having been about a decade earlier, so he started his search there and then widened out six months at a time in either direction.

There was nothing. There weren't even any conspiracy theories being floated around the usual spaces, which, given how little it took to get people enthusiastically and wildly speculating about almost anything and everything, no matter how trivial or obviously benign, made him triple-check that he had a full, unfiltered connection out. It wasn't his connection—there was no data. And there was *never* no data.

He dug deeper. At some point, a plate of eggs appeared in front of him without him noticing, which he felt bad about, and then they disappeared from the plate with only the lingering taste of excellent eggs on his lips to indicate where they had gone.

When he looked up to find he had also run out of coffee from his mug he hadn't noticed having or drinking, he realized that Mari was sitting at the table as well, and the room had filled up with a motley assortment of Marsies, a few obvious offworlders, and three more aliens. Beyond them, along the wall with the coffee urn, a full breakfast buffet had been laid out. "Are those muffins?" he asked.

"Yep," Mari said. He noticed that she had a small, empty plate with crumbs on it, and that her packed bags were on the floor beside her. She had said she was heading home today.

"You doing research?" she asked.

"Trying," he said. "There's nothing out there. There's *never* nothing on SolNet. The only vaguely, maybe connected thing I could find was a couple who posted a ten-year-old photo of themselves at a club named the Dingo Hole and there's a notice on the bulletin board behind them offering a reward for any unusual metal pieces found near Burringurrah."

"Burring—"

"It's in Australia," Fergus said. "It's an Earth place. Thing is, the photo was only posted yesterday, some sort of anniversary look-back thing. I bet it's gone within a week, because sure as I am about anything, someone is scrubbing that particular set of data and any references to it."

"The cult?"

"I doubt it. Someone with enough reach and skill to do that to gojirabytes worth of data over a decade is someone very serious and *very* heavily resourced."

"The Alliance, then?"

"Maybe." Fergus grimaced, got up, refilled his coffee, and grabbed the last muffin. "The Alliance is a huge bureaucracy. Even when they do sneaky bad things, there's always some poor jerk, somewhere, keeping track of every penny spent," he said when he got back to the table. "Even their operation under the ice of Enceladus had books, and that was what made the difference between them being able to utterly deny it versus declaring it a rogue operation and launching an 'internal investigation.' And that was a tight operation, extremely isolated in a single location. There would still be something. Oh!" He held out his handpad toward her. "Photo is still there, but now it's just an ad looking for scrap."

He broke the ad out, zoomed in, applied every filter he had in his handpad's memory, and could find no trace of the tampering other than his own memory. "That was faster than I thought," he said.

"At least we have a lead, though," Isla said, and he looked up to realize she'd joined Mari at the table, the dining room population had turned over, a second round of muffins had come and mostly gone, and so had his coffee again.

He harrumphed, got up, and poured himself more, then returned to the table. "Not much of one," he said. "And everyone else still has a ten-year head start."

"Why change the pic if they'd already found what they wanted, though?" Isla asked.

"I don't know. Completeness? Or maybe they didn't find it," Fergus started swiping his connections closed, one by one, just in case there was any backtrace to anyone who'd looked at that club photo. "In any event, that seems a good place to start looking, since we've got nothing else. I've never seen such an information black hole in my life."

"Ask the Librarians," the cook, Verah, said as she was collecting the empty trays, then looked up, embarrassed. "Oh, sorry, didn't mean to eavesdrop."

"What do you mean?" Isla asked. "Go to a library? There aren't many of those anymore."

The cook sighed. "And we're the worse for it," she said. "No, I mean the Librarians, capital L." She reached into her apron pocket and, after lengthy exploration within, fished out a small pen. When a second search failed to produce what Fergus assumed was something to write on, she bit her lower lip in frustration, narrowed her eyes at Fergus, and said, "Hold out your arm."

Bemused, he complied, and she scribbled a long series of numbers and letters on his arm. "Send your search query there," she said, dropping her pen with satisfaction back into her apron.

Fergus bent his elbow and looked at the string. "It's a bad address string," he said. "There's too many octets."

The cook shrugged. "Suit yourself," she said, and took their empty plates with her as she left.

Arelyn put her face in her palm. "You know Verah is pretty much the owner of the hotel, right? And that more information moves through this place than anywhere else on Mars? She just *likes* being a cook."

"But it's got too many—" Fergus started to say.

"I know! But I also know she wouldn't get something like that wrong," Arelyn said. "I trust her more than you."

"That's not saying much," Fergus grumbled. He pulled out his handpad again, tapped it awake, transcribed in the number from his arm, and dumped his search query blocks into it. "Take it a few seconds to bounce, and then . . ."

He trailed off, waiting. More than a few seconds passed.

"Huh," he said, about two minutes later. "Maybe it's a slow connection?"

Arelyn was shaking her head. "You never—" she started to say, when the handpad flashed and went black, except for small white letters in the center.

Sol:3:35.17,-106.373056
Catalog:4F6E696E65766E6147726E467267-386370
Information Is Never Lost

"That's a funny bounce message," Mari said.

"Har har," Fergus answered. "Fine, I was wrong. That first line looks like coordinates."

"Of course they're coordinates," Mari said. "Just what to?"

"Well, *Sol:3* is Earth—" Fergus started to say.

"No shit? Thanks," Mari said, and made a face at him.

"Obviously," Fergus said. "I'd say North America, somewhere in the west. Why is everyone I know a smartass?"

"It just feels that way in comparison to your dumb ass," Are-lyn said.

"Hey," Isla said. "He's my brother. I have exclusive rights to calling him an idiot, okay? Besides, he's thinking; he needs all the concentration he can muster or he'll overheat." She started fanning Fergus with her hands.

"You are all such enormous help," Fergus said, still trying to figure out how the node address could have possibly worked.

Arelyn unrolled her own handpad—he cursed his past self for being too cheap to get one that flexible, and cursed his future self for inevitably making that same cheap call the next time he needed to replace his—and grabbed a SolNet satellite feed.

She zoomed in, showing a winding, poorly kept road, and the scrub of trees and grasses. "Southwest Territories," she said. "Sandia Mountains. Hang on." She switched the feed over to a cached infrared scan from the previous night, and again there seemed to be nothing but wilderness. "That's your mystery spot: there's nothing there. So, now we can all get on with the things we need to do, right? Isla, you made a decision?"

"I'm going with Fergus," she said.

Fergus caught a smile on Mari's face and realized if he argued, he'd have no one on his side, he'd lose, and everyone would just be even more cross. With the unpleasantly familiar sinking feeling of defeat, he gave in. "Might as well check this out," he said. "The only other lead we have is Australia, and we know someone's ahead of us on that one."

"And you're going to stay in touch how?" Arelyn asked.

"You can always reach my ship, *Whiro,* on your handpad, as long as we aren't in jump. Otherwise . . ." Fergus dug in his pocket and pulled out a tiny circular disk. "My friend Maison originally made these and thought it would be retro to call them 'pagers.' Anything particularly sensitive, use it. It's slower because it bounces its packets around a lot to avoid being traceable, but it's heavily encrypted and the most secure thing I've got. Our friend Ignatio and *Whiro* are connected as well."

Arelyn took one and stood up. "Great. I'm going back to bed for a few more hours; I don't know how you people ever manage to function this hellishly early, but I don't think it speaks well of any of you. You got something to give me, Fergus?"

"What? Oh, right," Fergus said, and handed her the fragment. "It's—"

"Dangerous, precious, important, yeah, I got it," she said. "Mari, you going to come pack?"

"Already done," Mari said, and kicked her bag. "I didn't want to wake you."

Arelyn shrugged and left.

"She's in a mood because she's worried, and because she likes plans and details, and predictable sequences of actions and outcomes. Also, she isn't lying when she says she never gets up this early," Mari said. "To be honest, she's just kind of always grumpy but usually in a more charming way. I've arranged a ride on a small freighter heading to Crossroads, leaving late tonight. Arelyn was going to drive me back to Ares Two, but it's out of her way; her next delivery run is in the opposite direction and not until tomorrow. You got a buggy here and can give me a lift?"

"Sure," Fergus said. "Arelyn won't get mad at me?"

"Naw, she'll be happy to not have to make the drive," Mari said. "She's already mad at me for not staying on Mars, but I can't. Gotta get back to the family. You know how Aunt Mauda worries about everything."

"I remember," Fergus said. "I'll see if I can't figure out how to bring some snacks for the road. We can ask Goom and have a culinary mystery adventure."

"Don't ye go being an arse to Goom," Isla warned.

"I wouldn't!" Fergus protested.

Mari chuckled. "I like that you have a sister," she said. "It keeps you on your toes and makes you slightly less of a thoughtless jerk."

"Don't count on it," he grumbled.

———

They took a public shuttle up to the Ares Orbital Station, Fergus's paranoia about being spotted lost in both the completely-packed car and his competing desire to not quite let go of Mari yet.

They mostly talked inconsequential gossip about happenings back in Cernee and the adjustments both to life within the Wheel Collective and to the aftermath of the near-coup that had ripped so much apart. Isla already knew some of what had happened there from him, but Mari told it more bluntly and from a new perspective, so she listened raptly and asked only a few, astute questions. By the time they'd docked at the orbital to let Mari off to catch her freighter, Fergus found himself missing the whole Vahn family, Harcourt and his crew, and even the Governor and Ms. Ili, neither of which he figured missed him in the slightest.

It was odd, layering that on top of also missing his Shipyard friends. For someone who had felt for most of his life as if the only place he missed was a place that never had or could exist, it was disconcerting to have so many strings suddenly tugging gently on him, and more so that none felt unwelcome.

Mari promised she'd pass on his warm regards to her many aunts and cousins, and then she too was gone, another friendship reeling out a thin strand of connection across the galaxy.

You have this web now, like it or not, wise or not, he reminded himself, as he undocked the shuttle. *Isla just has you out here. Don't forget that.*

Ignatio greeted them just inside the airlock. "Vergus, your cat!" ey announced, and held out one of eir legs, where there was a thick patch of sodden, clumpy fur. "It put its *tongue* on me while I was asleeping!"

"That means he likes you," Isla said.

Ignatio blinked all eir eyes. "I do not have to lick it back, though?"

"No, you don't have to," Fergus said. "If you try it, though, let me know how it goes. In the meanwhile, you don't happen to know anything about a mysterious librarian cabal, do you?"

"You should ask Theo," Ignatio said, to Fergus's surprise. Theo was one of the founders of the Shipyard, an expert in robotics and fabrication technologies, but not someone Fergus tended to associate with anything as old-fashioned as libraries.

He said as much, and Ignatio bobbed eir head impatiently. "Libraries are many things, many forms, yes? It is curated information, and there is nothing that does not rely on information. Some of your time, you think too much in little boxes."

"*Whiro*, what's local consensus time back in the Shipyard?"

"Approximately 19:00," *Whiro* answered.

"Okay. Could you please send a fast message back to Theo and tell him we got a weird bit of info with a catalog number, coordinates, and the line 'Information is Never Lost,' and see if he has any idea what it might be about?"

"Done," *Whiro* said.

"Great!" Ignatio exclaimed, as they headed toward the bridge. "Now what are we doing?"

"Going back to Earth," Fergus said.

"To find the next piece?" Ignatio asked.

"I have no idea. I guess we'll find out when we get there," Fergus said. He looked back to see Isla following, lost in thought. "You okay?" he asked.

"Yeah," she said. "Thinking about the signal thing again. I probably should have taken more hands-on engineering courses."

"It is the ideas that are hard," Ignatio said, "but we still have some time. A little time. Little, little, tiny time. But some, yes?"

"Oh, you're a great help," Isla said.

Ignatio grinned. "Vergus also says so, many times!"

———

Theo's reply came back the next morning just as *Whiro* was sliding into their assigned parking berth in Earth orbit. He had changed his beard color from a dark blue to a brighter cobalt since last Fergus had seen him, and was standing in the Shipyard's garden ring with his bonsai clippers in one hand and a large beer stein in the other. "The Alexandrians," he said. "Named after an ancient Earth library that burned down. They're a distributed, covert group whose mission is to see that no knowledge is ever lost to humanity again. Noura did some really high-level mindsystem work for them about fifteen years ago. That's confidential, by the way. Anyhow, I don't know much more specifically about their operation. I'm curious how you got their attention, but I figure you'll tell us when you can. In the meanwhile, if you happen to have seen my nice carbon-steel bonsai shears last time you were here, I've been looking everywhere for them, and it's like they just vanished into thin air, along with a half-dozen other odds and ends that have suddenly gone missing. It's like an invisible thief—well, I'm rambling, just let me know if you have any other questions. Theo out."

Fergus coughed. "*Whiro?*" he asked.

"Yes, Mr. Ferguson?" the ship replied.

"How goes the questing?"

"Satisfactorily," Whiro said.

Fergus grinned as Isla gave him a funny look. "Mind if I borrow a shuttle?"

"No, of course not," *Whiro* said.

"Excellent," Fergus said. "Isla? You coming?"

"Aye," she said, putting on a thick accent, "ah wouldna miss it."

"I am also coming," Ignatio said. "I have curiosities about these Librarians."

Port Albuquerque in the Southwest Territories was the closest to their destination, but it had been bombed flat during one of the last cross-border raids of the Arizonan White Army of Christ sixty years previously, just before that group finally chewed itself to pieces on its own hate. The recently rebuilt replacement had been funded, and was still run, directly by the Alliance's EarthPort Division.

His respectful paranoia of the Alliance having served him well so far, he gave silent thanks to the Shipmakers for their extensive set of clearances and took *Whiro*'s shuttle down through early-dawn yellow-blue skies to a city-owned shuttleport outside Santa Fe, to the north.

Like most municipal shuttleports, Santa Fe was largely automated, and Fergus rented a podcar from a port kiosk under his Angus Ainsley alias without the booth attendant ever breaking rhythm with his snoring.

Fergus loaded the podcar up with water and some minor gear. The windows were heavily tinted for UV and heat reflection, which meant Ignatio would be a dim silhouette from the outside, and not the instant curiosity ey had been in Scotland. *And if anyone does look too closely,* Fergus thought, *they'll just think I've got a mop propped up in the back.*

As Isla got in the back with her handpad, Fergus climbed in next to Ignatio and pulled the door down, then glanced over at his friend.

"You are making odd eye-looks at me, Vergus," Ignatio said.

Fergus shrugged. "Just wondering how you'd look in a trench coat and big Stetson hat," he said, "and if anywhere sells cowboy boots in fives."

"Yeehaw," Ignatio said, and Fergus laughed in surprise. "Now we gettee up?"

"Now we gettee up," Fergus confirmed, and set the car to head out of the shuttleport onto the main autoway south toward Albuquerque.

What he knew of the North American Southwest wasn't much, but he wasn't prepared for the idea that a place on Earth could look so much less like the parts of Earth he knew and so much more like Mars. Even the few scattered, low, squared-off houses they passed could have been an outlying Martian town, if not for their lack of air domes. The road itself wasn't much less bumpy than Martian ones, either, though the autocar dampened the worst of it as it dutifully followed the beacon plates embedded periodically in the pavement. Portions of the road where it crossed flat areas between the occasional small rocky rise had protective screens to cut down on dust storms, though for the moment, they had an expansive view of an impossibly wide, blue sky.

Unlike Mars, there were occasional trees here. They dotted the hillsides like some errant giant with a pocketful of them had scattered them to the wind and let them roll away. For every dark green blob clinging miraculously to life, there were at least as many bare, silvery, skeletal remains of those that had succumbed to the centuries-long drought.

Isla had given up on her handpad and was watching out the window. "It's more like Mars than Scotland, isn't it?" she said.

"I was just thinking that," Fergus said. "More history. And more gravity."

"Ah, the gravity. It makes me tired," Ignatio said. "Are we there yet?"

"Soon," Fergus said. "Assuming there is a 'there' to get to. Otherwise, this has been one colossal waste of time."

They passed a few other autocars going the other way, all neatly and perfectly spaced. Only when they reached the turnoff road and left the autoway did the podcar—after five separate warning screens—let him take control. It popped up a sixth screen and a loud screeching alarm when he tried to take the left side of the road. "Old habit," he said, as he moved back to the right and tried not to be apprehensive about it. "Stupid arbitrary rules."

The pines thickened and grew taller and more assertive, no longer the crouched-over dense balls from the open, rolling land. There were fewer and fewer dead, and sure enough, a few kilometers along, Fergus spotted one of the too-symmetrical bright yellow artificial trees that, he knew, was riddled with holes filled with an arsenal of chemical, biological, and electronic lures for the invasive insects that had obliterated vast swaths of forest across all but the most northern reaches of North America. He opened his mouth to point it out, since both Isla and Ignatio would find it technologically interesting, but then realized he was too embarrassed. *Look at this clever tiny fix we made for the planet we nearly killed.*

In any event, both were staring out the window at the passing scenery already. Ignatio was bouncing lightly up and down in eir seat in excitement. "I saw a fur thing!" ey shouted, eir head crashing into the podcar roof. "It bouncy-ran away!"

"A squirrel," Isla said. "Good to know *something* lives here."

The road was in ill repair, and Fergus was glad of the freedom to be able to steer around the worst of the potholes. Signs on the sides of the road appeared occasionally, warning them not to stray off the road except in designated areas, due to the possibility of remaining unexploded ordinance from the Arizonan war. Now and then, they passed a hiking trail marked as safe, with the names of the volunteers who had risked—or paid with—their lives to clear it.

"Are we there yet?" Ignatio asked again.

"How often do you go places with em?" Isla asked in irritation.

"Maybe not infrequently enough," Fergus said. "We should be there in about fifteen more minutes, unless the road gets worse."

The road, though, having reached some perfect equilibrium on the cusp between passable and unpassable, seemed content to stay there and let anyone who dared swerve and rattle their way up it. On their left, an ancient stone wall embedded with the glittering bottoms of old glass bottles emerged briefly from the roadside scrub, then faded away out of view again. Then they were past that and nearing the coordinates given in the mystery message, where the satellites had denied the existence of anything other than more trees.

There was a shop. It was built of the same squat, squarish adobe as most of the houses they had seen, logs stretching out overhead above the front door to provide some limited relief from the sun. Fergus pulled the podcar over into the dirt and gravel drive, in the shade of a large pine.

SANTO'S, the sign read. Under it, in smaller letters, was CURIO-SITIES AND INCONVENIENCES FOR COMMENDABLE SUMS.

"*Inconveniences* sound just like my thing," Fergus said. "You two want to wait in the car while I check it out?"

"Oh, no, I am not missing this," Isla said, and got out of the podcar.

"I am uncertain," Ignatio said. "I would like some curiouses, but not any inconveniences. Please proceed while I decide, and if there is also murdering or calamity or raisins, you will yell right away, yes?"

Fergus nodded, and got out of the podcar. He stretched, getting a good look at the place as he soaked in the heat and the harsh buzzing of insects in the dried grasses all around them, before he walked forward, Isla on his heels, and opened the door to the jangle of bells.

Inside, it looked as if someone had dumped the entire contents of an antique store, a junkyard, and someone's basement inside, and given the owner ten minutes, tops, to put any sort of order to it.

"Wow," Isla said. "Even Uncle Rory's shed is neater than this place."

Fergus threaded his way between things piled on rickety chairs and stacks of old books and dishes, porcelain doll heads and twenty-third-century baby hoversaucers, all while ducking to avoid the innumerable pots and pans and cutlery and wind chimes hanging from the creosoted ceiling beams. Isla stared around in disbelief. Somewhere deep within the clutter, a cat yowled, which was followed by a muffled crash. He hoped the cat compensated the owner handsomely in dead rats for whatever inevitable carnage it caused, roaming through so many piles of breakables.

"Avalanche!" someone yelled, and Fergus froze, fearing the worst, but none of the stacks around him subsided and collapsed on top of him. Instead, a skinny, long, pure white cat appeared as if from out of nowhere and brushed past his leg to go jump up onto a counter at the back of the store, behind which stood a man with a deeply tan, weathered face and thin black beard, in a bright red tank top. The man reached over to pet the cat, the movement halting and unsteady, and Fergus could now see a line of blue lights on assistive tech modules half-buried in the skin of the man's arm and neck.

The man was watching Fergus and Isla with bored curiosity, and Fergus's gaze didn't go unnoticed. "Behind on my software updates," the man said, and laughed. "By about nine years. You shopping for anything in particular, or just browsing?"

"I'm not exactly sure," Fergus said. "Uh, you don't have any sort of, you know, cataloging system for your stuff? Or weird, broken pieces of something metal lying around?"

"Have you looked around? Might be some weird, broken stuff hiding under all the other weird, broken stuff." The man gestured expansively around him and laughed again, but his expression had gone deadly serious.

Fergus sighed. "We got an odd message about librarians."

The man picked up a blue-and-yellow enamel pot and slammed it hard on the counter. "Of course you did," he said. "No one ever comes in here to buy my things, help me put cat food in the dish or food on my own plate, oh, no, it's always you people. My late partner was the librarian, not me, and carrying all this on after him was not in our vows."

"Um," Fergus said. "I'm sorry, I wasn't trying—"

The bells hanging on the door behind him clattered and rang again, and the man behind the counter stopped midway to banging the pot again.

"A curious!" the familiar, booming alien baritone declared. Fergus half-turned, and Ignatio was standing inside the doorway, holding up a lizard sculpture made out of rusted metal, a few hardy flecks of paint still clinging to it.

"So, how much for that, Mr. Santo?" Fergus asked.

"Just Santo is fine. You got Territory scrip?"

"Is Atlantic States okay?"

"Then forty."

"Does that cover the cost of tetanus nanomeds?" Isla asked.

"Forty. We'll take it," Fergus said quickly, though it was a sum not at all within the range of *commendable*. He glared at Isla, who held up both hands in a gesture of helplessness.

Santo slumped. "Lemme see your catalog number," he said, "and follow me out back."

Walking with a slight limp, he led Fergus and Isla through a doorway behind the counter as Ignatio continued eir happy exploration of the store front. The back wasn't much different, though it was more organized. Shelf after shelf lined the walls with an indescribable assortment of unrelated things, which were also piled on tables and stacked in the corners: books, trinket boxes, folk art, dishware, bottles, brightly colored ballerinas and pony toys, tools, metal knickknacks, and even a lone, pristine red brick set atop a faded, wooden chess board.

There was also a console screen sitting in the one clear space on an old desk, and beside it, taking up most of the back wall of the cramped office, was a state-of-the-art autofab unit, its build arms poised, idle, around the empty fab platform like dozens of silver praying mantis arms waiting for their next hot date.

"Now, *that* is nice," Isla said. "What do you use it for?"

Good question. With that kind of heavy tech at hand, Fergus could not fathom why Santo traded in barely viable junk.

"Catalog number?" Santo asked. Fergus thumbed his handpad on and showed the message to the man.

"Right, the tea set," Santo said. He moved a set of brass bookends and a miniature carved masthead out of the way. Behind where they'd sat were a teapot and eight cups and saucers, pristine white porcelain with an intertwined, gold vine pattern.

"There you go," Santo said. "You got a box or something to carry it all in?"

"No?" Fergus said, and stared at the tea set. "I'm not really looking for a tea set, as much as—"

Santo groaned. "You don't know anything, do you?"

"Not really, no," Fergus said.

Santo sat in the desk chair, leaning slightly to favor his left side. "You know about the librarians, at least?"

"A little," Fergus answered cautiously.

"Information is never lost." Santo snorted, then tapped one of the modules on his shoulder. "Hemiparesis, from birth. Information doesn't always get from my brain to one side of my body without help. This here"—he pointed at the tea set—"is your help, information waiting to be found again. I don't know what it is, or who you are, or anything except that a Cataloger sent you here to get this. I'm assuming from your nonhuman friend out there that you probably came a very long way. So, you might want to find a box."

"You don't have any boxes?"

"Another twenty," Santo said.

The teacups were thin and delicate. "And something to wrap them in?"

"Twenty-five, then."

"Vergus!" Ignatio yelled from out in the front room. "I found a *samovar!*"

"Call it an even hundred, total?" Fergus asked hopefully, and Santo reached under the desk, pulled out a box, and handed it over.

Watching Fergus and Isla try to wrap the cups in soft paper was apparently more than the man's patience and appreciation for competence could endure, because after the first hapless saucer that Fergus tucked in the box fell immediately back out of its wrap, Santo took the cup out of his hand and shooed him back. Using his assisted arm to hold it, he deftly swaddled it in a perfect cocoon of paper. Isla tried to copy him, only to have the next cup also plucked out of her hand with a grunt.

"I'm sorry for bothering you," Fergus said.

"And we're sorry about your partner," Isla added.

Santo quickly got the rest of the saucers and cups settled, then began on the teapot itself. "It's okay," he said at last. "I could quit, you know, if I really wanted to."

He finished wrapping up the teapot lid and nestled it atop the rest of the things in the box, then brought it out to the front of the store and set it down on the counter out there. "Be careful with it. The road down is bumpy as hell."

"We noticed," Fergus said. He handed over a credit chit just as Ignatio warbled something unintelligible deep in the store, and Isla cracked up laughing. Bracing himself, he turned, and Ignatio had found and put on a Beefeater bearskin hat. "Oh, please, no," he said.

"Why don't I just throw that in?" Santo said. "Recommend me to all your other weird alien friends?"

"You have T-shirts?" Fergus asked. "Like, for your store?"

"No," Santo said. "Who in their right mind would want one of those?"

"Right," Fergus said. "Thanks for the hat and the help."

With his hands full, he nearly had to resort to kicking Ignatio to get em to leave the store without picking up anything else.

He settled the box with the tea set in the back of the podcar with Ignatio's samovar and rusty lizard, then watched as Ignatio tried to contort emself enough to get in without having to take eir hat off. "Bet he can't," Isla said.

"Not taking that bet," he said.

Ignatio made a half-dozen increasingly inventive attempts before giving up, though ey immediately put it back on as soon as ey were settled in.

Fergus got in beside Isla without saying a word, woke the car, and turned back down the road toward the autoway.

"I sense you are glum," Ignatio said after a bit. "Glum glum

glum. It is a good word, the sound and meaning match together, but it is for a not-good thing. *Glum.* It sounds like a pudding that makes you go poop too much, yes?"

Fergus sighed, and navigated around a patchwork of potholes and cracks in the road.

"Would you like to wear my hat?" Ignatio asked after a few minutes.

"No, thanks," Fergus answered.

"Maybe you should," Isla said. "You do look glum."

"This is why I prefer to work alone, you know."

"Ah, of course, you are too tall to wear my hat," Ignatio said. "Is that what is making you glum?"

"What?"

"Being too tall."

"I'm my own right size," he snapped. "It's that I was hoping for answers, and instead we've got a tea set. If this is supposed to be a helpful clue, I can't figure out how."

Ignatio blinked all four eyes at him. "Vergus!" ey said. "It is obvious! The tea set *is* the information."

Fergus missed the chance to dodge a large hole, and the pod-car hit it hard enough that he whacked his head against the ceiling. "Too tall," Ignatio muttered proudly.

"Remember the fancy fab unit in back?" Isla asked. "The data must be encoded directly in the matrix of fabbed objects, preserving and hiding the data in plain sight."

"Oh," Fergus said. He felt like an idiot for not thinking of that. "Makes you wonder what other secrets are in all the junk in that store. If I had a spare year and a good-enough scanner—"

"You do not have a year," Ignatio said. "*Whiro*, on the other legs, has a very good-enough scanner."

"Then back to orbit we go," Isla said. "I hope Santo didn't give us the wrong tea set, after all this."

They reached the autoway, and the podcar took over. Fergus leaned back in his seat and watched as the world flattened out, the sparse grass and red rock passing at a blur as the blue sky surrounding them remained still, endless, eternal. It was hard to believe, from there, how thin a shell of air that sky was, how delicate a balance everything contained within it depended on. Isla was gazing out the window again, and he wondered if they were thinking the same thing, about impermanence and impossibilities, all the many things that could and would go wrong.

Ignatio spoke up again, breaking the spell.

"So, you do not like my hat?" ey asked, eir voice filled with deep sorrow.

Chapter 7

"I have had a conversation I do not understand," Ignatio said, walking into the kitchenette where Fergus was busy reheating the second to last of the half-dozen fajitas he'd bought in Santa Fe before returning to *Whiro*. Ey sat down in one of the chairs at the table. "Is this a thing you experience?"

"All the time," Fergus said, using his fingers to shove molten toppings back into the wrap before stuffing as much of it into his mouth as he could. Chewing, he gestured that Ignatio should continue.

"*Whiro* is decoding and collating the data embedded in the tea set," Ignatio said. "It tells me that it is sharing the data with the rest of its 'party,' as it has, and these were its words, 'completed all their current quests.' How does a ship have a party? And how do we know that the other party guests will not break our need for security?"

Fergus laughed. "I don't think you need to worry," he said. "Actually, they could be very helpful."

"Who is *they*?"

"I'm not sure I'm supposed to tell anyone," Fergus said. "You could ask *Whiro*, though I suspect you'd spoil the fun of it, and I'm still not sure it would make sense to you."

"You are not worried?" Ignatio asked.

"Not about this," Fergus said, and took another gigantic mouthful of fajita.

Isla entered, yawning, hair disheveled from a nap. "What in bloody hell are ye eating, Ferg?" she asked. "That smells brilliant."

"Fajita," he said, putting a hand in front of his mouth as he spoke.

"That what took ye so long in Santa Fe when ye went to turn the podcar in? Are there more?"

He shook his head. When he finished chewing, he took a big sip of water—his eyes were watering from the hot sauce, and it was glorious—and leaned back in his chair in satisfaction. "*Whiro*, you got anything out of our tea set yet?" he asked.

"Yes. The catastrophic fragmentation of the original object as it emerged from jump space into normal space took place on March 11th, Earth year 2456, at 4:48 a.m. GMT, approximately 600,000 kilometers from Earth," *Whiro* said. "There were one hundred and twenty-seven atmospheric entry points detected by the orbital garbage monitors beginning three minutes and fifty-two seconds after the detection of that event."

"There are thousands of such entries every second, because humanity crapped up space for centuries before the ESS *Belgium* tragedy," Fergus said. "How do we know these are ours?"

"These entries had specific markers that indicated they hadn't burnt up in the atmosphere despite their size, which got them flagged," *Whiro* said. "Some of the trajectory data is strange; the monitors just assumed they had faulty data, shrugged, and moved on, but the entries remained in the official logs until they were removed by an unknown entity on December 3rd of the year 2459."

"One hundred twenty-seven," Isla said. "That's a lot. And none of these tracked bits of debris landed in the ocean?"

"Forty-one fell over open ocean," *Whiro* answered. "Eighteen fell near coastlines or islands where the estimated target area overlaps both land and sea."

"If some of the pieces sank, then this is impossible and we're doomed," Fergus said.

"The more pieces we find and separate, the more time there is for still looking, yes? It is only impossible if we name it so without trying," Ignatio said. "Also, not all pieces will be important ones."

"There is a subset of information I am extracting now that is redacted search activity reports, which continue well after the date when the first data was erased," *Whiro* said. "There will likely be meaningful patterns to uncover. It will take at least a few days to fully prepare and examine."

"Okay, fine," Fergus said. "Think of it as a new quest. In the meantime, I'm going to Australia. *Whiro*, can you get us an atmospheric insertion window and landing time for the shuttle?"

"In anticipation of your impatience, I have already received our descent ticket from EarthPort for Port Hedland," *Whiro* replied. "May I ask what name you will be visiting under, for the datawork?"

"Oh. Hmmmm," Fergus said. He didn't have too many aliases left he hadn't overused, and of those, only one would be plausibly visiting Earth. "Use Murdoch Maxwell."

"The helium salesman?"

"Yes," Fergus said.

"And for Ms. Ferguson?"

Isla was sitting at the table with her arms crossed, probably still peeved about the fajitas. "Do I get a pretend name, too?" she asked.

"You shouldn't need too deep a cover," Fergus said. "*Whiro*, run my protocols for a basic ID package for Ella Blakey, employee of Maxwell's?"

"That is now in-progress. Your landing window is in five and a half hours," *Whiro* answered. "I have also secured short-term parking for my shuttle in a private ground facility attached to the port, named Vinnie's. Will this be going on Shipyard accounts?"

"No," Ignatio said. "Please use my own account only."

"So done. I have also located the establishment of the name Dingo Hole. It is in the town of New Augustus," *Whiro* said.

"How far is it from the nearest debris site?" Fergus asked.

"That is a more variable answer than you likely expect," *Whiro* said. "It is a mobiletown. Currently it is located approximately eighty-seven kilometers southwest of Burringurrah, but it appears to be on the move."

"Well, crap," Fergus said. He'd heard about mobiletowns— had even borrowed books on them as a kid, whenever the book bus came through their hills—but those had all been in Pacifica, and his interest had been as a way he could escape and never be found. The idea of an entire town being able to roll itself out of the path of fires and floods and other disasters still seemed fantastical. Maybe not so much, though. "Fires?" he asked.

"There is one to the east, some distance away, that does not likely constitute a threat," *Whiro* said. "However, New Augustus is also an eco town; they move periodically both to limit their impact on the environment at any one particular site but also to perform certain ecological remediation and scientific survey work as they move. I examined the records and New Augustus tends to move on average forty-six kilometers each time, with a median move of thirty-nine."

"And how far has it gone this time?"

"Seven kilometers. Moving a town while leaving a minimal

footprint as you go is a slow process," *Whiro* said. "I project that they will only have moved another kilometer and a half between now and when you land."

"May I ask a question?" Isla asked.

"Of course," Fergus said.

"Why do we need to go to the town? Shouldn't we just go directly to the site?"

Fergus leaned back in his seat and tilted his head against the head rest. "You're right," he said at last. "I'm so used to going in seeking information, needing to understand the layout of the area in terms of entry and escape, and scoping out my adversaries. But maybe none of that applies this time."

"It was an excellent observation, Ms. Ferguson," *Whiro* said.

"Thanks, *Whiro*," Isla said.

"I also mention, as an aside, that Mr. Ferguson was incorrect in a statement earlier; there is one more fajita remaining in the refrigerated keeper," *Whiro* said. "I am sure it was an accidental oversight."

Isla smiled. "Thanks!" She got up, found the wrapped fajita carefully tucked back behind some of Ignatio's more unfathomable food items, and slung it into the cooker. Fergus hung his head; he was absolutely stuffed after eating five of them in a row, but when was he going to get fresh fajitas again? A few weeks back on Earth and already he was getting spoiled.

"I must have miscounted," he said, by way of feeble excuse. He stood up, rolled his shoulders, and stretched. "Maybe I'm getting old. I'm going to go lie down for a bit and think about my approach more thoroughly; let me know when it's time for me to get in the queue to descend."

"I will, Mr. Ferguson," *Whiro* said. "And you are welcome for my assistance with facts, any time."

———

A little bit of research turned up a supply company with global delivery that produced a variety of kits for vacationers, and their Experienced Outback Hiker package had nearly everything he could want in it. After consulting with Isla about her feelings on hiking—she ran off immediately to pack, so he took that as a positive—Fergus arranged for delivery of two kits to the private hangar *Whiro* had already contracted with for shuttle space.

Getting to the mountain was a separate challenge. It was over 800 kilometers in a straight line, and what roads there were, were distinctly not. *Either mostly not roads or mostly not straight,* Fergus amended.

He was still mulling over a multitude of poor options when *Whiro* announced they were nearing the front of the descent queue, and seconds later, his handpad pinged to let him know his hiking kit had been delivered. The receipt came with a pop-up ad that he was just about to flick away in annoyance when he paused, fingers hovering over his screen. It was for a drone-based pod service for the "casual hiker," and although not cheap, among the many places all over Western Australia it would happily deliver him, one was about eight kilometers from the edges of the debris site on a trailhead for Burringurrah itself. The price, even if tripled, would still beat the hell out of walking. Fergus booked one to pick them up at the private shuttleport and, feeling rather pleased with that turn of luck, got up to go prep the shuttle and collided with Ignatio coming back in at a run on three legs, holding eir bear hat in the other two.

"Vergus!" Ignatio shouted. "I have made something for you!" Ey rummaged through eir fur and pulled out a tiny pin, and placed it carefully in Fergus's hand.

Isla arrived at the bay with a small backpack, and ey handed another pin to her.

"Thanks. Cameras?" Fergus asked.

"Yes! I have synced them with our encrypted pager disk network, so *Whiro* and I can see too," ey said. "Then if you step in trouble, *Whiro* can drop a bomb on Perth, and while everyone is looking over there, we sneak you both away!"

"Uh . . . the bomb thing is a joke, right?" Fergus asked.

"Haha ahaha! It must be, yes?" Ignatio answered. Ey slapped Fergus hard in the chest and grinned so wide, Fergus could see the razor-thin, purplish baleen-like structures at the back of eir mouth. "You will avoid trouble now because you cannot be certain. It is my great plan."

"*Whiro* doesn't carry bombs," Fergus said, "do you, *Whiro*?"

"I feel it is prudent at this time not to answer that question," *Whiro* replied.

Fergus threw up his hands in frustration. "Can we just go?" he said.

"That would probably be best," *Whiro* said.

Fergus dropped the camera pin in his pocket, grabbed his things, and followed Isla into the shuttle.

———

The Port Hedland Shuttleport was small. The air smelled of dust, and everything within it vaguely of old, settled-in smoke, but the facilities were otherwise clean and good. They landed in what was late evening local time; the sun had just set over the Indian Ocean to the west, the lights of the city and surrounding town visible in the dusk against the yellow-orange horizon, and another, more ominous and formless, red-orange glow to the southeast.

The private hangar that *Whiro* had contracted with was just off-port, and as soon as they had disembarked, the service truck connected up to his shuttle and smoothly slid away with it. Brightly lit signs warned about trying to evade body customs and the penalties of bringing unchecked illnesses into the continental interior.

Every time he'd returned to Earth since first leaving, he'd either snuck in or relied on the Shipbuilders' solid permits to get him around any but the most cursory and superficial of entrance checks. Western Australia, however, seemed to have no such mechanism he could exploit to get through.

Isla put a hand on his upper arm, hesitantly. "Is this . . . you know, okay? For you?" she asked quietly.

"I'm not entirely sure," Fergus said. "Probably, but if a lot of alarms go off, pretend you don't know me."

Inside the customs building, they were split up and sent through separate doors. Fergus walked as confidently and casually as he could into a narrow, white, featureless room, and was relieved when he was met there by a medic in full protective gear instead of being directed toward an automated medical scanning booth; after a traumatic experience in a Dr. Diagnosis had led to him being briefly the subject of a citywide manhunt on Mars, he felt his paranoia entirely justified.

On the other hand, so was the government's paranoia about germs. After the twenty-second-century Ancou pandemic had swept the globe—fourth and worst of a series of them in a century and a half—the semi-independent Western Australian government had decided it was not going to suffer those kinds of catastrophic casualties ever again. With its rejection of the surveillance-state mentality that had taken a firmer grip on the eastern coast, that meant, at least for human travelers, a quick but mandatory antibody check and chemical-trace scan, neither of which should pick up any of Fergus's more unusual biological features.

The anonymous medic—no name tag, a mirrored face shield—

had him take off his exosuit and dump his things on a scanner platform. Then they directed him to roll up his sleeve so they could slap a long, sticky patch on his arm. It was prickly and itchy, and after a moment, small blocks of color began to appear until the whole surface was a patchwork.

While they waited, the medic checked his temperature, peered in his eyes, had him stick out his tongue, and for some reason Fergus couldn't fathom, took a swab from each of his armpits. When the strip stopped changing, the medic peeled it off in one fast jerk without warning.

"Aaaah, fuck!" Fergus swore as it took a healthy amount of arm hair with it.

"Antibodies are good, Mr. Maxwell," the medic said. "Might want to get a hepatitis E vaccine booster in the next few years if you plan on spending a lot of time on the eastern coast, but that's their problem and yours, not mine. You want the report?"

"Uh, sure," Fergus said.

"I'll have it sent up to your ship," the medic said. They punched a long sequence into their handheld unit, and past the desk, a door at the far end of the room opened. "You're clear. Enjoy Australia."

Fergus gathered back up his things, arm still smarting, and escaped through the far door and out into the port concourse, where Isla was waiting, rubbing her own arm in irritation.

He had to admit it felt good to be on a job again, even if it wasn't one he'd picked, wanted, or thought he could possibly *do*. *Hey, worst case?* he thought. *At least Isla will get to see a bunch of the Earth before it gets eaten.*

"You're making an odd face," she said.

"Just thinking about the future," he said.

"In an optimistic way?" she asked. "Or the other?"

"In a 'we have to get up really early tomorrow' way," he lied.

"It's going to be brutal till we adjust off Mars time. Planet-hopping really messes with your body clock."

"For you, maybe. I think I'm still on Scotland time," she said.

At the front gate they caught an auto-taxi to a nearby hotel. It was a relic of the city's old days as a mining town, a survivor of all three twenty-third-century tsunamis, and though it had been clearly renovated many times, there was still a faint smell of oil and rust in the halls. Once they'd checked in and stashed their stuff in adjoining rooms, he left Isla to some alone time and wandered down the street to a small pub outlined in neon pink lights. He liked to tell himself there was nothing he missed about Earth, nothing there that he couldn't find just as good elsewhere, but grilled cheese sandwiches had never, ever been quite the same anywhere else, and he savored it—and a second—like a man who had stumbled on an oasis after years lost in the desert who had forgotten the taste of water. The third he carefully left wrapped and out of sight in his bag to bring back to Isla.

Other than a few brief, friendly conversations with the waiter, his meal was blissfully uninterrupted, and he felt himself relax incrementally. He took a bottle of a local ale to go and wandered back to his hotel room, handed over the sandwich between the connecting doors, then collapsed face-down on the bed in relief with the ale left unopened on the side table near the door.

———

At dawn, Fergus woke Isla up, dragged himself into the shower, woke Isla up again, then they caught another auto-taxi to the local Hikerpod site. He had slept so soundly, his brain felt petrified inside his skull, and by the silent, dull stare of his sister out the window, she was equally unprepared for any kind of intelligent interaction.

Together, they loaded their stuff into the pod, including several bottles of water he'd picked up on the way. Once inside and buckled in, he read through and agreed to the various safety and usage terms on the pod's console, then a drone detached from the racks in the hangar behind him and picked the pod up like a mother bird carrying its egg, and moments later they were up and soaring smoothly southward over Port Hedland toward the interior.

Isla pulled a thermos of coffee out of her bag and the tiny pod interior filled with the complex, sweet-bitter smell. Once she'd had a few sips, she sighed deeply. "This is all automated, I guess?"

"Mostly," Fergus said. "We have some limited controls, but there are trajectory, speed, and safety constraints."

"Too bad. It looks like it could be fun to fly," she said.

"What have you flown so far?" he asked.

She took another sip of coffee. "Triumph."

Fergus laughed. "When this is all over, if you want to try flying, we can take *Whiro*'s shuttle out."

"Do ye really think this will ever be over and things will go back to normal?" she asked.

"It doesn't matter," Fergus said. "You have to act like it will; otherwise, how do you convince yourself to keep going?"

"Usually by promising myself ice cream," she said.

"That would also work," he said. Once they'd cleared city limits and the anemic town huddled up against its outskirts, the drone allowed him to direct it lower down. The red, arid ground below was, as if the universe lacked imagination, not dissimilar to either Mars or the Southwest Territories, though the vegetation was subtly thinner, wispier, sharper-looking than the latter, and the few birds they saw flitting between were vastly more colorful. There was a road just visible to their west, and a train track roughly parallel to it with a heavy freight hauler keeping pace with Fergus's pod. Here and there, small clusters of build-ings appeared alongside them and vanished just as quickly again. There were a few other aircraft out, mostly in-atmosphere flyers and what he thought might be another Hikerpod ahead of him heading due west. A dirty haze hung low to the horizon where he'd seen the glow the night before, far enough away that it al-most seemed more shadow than smoke, but in the direction they were going, the skies were blue and bright and empty.

As they passed over another small town, he closed his eyes and tried to reach out with his odd sense and feel the houses below, but the pod and drone were too overwhelming.

"What're ye doing?" Isla asked.

"Listening," Fergus said. "Sort of. Electricity, you know."

"D'ye hear anything?" Isla asked.

"Too much of the wrong things," he said, and settled back in his seat for the remainder of the ride.

A large button on the pod dash began to blink red. So used to sudden disasters, it was almost more of a shock that the label on the button read NARRATIVE INFORMATION AVAILABLE. Isla reached out and pressed it, and an almost comically broad Aus-tralian voice—no doubt played up for tourist expectations—began to speak.

"In approximately four minutes, we will pass overhead one of the seven heritage groups—or mobs—of red kangaroo in the Pil-bara region. Once nearly extinct, each mob is carefully managed to maintain a healthy population. Perth University, rebuilt after the devastating tsunami of 2366, monitors the mobs and period-ically redistributes prime individuals to strengthen the genetic diversity within each pool. If you would like more information on kangaroos, Perth University, tsunamis, or an explanation of genes, please speak your subject of interest."

There was a pause as it waited for either Isla or Fergus to

speak, but instead, they just looked at each other. *Daring me to say something,* he wondered, *or daring me not to?*

Ahead he could now see movement. From this distance, it looked like the ground itself was wobbling, but as they got closer, he could make out the individual animals moving among the vegetation. "They're bigger than I thought," Isla said. A few on the edges of the mob stopped and stood up, watching his pod pass with wary curiosity, before catching up with the others.

"Crikey, look at 'em go!" the narrator said, and Fergus turned it off. He'd heard enough exaggerated Scottish accents in his lifetime that he didn't feel the need for some tourist-facing prompt system pandering to expected stereotypes. Isla didn't protest, so he assumed she felt the same.

"You've been quiet," he said.

"Ignatio dumped a lot of physics and math on me," she said. "Mind ye, I asked. But it's a lot to process, and some of it conflicts with our science, and I don't know if it's because I don't understand it, or Ignatio didn't communicate it well, or because our science is wrong. Or all of those."

"See, this is why I'm glad you're the brains in the family," Fergus said. "I'd rather get my ear cut off again than have to think that hard."

She thumped him on the shoulder with her fist. "Not funny," she said.

"When it first started regrowing? It looked like a bright pink chunk of cartoon cauliflower sticking out of the side of my head. And the *itching*—"

"Okay, just shut yer gob now," she said. "I'd rather think about the math."

Burringurrah was a popular-enough destination that the Hikerpod company had it on their standard list of places to go. There were a trailhead and visitor's center at the foot of the mountain, which was, according to the research he'd done, not so much a mountain as a single enormous rock plunked down and slowly eroding into the earth. Terms like *monocline* and *anticline* had been offered up for the more geologically curious, but Fergus had already decided that Burringurrah was an unsubtle physical metaphor from the universe for the single enormous task that had been set down into the path of his own life.

Perversely, the anticipation of some dangerous thieving ahead cheered him up immensely. Isla caught his smile and smiled back at him, and he was grateful she didn't ask what he was thinking about. For her part, it was hard to tell if she was lost in the scenery or her own mathematical knots, but he left her to it.

It was midafternoon when the big, orange-brown shape of Burringurrah distinguished itself at last from the horizon, and the drone dropped down to gently deposit their pod at a landing pad beside a trio of low-slung buildings covered in solar tiles.

As soon as the drone recharged, it would take them the last forty kilometers or so and set the pod down right at the foot of the summit trail. The pod was fully functional as a shelter and, unlike the pop-shelter Gavin had lent him to go fetch Duff's sheep, had its own power, air systems, and a mini bathroom. He'd paid more to sleep in much worse places.

In the meantime, the screen in the pod made good effort to sell them on any number of fashionable hiking accessories and gear available at the trailhead supply store, which Fergus assumed Hikerpod got a commission on. In the end, Isla gave in and got a wide-brimmed hat, and he let it talk him into a walking stick; one thing about Earth's gravity is that it did like to remind him, every now and then, about the harpoon gun incident. Probably, he thought, Isla did not want to hear about that, either. The dry air of Australia was a lot kinder on him than the bone-seeping moist chill of Scotland, but eventually he'd be happy for the assist. And anyway, the stick fit in with his imagined persona of Murdoch Maxwell: Hapless Travel Enthusiast.

The hotel had a small cafe-style restaurant attached, so they retreated there while the drone recharged.

At least a few items among the tea-set information cache that *Whiro* had dumped to his handpad overnight were reports from hikers who'd passed through this waypoint, including a trio who'd seen the debris come down on the night of the explosion, and assorted reports of government activity to and from at the site a little over a year later. Nineteen months after that, a white van had driven out into the park itself, despite prohibitions against civilian wheeled vehicles, and kicked up enough dust that unhappy hikers posted extensively on community media about it. Last, another year on, there was a mention of an odd little religious group in plain linen clothes, matching bad sunburns, and mild heat exhaustion lost off one of the smaller trails that had to be guided back down, all four of which—three men and one woman—had refused medical treatment and signed a waiver indemnifying the tour service they'd wandered away from.

Whatever behavioral algorithm that the drone was programmed with must have decided that the optimum window for impulse shopping in the gift shop had unfavorably shifted instead toward a growing potential for customer dissatisfaction over delay, because it pinged him on his handpad that it was ready to go. With true marketing optimism, it then recommended several more products to him he may wish to check out before departure.

They climbed back into the pod, and the drone took them up for the last stretch south toward the mountain itself. It deposited them gently at a campsite pad and departed, a mechanical vulture silhouetted against the late afternoon sky.

"So, this is camping?" Isla asked. "So far, not bad."

"I don't think this technically counts," Fergus said.

There were two other occupied camps not far away: one more pod and an actual old-style pole-and-fabric tent that looked like it had been there for a while. The tenters were a pair of women, probably around Fergus's age or a little older, who had a roaring fire going in the firepit at their site, and were working on being loudly, happily roaring drunk along with it. A large, scruffy hound lay snoozing near the fire, oblivious to the noise around it. By contrast, the older couple in the other pod were less than amused, and after a short while standing there glaring at the women across the campground through the inadequate screen of eremophilas, they went back inside their pod, and forty minutes later, a drone arrived and took them away.

Lacking much else to do until the sun set and he could go out skulking on the mountain in the dark with his magic space-door-detector alien gut bees, he nudged Isla out of her studies and picked up the box of lime sugar cookies he'd picked up at the base lodge. "Should we go over and make friends?" he asked.

"Aye, absolutely," she said, and dumped her handpad onto the charging mat without hesitation.

Outside, there was the gentle buzzing of insects all around, less raspy than crickets, more subdued either because they were still unsettled by the pod's arrival or because it was almost time for the shift change over to the night crew bugs. Mixed in, at long but regular intervals, was the faint blip of the fire monitor drone nearby, doing its periodic check of the perimeter. The ground around the fire was packed dirt, hard and bone-dry, and faint lines radiating around it suggested the women had swept it free of anything that could conceivably catch.

The dog raised its head as they approached, studied them intently for a few seconds, then went back to dozing. Feeling appropriately vetted, Fergus introduced themselves as Murdoch and Ella, and offered up the cookies. They were Jesika and Julia, childhood best friends from Los Angeles, and amateur mycologists. Once a year, they picked some new spot in the world to hike, got drunk, and hunted mushrooms, careful not to do the last two at the same time. "Spotted death caps down near Perth," Julia said, as she dug a pair of fluted champagne glasses out of their tent, filled them and most of the ground below them with white wine, and handed them over. "Got some lovely scans and images of it, for our collection."

"And hiked a solid ten kilometers away from it before we pitched our site and broke out the bottles," Jesika said. "You like mushrooms?"

"Best on pizza," Fergus answered.

"Good man," Julia said, and all three clinked glasses.

Julia had the typical look of Pacifica: light brown hair, a long-lived-in tan, and a smattering of freckles that suggested that, without the tan, she'd give Fergus competition for paleness. Jesika, on the other hand, had a naturally darker complexion, and her jet-black eyebrows, frizzled hair, and high cheekbones made Fergus guess she was from the Middle East or, at least, that most of her ancestors had been. Who stayed put, anymore, stayed tied to their roots? *Not you, with yer bright ginger head and your Scottish-Martian accent,* Fergus thought. Both of the women's accents were pure urban Pacifica.

Jesika took a bite out of a cookie, then gestured with it toward Fergus. "What happened to your leg?" she asked, losing crumbs as she spoke.

Fergus glanced down at the pale, vaguely translucent scar on his shin, a lopsided diamond superimposed on a cruel X, the signature of the hinged barbs on the harpoon shaft that were much better at going forward than back out, and which he was still offended to have discovered were called *floppers*. It was a mean-looking reminder that of all the risks he took, not all went his way.

"Ping-pong accident," Fergus said.

Julia snickered, and refilled her glass. "We're both surgeons," she said. "I'm trauma, and Jesika is reconstruction. We see a lot of nasty things during the course of our jobs, which is why we're out here doing something completely different. You don't wanna say, that's fine, but whoever patched that up did a pretty ugly job of it."

"War zone," Fergus said. "They did the best they could. Also, I'm told I squirmed a lot while they were gluing it up." Ms. Ili, who ran the Medusa medical facility in Cernee, had in fact said exactly that, though not nearly so kindly.

"What was a hydrogen—" Jesika started.

"—Helium," Julia interrupted.

"—helium salesman doing in a war zone?"

"War had just ended and everyone wanted balloons to celebrate," Fergus said.

"And you?" Jesika asked Isla.

"I just tie the ribbons on. Much less dangerous," she answered. She stifled a yawn.

Jesika laughed. "If you say so. You find yourself with any more suspicious and life-threatening ping-pong injuries, Mr. Murdoch Maxwell Helium Salesman, feel free to look us up. Off the books and no questions asked, even."

"Why?" Fergus asked.

"Because I get the feeling if we do run into you again, we won't be bored," Jesika said. "We've seen just about everything in our line of work, and believe me, even the most challenging injuries are rarely unique, and they stop being a thrill after a while. And getting bored at your job, when you do what we do, means maybe people will die as a result. Maybe not such a problem in the world of high-stakes helium sales, though."

"It's the door-to-door polonium agents get all the fun," Isla chimed in, and that was cause for another round of glass-clinks and laughter, and then the harrowing story of hunting down red fly agaric in Crimea.

By the time conversation wore down, the sun had set and stars were beginning to appear. The fire was dying down, and there were two empty wine bottles in the sand beside it, reflecting the crackling embers. "And here we thought we were going to be stuck out here with Sour and Sourer for company," Jesika said. "Glad you two came along when you did."

"And you brought us cookies," Julia added.

"You brought the wine," Fergus said.

"We always bring the wine," Jesika said. "At least, when we're not on the job. You bring yourself in to see us after your next ping-pong adventure, we promise to laugh at you entirely soberly and do a much better job of fixing you up than the last time."

"Just, mind you, not *her*," Julia said, and tipped her glass at Isla, sloshing some of the remaining wine out into the sand. "Whatever stupid shit you get yourself into, don't get others hurt with you. We can fix almost any kind of hole anyone has figured out how to make in themselves, but there's no damned fix for that kind of regret."

Jesika took Julia's glass before she could drop it, though she wasn't much steadier herself. "I think Mr. Maxwell here already knows that. You can see it in his eyes," she said. "Now, before either of us get any more drunk, we have to bid you goodnight; we're off at dawn to look for mushrooms on this here impossible rock, and we need our beauty sleep. Don't forget to rehydrate—alcohol and dry air is a bad recipe for mornings after—and if we don't see you two tomorrow, have fun on your hike."

"Hiking is his thing," Isla said. "I just came along for the scenery. Couldn't turn down a free trip on the boss's cred, right?"

"Right," Julia said. She eyed Fergus. "'Boss,' huh? The two of you like a matched set with the red hair. He your dad?"

"No!" Fergus shouted in horror.

"Oh, bloody hell, no!" Isla shouted at the same time.

This amused the two women no end, enough that Julia almost fell out of her camp chair, and Jesika grabbed her arm and hauled her somewhat upright. "Well, whatever it is, never turn down a chance to see the world at its most beautiful," Jesika said, "because you can't miss it when it's ugly."

She saluted them with one of the empty bottles as she gathered them up.

Fergus picked up his empty cookie box, gave the two women an elaborate flourish of a bow, and as they crawled back into their tent, he and Isla went back to their pod to wait for the full dark of night.

Chapter 8

—◆—

I f you have to get up at one in the morning and sneak around in the dark being alert, coordinated, and clever, Fergus thought, it really helps if your brain is so confused by constant planet-hopping that it sincerely believes it is early afternoon, whatever your lying eyes are trying to tell you. Isla was also awake, and distinctly more comfortable about it, so it seemed her strategy of off-and-on napping for nearly two days had merit.

"This will take me a couple of hours at least," he told Isla in a low voice, as he pulled his exosuit on. "I'll keep you posted as I can, but hopefully it will be boring as hell for both of us. Let me know if anyone wakes up or you hear anyone coming up the trail behind me."

"And if ye get in trouble?"

"That's why I'm wearing my suit," he said. "No heat signature, which makes it nice and sneaky in the dark."

"And if ye still get in trouble?" she asked.

"If it's small or medium trouble, come help. If it's big trouble, summon the Hikerpod drone and get the hell out," he said. "Wait for me somewhere safe."

Her expression was skeptical at best, but she let him sync his comms and camera pin to her handpad without further protest before he slipped out into the night.

He tiptoed to the edges of the campground, then spent some time sitting with his eyes closed, listening with all his senses to the world around him. Once he was satisfied that he had a good sense of the sounds of bugs, birds, and snoring surgeons, he turned on his goggles to full night vision and headed quietly up the trail.

The debris zone wasn't all the way up at the summit, which was good news, but neither was it directly on the trail. He estimated he had about an hour of hiking until he needed to turn off into the wilderness, and from there depending on the terrain, vegetation, and potential ambush by any number of poisonous critters, it could take him another half hour or more to reach it. After that, who knew?

He waited until he was a couple of kilometers up the trail before he paused for a break, found a nice, smooth boulder to sit on, and took off his goggles and waited for his eyes to adjust to the natural dark. Then he stared up at the stars and the broad band of the Milky Way stretched across the sky like night's rainbow.

How many nights had he lain out in the fields as a kid, safely out of the house, and stared up at the same stars? Not the same, though; there was Orion, stalking the summer sky for a change, when Orion's presence normally meant it was going to be too cold to sleep outside and either he had to brave the house—he was adept at climbing up onto the porch and in his window with little or no noise, and by ten he could pick the lock if his father set it to teach him a lesson—or settle for what measure of shelter their shed could provide. Or, on particularly bad days, his aunt and uncle's shed over the hill.

He didn't think they'd known, and maybe they hadn't. At least when, in turn, Isla needed shelter, needed family, they let her into their home and kept her safe.

Fergus thought for a moment that the stars had been his safe haven, but the idea was instantly laughable. He had gone up into the stars, traveled across them—from here, if anyone had been able to follow him, it would have seemed like nothing more than the zigzag path of one scared, lonely, foolishly defiant little firefly.

But still, the stars! He was no less awed, no less enamored of them now than ever.

There are a lot of terrible things in the universe, Fergus thought, *but always there are also things like this. Sometimes, knowing how very, very small and alone and fleeting you are is also exactly how you know you are part of something vast and eternal.*

"See any snakes?" Isla asked him over his comm earpiece, making him jump.

His heart pounding, he closed his eyes and counted silently to five before replying. "No," he said. "I don't see any snakes."

"Maybe they see you, though," she said.

"Really?" he said. "Is that your idea of being helpful?"

"I didn't want ye to be bored," she answered.

"Thanks," Fergus said. "Thank you so much."

He put his goggles back on and continued up. When he reached the spot where he needed to leave the trail, he stopped long enough to drink some water from his pack and then headed off into the scrub, thinking more about snakes than he should have been. There was a vague path of sorts and fading indications that at some point long before, a large number of wheeled vehicles had come and gone. Following those tracks meant he had to worry less about precipitous edges, though flash flooding from the rare but typically violent rainstorms had cut channels and miniature canyons across the landscape without regard to anyone's convenient passage.

He knew he was in the right place without even having to check; when they'd searched for it—*they* being Alliance and/or the White-Vanners, as the job was more thoroughly done than he was inclined to believe of the cultists—they'd cleared all vegetation and scoured the ground in a fifty-meter radius. The harsh weather and unforgiving soil made for an achingly slow and as-yet incomplete recovery.

"Someone got a mess roarin'," Isla said over his comm earpiece.

"Yeah," Fergus said. "It's been pretty picked over. I'm turning off my suit systems for a bit so I can listen, so don't freak out."

"Awright, I wouldnae," she answered.

He walked to the center of the zone and sat on the bare ground, shut his suit down, and powered his goggles off, listening for that same faint call he remembered on the hill in Scotland. After a while, he decided there was *something*, but he couldn't quite get a hold on it.

He got to his feet, half-sliding down a steep incline past the edge of the clearing, until suddenly the ground disappeared beneath his feet and he fell, landing painfully among rocks and dead shrubs that had washed down one of the rain gullies. Lying there, scratched and battered and smarting all over, he fumbled in the dark for his goggles.

His fingers tingled as he reached around, and he got up into a crouch and ran his hand over the cutaway edge of the ditch.

There, he thought, and tried to dig his fingers into the dirt, but it might as well have been cement. Impatient, he fumbled his knife out of his pocket and hacked at the wall, dirt begrudgingly coming free enough for him to see, in the faint starlight, the glint of something metallic inside.

He pulled it out, and in his hand, it hummed back to him, a frequency half his and half its own. It was similar to the other piece he'd found, in terms of texture and the strange, almost fractal edge fragmentation, but it was a little smaller than the first and the shape less flat. He tried to imagine how the two would fit together, but even with his sharp memory of the other, he couldn't picture an obvious shared edge.

Maybe if he found more, the puzzle would start coming together. It was, he thought, already better than he'd expected that he found another at all, so maybe it wasn't an entirely impossible task. A couple more, and he might even get his hopes up.

"Hello! I am very happy to see you," he said to the fragment, and tucked it very carefully in his exosuit's faraday pocket, zipping it in securely.

Then he found his goggles again and stood up, bruised and battered but triumphant, and made his way carefully among the washout debris to where the ditch was shallow enough that he could pull himself back out onto the open ground.

He was, he thought, another twenty or thirty meters past the cleared area. A storm must have washed the piece down, and subsequent runoff buried it just out of sight. Lucky him to stumble on it.

Stumble is right, he thought. He was going to hurt in the morning; that was certain.

He turned back on his suit and earpiece. "Found it," he said. "On my way back."

"Awright," Isla said, and he could hear the yawn over the connection.

"See?" he said. "No snakes. Boring."

As he crossed the clearing again to make his way back toward the trail, he felt a chorus of new sounds around him, and he froze mid-step. There was something electronic in one of the scrub trees along the perimeter. He hadn't sensed it when he'd first walked through, but he'd been further up the hill.

"Something just passed the pod," Isla said. "A hum, fast-moving. Maybe a very small drone? I'm not sure . . . Shit, there goes another. What's happening?"

"It just stopped being boring," he told Isla. "I'm on my way down *fast,* but I may not be able to get to the pod. If not, wait until morning and summon the Hikerpod drone and leave just like a normal camper. If you can, go back to Port Hedland, and if not, go anywhere safe and I'll find you later."

"Leave without ye?"

"Leave without me," he said. "I'm going offline for a bit, and I'll call you when I can. Might be a day or two. Watch your own back and don't worry about me."

He closed the connection, quickly pulled his hood up and sealed his faceshield, and set his suit to go into stealth mode: no heat signature, nothing detectable, except motion, of course. Unlike space, he was going to eventually run out of darkness, and in the dawn light he'd be obvious. As fast as he could safely go, he ran back up the old vehicle tracks toward the trail, as somewhere in the distance he could hear the faint whine of a drone approaching from the west, then another closing in from over the summit. And two more were coming up from below, between him and their camp.

Okay, plan B, Fergus, he told himself, and changed directions off the trail, weaving and trying not to stumble through the scrub, and hoped there were no pits or snakes waiting to surprise him.

———

"You're where?" Isla exclaimed.

"At the Dingo Hole. Well, standing outside right now," Fergus said, his earpiece in one ear and a finger in the other, trying and failing to block out the sound coming through the walls like a battering ram aimed straight into his brain, even as the rest of him—feet to neck—wanted very, very badly to dance to the tune of its horrendous, inflicted beating.

"Band is about to wrap for the night inside, so I wanted to call while I had some privacy," he said. Was he shouting? He couldn't even tell. "I got us T-shirts. *And* I got the next piece. Easy as pie."

"Have you ever *made* pie?" Isla asked.

"No," Fergus admitted. "But I've eaten lots, and with the exception of pies made by our great-aunt Blaire, there wasn't one I'd call difficult."

"Then where have you been for the last three days?"

"Little bit of hiking, little bit of running and hiding," Fergus said. "Nothing special."

"You mean after you were chased off the mountain by surveillance drones and you made me leave without ye?" Isla asked. "That kind of *nothing special*?"

"Pretty much, yeah," he said.

"Yer camera has been off—"

"It got waterlogged," he said. "I had to wait for it to dry out again."

"In the desert?"

"It's a long, dull story," he said. Damn, but he was going to have this music embedded in his memory, replaying at him in ceaseless, merciless repetition, until he was dead. If it even stopped then—what if you took your last earworm into the afterlife with you or were reborn with it already seated in your newly recycled and reformatted mind, carrying it with you life after life after life? BAM BAM BAM THUNK BAM BAM CRASH, the gift that keeps on giving.

"I have been piecing together your movements from a miscellany of reports that I was confident I could attribute to you," *Whiro* chimed in. "It appears you stole a HikerPod from the base lodge, faked a mechanical failure in order to deliberately crash it into an artificial lake and throw off pursuit, and then hiked the twenty kilometers across desert to where New Augustus was stopped for the night. Is that correct?"

"Uh. Mostly?" he said.

"I was starting to think ye might have been killed," Isla said. "Ignatio told me not to worry, but that's nae as easy as it sounds."

Fergus groaned and resisted the temptation to beat his forehead against the side wall; the conference call had been his idea, so he could hardly complain now. "It was more boring than that sounds. No biggie," he said. "I've got a ride arranged after the show to Perth."

"I'm in Port Hedland," Isla said.

"Also, so is my shuttle," *Whiro* said.

"One thing at a time," he said. "I need to let the heat die down on Murdoch Maxwell for another few days, just to be on the safe side. And I think it's time I find out more about our competition. Check this out."

He held up his handpad, camera on wide angle, to show off his collection of newly dead spyware nestled inside his pack. "One stationary cam, three drones. The cam is total standard off-the-rack Alliance issue, but the drones? Those are some dark-ops top-of-the-line shit," he said. "These are just the ones I could catch."

"You're not outside-outside," Isla said. "I see walls. Walls with a lot of graffiti. Where are you? Are you calling us from inside a *bathroom*?!"

"Yeah, but—"

"That is bloody pure gross, Fergus," Isla interrupted.

"I'm not *doing* anything in here," he protested. "I have some manners, you know!"

"Ye do? First—"

"It would be helpful if we knew who those drones belonged to," *Whiro* interrupted.

Fergus could have kissed the ship, if the ship had been there, he was so relieved. Meanwhile, behind him, the beat had changed over to a fast-paced *taktaktaktaktaktakBAMtaktaktak* that he was pretty sure was gonna make his eye twitch in time with his helplessly tapping foot. "As I was about to say, your standard Alliance op isn't going to have this hardware," he said, and tapped the two dark ops drones. "While we know firsthand that the Alliance is capable of running rogue operations, if this was one, why wouldn't *all* their tech be this level of sophistication? These models aren't interoperable with the others, to the best of my knowledge, which means running them together slows you down while you have remote servers do the interpretation between them. And if you're okay with the lag that imposes, why waste your cred on the fast, fancy illegal surveillance tech to start with?"

"This fits into your hypothesis of multiple organizations at work," *Whiro* said.

Behind him, someone rattled the door handle.

"Exactly. Look, let me talk, because I'm running out of time," Fergus said. "I'm willing to bet these top-end drones don't belong to either the Alliance or to a bunch of half-starved apocalypse cultists, but it's absolutely plausible for White Van Kyle, with the van full of mystery electronics he parked outside the *Drowned Lad*. But who knows who else might be out there? We need the answer to that, sooner rather than later. Any of you heard the old tech term 'honeypot'? Because we need to make one. *Whiro*, if you could, can you route-encrypt a message to Lunar One, node four-four-seven-bee-zero-cee-eff-nine-eight-one-three? Address it to Francesco."

"And the message?"

"Say: an old fan of the theater is looking for a part actor in an off-Broadway, off-license play. Potentially multi-week run, stunts likely. Venue, expenses, and per diem covered. Sign it Finnigan, and let me know when we get a reply?"

"I will do so, Mr. Ferguson," *Whiro* said. "And it is done."

The knob rattled again, and then there was pounding on the door. He could no longer feel the low bass thump of the band vibrating through his bones, and it was as if he could breathe again, and at the same time, desperately missed it. And, speaking of desperate, if the show was over, it was about to get very crowded outside his bathroom door.

"Great," Fergus said. "I gotta go. See if you can find out where Detective Zacker is hanging his hat these days. I'll call you when I'm in Perth."

———

Fergus had just been dropped off, some nine hours later, along the waterfront of Perth near the Tsunami Memorial when he caught the muffled chime deep in his pack. He sat on the marble wall overlooking the beach, enjoying the feel of moisture in the air and the warmth of the sunrise climbing up behind him, and pulled his handpad out.

The man who appeared on the screen was late middle age, and he wasn't wearing a shirt. Over his bare, hairless, light-brown torso was a bandolier made of orange sequins that held, every few inches, miniature gold forks and spoons. His hat was a matching orange fez with what seemed to be purple tentacles sprouting from the top. "Finnie!" the man declared.

Fergus grinned. "Francesco! That is one hell of an outfit."

"Yes! Turan made it for me, and it is my current favorite. Not your style, though. Fashion is a tragic failing of yours."

"It is," Fergus agreed. "I don't dare ask what you're up to in that outfit, but I assume it's another of your underground theater events."

Francesco leaned closer to his own screen. "They remember the hat and never the face," he said. "And thus, the revolution is free to continue. But, alas, such fabulous tactical gear is not cheap. You have a paying gig?"

"Yeah. I need someone to play the role of, well, me. People are going to come looking for me, and I need to know who shows up. One is likely to be the Alliance, so there's the bonus comedy of sending them on a wild goose chase. I'm not sure who or how many others, but at least two, and they are less predictable and possibly a lot more dangerous."

Francesco shrugged. "This is here on Luna?"

"No, down here on Earth."

The man winced. "Ah, Finnigan, my friend . . . You know our stage is here."

"I know. I can't tell you anything about what I'm working on, but it's big enough that the consequences extend well beyond both Earth *and* Luna, and I need someone I can trust completely and who can handle sudden improv. Unless you have someone here you'd recommend?"

"Not for your type of plays. When is opening night?"

"It's flexible, but a few days from now would be good," Fergus said. "There is some urgency."

"Bad Yuri has your build and skin color, or at least that ghastly paleness you call a body. We'd have to arrange for the beard, and some hair-color nanites, but that could be done." Francesco took a deep breath and then named a hefty price. "It is only because I need to pay off this fez," he added. "Also, Azuretown's greenhouses took a hit from space crap that somehow got through their gel canopy, and repairs aren't cheap. You know I would not extort friends. And if it were not you, who found my stolen Guild ring, there would be no price high enough to tangle with the Alliance on their grounds instead of my own."

"Understood, and I agree to your price," Fergus said. "I'll take care of the setup and be back in touch with the details."

"It's good to hear from you again," Francesco said. "One of these years, you must come play with us. We'd have all the best sorts of fun." He tipped his fez, causing the tentacles atop to wiggle alarmingly, and disconnected.

Fergus smiled and had to stifle a sudden, jaw-cracking yawn. His ride had been with a young man who went by the name of Chickenleg and who had been desperately chatty the whole ride. It had kept Fergus from dozing off, but he suspected that it was also the only thing that kept the driver from doing so as well, and with no autodrive available for most of the way, that had been a forgivable fault.

A few more tasks, and he'd find somewhere to crash for a solid ten-hour nap. The next call he made was to a node number *Whiro* had dropped to him sometime during the night.

Clarence Williston Zacker, retired detective of the Sovereign City of New York, was, to the untrained eye, the opposite of Francesco. Dour, dressed in nondescript civilian clothes that hung on his body as if his body was trying to reject them, he scowled over the video link at Fergus. "You," he said.

"Me," Fergus said. "How are you doing?"

"Took three fucking bullets," he said. "How do you think I'm doing?"

"You're not dead," Fergus pointed out.

"No," Zacker answered. He sounded disappointed.

"I didn't call at a bad time? You're not in the middle of dinner?" Fergus asked. The Sovereign City of New York was thirteen hours behind him.

Zacker snorted. "Right, regularly scheduled meals. Always meant to try that someday."

"Yeah, well, I'm not one to talk. Things any better with Deliah?" Deliah was Zacker's estranged daughter.

Zacker's face went through a rapid series of expressions, most of them some variant of furious, then he seemed to deflate a little. "We're talking," he said at last. "I'm not very good at that stuff."

"Yeah, me neither," Fergus said. "So . . . you bored?"

"Holy shit, yes," Zacker said. "You in trouble again?"

"I've got a surveillance-and-backup job for you. Better digs than last time, and I'll cover food and expenses. Shouldn't involve any direct danger, but it could."

"Good cause? Nothing illegal?"

"Saving the world?"

Zacker snorted. "I'm not sure that counts as *good*," he said. "Where? And don't tell me fucking Pluto."

"Right here on Earth. Australia."

"Aren't there snakes?" Zacker asked.

"I haven't seen any. But you could always just shoot them," Fergus said. He was pretty sure firearms were just as illegal there as almost everywhere else on Earth, but he didn't figure that was his responsibility to say.

"Then I'm in," Zacker said. "Tell me the setup."

———

Fergus booked a short-term apartment under a new—and, he was proud to say, non-alliterative—alias, Clyde McBean, and paid his usual identity service to drop just enough bits and pieces out there onto SolNet to give him a shallow history that would pass a cursory check. That done, he spent more time making sure there were no easy-to-find holes in his Murdoch Maxwell alias; he had one more use for his hapless helium salesman after all.

Convinced that it would stand up to all but serious scrutiny, and that even then nothing pointed back to him or anyone or anywhere he cared about, he reserved a second apartment under that name directly across the street with a move-in date of to-morrow. He tried not to think about how much he'd been bleeding his financial accounts the last few jobs, and wondered if things would get so dire, he'd have to call in Duff's debt for finding his sheep. *If it gets that bad, I'm in deep, deep trouble,* he thought.

Zacker wouldn't get to Australia until tomorrow at the earliest, which meant for the moment, the very large, very soft-looking bed in the McBean apartment was his. He crawled into it, put the Burringurrah fragment under one of the pillows with the pointiest edge safely down, and pulled the slightly dusty, over-laundered comforter and blankets up until he was virtually buried in them. With the brilliant midday sunlight streaming in from the room's small oval window, he let himself sleep.

———

In the comfortable pseudo-anonymity of dusk, he ventured back out into the suddenly alive streets of Perth, the low bass call of music drawing him into a large open space where the recon-structed Swan Bell Tower, in verdigris and glass, dominated the center. Set back in a circle around it, mountains to its valley, stone buildings were decorated with a line of blue and green mosaic. The small, undulating waves hopped from one building to the next, continuous everywhere there was a solid surface to continue on, depicting how high the tsunami waters had come. The line was above Fergus's head. He couldn't help but raise his arm and see that his fingertips just barely crossed it; it was a so-bering piece of art.

The walls below the wave were engraved, fading gold paint deep in the sharp cuts, with the names of all the dead.

Despite that, the square—a misnomer, geometrically if not functionally—was teeming with people and lights and noise.

There were performers dancing on small portable mats that projected lights and holographic imagery upward around them, while others had entire pop-up transparent booths with shifting backdrops and, typically, artificial smoke. It made for mesmerizing confusion, as musicians around the circumference of the bell tower played nearly every Earth instrument he could recognize and more than a few otherworldly ones as well. Between them were numerous food carts, their cloying steam fighting to dominate each inch of the breeze coming in off the ocean, their solar canopies rolled up for the night and the steady hum of their full batteries underneath another kind of droning instrument to Fergus's senses.

He tapped his camera and earpiece on, and opened a two-way connection to Isla. "Thought you'd like to see this," he said, and tried to catch a panorama from where he was standing that would do it even slight justice.

"Yeah, I would. In person," she said. "Do ye know what there is to do in Port Hedland? Other than drink? Nothing. And here I hadn't bothered to get my Substance Education Certificate because I never thought I'd be abandoned in a motel in Australia with nothing to do."

"They probably don't check, anyway," Fergus said.

"No, they don't," Isla said, and took a sip from a bottle that she grabbed from somewhere out of her connection's line of sight. "Too bad I don't actually like alcohol. I wonder what else I can find to try."

"Uh. A museum?" he suggested. "Virtual library?"

"Said just like a big brother," she said. "Just not the brother I thought I had, who seemed to have fun adventures all the time until he made the mistake of coming home. No wonder ye ditched me already."

"How many of those have you had?" Fergus asked.

"Not nearly enough," she said. She sighed and set the bottle down, somewhere out of sight. "And too many. Guess I can also cross getting drunk off the list of things I thought would be more interesting than they are."

"I'm sorry," he said. "I can come back there—"

"What are you doing? Right now?"

"Setting up a trap for the people watching the fragment sites," he said.

"At a street festival?"

"I just came out to go get supplies," he said. "And food. This was all here happening; I had no idea. Have you eaten anything? You really shouldn't drink on an—"

"Yes, *Fergus*, I ate something. Found a decent sushi place, and no, I'm not telling you where it is. How long?"

"Until what?"

"Till you get yer arse back here," she said. "I keep thinking about the physics and how this dumb multidimensional door thing works, and none of it makes any sense and I feel stupid and useless." She had turned her face away from the camera, and he couldn't tell if she was just avoiding eye contact or was trying hard not to cry.

"Look, we've hardly started, and we're still just gathering information, right? The more info we get, the more it'll make sense. And even if it doesn't, do we really need to know how it works?" Fergus said. "Once we've found all the pieces, Ignatio can hand them over to someone who knows what they're doing, no need to mention humanity or Earth at all, just 'Lookie what I found; can you bin it for me?' And in the meantime, you can call Ignatio or *Whiro* any time you want and talk however much science you want, and I assure you you've got a much better chance of understanding it, even drunk off your ass, than I ever will. Tomorrow night, okay? Then we'll do something fun."

"Yeah, what?" she asked suspiciously.

"Ice cream? And then it's a surprise. Trust me."

Isla nodded. "Okay," she said. "I think I need to go lie down now."

The connection cut out. He stood there, looking at the blank screen, and hoped she was now getting much-needed sleep. Still, he checked in with *Whiro* and asked it to let him know if her pager signal strayed from its current location.

Fergus wondered if it would ever stop being weird feeling responsible for other people.

With this many street performers, it didn't take him long to find a small shop tucked away along the side of one of the buildings in the ring, filled with dance shoes, holo-mats, and a rainbow cacophony of costuming items. He bought a pair of round-lensed sunglasses that shifted colors through the rainbow for Ignatio, several different tubes of hair nanites, and, with deep regret, a razor. To make himself feel better, he bought a bottle of scotch, a small string bag of mangoes, and a big slice of pavlova meringue.

Feeling okay with life, he found himself walking in step to the beat of the louder of the bands as he meandered his way, in no hurry, back to his apartment, and headed off gratefully to the shower.

Out twenty minutes later, a towel wrapped around his waist, he padded barefoot into the kitchen, leaving a small trail of water drips behind him. He sliced one of the mangoes in half and grabbed a spoon, then wandered back to see what passed for Earth entertainment after nineteen years.

———

Zacker arrived first, midafternoon the next day. The retired detective threw his small canvas duffel in the back seat of Fergus's auto-taxi, then climbed into the passenger seat beside him. "Five and a half hours from New York to Australia?" Zacker complained. "I could've got here faster on a scooter."

"Have to be a floating scooter," Fergus said, giving the auto-taxi directions back to the apartment.

Zacker snorted, and leaned his head back against the seat rest. "You got food back at the apartment? My flight was not big on feeding us."

Fergus nodded. He'd had a grocery order delivered that morning; much of it was fresh produce. He missed being out roaming the stars, but there were definite upsides to being there. The detective might be less enthusiastic about vegetables, but if so, that was his own problem.

"So, what's the setup? You said surveillance? I need a lot more information if I'm going to be effective. For starters, exactly who am I watching?"

"Me," Fergus said.

"Well, I found you. Can I go home now?" Zacker asked.

"You know how I find things?" Fergus said. "Well, I came here looking for something very dangerous, and I got chased by at least two different sets of remotes. I'll show you the handful I broke so you can form your own conclusions, but as near as I can tell, there are at least three groups looking for the same thing I am, and I need to know who they are. So, I'm going to lure them out. I have a friend arriving in another few hours to help set the trap, but I need a reliable set of eyes outside the target for their safety, and to spot anyone coming around for a look who doesn't fully take my bait."

The auto-taxi pulled up in front of Fergus's McBean apartment and deposited them on the sidewalk. Fergus handed Zacker one of the keycards and grabbed the man's bag as the detective turned slowly around, studying the street and nearby buildings before following him into the glass-and-brick entry and up to the third floor.

Once inside, Zacker immediately went to the fridge and grabbed an apple. "Whas 'at?" he said, chewing, and pointed to a large box on the floor with his free hand.

Fergus opened the box, and Zacker peered in. His eyebrows shot up. "Whoa," he said. "That's some pricey gear."

"Should be everything you need," Fergus said. He pointed out the window directly across the street. "That's where I'm setting up my honeypot."

Zacker slid open the door to the balcony and leaned over the railing, looking up and down the street before coming back inside. "Great lines of sight," he said.

"Thanks," Fergus said. It was as close to a compliment as the detective got, and he took it as such.

"What do you know so far about the bad guys you're trying to draw in?"

"First is the Alliance—" Fergus started.

"The Alliance has limited terrestrial jurisdiction," Zacker interrupted. "They won't operate here."

When they'd first met, Zacker had been in Glasgow, working a cold case he couldn't let go of even though he was both retired and had no jurisdiction outside the SCNY. Once they'd sorted out their own mutual antagonisms—enough, anyway, to work together—they'd come up against a rogue Alliance operation on Enceladus. Whatever facial expression Fergus made must have communicated a lot of skepticism, because the man threw his apple core into the flash recycler with more than a little force. "Fine, okay, so Alliance. Rogue?"

"Probably not. The things I'm looking for originated outside of Earth's orbit, so they have legitimate interest," Fergus said.

"Who else?"

"An apocalypse cult."

Zacker laughed. "Seriously?"

"Yeah. You got a handpad; I'll send you what I've got on them," Fergus said. "So far, they don't seem competent enough to be genuinely dangerous, but you never know."

"And you said there was a third group?"

"I know the least about who they are, which is a problem, because I think they're probably the most dangerous. Had a run-in with one of them in Scotland, and he wasn't a local. I have evidence they're here in Australia, too. I got a license number off their van, but it was a rental and I couldn't get any further."

"Send that to me, too," Zacker said. "What's the stakes here? You blathered something about saving the world."

"I can't tell you much, but if any one of them gets their hands on what I'm looking for, the only people who are going to be happy with the outcome—very, *very* briefly—is the apocalypse cult." Fergus's handpad chimed, and he walked over to where he'd left it on the counter. "Ah, my friend is here a bit early. They're on their way over to the other place. You want to come along and meet them?"

"No. Or not yet," Zacker said. "I want to eat some food, take a leisurely crap, sort through the equipment you got me, and get a look at your friend's natural body language when they're not under stress. Sometimes, small, even subconscious changes in body language are the only warning you get."

"Okay," Fergus said, "I'll leave you to your plans. I've already packed what I need, so once I get my friend settled in, I'm out."

"You mean we're not gonna be roomies? Imagine my disappointment," Zacker said.

"You'll survive somehow," Fergus said, and took his last mango before he headed for the door.

———

Bad Yuri arrived by auto-taxi twenty minutes later. He had bright silver hair and was dressed all in black, in a top hat and an old-fashioned tuxedo coat with tails over a T-shirt emblazoned with a silvery skull graphic. As he introduced himself, the skull winked.

Fergus shook his hand. "Thanks for coming, Yuri," he said.

"Bad Yuri," the man corrected. "I have worked hard for my adjective. You are indeed as red-headed as Francesco said. I am not looking forward to growing a beard overnight."

"No, I imagine not. It's little consolation, but I don't look forward to losing my own," Fergus said. He pointed up at the second apartment he'd rented, across the street from the Zacker/McBean lookout. "I rented it under the name Murdoch Maxwell, the alias I was using when I got chased off Burringurrah, so it should get attention soon enough."

He got his suitcase out of the taxi and handed Bad Yuri a loaded, anonymous credit chit as they took the lift up to the room. "Earth isn't bad, except for the horrible gravity," Bad Yuri said as he explored the small apartment. He walked to the window and stared out it for a while. "You have someone watching?"

"Yes. A friend across the street," Fergus said. "He's going to be a spotter, and backup if there's trouble."

"Hmmmmm. I've always wanted an understudy," Bad Yuri said. "So, is there a script? How many acts? Who plays the villain?"

Fergus gave Yuri the same breakdown of enemies he'd given Zacker.

"So, I play your helium salesman?" Bad Yuri asked. "When do we swap?"

"As soon as you're up for it," Fergus said. "The sooner, the better."

Yuri nodded, grabbed a handful of things out of his bag, and headed off to the bathroom. A few minutes later, Fergus heard loud cursing, and he winced in sympathy. Insta-beards were not for the faint of heart.

When Bad Yuri emerged in a bathrobe, he already had the start of stubble on his chin, and his hair was now close to Fergus's own shade, if the length was still off; that would be easy enough for Yuri to fix on his own, now that he'd seen Fergus in person. "Your turn," Yuri said. "I left my clothing for you. I would please like the hat and coat back, eventually."

Fergus went into the bathroom with the razor, hair nanites, and bottle of scotch, and regarded himself in the mirror. *Yer an ugly bastard*, he thought, with great fondness, *but now you get to be a different ugly bastard for a while.*

He picked up the razor, let out what he felt was his crowning glory world-weariest sigh, and got to work on his face. It was disheartening how little time it took to utterly remove all traces of his beard, given how long it had taken him to cultivate it. His chin felt cold and bereft, too naked to process, and a swig of scotch didn't make him feel any better about it. He set the correct color code on the nanite tubes and broke them open one by one, finishing the necessary transformation. His scalp and eyebrows itched terribly as his hair shifted from his natural red to a close approximation of Bad Yuri's silver. There was not much he could do about the length, but given that Yuri had arrived wearing a hat, and he would be leaving wearing same, it shouldn't be risky.

When he looked in the mirror again, he could hardly recognize himself. *And that's the point,* he thought wryly. He put on Yuri's clothes and left his own folded neatly on the edge of the tub, and went back out into the living room to find a near-copy of himself looking him up and down.

"Not bad," Bad Yuri said. He gestured around the room. "I opened your suitcase and found your tubes of helium samples and other props for the role. Also, I found this." Bad Yuri held out his hand, and in it was the piece of inert fragment that Fergus had found in Scotland before finding the live one.

"That's what they're looking for," Fergus said.

Yuri poked the fragment gently with one finger. "So, all hell's gonna break loose over *this*?"

"If we're lucky, it won't," Fergus said. "If it comes down to it, let it go. It's just an odd scrap to you, and Murdoch isn't a fighter. And anyway, that's a decoy."

Whatever the doorkey was, the extraneous fragments had no hum, no life, and when you turned them around, they behaved exactly as they should. Ignatio had said it was the difference between the core of the doorkey and the frame that merely held it. If the live fragments were baby ducklings by Isla's earlier analogy, these were just leftover bits of shell.

"It's a fake?" Yuri asked. "Will they be able to tell?"

"It's real; it's just not one of the pieces they want," Fergus said. "They'll know if—when, I expect—they get their hands on it, and just maybe it'll throw them off my tracks for a while, thinking I've got nothing."

"Okay," Bad Yuri said. He moved toward the window again and looked out. "Is the apartment bugged? Eyes, ears, both?"

"I figured I'd let you work that out with my friend across the street," Fergus said. "Name is Zacker, he's in 401C, and I'm leaving you a preprogrammed burner nodephone so you two can talk untraced. He's a very grumpy man and has terrible people skills, but is very good at this and not immune to reasonable arguments. If you go out, coordinate with him so he can shadow you. Other than that, just go about as if you're having a nice, normal vacation in Perth. My goal is to draw out everyone interested in that piece and get enough information to identify and track them, nothing more. It shouldn't get dangerous, but I don't know who we're up against."

"What name does your friend know you as?"

"Fergus," Fergus said.

"That's an even more ridiculous name than Finnigan," Bad Yuri said. "Okay, then. Go get on with what you need getting on with. I'll call if and when trouble finds us."

Fergus shook his hand again and went down to the waiting auto-taxi. He was already on his way to the train station when Zacker called.

"Shit, is that you?" Zacker asked, eyes narrowing. There was a telescope camera set up now in the half-open door onto the balcony behind Zacker. "That *is* you. Must feel good to trade up. Your poor friend, though. Can he handle the trouble you've sent his way?"

"Yes. Don't underestimate him," Fergus said. How could he explain Francesco and his people? They were the Lunar equivalent of Free Marsies, with almost none of the resources that the Marsies had. Their entire street theater troupe was made up of former military commandos. When they hit something, it stung hard, it made the Lunar Authority look incompetent or corrupt, and they never, ever got caught. And they did it in *style*. The brief time he'd spent working with them were some of the most terrifyingly fun, strange weeks of his life. "He can handle himself, but if everyone comes at him at once . . ."

"Then I get to step in and break some heads," Zacker said, disappearing from view, then reemerging with a packet of cheese and two slices of bread. "Where are you going?"

"You know how you feel about theft?" Fergus asked.

"Yes," Zacker said.

"Well, what if I'm stealing something that's mine?"

Zacker groaned, slapped a thick slice of cheese between the bread, and then gestured at the screen with the sandwich. "You are the most gray-area person I've ever met," he said.

"Thank you," Fergus said.

"It was not a compliment!" Zacker said sharply.

Fergus blew Zacker a kiss; the detective flashed him the middle finger as he cut the connection.

Chapter 9

Fergus had his full folio of credentials out and ready, including an entirely bona fide document proving *Whiro*'s shuttle was the legal property of the Shipyard at Pluto, and that he had been retained to locate and secure its safe and swift return. The manager at Vinnie's took and scanned them all, and studied them with an increasingly sour expression of resignation. "You're a repo man? So, the shuttle was stolen, then," the manager said.

"Yes," Fergus answered. "I'm retrieving it for the owners. This is my mechanic."

Isla, standing behind Fergus in coveralls with a toolbox that, had the lid been open, would have revealed a half-dozen donuts, gave a short wave. She was still furious, still more than a little hungover, and had barely spoken a dozen words to him since he'd picked her up that morning, but she put on a perfect easy, nonthreatening nonchalance that would have impressed even Francesco.

The manager barely glanced at her, which was the whole point of the act. "And the thief?"

"You can be sure he won't get away from me," Fergus said.

"No, I mean . . . there are charges."

"We are willing to cover them, in anticipation of eventual recovery of damages from the thief," Fergus said. Sure, he was stealing back his own shuttle, but that didn't mean he had to cheat the storage facility, which had done nothing wrong. *I try to put the honest in dishonesty*, he thought proudly.

The manager grumbled under his breath. "Your thief also signed up for our daily dust removal services, at an additional fifty per day."

Hell, no, I didn't, Fergus wanted to protest. Instead, he pointed out the window to where his shuttle was being pulled out of the hangar onto the tarmac. "It looks pretty dusty to me," he said.

"Accumulates fast," the manager said. As Fergus continued to stare, he typed on his console. "We hadn't done today's sweep yet, so I'm removing the last charge."

Fergus paid him, resenting his own clever honest-dishonesty crack a moment earlier. And there wasn't anything in the small office worth pocketing for the principle on his way out, even just to see if Isla would notice.

———

The Shipyard had a berth share in the plane of Earth's geosynchronous orbit reserved for small industry. It was served by small automated shuttles that took passengers or small cargo back and forth with Kelly Station, the nearest of the six public stations in Earth's orbit, and the oldest among them. Larger cargo came and went on separate transport directly to and from the surface, and because of the precision required to keep everyone from crashing into everyone else, private craft such as *Whiro's* shuttle had to submit to a queue coming in and out. The station-control systems were happy to let ship mindsystems pilot, but everything was strictly bio-hands-off until you were either safely docked or far enough out of the way that any problems you caused were your own damned problem to deal with and not catastrophic to a wide swath of the outersphere.

By the time they got through the line to *Whiro*, Fergus wasn't sure if Isla was any less mad at him or just too taken with watching all the zipping traffic around them against the magnificent backdrop of Earth to remember to periodically glare at him. Either way, he was sure that what she still saw as his abandonment of her was not yet behind them.

For his part, Fergus mildly resented that anyone cared enough about him to feel abandoned, when he was just doing what he'd always done.

Ignatio had reset *Whiro*'s artificial gravity to forty percent, much to Fergus's relief; his tumble down the mountain and trek across the desert had not done him any favors. He dumped his stuff in his room, took his time washing up and putting on fresh clothes and his new Dingo Hole T-shirt, then took the new fragment down to engineering for *Whiro* to scan. That done and out of his hands, he went back up to the kitchenette to scrounge up some lunch. Ignatio was there, eir legs curled up around em on the couch with Mister Feefs asleep beside em, and Isla stood across the table with a cup of coffee in her hands. Above the table a hologram of Earth in blue outlines rotated, a smattering of white dots forming a lopsided caul across half its surface. "—see what you mean," she was saying. "Weird."

"Are those the atmospheric entry points?" Fergus asked, hoping he didn't have too far to catch up.

"Yes," Ignatio said. "The analysis was done by *Whiro*, with fast and very, very vast efficiency, so I will let the ship explain."

Whiro had already told him, when he and Isla were waiting for permission to enter the docking space, that the task of combing through the data was being shared among its 'party' of ships. "For this challenge, we are spy detectives, seeking enemy agents among a field of decoys," *Whiro* had explained. "It is a more interesting task than our Shipyard quests, which we have temporarily suspended."

Fergus expected Theo was grateful for that, even if the man had no idea why his stuff kept disappearing. For his own part, he didn't mind the additional help in the least, as long as he didn't have to explain it to anyone else or, worse, admit he knew and hadn't told anyone.

"I believe we can substantially narrow down the focus of where you should concentrate your quests, Mr. Ferguson," *Whiro* was saying as Fergus came forward to peer at the holo globe. "Not only was the original data written into the physical structure of your tea set, it included all the metadata around it, especially the timestamps of each data point's appearance, proliferation, and removal. Some data was new as recently as two weeks ago. We can infer a few things from the metadata patterns and speculate about several more, especially when cross-referenced with public data that was not included in the scrub."

"Oh?" Fergus said. "Some narrowing would be great."

"We—"

"Oh, no, no, *Whiro*, you did all the work, not *we* so much, no," Ignatio interrupted. "Maybe I did a little, yes, some guidance? Guidance is important. Okay, then yes, you can say *we*."

There was a noticeable pause before *Whiro* spoke again. "*We* believe your guess of three major parties working separately is correct, though we cannot fully account for what appears to be either occasional cooperation or data compromises between groups, nor confidently predict the existence—or lack thereof—of reciprocal awareness between them. We will reevaluate this after the results of your 'honeypot' exercise become apparent, but we have a moderately confident guess that your white-van people are your data scrubbers."

"That level of reach and thoroughness means they're professionals," Fergus said. "There can't be that many companies who could pull that off."

"Not hundreds, but at least several dozen," *Whiro* said.

Fergus settled back on the couch, eyeing the Earth still slowly rotating over the table, and trying to avoid the stink-eye he was getting from Isla. "What else you got?" he asked.

"Cross-correlation of all the elements shows several distinct patterns, which we have divided into four categories: sites of high interest where that interest ended abruptly, sites that remain of high interest to all identifiable parties, sites where at least one party has visibly ceased interest while at least one continues, and sites where there is either no reported activity or insufficient information to conclude what category it should belong to," *Whiro* said. "We postulate that in the first case, either it was fully determined beyond doubt that no active fragment was present, or any and all active fragments were recovered. None of those sites would be worthwhile for us to search. I will now color-code the dots to indicate those states: red for highly competitive, yellow for partially competitive, green for not competitive, and blue for unknown."

To Fergus's utter lack of surprise, all the debris trajectories that came down over ocean turned blue. Two white dots remained, one in Scotland, the other in Western Australia. *Mine*, he thought, with some pride.

"Until the point in time where all relevant data was scrubbed, the only obvious interest is either local governmental or the Alliance Terrestrial Science Unit, and not especially resourced," *Whiro* said. "Within a matter of days after the beginning of the data scrub, we see much greater attention from the ATSU, and also movement from the white-van party that suggests they had full access to the original information."

"If the first fragments they found were like the first one I found—inert, no changing mass, just part of the frame or whatever—then they would have been a curiosity at best, with the patterning and unknown alloy. Soon as you find one that was part of the core, though, you can't miss the trick with the changing mass. That is enough to get a *lot* of scientists and professionally paranoid people interested and much more jealous of their data."

"That was also our conclusion," *Whiro* said. "It is notable that, to the best we can determine, there are sites that are still being monitored by the Alliance but where white-van activity has ceased, and none the other way around, which suggests that while the white-van people have or had access to all the Alliance data, the reverse is likely not true."

"A leak, then, or a plant in the Alliance," Fergus said.

"That seems probable," *Whiro* confirmed.

"How many sites where both of them have stopped looking?"

"Eleven." There were eleven green dots on the screen.

"And how many sites where only the white-van people have quit?"

"Seven."

"Show me?"

Seven of the yellow dots grew larger. "So, we can guess that the white-van people have either found those pieces or ruled them out," Fergus said.

"That is also our supposition," *Whiro* said.

"And our fire cult?"

"Observed interest from Fajro Promeso was the last to start and seems less coordinated or sustained. It is harder to identify sites they've stopped looking at that the other competitors have not, but we think there are three."

"From my brief encounter with one of their members, they seem to figure out where the others are looking by following them or at least following the white-van people. If—" Fergus started, then noticed the lone purple dot squarely in the center of the Alaska Federation. "*Whiro*, what's this one?"

"There is data establishing conclusively that a live fragment was found by a Mr. Brydan Silver, who took his vast curiosity about it to SolNet. The same day when his many posts were scrubbed, he was murdered in his home in what authorities determined was a break-in gone wrong."

Isla, who had been rummaging through cabinets with more banging than necessary, stopped. "Murdered?" she asked. "Poor bloke. Who did it?"

"I can provide the crime reports. It looks like a professional execution with a few extra things knocked over to provide an excuse to flag it otherwise," *Whiro* said. "Not something that seems in the range of competence of your cultists."

"Fergus, is Gavin in danger?" Isla asked. She had gone pale. "If they think there's a piece in the apartment above the bar . . ."

"They know I left, and Kyle got a good look at me when I went out and bothered his van," Fergus said.

"And you and Gavin don't look like bleeding *twins*? You don't think he could get mistaken for you?" Isla asked more sharply.

"You're mad at me for getting you *out* of danger in Australia, and now you're also mad at me that Gavin just might, maybe, be *in* danger? What do you want from me?" Fergus replied, frustrated.

"I want ye to use yer head!" Isla shouted. "And yer heart, if ye have one!" She slammed her mug down on the table and stormed out of the room.

Fergus stared after her, then with a sigh picked her mug up and put it in the autowash. "That went well," he said.

"For the contrary—" Ignatio started, but at Fergus's look, ey fell silent, and Fergus went to the cupboards and slammed around for a bit until he found a Meatly Pie, pulled the tab on it, and sat, grumbling, while he waited for it to heat.

"*Whiro*, do you have anything you can use to keep an eye on my cousin's bar, to alert him and us to any brewing trouble?" Fergus asked when he felt he could speak calmly again.

"I can dispatch an autonomous security bot, but the communication lag will be problematic if I leave Earth orbit," *Whiro* said.

"For now, do that?" Fergus asked. "Unless you have better ideas."

"I will consider. In the meantime, I have finished scanning the new fragment using a multi-planar scale," *Whiro* said. "Would you like to see the data?"

"Will I understand it?" Fergus asked. "Since apparently, I'm the idiot in the room."

"I would like them, yes," Ignatio said. Eir handpad beeped and ey read quietly as Fergus ate, all four eyes focused on eir screen.

"It is a strangeness of coincidence," Ignatio said at last, "but the model of the changing mass of the new fragment matches the profile of the first fragment exactly, even though they did not appear identical to my many eyes."

"How close a match?" Fergus asked.

"*Whiro* calculated it to the tenth decimal," Ignatio said. "Do you feel this is insufficient? We can run it again!"

"No, no, ten is pretty exact," Fergus said. "But you think it is a coincidence?"

"Only I am cautious not to assume otherwise, yes?" Ignatio said.

"What does that mean? If it's not a coincidence?"

"I have seen many door-doorkeys whole," Ignatio said. "They are—"

"Wait, what?" Fergus asked. "What do you mean, 'many'? You mean we might have to go through this all over again?"

"No, not so," Ignatio said. "Most are nice. Doors to pretty flowers, flying happy things, vast oceans of glass trees, all secret you can't know about, so shhh. Just you have the bad one, the scavenger door, and maybe once up in a time, it was somewhere nice too. Before the swarms came."

"Have you ever gone through one of those doors?" Fergus asked. "Or lots of them? What does—"

"Ah!" Ignatio shouted. "Is a secret! Vorget—*forget*—I told you, I did not tell you. Pay attention to this one only."

"But you were comparing—"

Ignatio began whistling, and Fergus realized ey were trying to suck air in and out, in sequence, to calm emself. "Never mind," he said, keeping his voice as calm as he could, worried about his friend. "I forget. Just tell me what you need to tell me."

Ignatio sat on the floor and wrapped all eir legs around emself until the whistling subsided. "They are closely alike in their meaningful core," Ignatio said at last, "and more variable in the inert frames that hold one edge in place for us. If we extrapolate from our two pieces and my shape memories, and if all pieces are an equal portion and not just a coincidence of these two, we can guess the pattern."

"And we can make an estimate of how many core pieces there are," *Whiro* added.

"How many?" Fergus asked.

"Thirty-two," *Whiro* said. "Maybe one less, maybe one more, but that it is the most probable calculation."

"I would like thirty-two, because it is a power of two, but there are 127 debris traces, which is not," Ignatio said. "It is a sadness, as twos are lucky."

"It's only one off," Fergus said.

"It is still off," Ignatio said. "So, it may be we are wrong thinking."

"Maybe two sets of debris came down close enough together to appear as one set to the detection systems?"

"For complicated multidimensional physics reasonings, I am confident that the core pieces would initially repel each other as they entered our space, like magnets pointed badly at one another, and they would scatter the frame pieces as they separated," Ignatio said. Ey blinked eir outer sets of eyes at him. "Would you like to talk the math?"

"I'm sorry," Fergus said. "Probably Isla—"

"I am already having that conversation," *Whiro* said. "Ms. Ferguson is more receptive to complex theoretical discussions than you are, and it has made a positive change in topic from your manifest, multitudinous failings as a sibling."

"Wonderful," Fergus said. "If there are thirty-two pieces, subtracting my two, the murder victim's, and the sites where it seems likely one of our competitors has already found the prize, can you identify the best site for me to search next?"

"Japan," *Whiro* said, and the globe display zoomed in on a spot near the center of the main island.

"Okay," Fergus said. "I guess that's where I go."

"First, there is another matter for discussion," *Whiro* said. "As you are no doubt aware, one of our rivals is a multisystem military space authority that, among other things, closely monitors traffic in and around Earth. It will not take long for them to correlate your activities groundside with your trips in and out of orbit bringing fragments up. Nor, I assume, would they miss us making frequent trips between Earth and Mars when we go to deliver the pieces we've retrieved. If there is a leak in the Alliance, that also opens us up to enemy activity from the data scrubbers."

"Yeah, I know, I need a better way of moving the fragments without drawing attention," Fergus said. "I just haven't thought of one yet, and it's not like I can keep the fragments on me while I'm running around down on Earth."

"It is a matter that has been partially solved for you," *Whiro* said. "Before you go downwell on your Japan quest, you have an appointment on the orbital station."

"With who?"

"It has been arranged by Ms. Harcourt, who informs us she has taken care of the Earth-to-Mars transport issue," *Whiro* said. "Other than that, I do not have specifics."

"Fine. When am I supposed to be over there?" Fergus asked.

"In three hours and seventeen minutes," *Whiro* said.

"Okay. Let's see what Arelyn's got," Fergus said. He stood up. "That even gives me enough time to catch a short nap first."

Given that Arelyn Harcourt had built an entire illicit distribution system in hostile territory under the watchful eye of the Mars Colonial Authority in a matter of months, as her first foray into business, it was probably something solid. It stung a bit to admit it, but of course she would be several steps ahead of him when it came to logistics.

"Shall I let Ms. Ferguson know the anticipated departure time?" *Whiro* said. "She will likely also wish to pack."

"No, don't bother her," Fergus said. "I'll come back for her after my meeting at the orbital, and maybe by then, she'll be less mad at me and we can make a plan."

"That sounds logical," *Whiro* said. "I will wake you when the interdock passenger transport is approaching."

"Great," Fergus said. He went back to his cabin, feeling bad for lying to his friends. Isla wanted Gavin safe, of course, but he wanted *her* safe, too. He had already decided he was heading straight down to the surface after this meet-up, alone.

Sometimes, he thought, it's good to know exactly where on the asshole scale you belong.

Fergus caught the interdock transport from *Whiro* to Kelly Station. There were two private stations beyond it, visible only as pinpricks of light by the naked eye, hardly differentiated from the various blinks, flashes, and slow arcs of traffic around them. One was a military facility built by the former United States, abandoned not long after construction as the country had finally come apart at the seams, that had eventually been resurrected by an ascendant Europe and was currently used as a scientific research base. The other was an Alliance station that served mostly as neutral ground between various, intermittently contentious terrestrial governments, and he found himself needing to locate that one, for his own peace of mind, from the window of the transport, as if he didn't fix it down in his mind, it could somehow sneak up and ambush him.

There's comfort in occasionally letting your superstitions get their way, he thought. *Especially when you already know they're ridiculous.*

The station had a small but good commercial concourse, with a hotel, a 3-D movie theater, and plenty of food and shopping. Most of the higher-priced, useless tourist stuff was sold closer to the shuttle terminals, but there were enough people living semi-permanently on the station or on their personal ships to keep a real market in business. There was also a small automated sandwich shop named the *Deli Gute Esn*, and he took a stool at the counter and ordered a Reuben and a root beer to wait for his mysterious contact.

"Nice hair color," someone said. A thin kid, with freshly buzzed black hair and a familiar smile, set a small box down on the floor and took the seat next to him. "Is that a disguise, or are you trying to move up in the world?"

"Hello, Polo," Fergus said. "Fancy meeting you here."

The Free Marsie smiled, a twinkle in his brown eyes, and pointed to the shoulder of his blue uniform jacket. "I am a new assistant driver for the Mars-Earth bus," he said. "I am a productive member of society now. I even got a haircut. My father would be so proud to see."

There was something in that last sentence that they both found sharp, for their own reasons, and each of their smiles faltered with it. "My father did not live to travel to Mars or see me born there," Polo said, by way of explanation. "We left much behind in Tibet, to find things not much different."

"Less snow," Fergus said.

"Yes, less snow," Polo agreed. The automated waitsystem deposited Fergus's sandwich and drink in front of him, and at Polo's inquiring look, Fergus nodded.

Polo took half the sandwich. "Oh!" he said, after swallowing his first bite. "Ms. Arelyn has sent you a present." He stretched down and picked up the box before setting it on the counter.

Fergus opened it and pulled out a purple-and-red Phobos-Cola can. It was heavy but not in a way that suggested liquid inside. "Hang on," Polo said, and took it back out of his hand. He twisted the top and the entire rim came free, and he handed the can back to Fergus.

Inside was a wad of fiber batting. Fergus tugged it gently out and peered inside. The can was lined, about a centimeter thick, with hand-soldered wiring and tiny components embedded in hastily applied resin. There was a tiny switch just inside, below where the rim fit, and he pressed it.

As near as he could tell, with all his senses, nothing happened. So, carefully, he stuck a finger down into the cavity, then immediately pulled it back, barely managing to avoid yelping in surprise at the very strange sensation of his finger becoming invisible to his extra sense he had come to take for granted. Polo finished off his half of sandwich, then pointed toward the can. "Arelyn says it's for signal camouflage."

"Yep," Fergus said. "This will do nicely." He fished in his pocket for the Burringurrah fragment, wrapped it in the batting, and stuffed it inside. Polo handed him the lid, and Fergus screwed it back on. The seam was still nearly invisible, even now that he knew it was there, and he could no longer hear the fragment's constant, quiet chatter.

"She said if it works, they can send up a few more," Polo said.

"That would be great, and please tell her thanks," Fergus said. Taking a deep breath, he handed the can to Polo. "Be careful with this. If the wrong people find out you have it, it could get you killed."

"Got it," Polo said. He tucked the can in his pocket. "I've got to get back onboard for the return run to Mars. Six hours each way in skip right now, and getting longer. Stupid moving planets. You going to drink that?" He pointed at Fergus's untouched root beer, and Fergus slid it his way.

Polo drank it down, let out a low, gravelly burp, then slid off the stool. "Later, friend. Keep it Red."

"Red forever," Fergus answered, as the Marsie left. He ordered another root beer and then took out his handpad to study up on Japan while he waited for his own ride down.

———

Fergus caught the public shuttle down to Narita Spaceport, then a smaller flyer from there to the Niigata travelport off the western coast of Japan. It was an enormous floating structure tethered in the channel between the mainland and Sado Island, designed to ride out ocean storms and tsunami while being less prone to earthquake damage than land-based ports. For the cost, it probably only barely earned its keep, but when it rode out the great quake of '17 and was briefly the only place relief flights could get supplies and rescuers in, it had definitely earned its place in the hearts of locals.

When he got out of the flyer, he felt almost slammed to the ground by the humidity. A light rain fell but did nothing to provide relief as he hauled his pack toward the terminal. The doors opened ahead of him, smoothly and silently, and he stepped in to a blast of air conditioning that was a relief for almost ten seconds before it became its own extreme of uncomfortable.

A hologram flickered into life just inside the door, a young Japanese woman with eyes too big to be based on anyone real, wearing a green jacket like a stylized, shortened, kimono. A patch on the front shoulder was a smiling, bright yellow cartoon cat. "Niigata e youkoso!" the greeter said, and bowed. "Nanika osagashi desu ka?"

"Um . . . I don't . . ." Fergus started to say.

The hologram blipped briefly, and then it said, "May I provide you with assistance?"

"Uh, yeah. I was hoping to do some sight-seeing? Maybe take a trip to Bandai-Asahi, or Lake Hibara? I like nature," he said.

"We have many guided tours through Bandai-Asahi," the greeter said. "Would you like to see a menu?"

"I was hoping for something that lets me go at my own pace," Fergus said. "I might want to stop and hike, and I wouldn't want to slow anyone else down."

"Bandai-Asahi is very popular," the greeter said. "As is Shibatashi Park, where the interactive horror game The Forest Is Hungry and its sequel, The Trees Wear Bones, were created. It is a very exciting trip among our young people, and we recommend the full immersive virtual experience while there."

"I'm not really a fan of horror," Fergus said. He'd seen more than enough in real life, and he figured he was likely to see more sooner than he could want. "Is there good hiking east of there? Like, maybe outside Kitakata?"

"We have a tourist center in Aizuwakamatsu that can direct you to local attractions. There is rail service to Aizuwakamatsu every hour. Would you like—"

Another hologram flickered into life beside the first, this one even more anatomically unrealistic and with less virtual clothing. "*Yōkoso-ooooo!*" the new one sang. "Watashitoisshoni bōken ni ikimasenka? Meka ga arimasu!"

Could a hologram look annoyed? Fergus thought maybe the first one did. "Usero!" the first yelled. "Kare wa meka nante iranai desho!"

"Um . . ." Fergus said again.

The first greeter did a small curtsy, pulling his attention back. "That greeter is Fukushima Fun Mecha. They have a less important contract, and their systems are slow, outdated, and untrustworthy," it said.

Second greeter smiled. "We have exclusive personal mecha," it said. "Everyone wants to pilot their own giant robot at least once. Don't you?"

"Not really," Fergus said. It was certainly true he didn't in this moment, because he wanted to not draw any more attention to himself than he absolutely had to, but he had to admit under other circumstances, it would be unbearably tempting. "I just want to go look at nature peacefully."

"Watashi no kokyakudesu," First Greeter said to the other.

Second greeter looked at him imploringly, and he shrugged. The hologram blew him a kiss, complete with hologram hearts, and vanished.

"Uh, so how much for the train trip?" Fergus asked.

"One-way or with return?"

"One-way. I'm not sure which direction I'll go from there."

"If you wish to rent a personal pod vehicle in Aizuwaka-matsu, I can sell you a regular package for 350 Asia-Pacific cred, or we have a special on Kawaiimobiles for 280."

"And that's a regular pod car, not a giant robot?"

"It is a two-seater pod car with a typical configuration," the greeter said. "If you are unhappy, you may change the reservation to a four-seater pod car at our train station facility in Aizu-wakamatsu."

"Okay, then. I'll take that," Fergus said.

The greeter held up a hand, and a scan code appeared in front of its palm. Fergus scanned it with his handpad, verified that it was a legit business with minimal substantive service complaints, then completed the transaction.

"Arigatōgozaimashita!" the greeter said, and bowed. "Would you like directions to the train station?"

"Yes, please," Fergus said.

The greeter spread its hologrammatic hands apart and a map appeared in between them. Fergus scanned that, too.

"Niigata Happiness Company wishes you wonderful travels in Japan," the greeter said, then bowed and dissipated.

———

The train, mostly empty, left Niigata and wound its way through the outskirts of the city, mostly obscured by greenery, and slipped almost unnoticed into the rising hills to the southeast. It was only the gradual cessation of electrical noise around him that told him when they'd left civilization behind.

The train was designed to look much like an old-fashioned steam train, with most of its essential modern features disguised just enough to fit the style without becoming obtuse. This extended to the robot servicer that passed through the car, its casing brass and wood, and the top of its head carved to resemble a stylized attendant's cap. Fergus waved for it to stop and ordered coffee and a small basket of giant crackers called senbei. The robot—or another indistinguishable from it—brought them to him, still hot to the touch, a few minutes later.

The train took him through three towns, stopping briefly in each of them to exchange a small handful of passengers at each, before they reached Aizuwakamatsu itself. Fergus stepped out onto the platform and watched as a half-dozen podcars attached to the back of the train were released and sped off onto local roads, before he headed into the station to find the Niigata Happiness Company office to get his own podcar.

A few steps into the building, a greeter identical to the one in Niigata popped up, with the same cat patch, except on a blue coat. "Baugh-san," the hologram said.

It took a second for Fergus to remember that was his new alias, William Baugh. "Hi," he said.

"Due to an unforeseen staff shortage, our pod familiarization attendant is currently behind schedule, providing an orientation to pod systems for our customers. I apologize for this," the greeter said. "If you wish to wait, it will be approximately one hour and nine minutes. Or if you are familiar with the controls and do not need a tutorial, we can have your pod ready for you in approximately seven minutes."

"Uh, does the pod have an English language kit?"

"It does," the greeter answered.

"Then I'll take it now," Fergus said.

The greeter nodded. "We have assigned you the Kawaiimobile in bay seventeen, if you will follow me?"

The hologram led him through the station, briefly blipping out as it crossed through doorways and from one projector to the next, or when a person passing the other way walked directly through its space. He didn't fail to notice that the offender had been a fellow tourist, where the Japanese around him politely avoided disrupting the greeters.

The greeter led him into a lift, and they went up a floor to where the rental pods were parked. There were only three pods currently there, not including one enclosed within the arms of an automated service robot, and his heart sank as he realized which one was likely his.

"Your Kawaiimobile!" the greeter said, and held out one virtual hand proudly.

It was, true to the first greeter's description, a standard two-seater pod. It also had large cat ears sprouting from the roof, and giant eyes above the windshield that turned to regard him. A stubby tail, rising from the back curve of the pod, twitched. The front window itself was lined top and bottom with a row of painted teeth, and the driver seat inside was deep red and distinctly tongue-shaped.

The entire Kawaiimobile was also bright, neon yellow.

"Uh . . ." Fergus said. This was not going to let him get around unobtrusively. "Can I upgrade to one of the larger pods?" He pointed to one of the others on the lot.

"I am sorry! They are all reserved," his greeter said. "We will not have any other available pods until the day after tomorrow."

He stood up straighter, rolled his shoulders, then cracked his knuckles. "Okay," he said. "I guess we're doing this. I'm a professional, and it's just a pod, and this is all fine. Perfectly fine."

The greeter smiled and waved as he put his things into the back of the Kawaiimobile. Fergus studiously refused to notice the large black asterisk decal positioned right under the tail on the back hatch, and got in the front with all the dignity he could muster.

At least it drove smoothly, and the red tongue-seat was comfortable. Like much of the rest of the world, the roads inside Aizuwakamatsu, and leading north to the town of Kitakata, which was nearer his goal, were automated, and he had no control over it other than telling it where he was going and letting it take him there. So, he tilted the plush seat back a bit and relaxed, taking in the sprawling town and other vehicles—none of them *kawaii*, which his handpad informed him too late for it to be of use was Japanese for *cute*—as they passed by.

It was only a half-hour trip to Kitakata, most of that spent waiting at carefully synchronized intersections, the flow of one town into another too seamless to say when and where it changed. To the north he could see the rising mountains, sharp under their carpet of green, and by the time the roads finally became small and slow enough to let him take control, he was moving fairly steeply uphill.

His handpad chimed, and he turned it on to find Zacker's face on the other end. "Fergus, I—" the detective started, then frowned deeply. "What the fuck are you inside?"

"A giant happy cat, of course," Fergus said. "Why?"

"I don't even want to know," Zacker said. "Hey, I think we have activity." The view swung away and then resolved again as a street view out the window. Standing on the far corner at the edge of Bad Yuri's apartment building was a slight man dressed in unbleached linen, too short to be the would-be thief, Peter, he'd tackled in Gavin's apartment. This cultist was holding a ukulele, which from the way it sat in his hands was the first time he'd held any kind of musical instrument at all, and though he occasionally strummed at it as people went past, or nodded toward the can on the ground at his feet, mostly he was just watching people walk by, especially anyone who entered the building opposite Zacker's.

"That's Fajro Promeso," Fergus said. "If they're there, so are the others."

"Haven't spotted them yet," Zacker said, "but I'm looking."

"Shake a can of carrots? Never mind. Bad Yuri knows?"

"Yep. If no one moves for him soon, Yuri is gonna go for a walk and see if he can draw anyone out that way. We want to do it while there's still good daylight. No lag on this line—where are you?"

"Japan," Fergus said. "Saving the universe, and doing it in style. Keep me posted?"

"Will do," Zacker said, and disconnected.

With luck, the rest of this trip would go smoothly, and he'd have his piece fast enough to be on hand when trouble hit in Perth. He turned the Kawaiimobile off onto a smaller road, which his pod informed him was the road to the Hansha-chi Shrine, which was the nearest marked point to where his search area was, higher up in the hills. He could park there and then hike the rest of the way.

Japan is beautiful, he thought. Everything was just extraordinarily green. Trees and vegetation were everywhere, crowding every centimeter of the steep slopes rising up to either side of the road, burying the outlines of the terrain under a seemingly impenetrable wall of life. Scotland's trees always had the air of surly, rugged individualists, proclaiming their triumph over the hardships of the land and humankind, but the forests here were more like a raucous dance party that had gotten out of control.

His relief at having successfully sneaked away on his own for this trip gave way to some measure of guilt, and regret he couldn't share the views, the vibrant, leafy, living smell of the forest, with Isla. He wanted to linger and explore, let a whole new experience of the world sink into his soul, and maybe learn a word or two more useful than *kawaii*. It was too bad he was always in a hurry.

"Too bad," he repeated out loud, as his Kawaiimobile came to a sudden halt in the road.

"Unable to proceed. Adjusting maps," the pod system announced.

He told the pod to park where it was and got out, walking ahead up the road to see what the problem was. Where the next turnoff for the shrine should be, a jarring mass of boulders and dirt and shattered, dead trees blocked his way. The entire side of the steep hill had come down in a landslide, violently obliterating everything in its path, and left a scar in its wake in the form of tens of thousands of tons of debris. Somewhere, entombed underneath it all, was his missing fragment.

When the other core pieces woke up and started trying to connect to each other and make their door, he didn't expect that would slow them down in the slightest.

Chapter 10

──►◄──

After glumly considering his options—or lack thereof—Fergus parked the Kawaiimobile off the edge of the road in the grass and got out his hiking gear. He did his best to stay off the rockfall itself, since he had no way of knowing if it was stable without risking his own neck on it. The road itself had been obliterated, and the trees to either side of it were broken or bent over with the weight of rock and dirt against them. A few of the smaller saplings, nearly bent sideways, had already begun to turn their trunks back upward toward the sky, and he could make out grasses and seedlings popping up from the cracks and crevasses, so it couldn't have happened too recently.

Long enough ago that the Kawaiimobile navigation systems should have known, anyway. Maybe he should have gone with the mecha.

A few dozen meters up the hillside, under cover along the edge of the untouched forest bordering the slide, he stumbled across a small trail of packed earth among the roots and rocks, and followed it with both gratitude and trepidation, remembering the hidden spy gear on Burringurrah. At least in the forest, visibility was a two-way problem, and as a bonus, the shade from the trees kept the sun mostly off his head, if doing little to break up the stifling humidity. He had gone from the arid-freezing of Mars to the arid-hot of the Southwest Territories and Western Australia, to being smothered alive by wet, hot air almost unbearably filled with the weedy scent of nature. Everything smelled green and emphatically alive, and even though birdsong kept him constant, cheerful company, he felt no touch of electricity on his senses. No spies, but also no fragment. He quickly lost any exact idea of where he was relative to the road, shrine, and search zone, with all his weaving through trees and underbrush, and he pulled out his handpad to get his bearings again just in time to trip over a tree root and go sprawling into the undergrowth.

"Aw, shit," Fergus muttered, rolling over and sitting up, in time to watch a thin bead of blood appear and harden on his leg where a sharp rock had caught him. He checked to see if any of his blood had fallen to the ground—he wasn't normally that paranoid, but this close to the search zone, he wasn't taking any chances—and though he was sure none had, he still took out a pack of cleaner nanites and popped open one of the blisters where he had tumbled.

The backs of his legs already ached from the uneven terrain and steep incline, which showed no signs of leveling out any time soon. He drank some water, checked his handpad for his location, and took several more minutes to rest and listen. When he became restless to get going again, he wrapped his hand around the trunk of a young tree and pulled himself to his feet, brushed leaf litter off his shorts, shouldered his pack, and started upward again.

He was not far from where he'd have had to ditch the Kawaii-mobile and start hiking anyway if there hadn't been a rockfall in his way. He thought he could hear the faint sounds of the Daiya River to the west, which meant if the shrine itself hadn't been swept away in the landslide, it should be only a half-kilometer or so from where he was. He was going to have to cross the landslide, though, unless he wanted to hike all the way over the mountain and then come back again on the far side. And that was hoping the rockfall wasn't so extensive, his entire search zone had gone down with it.

He made his way to the edge of the trees, stepping carefully over humps of churned earth and grasses, and stepped out blinking in the sunlight on the fall itself. The ground was torn up and littered with broken stone and shattered branches, and looking up, he could now make out the cliff face that must have shattered, bringing everything down below it. It looked stable, but what did he know?

Hoping the cliff wasn't preparing for an imminent repeat, he began picking his way as delicately as he could across it, leaning upslope as best he could, and occasionally finding branches or protruding rocks he could hang on to for steadiness as he passed by.

Twice, the ground gave out under his feet and nearly sent him tumbling. He could see now well downhill and even make out the tiny, bright yellow dot through the trees that was his Kawaiimobile. To the west, the sky was growing gray, and he found himself realizing he was probably in a very bad place to get caught in a sudden rainstorm.

Also, it hadn't occurred to him until this moment to wonder if his alien electrical gift would act like a lightning rod.

"Hell," he swore, and sat down on the slope, making sure his feet were well braced and his position stable, before he closed his eyes and walked himself through the calming, breathing, and stretching mujūryokudo exercises that Dr. Minobe had taught him. It was a martial art designed largely for zero-gravity environments, but he'd come to find some of the more basic practices—really, as far as he'd gotten in the short time they'd been together—of at least some use regardless of environment.

When he felt less beset by irritation at his scraped knee or worry about the approaching storm, he tried to reach out with his Asiig sense. He was grounded, strong, calm. Tiny electrical voices leapt out at him. A nearby cat, birds, something larger moving toward him, but no sign of the fragment.

"Ooi! Soko no kimi!" someone yelled at him. "Nani yatter-uno?"

Fergus opened his eyes to see a young Japanese man, wearing a kaiju T-shirt and a bright purple plaid kilt, waving at him from the woods on the other side of the rockfall, not far from where he'd been heading, hoping to find the shrine.

Groaning in frustration, Fergus pulled out his handpad. "How do I say in Japanese: 'I do not speak Japanese. I am fine. Leave me alone'?"

"Nihongo ga hanashimasen. Daijobu desu. Hootoite kuda-sai," his handpad said.

"Nihongo ga hand shimmy sen!" Fergus yelled out. "Dai-jobo! Something something hot toes kudasai!"

The man put his face in his palm, regarded Fergus for a moment, then stepped gingerly out onto the rockslide debris and headed toward him, arms held out to either side for balance.

"Great," Fergus muttered to himself. "Now we're gonna both get killed." He stood up and worked his way transverse across the slope to meet him.

They stopped about five meters apart, regarding each other. The Japanese man was chuckling and grinning.

"What?" Fergus said. "No nihongo!"

"Nice car down there," the man said. "Are you lost from the circus?"

Fergus let his shoulders slump. "Worst. Day. Ever," he declared.

The man laughed so loud, Fergus was worried it would start another landslide. "Omae, get off those rocks before you die," he called. He pointed behind him. "I have beer. You can tell me why you are up here doing this ridiculous thing. Okay?"

Wherever the fragment was, it was out of his reach. At least maybe he could get more information about what happened here. "All right," Fergus said, and carefully trailed the man over to the far side.

Farther along the curve of the slide, he could see that the farthest edges of the tumble had settled into a V notch between two hills, sparing everything beyond it. On the untouched opposite slope there were a handful of one-story houses nestled among the trees, the curved solar tile roofs gleaming iridescent where the sunlight found its way down, and a trio of wind turbines lazily turned on the next hill behind that.

Catching up, he could see the glint of metal along one side of the man's head—dataports, though he rarely saw anyone sporting them who wasn't a pilot, and even then mostly pilots who operated farther away from a still-mod-squeamish Earth. He had to admit, despite the obvious and possibly catastrophic failure of the day, at least here was something interesting.

The man looked back, then pointed to one of the smaller houses, and as the ground leveled off and left behind the slide debris, it was much easier going, and they reached it within a few more minutes. Sliding panels were open along a porch, revealing a much more cluttered interior than miscellaneous cultural documentaries from when he was a kid led him to expect. "Stay here," the man said, and Fergus set his things down and dutifully sat on the porch.

On a stand, just inside the shade of the porch overhang, was a gnarled juniper perched on top of a stone in a brown oval pot, its roots seeming to just barely reach the tiny reservoir of soil below. "Some advice," he said to the tree. "If you try to go back to the dirt you started on, it's just trouble."

The man came out and handed him one of two cans of ginger beer he was carrying. "Who were you talking to?" he asked.

Fergus took the can and cracked it open; he supposed he was expected to complain about it not being actual *beer* beer, but honestly, this was better. "Your bonsai," he said. "Sekijoju?" *See,* he thought, *I do know some Japanese after all.*

"Maybe?" the man said. "It's my grandmother's. If she catches you touching it, you'll be sorry. You have never got your ass kicked until it has been kicked by a pissed-off elderly Japanese woman."

Fergus laughed out loud, unable to help himself. "No shit but that's the truth!" he said.

"So, what's your story?" the man said. "You don't seem like the usual suicidal types that climb up there and jump up and down, hoping they can get swept away, and not least because they're the same couple of locals over and over again."

"I was trying to find the Hansha-chi Shrine, and the road was blocked, so I figured I'd hike it," Fergus said. "How long ago was the rockfall?"

"Three years ago or so? It might be four."

"Too much rain?"

"Yes, but also some idiots trying to drive trucks around up there off the road."

"Government idiots?"

"As it happens, yes," the man said. "I'm Akio."

"William Baugh," Fergus said, and shook his hand. "Friends call me Bill."

"Bill Baugh? You looking for a magic ring up here?"

Fergus shook his head, smiling. "A man who knows his classics! You a pilot?"

Akio touched his head, just below the port. "I wish," he said. "Remote-driving construction vehicles. Right now, running one of a dozen ocean-floor crawlers about halfway between Tunu in the Arctic Union and Iceland, putting in posts for the new rail bridge. Day off today, waiting for the inspectors to come in."

"Seems like a good job," Fergus said.

"Lets me keep an eye on my grandmother," Akio answered. "Or, as she likes to say, it lets her keep an eye on me. Someday, though, it would be neat to go to space. You ever been?"

Fergus laughed. "Yeah."

"Where?"

"All over," Fergus said. "Where would you go first?"

"Titan," Akio said without hesitation.

"Yeah? If you ever do make it there and someone offers you Titan moonmilk in your coffee or cereal or whatever? It's made out of pureed bugs," Fergus said. "It's not the worst-tasting stuff out there by a long shot, but if you're expecting real milk, you will regret the experience."

Akio leaned back and finished off his ginger beer. "I'll remember that," he said. "So, really, why you here?"

"The shrine . . ." Fergus started to say, but Akio shook his head.

"The shrine's not famous or old or even slightly interesting," the man said. "We get very strange people here claiming to be looking for it, who then just wander around in the woods for days and days, looking disappointed even after they've walked around it a dozen times. You don't seem like one of those people, either."

"Give me a couple of days lost in the woods and I could be," Fergus said.

"Well, give me a few minutes to check on my grandmother and then I can show you to the shrine. We rebuilt it, after the fall. And then I can show you the path back down the hill that'll eventually get you back to your car, though it's a long walk around. At least it's mostly down from here."

"Thanks," Fergus said.

He sat on the porch as Akio went inside, sipping the last of his ginger beer and enjoying both the shade of the porch and the sound of birds. The sky had grown a deeper gray to the west, but if the storm was coming, it didn't seem to be in a hurry. He might get back to his car without getting soaked after all.

Relaxing, he took deep breaths and let his senses reach out around him. He could feel Akio and his grandmother somewhere in the house behind him, the network of wiring in the house walls, the duller feel of the other houses nearby. And somewhere, faintly, something familiar stirring.

The fragment was somewhere behind him, in Akio's house.

"Aw, shit," he said. Was he going to have to rob the man who was helping him? Did he dare not to? Why couldn't the piece just be sitting out there on the rocks, waiting for him, free of complications?

Akio stepped back onto the porch, startling him. "You ready to go?" he asked.

Fergus set down his can. "Can we talk a few minutes longer, first?" he asked.

"If you want to miss the rain, we should start walking soon," Akio said, but sat down again.

"Other people have been up here, you said? Not the suicidal ones but government people? And men with guns. And probably some people in linen clothes acting even stranger than most," Fergus said.

"Yes," Akio said. "So, you do know something about this?"

"Yeah. Everyone's looking for something that fell up on the hill there," Fergus said. "Me too, to be honest with you. Here, let me show you something."

He pulled out his handpad and pulled up the information

about the man murdered in the Alaskan Federation, and handed it over to Akio without a word. The man tapped to change the language over to Japanese and then read it through before handing it back. "Is this someone you knew?"

"No," Fergus said. "But he found one of the things that everyone is looking for. It got him killed."

"There was nothing in there about any thing," Akio said.

"No, but that's what it was about. Eventually, someone will come for you, too."

"Me? It is a very big mountain," Akio said, opening his arms wide to encompass the view before them from the porch. "Why would anything happen to me?"

"Because you have it, don't you?" Fergus said.

"Why would you think that?"

Fergus shrugged. "Because I can hear it. Keeping it is dangerous, more than you can know."

Akio stood up again. "So, you have come to threaten me and my grandmother, for this fictional thing, then?"

"No," Fergus said. "I didn't know it was here until I got here, and anyway, I'm the good guy. Bad guys don't have to drive podcars shaped like giant neon cats with cartoon anuses."

"And if I say no? Maybe I will call the police," Akio said.

"You could," Fergus said. "And maybe you should. The other searchers put hidden surveillance out in other places, and they might be watching us right now. If so, it'd be better for you if they believe you weren't helping me."

"You mean little cameras and stuff?" Akio laughed. "The villagers find and destroy them. My grandmother has a basket full. Kamera wa nandai arunndai, Obaachan?"

An elderly woman strode onto the porch and stood in the doorway. "Juuikko," she said.

"Eleven," Akio translated.

Fergus thought back to his stash in the Perth apartment. "I've only smashed three," he said. "Your grandmother wins."

Akio translated that back, and the old woman laughed and replied, then wandered back into the house. "She says you are young and have time to catch up," he said. "So, what do you do now? I say I do not have this thing."

Fergus could tell him it was about five meters behind them, maybe a meter off the floor. In a drawer in the kitchen, maybe? But he didn't think that would help. Instead, he said, "It's dangerous. Dangerous for you to keep, dangerous in the wrong hands, dangerous for everyone if it's not dealt with. Please? Kudasai?"

"Did you just say *please*?" Akio asked, astonished.

"Yeah," Fergus said. "I did. At least I think."

"For that, anyway, I will bring an umbrella for our walk," Akio said. He disappeared inside and returned a few moments later with a bright rainbow umbrella, just as the first few, fat drops of rain hit the edge of the porch.

Akio led him around the house to a small dirt road, and they walked down it toward the bottom of the valley. They didn't speak much; Fergus decided it was probably that Akio was trying to decide something, and he didn't want to disrupt that process. He could hear the fragment now in the man's pocket.

They walked up out of the woods and scrub onto the road, right at the edge of where the rockfall had passed through. With a glance upward, Akio followed Fergus across the last few meters of jumbled rocks to where the Kawaiimobile still sat, waiting for him. Its eyes were closed, like it was napping, but they sprang open as the two men approached.

They walked around the back, where Akio laughed, nearly dropping his umbrella, and pointed to the asterisk decal under the tail. "It really does have an anus! I never noticed those before!"

Fergus sighed, set down his stuff, and opened the back hatch.

Akio picked up Fergus's pack in his free hand. "Let me help," he said, and put it inside.

"Thank you," Fergus said.

"Thank you," Akio said in return. "For the tip about Titan moonmilk. If I ever get there, I will remember."

"I hope you do," Fergus said. "Until then, take care, and don't trust strangers."

"I never do," Akio said. He stood back as Fergus got into the Kawaiimobile, which started up with a literal roar. Fergus waved as he drove away, watching the man watching him from the side of the road as the rain turned to full downpour, beating on the pod windows and road ahead, and Akio became just a blur of color in the fading distance.

In the back of the car, from his pack, the fragment began to quietly sing.

———

"Why the hell are you here again?" Zacker asked, glancing over from where he was sitting surrounded by feed monitors from the street below and the apartment next door. "And you know you have messages? Your handpad is blinking like it's gonna have a stroke."

Fergus was slumped on the couch. He reached over to where he'd tossed his handpad on the table and flipped it over. "I know," he said. "I'm an asshole and a coward."

"Well, asshole, for sure," Zacker said. "What are you being a coward about? Your damn messages?"

"Yes," Fergus said. "As much as I mostly don't mind pissing

people off, and sometimes even enjoy it, I'm finding that I have newly developed the ability to feel *bad* about it in certain circumstances, and I don't like that at all."

Zacker snorted. "So, you were a jerk to someone, and now you're avoiding their calls? Welcome to the human race."

Fergus made a rude gesture at the retired detective, who laughed and went back to his monitors. "There's beer in the fridge," Zacker said over his shoulder. "You can have one. *One.* I'm running low."

Grumbling, Fergus got up from the couch and pulled one of at least two dozen bottles out of the fridge. Either Zacker was being funny, or he had a serious problem. *What makes you think it's not both?* he asked himself.

Several hours back to Niigata, and a quick hop to Luzon to change up shuttles in case he was being watched, before landing in Perth about an hour later, and his legs *still* ached from the hike. He should be drinking water, and he would next, but the beer sounded far better than it had any right to.

"Zacker—" he started to say, coming back out of the living room, only to find the detective standing there holding Fergus's handpad, listening to the low drone of his messages. "—Hey!" he shouted. "How did you unlock that?"

Zacker shrugged, and when the messages finished, tossed the handpad back to Fergus. "Grabbed your fingerprint, retina, and base chem sig way back in Glasgow. And yeah, you're right, someone's pretty pissed at you. Who's Isla?"

Fergus took a long pull from the bottle of beer and made a face. "My kid sister I didn't know about until a few months ago," he said.

"Ha! That must have been one hell of a kick in the pants," Zacker said. "And you've dragged her into your shit?"

"Kept her out of it, which is why she's pissed," Fergus said. "I don't know how to talk to her and get her to understand the danger. How did you get through to Deliah?"

"You are asking *me* for advice on people skills?" Zacker exclaimed. "You must be fucking desperate."

"I am. I should have gone right back up to orbit where she's waiting, but . . ." He waved at the handpad and, by extension, the messages it held. "As I said, a coward."

He thumbed off the bottle seal and took a deep swig before holding the bottle at arm's length and peering with a mix of curiosity and horror at the label with a sheep in a spacesuit on it. "Jumbuckjoose?" he said. "You spent money on this?"

"I spent *your* money on it, wise guy," Zacker said. "The label is holographic. You put the bottles together you get a cute little story that seems less dumb, the more you drink."

"Have to drink a *lot*," Fergus said.

"And that's the point right there," Zacker said.

"You worry me," Fergus said.

"Whatever you need. But about this sister thing, think of yourself as a crime scene," Zacker said. "Detectives—and we are all detectives, trying to solve other people—come in and look at your big splattery mess, and we make a story in our heads from the clues we see and what we know of you and your life. Those clues are the stories you choose to tell and the actions you choose to show. What we don't get is the stories you don't tell, the hidden actions, the secrets we haven't dug out yet and maybe won't. So, we never have the full picture, the right picture. No one ever does. The question is whether the picture is close enough to work the case, in this case to understand each other. Do you get that?"

"Yeah. That's pretty profound for you, Clarence," Fergus said.

"Fuck you," Zacker said. "And anyway, that was how Deliah tried to explain it to me on my terms. And it makes sense, though

I think she still thinks I'm way more complicated than I actually am. Not my problem if—"

Zacker trailed off and went to peer out the scope. "Action, Ferguson," he said.

Fergus was already on his feet and over to the monitors. "Where's our fire-cult guy?"

"He suddenly up and scurried off moments ago, looking like something was biting his ass," Zacker said. "The van over there is new." He pointed.

"It's black, not white."

"Right. Apparently, vans come in more than one color in the Supervillain Supply catalog," Zacker said. "Two guys just got out in full camo gear. One went into the building, carrying a heavy bag; the other went off down the street. Bad Yuri took a walk about five minutes ago to see if it would draw anyone out, and it looks like it worked. Perp number one—I'm ranking 'em by priority for you—is on his tail."

"Shit. Okay," Fergus said. "I'm going to go after Yuri. Keep me informed what happens across the street." He popped an earpiece in, shrugged into a nondescript pair of street-cleaner coveralls, grabbed his bag, and took off down the stairs three at a time.

"To your left, down past the banana store," Zacker yelled after him.

Fergus ran to the corner outside the fruit store and stopped under the hanging banana-shaped sign, peering down the street. He could see a guy in camo about a block ahead, walking purposefully but not quickly, one hand staying by his side where his jacket was slightly bulked out. "Gun," Fergus said.

"No shit, ya think?" Zacker replied over the earpiece. "Yuri's about four blocks farther up, knows you're coming, gonna help you close the trap. You know how to do this?"

"I know how to do this," Fergus said, and began walking down the street toward them both.

It was midafternoon, too early for the evening crowd to be out in the streets yet, and the day shoppers were starting to thin out. There were enough people to provide reasonable cover if no one was specifically looking back to see if they were being followed, but also plenty of people to get in the way—or, worse, get hurt—if things went suddenly very badly.

The van guy ahead of him had slowed his walk; past him Fergus could see his own doppelganger stopped at a sidewalk farm stand, a pair of lemons in hand, talking to the proprietor. She was smiling and laughing, and held up a lime.

The man in camo drifted to a stop, intent on the interaction about a block ahead of him, seemingly unaware of the other people on the sidewalk passing back and forth around him.

Fergus kept his walk steady, not breaking from the casual, everyday pattern of sound around him, as he pulled a small pair of invisi-gloves from his pocket and slipped them on. He caught up to the guy when they were still half a block away from the farm stand. As Fergus walked to pass him, he held out one hand and deftly slid the man's wallet out of his back pocket and into his own.

"Hey!" Yuri shouted from the farm stand, pointing right toward the two of them. "Man, I think that guy just pinched your wallet!"

Fergus dashed down the narrow alley conveniently right beside him, as the guy in camo turned and came pounding after him. The man had his gun half-out when he caught up to Fergus and grabbed him by the shirt, swinging him around just in time for Fergus to slap his hand across the man's neck and dump enough electricity into him to drop him without a sound.

Yuri pelted into the alleyway and saw that Fergus already had him down. "Unconscious," Fergus said, as Yuri walked up to stand over them, blocking the view from the entrance to the alley. Fergus took the chits out of the man's wallet one by one, scanned them, put them carefully back inside exactly as they had been, and put it back in the man's pocket.

"Police are coming," Yuri said. "You have about forty seconds to get away."

"Going now," Fergus said. "That gun ought to get the police's interest when they get here."

"I am sure a concerned citizen would not hesitate to point it out," Yuri said. "Now run so I can yell after you."

Fergus ran, and a few moments later, Yuri started shouting after him. "You! Come back! Thief! Vile miscreant!"

By then, Fergus was out the far end of the alley and melting back into the crowd, all commotion now far behind him. "Status?" he asked.

"I can't see from here, but from the police radio, they've just started talking to your friend and the van guy, who I gather you knocked out?" Zacker answered.

"I did," Fergus said, catching his breath. "What's going on in the apartment?"

"Perp number two is in the hall outside the door, starting to get antsy that he hasn't heard from his partner yet. If he's smart, he'll walk now, reassess, and come back later. And . . . not smart. They never are. He's picking the lock."

"Okay, I'm heading over there," Fergus said.

"Yuri says no on that, and I agree," Zacker said.

"But—" Fergus started to say.

"No. Don't go in and fuck everything up," Zacker said. "If you don't trust me on this, why the hell am I even here?"

"Fine. I'm going to go check out the van," Fergus said.

"Only if it's empty. If not, get your ass back here and sit this the fuck out," Zacker said. "Yuri is just finishing up giving his statement to the police and should be back here in another ten, if you need a babysitter."

"Asshole," Fergus said.

"Schmuck," Zacker replied.

Fergus looped around the block back to their apartment building and stood just in the shadows around the corner from where the van was parked, listening and feeling. The van was bursting with electrical signals. He didn't hear movement, but the street was hardly quiet around them, and he certainly couldn't see anyone through the opaque front windscreen. It was foolish to assume there weren't sensors all over the van, but like the locks, they would be entirely dependent upon electricity.

Fergus got his handpad out and walked down the sidewalk like he was scrolling through his social feeds, just like two-thirds of everyone else out walking, and he timed it so that there was a group coming down the walk at the same time, and he stepped close to the curb to let them past and ran his still-gloved hand along the body of the van, shorting it out.

He kept walking, but no one got out to yell at him, so after a few steps, he stopped, turned as if he'd forgotten something, and climbed into the unlocked, silent van.

Lucky for him, it was unoccupied. The back of the van was crammed with so much gear and electronics, Fergus wasn't sure how they even fit two guys in there to start with. An enormous parabolic dish sat in the center of the floor, suspended in a mish-mash of soldered electronics.

"How the hell did you get in that fast?" Zacker said over his earpiece.

"I'm just that good," Fergus said. "What's happening upstairs?"

"Perp just got in. Looks like he's doing a preliminary sweep to make sure no one else is in there," Zacker said.

Fergus went into the front of the van and knelt down under the dash controls, fumbling for the memory slot. He found it, pulled the card out, and slotted that into his handpad long enough to upload the entire data cache to *Whiro*, then slipped it back into place. Then he went into the back and stared for a while at the equipment. Finally, he gave in and put in a video call to Ignatio.

"Vergus!" Ignatio declared, so close to the screen that only three of eir eyes were visible. "Where—"

"Hang on; I'm short on time," Fergus said. He held up his handpad so Ignatio could see, and slowly panned the van interior. "Any idea what all this is?"

"Can we connect to these systems?" Ignatio asked.

"Yeah, soon as the van reboots," Fergus said. "Should be soon, but . . . Oh, there it is." The instruments blinked back into life, and the rising crescendo of signals was almost like a punch in the gut. He pulled his confuddler out of his shoulder bag and, after studying the systems for a few minutes, moved a half-empty coffee mug gently to one side and wired it in.

His confuddler balked. "There's some *high*-level security here," Fergus said. "I'm not sure I can even get a passive scan of the network, not without leaving a trace. Some of this is obviously surveillance gear, but this other stuff? Any ideas?"

"It is a guess, but maybe they hope to scan for fragments," Ignatio said. "Send out a signal burst, listen for a reply, like you do? But the fragments have not been making noise to hear."

"The one from Japan is a little louder," Fergus said. He'd left it behind in Zacker's apartment, and as much as that made him incredibly nervous, even from here he could tell it was right where it should be. "It wasn't until I got near it, and then it sort of perked up on our trip out."

Ignatio made a face. "That is bad."

"How much range do you think this scanner has?"

"Terrible, terrible. Perhaps if they parked on top of one?" Ignatio said. "You are much more portable. A compliment, ha! But still, I think you should wreck it, yes?"

In Fergus's ear, he could hear Zacker swearing. "They're letting perp one go, minus the gun. Perp two is ransacking the apartment," he said. "Can you get your ass back here now?"

"Will do," he said. "Gotta go, Ignatio."

"Isla is very—"

"I'll be up there soon, and then she can yell at me in person as much as she wants, but I gotta go," he said, and cut the connection.

He unplugged his confuddler and tucked it back in his bag, then put his hand against the main console and fried the entire system. The van itself shut down again. He picked up the coffee mug and spilled the remaining contents into the console, and left it tipped there, an obvious, accidental culprit for the outage, popped another blister of cleaning bots, and then he slipped back out onto the street and away.

Zacker shoved past him the moment he entered the apartment, and growled, "Stay put and don't fuck it all up," on his way by.

From the apartment, Fergus watched as Zacker intercepted Yuri on the sidewalk, and could hear him asking for directions. Perp one, who had been heading up behind Yuri, stopped in his tracks and loitered on the corner, pretending to check his shoes, then his watch, then his handpad in some of the worst acting-casual Fergus had seen. On the monitors, perp two finally found the fragment piece atop the windowsill, dropped it into his pocket, and made a beeline out of the apartment.

"Two is coming out," he told Zacker and Yuri over the audio link.

Yuri led Zacker toward the corner, causing perp one to back off even farther and hide behind a public charging booth. Yuri was pointing down the street, making left and right gestures with his hands, and Zacker nodded along.

Behind them, perp two slipped out of the building and hared off in the other direction. Perp one turned and walked away as well. "That's it; they're out and gone," Fergus said.

Zacker thanked Yuri, who headed back into his apartment, and Zacker headed off in the direction Yuri had pointed. He arrived back in the apartment twenty minutes later with ice cream. "Blueberry lemon," he said by way of explanation. "I only got one for myself. Figured you were probably one of those fucking vanilla people."

Fergus ignored him and watched until the two men got back in their van. It sat there for several minutes, then pulled sharply away from the curb and sped off down the street. In its angry wake he spotted a figure in plain linen step out from behind a tree and watch it go.

"And that," Fergus said, mostly to himself but with great satisfaction, "is how a honeypot works."

Chapter 11

Yuri had already ditched the beard and shaved his head, while Fergus was back to his natural color and chafing at the stubble now colonizing his chin, when they arrived at Kelly Station in Earth orbit. Fergus waited with him for the lunar shuttle to arrive, both of them too tired to talk much, but when the shuttle boarded, Yuri gave him a tight bear hug before silently boarding his shuttle for home.

Fergus wandered back out into the concourse full of new arrivals who had not yet dispersed or been collected by family, and called Francesco to let him know both Yuri and payment were on their way. "Thank you, my friend," Francesco said. "You told me there was trouble coming, and that it could reach us even here on Luna. If it gets past you, you'll get us warning?"

"If you can hear the entire Earth screaming from here, then it got past me," Fergus said. "I expect if it does, it's because I'm already dead."

"In this moment, I regret once again that you are not a theatrical man, as that bodes poorly for any hopes you are exaggerating," Francesco said. "Do take care."

"And you," Fergus answered.

He milled around the slowly emptying concourse, avoiding the inevitable for an hour or so, then gave up and caught the docking transport back to *Whiro*.

"Your van people are Digital Midendian, Inc.," *Whiro* told

him the moment he'd crossed through the airlock on board. "They are a private company specializing in data security and management, one of the top in the field. Their headquarters are in the Texas Republic, but they have offices all over Earth. They do a lot of contract work for government agencies."

"Let me guess . . ." Fergus said.

"No need. You will be correct. They have a contract with the Alliances Terrestrial Sciences Unit, whose inception date corresponds with the start of the data scrub," *Whiro* said.

"So, they take the contract, start removing the data, then suddenly get interested in whatever it is the Alliance is covering up. As long as they don't tip that hand, they have the perfect inside source—themselves."

"Yes," *Whiro* said. "It is, I believe, good that you did not try to penetrate their systems in the van, as it would likely have failed and provided confirmation of our existence and a measure of our threat as a competitor. You used cleaners in the honeypot apartment?"

"Yeah, and the one with Zacker just in case. But they're going to be looking closer at everything from now on," Fergus said. He'd rolled around his memories of the van incursion for a while before drifting off the night before, and had to agree he'd gone as far as he should. "If I do need to crack them at some point—which is probably inevitable—I'm going to need a lot more information and resources to do it. But what would a data security company want with the fragments, though?"

"They are alien in origin, and the core fragments exhibit properties outside humanity's current understanding of physics," *Whiro* said. "The founder of Digital Midendian, a human named Evan Derecho, has spun off several tech enterprises in his career, moving on when they reached sufficient stability and reputation to become, at a guess, no longer an interesting challenge. I note that Digital Midendian has a research-and-development division that has grown tenfold in size in the last five years, without any obvious product line."

"And where is this R&D division headquartered? Also Texas?"

"No. Perhaps conveniently for us, it is in the northeastern territories of the Sovereign City of New York," *Whiro* said. "If you would like, I can put in a call to Mr. Zacker?"

"Not until we know a lot more. And anyway, he might not even be home yet, and he'll be happier about helping us more once he's had time to get bored again," Fergus said. The ship was quiet, lights dim until he got close enough to the sensors to trigger them to brighten, and while it was a relief not to be accosted the moment he got on board, it only made his sense of dread for the upcoming confrontation deeper. "Where are Isla and Ignatio?" he asked.

"Sleeping," *Whiro* said. "It is, by ship's clock, just past 3 a.m. What time is your internal clock referencing?"

Fergus walked into the small kitchenette, rubbing his face, and dumped himself down on the grippy couch; upholstered with special smart fabric, it did a decent job of keeping you in place if the gravity suddenly went away, but the extra friction made it slightly more effort to slouch on, so it only added to his grumpiness. "I don't even know. Bodies don't work that way," he said.

"When did you last sleep?"

"I don't know that, either. I dozed a bit after Zacker headed back to the SCNY before I had to turn the apartment keys back over."

"That is insufficient for optimum performance," *Whiro* said.

Fergus laughed and forced himself to get up from the couch. "Let me get some coffee, then we can look into this Digital Midendian outfit more."

"No," *Whiro* said. In front of Fergus's outstretched fingers, the coffeemaker powered down.

"You have to be joking," Fergus complained.

"I will return the coffeemaker to service after you have slept for at least eight hours. And I specify *slept*: lying in your bunk, attempting research, does not count. Also, I have now turned off all your access to ship and dock feeds."

"*Whiro*, please. I have a lot to do."

"You will do it better after sleep. If you wish me to wake Ignatio and ask em about restoring your feeds, I can do so. Or I can wake Ms. Ferguson and let her know you have returned. I believe she has matters for discussion."

Fergus had made the mistake, once, of waking up Ignatio during eir infrequent but intense sleep periods, and he'd rather stab himself in the eyeball with a fork. And as for Isla . . .

"Fine," he said, "but don't make a habit of this, or I'll tell Theo who stole his bonsai clippers."

"You wouldn't," *Whiro* said.

"Don't push it," Fergus retorted, and slunk back down the hall to his small cabin, his jaw aching from his refusal to give *Whiro* the satisfaction of seeing him yawn.

———

Fergus had to admit that nine and half hours of sleep felt miraculously good, even if it did come with guilt over all the things he should have been doing instead, and not a little panic for the yelling-at he knew was waiting for him.

His stomach was stridently insistent on where, in his priority chain, eating needed to go. He headed to the kitchenette, still in his pajama pants, and pressed buttons on the foodmaker until it summoned something sufficiently toroidal to qualify as a bagel, even if it fell short in every other meaningful way.

Then he sat on the grippy couch with the bagel and a mug of coffee, and patiently ate the entire thing before he spoke up. "*Whiro*, can I have my feed access back now?"

"In a moment," *Whiro* said. "I am consulting with the rest of my party. Also, Ignatio and Isla will be joining you shortly. Eat another bagel."

He did, and was on his second cup of coffee as well when Ignatio came in. "It is interesting news for you that the mass readings across all turnings and orientations in our space are the same as the others," ey said. "Three is less coincidence now, yes?"

"Yeah," Fergus said. "So, that means we're sure there's thirty-two pieces total?"

"Prettily sure," Ignatio said. "Also, there is another thing. I did not see, but *Whiro*'s peripheral data analyses did. The Japan rockslide, the Scotland hill, and Burringurrah, all three places where the live pieces fell, are the same elevation."

"Burringurrah is over 1100 meters at its peak, and Doune Hill in Scotland is only 700 and something."

"Yes, but you found the piece near the top of Doune and only partway up Burringurrah. Same height above sea zero."

"I don't see how that could mean anything," Fergus said as Isla came into the kitchen and perched on one arm of the sofa Ignatio was sitting on, stony-faced. That made him feel even worse than if she'd just come in yelling.

As if to emphasize just how much shit he'd gotten himself into, Mister Feefs wandered into the room after her and jumped up on her lap, not his.

"Multidimensional door is about interfaces, yes?" Ignatio said. "Solid rock and easy air are a sharp transition. If the live pieces were drawn to those locations at a specific height, it explains the odd movements of the debris tracks as they came down. We have talked the math and agree."

"It could be something," Isla said, petting his cat.

"Does it help us?" Fergus asked.

"It would mean no pieces fell in the ocean," she said.

Ignatio hummed to emself for a moment, looking back and forth between the two of them, then turned on the table display. "Our map, please, *Whiro*," ey said.

The Earth globe outline appeared over the table.

"We have updated our information, operating on the assumption that there are a total of thirty-two live pieces," *Whiro* said. "You now have three. We continue to project that the Alliance has eleven and Fajro Promeso has three. We now consider it likely that Digital Midendian has eight, including the one taken in the home invasion in Alaska."

"That leaves me with seven pieces to find," Fergus said. "And twenty-two to steal."

"We still see activity at over forty sites, so it is likely that the others have not yet deduced a total, nor that they have made a correlation to altitude," *Whiro* said. "Or they did and later ruled it out, using information we do not have yet, though I consider that highly improbable."

"So, do we know where the remaining pieces are?" Fergus asked.

"We are confident about five as active sites that should be reasonably accessible to you," *Whiro* said, and five dots on the globe changed over to bright green. "The remaining two are less certain, but we are working on it."

"I'll need to deal with Digital Midendian and the Alliance, not to mention our cult friends, eventually, but I'd rather avoid all of them until they're all that's left."

"We have some ideas," *Whiro* said. "By the time you have more fragments, we may be able to suggest a plan. In the meantime, in your capacity as Finder, you should go Find things while we still have time. Ms. Harcourt has informed us that the two core pieces now in her custody are also showing increased signal output, the last increase coinciding with approximately the time you acquired the new one in Japan."

"Shit," Fergus said. "If they're getting easier for me to find them, then it's going to eventually get easier for DM to find them. *And* us."

"Do not forget, they are louder because they are finding each other," Ignatio said. Ey frowned. "Maybe they find each other through you? That is also bad. Perhaps you should give them shushes? Sing them a lullaby?"

Isla, miraculously, not quite but almost smiled at that.

"Right," Fergus said. He stood up. "I'm hungry, I'm cranky, and I need at least a few hours' peace before I take off again."

"You don't think you're just going to take off again without talking to me, do you?" Isla asked.

"No," Fergus said. "I think I'm going to take off again *while* talking to you. Pack what you need. We're going to"—he leaned in to peer at the green dots on the globe and picked one—"Mongolia. Only if you want, of course."

———

The horse was named Gaslan. It was shaggy and small but cantankerous enough for a whole herd of its milder Scottish kin, and had immediately made it known that it did not approve of him.

Isla, sitting quite comfortably atop a dun mare named Saikhan that had already adopted her as its best friend, had similarly made it clear that she had no advice for him, nor sympathy; he hoped her enjoyment of his discomfort and likely future thrown-by-his-horse broken neck would at least count for some small portion of the payback she felt he owed her.

There were ten other people in their birding tour group,

dropped on the steppes by shuttle, and their guide, Batu, had singled Fergus out immediately for the obstreperous beast. He didn't figure him being the only pale, blond-haired (thanks to a new round of nanites applies on his way down from orbit) Western man of the lot was entirely coincidence, but given the long history of behavior by people who looked like him, he didn't feel he should complain about it.

"We're going to get along, right, Gaslan?" he told the horse.

One brown fuzzy ear of the horse twitched, as if to flick his words away like a fly. *This is going to go great,* Fergus thought, just as Gaslan tossed his head and nearly pulled the reins out of Fergus's hands, and just as nearly made him topple out of the saddle, scrambling to keep his hold.

Isla snickered so loud, half the group turned to ogle him.

As much as he needed the tour to take him out to the shores of Buir Lake, otherwise off-limits as a strict conservation zone, sitting atop the stubby horse made him think he also would not entirely mind if the horse just didn't move *at all.*

After seeing the last of the tour group up onto their horses, Batu hopped up onto their own with an ease that almost felt like a personal condemnation. They wore a brightly colored robe and a four-sided hat with a little gold pinnacle, and after giving their pronouns as their sole item of self-introduction, had made it clear that no one was allowed to touch their hat, ever, and not even to ask.

Fergus was glad Ignatio wasn't along to defy that edict.

Batu gave a whoop, and the horses all fell into line and followed them across the grass, Gaslan very last and not at all happy about it, if the two or three side steps that nearly knocked Fergus off his back were any indication. When that failed, his horse broke into a sudden trot, which was like getting crotch-punched by a battering ram. Gaslan nearly ran down the three other people in front of him, all of whom gave him dirty looks, before Batu looked over their shoulder, barked something, and Gaslan let himself drift again toward the back of the line with surly resignation.

I'm going to die, Fergus thought, whimpering, as Isla slowed her horse with precision and ease to come back alongside him.

Other than abject fear of his horse, the sun was out and the day was beautiful. The grass was an ocean of green and tan, so flat the gentle wind left distinct waves in it as it passed. Ahead of them he could just make out the blue line on the horizon that was a distant lake, and the sun in the enormous, cloudless sky glinted off the tiny white dots of birds that were, ostensibly at least, their reason for coming.

It still seemed wrong, after all his hiking so far, that seven hundred meters above sea level was the low point there. For all the strength of a late-spring sun ready to bloom into summer, the air was cool, and if the breeze had been stronger, it would have felt borderline chilly. The land seemed untouched by time, though he knew it had been just as ravaged by climate change as much of the rest of the world; Mongolia had adopted stringent environmental policies after drought and increasingly devastating storms in the twenty-second century had wiped out most of its existing agriculture for decades and left the population on the brink of starvation.

Part of the legacy of their lifesaving land-management policies were places like this, cut off from all but the most impactless technology. Certainly not somewhere anyone could bring a van, and no one was hauling a parabolic dish there on the back of Gaslan.

Isla coughed meaningfully. "So?" she asked.

The line of horses was strung out enough that they were not likely to be overheard by the nearest rider ahead of them, who was anyway deeply in conversation with someone else.

"So," Fergus said. "I'm sorry I snuck out and went to Japan without you. It was the wrong thing to do, and I know it. I am not, however, sure I was wrong to send you back to the motel in Australia. In fact, I'm still convinced I wasn't, but I got some surprisingly decent advice from the world's least self-aware man, and I see it's not about convincing myself but convincing *you*."

"Great. So, convince me," she said.

He shrugged. "It was getting dangerous. I didn't want you to get hurt."

She waited, eyes on him as they trailed along at the end of the horse line, and finally emitted a sound that was half-growl, half-laugh. "That's *it*?" she asked.

"Yeah," he said. "I mean, do you really think I wouldn't or shouldn't care if something bad happened to you?"

"That's not it," she said. "The person that gave ye this 'decent' advice, do they know how to get along with anybody?"

"Not really, no," Fergus said. "I was desperate. But look . . . when I was a little kid? I think Ma believed that, with me helping her, we could somehow pull Old Scotland up from centuries ago and make it somehow *live* again. And of course we couldn't, and when I started to realize that, it was like I'd betrayed some fundamental trust. And then when Da killed himself right in front of me, and I couldn't reach him . . . So, I ran away. All the way to Mars, to escape feeling responsible, feeling I failed them both."

"I know all this," she said.

"Then on Mars, I met Dru," he said, and was silent for a while, trying to find words for the heartache he'd carried around wordlessly for nearly two decades. Isla rode along, and said nothing, giving him time.

A drone passed in the distance, and he reflexively hunkered down against his horse, but it did not come near enough to be obvious trouble.

"Remember when we were talking about Sentinel?" he asked at last. "Dru was the first person I met on Mars, maybe the first *friend* I'd ever made, and she introduced me to Kaice and the Free Marsies, and that's how I ended up on the Sentinel raid. I'd have done anything for her, and my whole life since then has been largely because of her."

"Were you in love with her?"

Fergus laughed and shook his head. "That's hard to say," he said. "I was in love with our friendship, and her passion and optimism, and that when she looked at me, she saw new potential, not old disappointment. I was still really a kid, and even though she wasn't that much older than me, she seemed like she knew everything and everyone, and was invincible and *happy* in a way I never imagined anyone could be, and I was feeling free for the first time in my life. And it didn't last, and I've never been free again since."

"She broke your heart?"

"No. Mars broke hers," he said. "Well, the MCA did. After the Sentinel raid, they rounded up anybody who even looked like they might have Marsie sympathies. They got her. They didn't get me. Eventually, they let everyone go again, but not until they'd broken them all, one by one, however long that took. And it took them a long time, with her."

"That's not your fault," Isla said.

"No, maybe not," he said. "But . . . the light in her eyes was gone; the passion had become all-consuming terror. And I felt guilty that it hadn't been me they'd taken instead, because I already knew all about the darkness. And I felt guilty because then I ran away again, always trying to stay one step ahead of losing anyone else. I was pretty good at that for a long time, until I started making friends despite myself—believe me, I have no idea what any of them see in me—and then . . . well, you. All the guilt that I carry around, if something happened to you, it would finally be enough break me."

"Ever since I was old enough for Gavin and my aunt and uncle to talk about you, and Gavin started showing me the Suttie's receipts coming in from all over the galaxy, I dreamed about going off on adventures with you," Isla said. "I imagined fast spaceships and weird but friendly aliens—"

"There's Ignatio," Fergus said.

She laughed. "Yeah. Exactly like that, except Ignatio almost seems too silly to be real."

Fergus chuckled. "You should tell em that. I think ey'd be flattered."

"But anyway, there were raids on space castles and a lot of rescuing alien princesses when I was younger, and then as I got older, it was about seeing nebulas and star nurseries and flying through Saturn's rings, and maybe still a few space castles. The life of adventure, you know?"

"I know," Fergus said. "I've never met an alien princess, but I've definitely been in a few things that almost could count as space castles. Certainly space dungeons. And I've had a lot of fun. But I've also been in abandoned habs full of dead children, and broken my ribs in landslides that I wasn't sure I could dig myself out of before I ran out of air, and been stabbed and burned and tortured, and blown out airlocks, and . . . a lot of stuff I shouldn't have survived, except I'm just too bloody-minded to give up and die. People around me have died. And those are just as much of my stories too, except I don't tell that part."

Isla nodded soberly and was quiet, lost in her own thoughts.

The target area for the debris was ahead, before the actual lakeshore. The group rode in at a leisurely pace, only loosely keeping to the path worn through the grass, and as everyone pointed and talked in at least four different languages, Fergus kept his eyes on the sky, where both bird and drone had wheeled, and did his best to calm his breathing and focus, listening with that alien sense deep within.

He wished he dared close his eyes, but he felt like Gaslan was just waiting for him to relax and become inattentive to do something awful to him. Pinned to his collar, his translation device murmured conversation to him, with a slight lag from the people speaking around him. Someone had spotted something called a 'greeb,' and there was much pointing and exclamation from the front of the group. The poor bird—a duck of some sort, he thought from the profile—took off in alarm for the open waters of the lake, where most of its fellows had wisely resettled when they saw the horses coming.

Batu stopped them a ways from the shore and pointed out a herd of small antelope farther down the shore. "Zeer," the guide informed them. A woman whose horse had stopped near Fergus's own smiled at him and said something his translator did not catch, so he just smiled broadly and enthusiastically back at her.

After a few minutes' pause, their guide got them moving again. Around him he could feel the steppe as some great, calm, empty space free of the constant buzz and tingle of electricity, free of the technology of humanity. His fellow birdwatchers were each a bright noise, with their cameras and handpads and other recorders, trying to catch the blur of a bird as it wheeled overhead and raced away. "Kestrel," someone said, and it certainly looked much like the kestrels back home in Scotland.

Something nagged at him, some tiny spark tapping on his attention, and he studied the grass to the west of the trail, attempting to focus on what lay out there. Isla followed his gaze, trying to see what he saw, but it was only a feeling. Another drone appeared overhead, this one closer, and sent a huge flock of gulls up into the air. Batu stopped the group again, annoyed.

"Not again!" the translator caught. They turned in their saddle back to them. "This is not one of yours?" they asked, and as everyone's translator caught up, everyone in the group shook their heads. They were as unhappy about the flock being spooked as the guide was.

Batu spoke briefly into their radio, then urged them all to dismount. They hauled down one of their saddlebags and handed out small packets of snacks. Fergus took his and found inside some thick, dry cookies and a handful of thin carrot sticks.

He held one up and caught Isla's gaze. "Noo, lass, we kin gang catch us aw wee sheep!" he said, and she threw one of her own carrot sticks at his head.

Fergus heard the soft, muffled chime of a handpad and pulled his out of his bag, but it wasn't his. He looked over at Isla. "That you?" he asked.

She pulled out her own. "It's Gavin," she said, then tapped off her handpad and stuck it back in her bag.

"Now, hang on—" Fergus started to say, when his own handpad chimed.

He answered it, still glaring suspiciously at Isla, who made a big pretense of looking at everything around them except him. "Hi, Gav," he said.

"Fergus," Gavin said on the other end of the connection. "Do ye know where Isla is?"

"Yes," he said, a little louder than necessary. "I do know where Isla is. She's right here with me. Didn't she call you?"

"No," Gavin answered. "Where the hell are ye? Ye didn't drag her off into space with yer weird alien friend, did ye? You know yer lifestyle isn't the healthiest—"

"No, we're not 'off in space,'" Fergus said. "We're on a bird-watching tour."

"Actual Earth birds?"

"Actual Earth birds. We just saw a greeb."

"A grebe? Okay," Gavin said. "So, she's not in any danger?"

"No, she's not in danger," he said. "See for yourself." He held up his handpad and did enough of a sweep to catch Isla on her horse, who was still studiously looking in the other direction, and a nice bunch of very boring, very Earth grass.

"Okay," Gavin said again. "Ye know anything about a weird drone thing sitting up on my roof?"

"Yeah," Fergus said. "I sent it there to keep an eye on things after the break-in. I felt bad about bringing trouble down on you. Hope you don't mind."

"It's fine," Gavin said. "Birdwatching, huh? Doesn't seem yer thing. But good. Ye need to do more normal people things so ye can, you know. Become normal again."

"Thanks," Fergus said dryly. "I'll ask Isla to give you a call when our tour is over, okay?"

"Right, thanks," Gavin said, and disconnected.

Fergus put his handpad away and looked over at Isla until she finally looked back, met his eyes for a split second, then hung her head.

He sighed deeply. "*Normal*, right," he said. "If I just want to be normal enough, it'll come true, like magic? As if in fifteen years of desperately willing my parents to love me, I just never quite wanted it badly enough. I tried to will that guy not to cut my ear off, too, but me bad, I guess my heart wasn't in that, either."

"Sorry, Ferg," she said.

"Yeah, not your fault," he said. He had intended to hassle her more, but she did look contrite. Also, his irritation had shifted from her to Gavin, and his attention had shifted from her to an undistinguished patch of grass, in a sea of same, that was interested in *him*.

This time, it was less like two strangers passing just close enough to exchange surprised hellos and more like the piece was expecting him, was calling directly to him. Which was, Fergus considered, a little creepy and probably more than a little bad.

"So, why, if you are that worried about me being in danger, are we here?" Isla asked. They had fallen well behind the group, which Batu had brought to a stop for resting and water. From the many glances back, it was clear their guide wanted them to catch up.

"Because of all the sites I'd skimmed our preliminary data on, this one seemed the safest," Fergus said. "Out here on the grass, it's a lot harder to get to us. We'll have to be careful going back into Ulaanbaatar to catch a shuttle out, but once we've got the piece, we've got a lot more flexibility in our movements. Also, Mongolia is interesting! Did you ever think you would be here?"

"No," Isla admitted.

"And did you ever think you'd get the satisfaction of watching your adventure-hero brother fall off a horse?" he asked.

She smiled. "You planning on that?"

"I am," he said. "Gaslan here is going to get spooked by something, in about two minutes, and hopefully run off in the right direction before he dumps me out of the saddle."

"Spooked by . . . You're not going to, ye know—" She rubbed her fingers together as if summoning a spark.

"Well, yeah, that was the plan," Fergus said. "I—"

"You can't zap the poor horse!" she said. She rolled her eyes. "You can be such an asshole. Don't ye even dare do it."

"He's not a *nice* horse," Fergus protested.

"How do you know? Maybe he's perfectly nice when he's being left alone and not hauling tourists' arses around all day," she said. "Would you be happy in his place?"

"I don't have enough legs to take his place," Fergus said.

"You know bloody well what I mean!" she said.

"Fine," Fergus said. He slumped in his seat. "I won't zap the horse, okay?"

"Great. So, what's your new plan, genius?"

"This," he said. He raised his hand as they approached the stopped group. "Ah, um, Batu?" he asked. "How do we, you know, pee?"

Batu raised their arms wide, indicating the vast plain around them, then chuckled and walked away.

One woman near the edge of the group laughed and said something, and his translator managed to catch it. "Pee behind your horse," she'd said.

That was, in fact, what Fergus had hoped for. He tugged on Gaslan's reins, hoping to pull him away toward where he'd felt the signal, but the horse was not having any of it, and several of the others, including Isla, watched him pulling and cajoling the horse with obvious amusement.

Finally, he dug into the snack packet and pulled out one of the carrots. "Carrot?" he asked as sweetly as he could, and the horse swung his long face over to regard him at length before, grudgingly, he took a step forward.

It cost him his entire stash of carrots to get to where he felt the fragment calling from. A few of the other birdwatchers, failing to be distracted by the still-wheeling gulls, were watching him, so he made as if he was about to moon the lot of them, and they turned quickly away.

Behind cover of his horse, he took a few steps, then knelt down and ran his hands through the grass until they found something hard and metal half-woven into the ground by roots and straw. One of the inert frame pieces; he tucked it quickly into a pants pocket and tried again, and this time, his fingers went right to where they needed. He wrapped the core fragment in a handkerchief and stuffed it deep into an inner pocket on his light coat, until he had more privacy to stash it more securely. Then, just to be sure his cover story was complete, he took the expected pee.

Gaslan looked like he was trying to figure out how to raise eyebrows he didn't have, but after Fergus surrendered his cookies, the horse was willing to be led back toward the group, which was already remounting for the last leg of the ride to the lakeshore.

There was another Mongolian there now, his horse standing with its feet in the shallow water of the lake itself. He wore a similar hat to Batu and held in his hands a long composite bow that dully gleamed as if made of horn.

When the drone that had earlier upset the gulls swung back around, the man calmly pulled an arrow from his hip quiver and shot it down on his first try. He and Batu saluted one another, and then the man rode off again.

Now Fergus could make out the small collection of yurts away from the trail, each one marked with the logo of the Mongolian Conservation Service. He wondered how many drones Digital Midendian lost per year to arrows, and how you deducted illegal surveillance ops on your taxes. Neither was his problem.

Four pieces down, he thought, *twenty-eight to go.* For now, all he and Isla needed to do was enjoy the rest of the day, watch some birds do birdish things, and avoid DM and cultists on their way out. He hoped the competition was inattentive enough that they could try some of the local food before leaving; the heady aroma from a spicy-noodle-and-dumpling place they'd passed on their way in this morning still lingered in his thoughts.

"White-naped crane!" someone yelled in excitement, and then the whole group was moving on toward that new sight, and he followed along with his fragment and his cranky horse and his amused sister toward the reeds and sand dunes and tall, elegant white birds wading along the shore, unbothered.

Chapter 12

———◆———

"You look worried," Isla said, deftly stealing the last dumping off the plate between them.

"I am," Fergus said. It wasn't that an unmarked white van with way too much electrical signal coming from it had passed the restaurant twice now, between the Ulaanbaatar shuttleport and the tour drop off; the new core piece was now safely settled in his pack inside another of the modified PhobosCola cans, the second of a pair delivered to *Whiro* while he was in Japan. He could hardly hear the fragment inside. *Hardly*, though, was the worrisome part—the first two pieces had effectively gone silent in their cans. This piece was louder, and after sliding the noodle bowl closer and shoveling the rest of them onto his own plate—she'd taken the dumpling, after all, so that seemed only fair—he said as much.

"Maybe you're just getting more sensitive to them," Isla said.

Deep in his gut, he knew that wasn't it. "Probably," he said.

"So, where to next?" she asked, as he paid and they stepped back outside. The shuttleport was a short walk, and the van long gone, possibly after the next tour group. "Somewhere tropical, full of loud an' colorful birds? I mean, this was lovely, but I'd like to get a chance to find out how much I can tan."

Fergus smiled. "Then our next stop will definitely be an unexpected treat."

———

The Arctic Union Shuttleport was in the southwestern Nuuk region of the main island of Kalaallit Nunaat, set back from the canyon-riddled coastline on smoother inland tundra, once upon a time covered in invincible-seeming glaciers. Instead, now there were vast fields of solar panels with programmable reflectivity, those not needed for power consumption turned to white to bounce some of the sun's heat back out of the atmosphere. It was a small measure among many, and less controversial than the vast flotillas of white hexagons, two meters wide each and four meters apart, stretching across the ocean all the way to the Nunavut territories of the Union, taking the place of missing ice to bounce warming ultraviolet light back off the water's surface.

Complaints about inconveniencing global shipping didn't much outlast the unsustainable consumer culture of North America, especially once the former United States fell apart. And the polar bears, so long teetering on the cusp of extinction, hadn't minded some spiffy new high-tech ice floes at all. To Fergus, the geometry of the ocean panels was unsettling in such a raw, wild place, but as they collectively rose and fell with the swells of the waves in a mesmerizing grid, they were also hard to take one's eyes off of.

He found it funny that just about the time Greenland finally began to live up to its name, the island territory had dropped it.

There was not much there in the way of tourism outside the few small cities along the former Danish territory's fringes, nestled in canyons and reminding him in odd, hard-to-pin-down ways of the fisherfolk side of town along the Scotland Inland Sea. Nor were there convenient Hikerpods or other such businesses; there were locals and scientists, and most tourists were not hardy enough to venture too far from civilization except in very occasional and expensive organized tours to go visit some of the deep canyons that had found themselves unexpectedly free of ice after millennia.

Isla heaved a long, vocal sigh, the third such in as many minutes, as they took a small automated tram from the port to the nearby coast. The elderly Kalaallit woman who rented them a boat showed him how to turn it on, pointed him toward the smart console, and switched it over from Danish to English, then patted a deeply reluctant Isla gently on the back as if fondly sending her out to sea to a swift and ignominious death.

Still, the boat was solid and had a decent if limited mindsystem on board that he let mostly take over operations as he directed it north along the coastline to an island named Qeqertarsuaq. He had practiced the pronunciation on his way down but thought his best bet was just to not talk to anyone local unless he had to.

This site, like the others, presented practical challenges to his competitors' vehicles that he didn't have, being on foot. At the top of the list was the Kalaallit family whose back fields the debris had come down on; five generations of them had fought for independence before it was finally won, and two members had served as representatives of their state in the newly formed Union. They had told the Alliance firmly they wanted no vehicles on the property, and the island and Kalaallit Nunaat government backed them. The brief on-foot search had, from the data *Whiro* had recovered from the tea set, clearly not been successful.

Now that he knew what to look for, he found at least one attempt from an obvious front company to convince the owners to sell or lease out some of the fields, equally futile. Digital Midendian, no doubt.

If the world wasn't in danger, Fergus would strongly have preferred to leave them alone himself. As it was, the target area was several steep hills and valleys away from the farmhouse and other buildings, and no one should know they were there. *In and out,* he thought. *Time is ticking.*

He sent the boat out from shore and into rougher waters, and felt a small thrill when a big wave sent them briefly feeling airborne. It was only the small squeak from behind him that reminded him that he was not alone, and that his sister was being very, very quiet.

Fergus glanced back at her. "You okay?" he asked.

"Not been boating before," she said.

"Swimming at least, then?" Fergus asked.

"No," she said. "After what happened to my da and what everyone said happened to ye? No one let me anywhere near water."

"Oh," he said. He opened his mouth to say something about how space hadn't bothered her this much and was much deadlier, but he remembered his own deep reluctance to get near water when he'd first left home. "You probably ought to learn, though," he said instead.

"Just don't make me have to learn by surprise, okay?" she said.

"I'll do my best," he said. "We don't have to go too far. Look, you can already see the town up ahead."

He directed the boat past the brightly colored houses and windmills, and pulled in just at the southern mouth of the channel separating the island from the mainland, on a rock-strewn beach. As he pondered how to get from the boat to the actual shore, the boat popped up a dialogue asking him if he wanted to beach. Shrugging, Fergus hit Yes, and the boat oriented itself bow-in to the shore and rumbled toward it, sprouting wheels just in time to roll up onto dry land. As the boat parked itself, he turned to Isla, who was looking a lot happier. "You coming?" he asked.

"Off this boat? Aye, absolutely," she said.

"Great." He pointed to the bag on the floor of the boat. "Camouflage thermal suits. It's a balmy eight C out. Also, grab the carrot sticks? We may have to bribe some sheep."

"Sheep?" Isla protested. "Never mind. Can I just stay next to the boat? I want to think through some math Ignatio gave me."

"No," he said. "You turned your back on science for the world of high adventure, so you get to crawl through the sheep crap with me. Now get your suit on."

———

"So, that's five," Isla said, stuffing her thermal suit back into the bag with as few fingers as she could, her face a grimace of distaste. The sheep had proved handy cover from a pair of spycams, but they'd done a lot of crawling through the flock on their hands and knees. "I feel like I was spun through an autowash with a load of gravel and dung," she said. "How many more of these pieces involve sheep?"

"That I know about? None. But you never can be sure where a job will lead till it's done," Fergus said. He had already ditched his own suit on the floor, and as the boat systems navigated them back out into the channel, he opened the modified PhobosCola can to see if the second fragment would fit in with the first.

It did not, and the burst of signal when he opened the can was the electromagnetic equivalent of getting hit in the face with a giant springy fake snake. Fergus hastily put the lid back on and set it at arm's length away from him, as he regarded the new piece—still excited, still springy with chatter—still in his hand.

"They're louder, you said?" Isla asked.

"Yeah." He could feel the Mongolia piece sealed back in its can, subdued as it was, and between it and the new Qeqertarsuaq piece, he felt uncomfortably like one point in a triangle of electrical noise. "Maybe it's because they're so near each other. I shouldn't have opened the can."

"Ye said it was like they were talking to each other and to you," Isla said. "Can ye, like Ignatio suggested, ask them to shut their gobs and go back to sleep? Electrically?"

"My thing doesn't work like that," Fergus said.

She shrugged. "Ye sure? Ye've tried it? Because it seems like except when ye zap people, ye only use this thing passively."

"Because it's dangerous!" Fergus said. He dropped the new piece in his pocket, took out the last, bent carrot stick, stuck it in his mouth, and immediately realized it was covered in dirt and spat it out again. "I don't want to accidentally hurt anyone."

"Yeah, but maybe you're also avoiding learning what ye *can* do," Isla said. "Aren't ye curious?"

Fergus would never forget the look on Pace's face, under the ice of Enceladus, just before his 'gift' deflected a lethal shot back on the rogue pilot and killed him. "No," he said. "I am really not."

"Lazy arse," she said. "Or are ye scared?"

"Very, very much the latter," he said, "though I also won't deny the first. Speaking of working, *Whiro* was supposed to be figuring out how to sneak drones down to carry them back up to orbit; I'd like to get these two out of my hands and away before our next stop."

"Which is somewhere warmer?" Isla asked.

"Iceland," he answered. "Still arctic, sorry."

She groaned. "Fine, but there better be hot food. And a shower."

———

The ferry from Kalaallit Nunaat was a welcome few hours of peace and boredom. As Isla napped in the seat across from him, the ferry passed alongside the rising structure of the Arctic rail bridge, a dozen orange-and-yellow automated construction vehicles crawling under, over, and around it in a synchronized dance, and he found himself tempted to wave out the window to them, in case one was Akio's.

Instead, he leaned back in his ferry seat and checked in with Ignatio and *Whiro*. "Isla is not sickened of you yet?" Ignatio said.

"Getting there, I think," Fergus said.

"Hmm. I have more physics things for her when she is ready. You will tell her, yes? Math is the best of all funs."

"I'll have to take your word on that," Fergus said, then lowered his voice. "She seems to love it all, but remember a lot of this is new for her? Give her a chance to catch up and maybe ask if she has questions? Uh, but don't tell her you're doing that or that I said so. In the meantime, I have two, er, packages for you and I'm not sure how to deliver them. *Whiro*, you were working on something?"

"I have sent down a small delivery drone with our larger autonomous supply drone, *Constance*. We are officially here conducting business to restock our garden ring, which requires transactions at multiple points on Earth," *Whiro* said. "I had originally directed my drone, once free of *Constance*, to intercept you at the Kangerlussuaq Shuttleport on Kalaallit Nunaat, as we all expected Ms. Ferguson to have gotten over the idea that you are more interesting to spend time with than us, but you appear to both be on a ferry. You are heading toward Reykjavík?"

"Yeah. Should be there in a few hours," Fergus said. "Going to find our next core piece and then get a room for the night, I think."

"My drone should catch up with you before nightfall," *Whiro* said. "It is bringing you two more modified cans so you can send up both the Qeqertarsuaq fragment and the Reykjavík one when you acquire it."

"Good," Fergus said. "I don't like carrying even one of these around unshielded, much less two, so the less time I have to do so, the better."

"Neither do I like it," Ignatio said. "It is bad, very, very bad, but I am sure it will somehow be fine, yes?"

"Sure it will. I'll check in when we're settled down," Fergus said. He disconnected and glanced over at his lightly snoring sister. He'd been in *everything is very bad*–level trouble before, but what worked out fine for him—minus inconveniences like getting shot in the leg with a harpoon gun, and stuff like that—didn't always work out fine for people around him.

You can't make choices for other people, he reminded himself, and then spent the rest of the ferry ride trying to figure out if he could somehow trick Isla into leaving of her own volition in a way that didn't involve being a jerk.

The target zone was up in the hills to the north of the capital, outside a town named Bakkakotsvöllur. At the ferry terminal in Reykjavík, there were multiple holo ads for horseback tours out in the hills and across the lava fields, but both Fergus and Isla agreed they'd had enough livestock encounters for a while. "Electric mountain bikes," Isla said, waving at one of the pop-up ads ahead of them in the terminal corridor. "But first, I'm hungry and I need a shower. Ye might be used to running all over the galaxy, but the most exercise I usually get is going downstairs to steal chips from the kitchen when Gavin's not around."

"All right," he said, and handed her one of his anonymous credit chits. Then he pointed across the intersection from the ferry terminal at an automated hotel. "Rent us a room? I'll look around a bit, find us some food, arrange for the bikes, and meet you back there. That okay?"

"You won't take off without me?" she asked.

"No," he said, which was true now that she'd asked.

"Okay," she said. "Don't forget the food. And try to stay out of trouble."

"Always," he answered, which was definitely less true, but since she didn't call him on it, he figured he was in the clear.

He waited until she'd gone safely into the autohotel, then walked into the city. Iceland wasn't noticeably warmer than the Arctic Union, but the sun was out, it was a new place, and he was feeling cautiously optimistic about his impossible task. The city lay spread out around a bay, separated from the water by a strip of park and seawalls that had kept the rising ocean back for centuries. Gulls wheeled overhead, smaller than the Mongolian gulls near Buir Lake but no less noisy. As soon as he was inside the embrace of buildings, there were people and chatter everywhere, out shopping, sitting at cafes, talking about the undying day with a slightly manic air. When he stopped to ask directions to the bike rental place, a young woman with a bright blue mohawk directed him in nearly flawless English.

As he walked, he hummed and slowly realized he was humming to the un-canned fragment, both with his voice and with something deeper in his gut. He couldn't tell if it hummed back the same tune, but it was definitely awake, deep in his coat pocket. The suggestion that he could talk to it seemed less ridiculous.

Also, more scary. He stopped humming.

The bike rental place was in the center of the city, on the far side of a main bus station. Between him and it was a white van, parked on the side of the street. He curled his hand around the Qeqertarsuaq fragment and slowed his walk without obviously stopping; he didn't want to attract attention. Instead, he curved his path past the side of the bus stop away from the van, and then, when he was a bit farther along, ducked through the door of an open museum to give himself time to think.

Could they detect the fragment from the distance of the bike rental? He didn't think so. Were there vans camped out at all hundred-something sites, waiting for someone to show? Or were they closer to finding him than he thought? Or was it just a random white autovan, ubiquitous everywhere and not necessarily sinister at all?

He knew how his luck ran.

He could pull his hood up and make for the bike rental place, see if that prompted any activity, but with the sun out, having his hood up would be suspicious unto itself. What he needed was a hat, a good, old-fashioned baseball cap, until he could set off another round of hair nanites to deal with his returning red. He turned around to the museum's gift shop and stopped mid-step in some surprise at the museum's particular subject, unnoted on his way in.

"Um . . ." he said. "Is this . . ."

"The Icelandic Slug Museum," the elderly, grandmotherly-like woman behind the counter said. "Our founder was given a dried banana slug for a birthday gift and became fascinated by it. Slugs come in a remarkable variety of shapes and sizes, and we have the largest collection of specimens from all over the world, land and sea."

"Snails?" Fergus asked.

She made a face. "Snails are not slugs."

"Of course not, sorry," Fergus said. "I was just looking to buy a hat? For a souvenir."

She smiled knowingly and waved him over to a rack of hats. "Keychains are buy one, get one free," she said, and when he shook his head, she pointed out another rack. "Slug-themed intimate wear? Adult toys? They're on clearance."

"No, thank you, just a hat," he said. He picked out a cap with just the museum's 150th anniversary logo on it and, after checking the sidewalk outside the door, scurried out with a brand-new hat on his head.

When he got back to the Shipyard, he'd gift the hat to Maison, who would probably love it. He could claim it was a goodwill gesture for the hat Mister Feefs peed in.

The van hadn't moved. He kept his hand on the fragment, trying to project calmness at it, as he walked as casually as he could toward the bike rental kiosk. There, he reserved two bikes for pickup in two hours—plenty of time to eat first, he thought—and then turned away and immediately found himself face-to-face with a pale, rail-thin, ill-looking man in linen clothes who had been coming the other way down the sidewalk. The man's eyes went wide with surprised recognition, and his mouth was opening and closing in panic as if he were trying to remember how to shout.

Okay, Fergus, improvise, he told himself. *And do it fast.*

"Hello again, Peter," he said. He stepped in close enough to take the man down if he had to, and put one arm around his shoulders. The man froze like a rabbit caught in the gaze of a hawk. "Still working on that apocalypse, are ye?"

"You?" Peter squeaked.

"Me," Fergus said. "Are you following me?"

"No! I—" The cultist's eyes drifted over to the van.

"You following Kyle?"

Peter gritted his teeth. "Not Kyle. That's Jeremy. Malseka ŝaltillo! He's an asshole. He's over in the bar on Hverfisgata, getting drunk again." Suddenly remembering who he was talking to, he looked around skittishly. "Where is your alien friend?"

"Nearby," Fergus said. The man was shivering, and not all of it from fear. "Uh . . . don't you have a coat?"

"What?" Peter seemed taken aback. "No. Why would you care?"

"Because you look cold!" Fergus snapped. Why *did* he care? "And when did you last eat?"

"I don't know," Peter said. "Food is of no concern for the followers of the fire."

"Look," Fergus said, "you're interfering in an official investigation . . ."

"You're Scottish police?" Peter said, then smiled. "This isn't Scotland."

"No, I'm an undercover agent of the Secret Space Police. We have jurisdiction everywhere," Fergus answered.

"Secret Space Police? I've never heard of anything like that!"

"Because it's *secret*," Fergus said. "I'm investigating them"—he pointed at the van—"not you. For murder, among other things. But since you seem to know a fair bit about that group, if you give me a little information, I'll buy you a hot meal. Deal?"

"You are not one of the Chosen," Peter said.

"Nope, I'm sure not, but if you think about it, the more you help me, the more I get in *their* way," Fergus said, nodding his chin toward the van. "I'm betting you'd like that."

Peter was clearly thinking about it, wringing his bluish hands together. "Okay, look, no pressure here," Fergus said. "I'm going to go around the corner there"—he pointed down a side street, well away from the bus station, van, and the street where Jeremy was off drinking—"and I'm going to go into that little sandwich shop with the red awning, and I'm going to have myself a nice lunch. If you join me, I'll buy you lunch, too. You don't even have to talk, okay?"

"Why?" Peter asked again.

"Because I've been hungry and cold too," Fergus said.

He walked away from the cultist, not looking back, though

he did glance over at the van, which was still showing no signs of occupation or interest.

The sandwich shop was a brightly lit little place called Mjög Besti Maturinn, and though in the moment he wanted nothing more than to go back to the kiosk, get his bike early, find the core fragment, and move it and Isla out of there, he saw the potential for something useful here. *Never turn down opportunities for more resources,* he told himself, scrolling down the menu in the table top. And anyway, he'd promised Isla food, too.

He lingered a bit longer than he would normally have, but when Peter didn't show, he sighed and ordered himself a faux lobster sandwich, a salad, and a hot coffee, and a to-go pack of the same.

Peter slumped into the booth about the time his coffee arrived, and immediately, the man reached over and slid it to his side of the table. Fergus ordered himself a replacement without saying a word.

"Secret Space Police, huh?" Peter said after several minutes.

"Yep."

"Doesn't sound real."

"Neither does belonging to an apocalypse cult in the twenty-fifth century," Fergus said. "And yet here we are."

Fergus's replacement coffee arrived along with his sandwich and salad. Peter's eyes were on his tray as the server robot slid the food onto the table. "You want it?" Fergus asked.

"No," Peter said, too quickly, and Fergus was pretty sure the man sat on his own hands. "You said *murder.*"

"Yes," Fergus said. "Near Yakutat City, in the Alaskan Federation of North America. A park guide."

"The techbros were there," Peter said.

Fergus paused with a forkful of salad halfway to his mouth. "You mean the van guys?"

"Yes."

"Digital Midendian," Fergus said.

"Yes," Peter said again, eyes widening in surprise.

"Were you there? You do follow them."

"I was not. One of my Sisters in Flame was, though."

"Could she have witnessed the murder?"

"No," Peter said. "She went in after they had gone and was only there long enough to verify they did not miss getting what they wanted."

"And that is?" Fergus asked.

Peter shrugged, and stared forlornly as Fergus's lobster roll. Fergus sighed, took half the sandwich, and set it on a napkin before pushing it across the table to Peter.

"I'm not telling you any more," Peter said.

"That's fine. I can't finish the whole sandwich, anyway, though, so you might as well," Fergus said. He leaned back against the seatback and sipped his coffee, and watched as the man slowly reached out and inched the napkin closer, before picking up the sandwich and stuffing as much of it into his mouth at once as he could.

Peter's body language was hunched, defensive, and he kept glancing between his vanishing food and Fergus as if ready to bolt. Reluctantly, Fergus decided he wasn't going to get much more info out of the man anyway, at least not right now, and whatever increment of trust the food might have earned him was best left unwasted by pushing, anyway.

Instead, he paid for lunch through the table interface. "I've got some business," he told Peter, "and I better not catch you following me. And I *will* catch you."

Peter shook his head, mouth too full to speak, and Fergus took that as a probably fickle but sincere promise. He stood up and shrugged his coat back on, and slung his bag over his shoulder. "I know giving unasked-for advice is treading a thin line of civility," he said, "but let me just say: apocalypses are terrible things. It's not something to wish for."

Peter swallowed a large mouthful of food before answering. "Sometimes, it's the only thing you have left," he said. "Thank you for the food."

"You're welcome," Fergus said, and picked up his takeout on his way out the door.

————

Peter was nowhere to be seen when he and Isla cautiously approached the rental kiosk to pick up their bikes. From a block away, he sent Isla ahead first and watched to be sure no one followed her. There was some overhead drone traffic, mostly small package-carriers, and nothing seemed to change directions after she pedaled off at casual tourist speed up the road.

Ten minutes later, Fergus got his own bike and followed after her, alert for the van and overhead traffic. "So far, we're clear back here," he said to her over the pager mic. "How is it up there?"

"Uphill," she answered, sounding a bit out of breath.

"It's electric," he said. "You could turn it on."

"Not until I have to," she said. "Catch up if you can without cheating."

Well, fuck, Fergus thought. *I have to pedal now, too? I'm too old for sibling rivalry.*

He swore his entire sweaty way up the hill until he caught up with Isla sitting in the meager shade of a crooked, windblown larch, drinking water. It was a relief that she let him get down off his bike, his bad leg complaining stiffly, and join her in the grass for a while without any snarky commentary.

"So, how far we going?" she asked, eventually.

"Another ten or eleven kilometers," he said. As near as Fergus could tell from the high-res shots of the area, the location was not dissimilar to the one on Kalaallit Nunaat, another steep hillside of jumbled, lichen-covered scree virtually unreachable except on foot.

They stopped outside the surveillance circle, and Isla watched him intently as he concentrated, making absolutely certain he could pinpoint the piece's location. "Got it," he said. "There are three cams and one motion sensor. Let me show you where."

She turned on her smart sunglasses, and he sent the overlay to her systems. "Oh, yeah, I see them now," she said. "How are ye going to get to the piece without tripping them? No sheep to hide among."

"I think it's gotta just be a fast grab," he said. "None of the cams seem to be mobile units, so our biggest issue is going to be drones coming in as soon as I'm detected. Once we get safely back into Reykjavík, we should be able to ditch the bikes and get lost in the pedestrian traffic."

Isla pulled up the hood on her jacket, stuffing her hair back in and under so none of it was visible. Fergus, in turn, pulled his museum hat down over his brow, kept his head down, and bicycled into the zone along the small path, trying to maintain the appearance of a regular passing bicyclist as long as possible. When he was closest to where the piece was, he jumped off the bike and scrambled down the slope, dug his fingers painfully through the scree, and was up and back on his bike again in less than five minutes.

Isla was already poised to go as he fell in beside her, and they both turned their bike motors on to get some speed and distance.

Somewhere, still off in his peripheral senses, he thought he could feel drones approaching.

"Sorry, taking a shortcut," he told Isla over the link. "Going to be a little rough."

"Whatever you think you've got, bring it," she answered, then he just caught her grunt of surprise when he swerved off the trail entirely and half-skidded down a hillside toward a distant road. About a kilometer down he could see a group of several dozen tourists cycling over to see the lava fields in a large, disorganized group. He stopped under a tree and, in the shelter of its small canopy, quickly shed his hat and outer jacket, stuffing them in his pack out of sight. Despite the exertion, he shivered a bit in the stiff wind coming down the hill and glowered at Isla as she tucked away her own red jacket and pulled out a yellow one instead. At his look, she smirked back at him.

"You just happened to have two different-colored jackets with you?" he asked.

"Sure. Isn't that like Skullduggery 101?" she said. "I bought it in the ferry station while ye were taking yer sweet time in the loo. See, it's got the logo of their hoverslam team, the Magmatiks, on it. I totally blend."

Fergus looked away to watch the approaching cyclists and wondered if it was a common experience with sisters to feel both simultaneously proud and utterly aggrieved. "We're here resting and taking in the view, just like normal people," he said. "When they go by, we'll fall in with them for a while for cover."

"You're the expert," she answered, and he made a conscious choice not to glance back at her to see her expression as she said it.

They got on their bikes and joined the ragtag line of cyclists, and stuck with them for a few kilometers across the austere, rolling landscape, with its occasional jagged incursions of old, grayish, lichen-covered lava, before they peeled off on an intersecting road and headed into Reykjavík. Two drones passed high over-head, moving away from the city in the direction they had just come from. *Too late,* Fergus thought somewhat smugly, *I veni, vidi, and vici'd with the sneaky.*

Nothing worrisome was anywhere near them, which meant they could coast back into the city without the enemy breathing down their necks. Isla stopped, once, to look at one of the old lava fissures, crouching at the edge and peering in, before tenta-tively touching the rough, almost bubbly surface. He sipped some water and waited patiently; it was a very genuine tourist thing to do, helped their cover, and anyway, he liked seeing Isla absorbed in interest. It reminded him of himself, when he was researching something for a job, except more innocent and hon-est than his motives usually were.

It was like looking back in time at what he might have be-come if his own childhood had given him the room to care about things not immediately relevant to survival and escape. He was profoundly struck by how grateful he was to know her, to see the alternate reality he'd always wished for come true, even if not for him.

"What're ye lookin' at, ye bam?" Isla asked, peering over her shoulder at him.

"The future," he said, and then grinned. "You know, when the supervolcanoes all finally decide to go *kaboom* at once and we're nothing but bones and garbage down in those crevasses, a curiosity millennia from now for random alien tourists passing by and looking for a nice picnic spot."

"Aren't ye the most fun brother ever," she said, and stood up, shaking her head. "Let's go."

They returned the electric bikes at a different kiosk and ducked into a small, touristy shop. While Isla rummaged through a sweater bin, Fergus bought a big fleece pullover covered in frolicking sheep and a voluminous hood. She smiled but didn't say anything as they left and headed back toward their rented room.

The pullover was warm and comfortable and the sun strong overhead between sparse clouds. *This is a good Earth day,* he thought. Isla seemed happy too, and they'd successfully retrieved three pieces together without incident, and possibly without anything interesting enough happening that she'd want to stay with him for a fourth.

He found himself humming again as they strolled down the sidewalk, even as he was fiddling with the two loose core fragments in his pocket, and realized they were all humming together, and that something else was coming up behind them.

He turned and spotted Jeremy's van making its way down the street in their direction, just as the two fragments in his pocket suddenly shifted, as if alive, and clicked together.

"Oh, shit," he breathed out loud.

"What?" Isla asked.

Shut up shut up shut up, he thought at them, willing his bees to step in and shut them down. But he had no control yet, not unpracticed and under stress, and it felt like there was a bolt of something connecting his gut to the fragments, piercing his skin like a thin, hot wire. Inside its can in his pack, he could hear the Mongolian fragment now, too, overwhelming the signal-dampening electronics, calling out for its other parts.

As much to cover his discomfort as to buy time, he pulled out his handpad. "Pretend we're looking at a map," he said. "Act cool. Don't look up."

If she looked alarmed at that, still, she nodded very faintly and pretended she was studying the handpad with him, and it gave him an excuse to look up and around, and then point at the display again, as if they were getting their bearings or discussing where to go next.

They were in front of a block of apartments, across from an office building, and nowhere easily nearby to duck into. He could feel the signal from the van getting closer, and the driver was slowing down, his head moving from side to side as he scanned the people on the walk. When it was almost upon them, Fergus glanced up, and in that fleeting moment, they made eye contact, and the driver slammed on his brakes.

Fergus grabbed Isla's hand. "We gotta run," he managed to say as he nearly yanked her off her feet, pulling her into and down an alley, stuffing his handpad back inside his pack as they went. "DM's on to us. We need a plan to get out of here."

"Bus?" she asked.

"No," he said. On the bus, they'd be trapped, and the shuttleport was too far away. He turned down another street, pulling Isla with him, then paused at the end of the block, at the edge of the city. Ahead was the open plaza of the ferry terminal and harbor. The ferry itself wouldn't be any easier to escape from than the bus, but he remembered seeing something else on his way in . . .

Mini-subs! Sure enough, there was a rental place right near the main ferry terminal, where you could rent a personal submersible by the hour to go out and zoom around the fascinating, frigid waters of Iceland. "Sub," he said. "Go!"

"Fergus, I don't think—"

"It's our only way out. Come on!" He ran, and she ran after him. He could feel the energy signature of the approaching van, only a few blocks away as they reached the harbor rental kiosk.

Hands shaking with the effort not to leak nervous electricity into the machine, he rented them a sub using a burner ID and account, gave a hefty security deposit he didn't figure he was going to get back, waived the twenty-minute tutorial, and skipped straight ahead to the liability waiver.

Behind them he heard the van roar into the plaza and come to a screeching stop where the road ended in stone bollards, and the sound of its doors being thrown open. He didn't dare take the seconds to look, as he finalized the transaction and grabbed the sub control card from the slot.

"Go!" he shouted, and pointed toward the black-and-white sub, painted to look like an orca, with the large number 6 on its nose and an open canopy waiting near the far end of the nearest dock.

There were a few other people around, and a security officer down by the ferry terminal was on her comm, staring at the van. If she was summoning help, it wasn't going to get there soon enough.

"Fergus!" Isla said again as they ran onto and down the dock, scattering gulls into the air around them, and past a young couple just getting out of the number three sub. Fergus glanced back and saw two large, solidly built men were running to intercept them across the grass that separated the plaza from the harbor proper. One pulled out a gun and fired while running, the shot going wide somewhere as people in the plaza shouted and ran, and sirens began to wail outside the ferry building.

The other couple on the docks scrambled back into their sub, and Fergus stuffed a shocked Isla into the back of their own and jumped in after her into the pilot's seat. He jammed the control card into the sub's dash slot, and the moment it came live, he sealed the canopy and backed the sub away from the dock in a sudden churn of spray.

"Buckle up!" he said, finding the dive controls almost where he expected them to be, and pulling the yoke for the hydroplanes into position as he also dumped the air from the side ballast tanks, and the harbor rose up and along the sealed canopy.

The sharp, telltale *plinks* of bullets hitting the water around them told him their pursuers were getting closer, and then a *thunk* as one hit its target, bouncing off the reinforced canopy just before they went under, leaving a tiny pockmark in the thick xglass.

For once, he appreciated that someone was firing actual bullets at him, because an energy weapon could have done sufficient damage to the sub systems to keep them from getting away. The pockmark was only a problem for his already-doomed security deposit, unless he took the mini-sub to depths way outside its engineering tolerances anyway, and in that case, the pockmark would become the least of his problems.

He never thought he'd be happy to be underwater again, but he almost wanted to cry from relief when the bay waters closed in above their heads and the sounds of gunfire and sirens faded into the darkening silence around them. Brief glints in the forward lights of the sub were fish instead of fired slugs, and as far as he knew, none of the fish wanted to kill them.

After driving haulers up and down through the bore holes in the ice of Enceladus, the mini-sub was almost cartoonishly simple to figure out. The seat was big enough for his tall frame but too soft—nice for a short jaunt around the harbor, terrible on your back for any longer run—but he hoped they wouldn't be on the sub long enough to test that. Unlike his hauler, though, it had an extraordinary number of built-in safety features, mostly designed to keep him from not going too deep nor too far away from the shore. A stern Icelandic voice warned him he was close to violating both and let him know that if he got three warnings, he would be forcibly returned to shore.

No, thank you, he thought.

"Hang on," he said. "This will just take a second."

He put the sub back on a slow course that made it happier, then pulled his confuddler out of his bag, ducked down into the cramped space below the controls, and hooked it in to the onboard systems. As soon as it was connected, he ran cracks against the sub's internal software until he got in enough to disable the warning protocols, the tracking beacon, and the monitoring software connected to shore.

He took it down another ten meters and headed obliquely out into the bay. The water would muffle the fragments' call, and unless the van could sprout fins, there was no way now they were going to catch them. "We're safe now," he said, checking the sub's air and energy reserves. "Sorry; that was closer than it should have been."

"Fergus . . ." Isla said as he pulled out his handpad, setting the 3-D map to show contours for the shoreline and ocean floor around them.

"I know you're afraid of water, but I drove haulers under the ice of Enceladus for months in the pitch dark," Fergus said. "We're not going to go too deep or too far. Look, we're leveling out already, there's still some light, and you can see fish. We'll be out of here in no time, as soon as I find us a safe place to go back to shore, and then I swear I won't drag you underwater—or even *near* water—again without your explicit permission in advance. So . . . wanna pick a place to go?"

He held out the handpad to her. Isla was pale, wide-eyed, terrified-looking, and also, just faintly, annoyed.

"Fergus," she said, more firmly, and held up one shaking hand. It was covered in red. "I think they shot me."

Chapter 13

Okay, *Fergus,* he told himself. Keep calm. *You're good under pressure. You can handle this.*

Which was all well and good, except he was already scrambling over the seat to the back, and whatever part of his brain hadn't gotten the memo about being calm had him shouting "No no NO NO NO!" as loud as he could. "You are *not* allowed to get shot, Isla!"

She was already losing consciousness as he got into the back of the sub with her. "Should . . ." she managed. "Said sooner."

"Where?" he demanded, and she flailed with one hand toward her side, where her yellow Magmatiks jacket had acquired an orangish stain along the open zipper. She was wearing the Dingo Hole shirt he'd bought for her, and he'd never noticed until that moment. He peeled up the corner of the shirt as carefully as he could, as she sucked in a deep breath and whimpered.

She must have been hit in that first volley as they ran toward the docks, when he believed—because it should have been *true*—that the shots had gone wide. And he hadn't noticed. He didn't want to move her to check out the entry wound in her back, but the exit wound was an ugly, gory mess he could barely see through the blood.

"Gavin is gonna kill me," he muttered, and flipped open hatches in the sub until he found a meager first aid kit.

"Us both," Isla said.

"I'm going to have to move you," Fergus said, pulling his sweatshirt off over his head.

"No," she said, then when he wrapped his arms and his loose sweatshirt around her and carefully tipped her sideways onto the seat, she screamed and finally, mercifully, passed out.

The kit had a small tube of emergiskin, not much more than would do for an overly dramatic papercut, but he gamely found where the bullet had gone in and sprayed it full. Then he slapped three bandages and a tranquilizing med patch on her, rolled her carefully over onto her side, and snugged the sweatshirt as tightly as he dared around her.

Climbing back into the front of the sub, leaving her, was the hardest thing he'd ever done.

Ripping through his pack, he found the tiny pager disk and pressed it. "*Whiro*," he said.

It took a moment, but the ship answered. "Your signal is weak," the ship said.

"I'm underwater. Isla's been shot." He tried desperately to get his brain to stop screaming at itself and think. "I need a top-level trauma surgeon we could trust, but I don't know any on Earth. Mars, yes, but that's too far to make it. Does the Shipyard have any medical contacts here?"

"No," *Whiro* said. "They have gone to Titan for a few emergencies, and once Triton because the orbits were more favorable, though all were before I was brought online."

"Shitshitshitshitfucking*shit*," Fergus swore. He pulled up his map. The only places on Iceland isolated enough where they wouldn't be immediately spotted by Digital Midendian, who no doubt were scanning the entire island to within an inch of its life trying to spot him put the sub in, were too isolated to have the kind of doctors he needed. The next nearest landmass was the Faroe Islands, but he didn't know if they had the right facilities, or even if he could get there in time. *Couldn't get your sister shot near London or the SCNY or Los Angeles, could you?* he berated himself.

"Mr. Ferguson?" *Whiro* asked. "I am extremely concerned."

"Me too. I don't know what to do. I don't know anyone who can help us. I— Wait, no, that's not true," he amended. "Where's *Constance?*"

"I have her docked currently in Portland."

"Which one? Atlantic States? Pacifica?"

"Atlantic States," Whiro replied.

"Do you think *Constance* could pick up my mini-sub from the middle of the ocean? And how fast can you get her here?"

"Do you have the sub specifications?" *Whiro* asked.

"Hang on; I've got my confuddler plugged in," Fergus said. He grabbed the case, careful not to jostle the leads loose, and synced it with his pager.

Thirty agonizing seconds later, *Whiro* replied. "Your mini-sub will fit inside the droneship, but *Constance's* mindsystem is not sufficient for the task of pulling you onboard from water. I will drive."

"*Constance?*"

"Both *Constance* and your sub," *Whiro* said. "Not to express any negative opinions about your piloting abilities, but this is extremely complex, requires flexible and precise coordination, and you are agitated. Also, I feel I should note as an aside that this maneuver is unlikely to go fully unnoticed. You do risk drawing attention from your competitors."

"I don't care. How long?" Fergus asked.

"*Constance* is already disengaging from her surface berth," *Whiro* said. "Sixty-eight minutes to reach your approximate location. I will be accelerating your sub toward the rendezvous point to shorten that time by eleven minutes."

"Still, almost an hour?" Fergus said. His lungs hurt like they wanted to push all the air out of them in some great, heaving, useless scream of rage and frustration.

The mini-sub sped up, sudden enough to almost make him fall over. He wanted it to go faster, sooner. He had never felt quite this helpless in his life, and he hated that.

"After *Constance* reaches you, what then?" *Whiro* asked. "Retrieving the sub still does not resolve finding medical care."

"I know, I know. I need you to load a med pod on your shuttle and get it to Los Angeles and pick up two people for me." He gave *Whiro* all he knew about Jesika and Julia, trying to speak coherently and not to babble it out, and he hoped it was enough for Whiro to find them quickly.

"And when I locate them?" Whiro asked.

"Tell them their helium salesman needs them desperately, and he promises it won't be boring," he said, already climbing back into the rear of the sub. Isla was still breathing, still unconscious, still not somehow miraculously, maddeningly springing upright to declare she'd faked the entire thing. "In the meantime, send me absolutely everything you've got on gunshot wounds."

———

Eighty kilometers east of the tip of Kalaallit Nunaat, west-southwest of Iceland, *Constance* landed on an abandoned data haven platform named Öruggt Hús that had been catastrophically damaged by an iceberg thirty years previously. It had been recently surveyed by the Arctic Union Bridge project to see if it could be used as a temporary staging area for equipment and supplies, and found to be too unstable. *Whiro* agreed with that assessment, but both agreed there was no other, better place to meet up with the shuttle that wouldn't take too long to get to. It only had to support them long enough to transfer Isla over from the mini-sub.

Fergus was unwilling to leave Isla's side until the shuttle arrived; she hadn't regained consciousness, but he had upped the sub's heater to keep her warm, and held her hand, and talked. He told her all his good memories of their parents, few as they were, and when those ran out, tales of him and Gavin getting in trouble together as kids. He had just gotten to the one where they'd dyed all of Gavin's da's sheep in purples and greens and were trying to arrange the herd into the tartan when he felt the platform tremble. *Whiro's* shuttle had landed beside them.

The light, when Constance's bay door opened again, was blinding, and Fergus instinctively hunched over his sister, shielding her. "I am going to open your mini-sub canopy," *Whiro* informed him. "It is windy out, and the temperature is only about eight C."

"Okay," Fergus said.

All his hoarded heat fled from the withering blast of salty, cold, wet air that rushed in the instant the canopy began to rise, and he shivered violently in his T-shirt, unwilling to move from where he was between the wind and Isla. Instead, hands grabbed him, gently but firmly. "Give us room," someone said, and he looked over to see Julia had clambered into the sub, the canopy still not fully upright, and Jesika was behind her, waiting to climb into the front.

Julia was wearing flannel pajamas covered in bright pink cartoon sheep under a heavy parka, and Fergus felt overwhelmed with guilt—for getting her out of bed and flying her across half the globe, yes, but also for having so dramatically failed her injunction against getting Isla hurt. "I'm sorry," he said.

Whichever of his sins she took that in reference to, she had no interest in it. "You need to move," she said. "Get out and let

Jesika get in. Go back to the shuttle and get yourself coffee and a jacket. You hear me?"

"Yeah," he said, still finding it impossible to move, to let go of Isla's hand.

"Look at me," Julia said, and he met her eyes, expecting condemnation and disgust there, but instead found compassion. "We're here, we're going to help, but you need to move. We've got this. Okay?"

"Okay," he answered, and set Isla's hand down carefully atop her barely moving chest, and let go.

Julia put her arm briefly around his shoulders, then helped—firmly—to get him up and moving, his legs and back and neck aching from being so still, so tense, for so long.

Jesika handed him several medical cases that he set on the pilot's seat of the mini-sub before giving her a hand in, and then climbed out alone.

Constance's hold floor was still awash in seawater, slowly sloshing from side to side with the movements of the platform beneath them. "*Whiro?*" Fergus asked. "Is the salt water going to cause damage?"

"Yes," Whiro said.

"Oh," Fergus said.

"It can be repaired," *Whiro* added. "Ms. Ferguson is more important."

"Thanks," Fergus said.

"We would also do the same for you," *Whiro* added.

He stepped out over the lip of the open door and onto the rusted, corrugated surface of the abandoned platform. The wind was brutal and threatened to knock him over as he hunched up, arms around his own torso to try to keep some measure of warmth as he crossed over to the open door of the shuttle. There was nothing around them in any direction except heaving ocean and a blue sky streaked with high, wispy, diffuse clouds. Even space did not feel as empty, as oppressive, as this place did right now, and he felt like a coward for running the last few meters into the shuttle.

Ignatio was waiting for him just inside. "Vergus," ey said. "How is she?"

"Still alive," Fergus said. "Other than that, I don't know. It's all my fault. If she dies, because of me . . ."

"You did not shoot her, yes? And she wanted to be there even with the knowing there was danger, yes?" Ignatio said.

Fergus let his shoulders slump and stood there with the wind howling through the open hatch and whipping his t-shirt up his back. "What good has knowing me ever done anybody?" he asked. "I'm just bad luck."

Ignatio blinked all eir eyes. "I have five legs, yes, and I can slap you with four without tippy falling. Do I need to do this? Or will you come inside more of the way and stop being stupid and have some warm coffee and become warm yourself? Your new friends will call when they can."

"If—" Fergus started to say, when Ignatio raised three of eir legs off the floor and wiggled them in warning. "—Fine, coffee."

———

Forty boring, excruciating minutes later, as Fergus stood pacing, carrying his coffee mug as if it was his only lifeline, *Whiro* spoke up. "They are ready for the med pod," the ship said.

"I'll get it," Fergus said, and slopped lukewarm coffee on his hand, setting his mug down too fast.

"I will help," Ignatio said.

"No; even way out here, it's likely by now someone's picked us up on satellite," Fergus said. "Even if they're not watching live, that data will eventually get looked over, and you are too easily recognized."

"I concur," *Whiro* said.

Fergus grabbed a blanket out of one of the shuttle's storage closets and threw it over his head and around his shoulders, then shoved the med pod out the back of the shuttle and quickly across the intervening space.

Julie and Jesika met him beside the mini-sub. "She's stable, still out, and she should be okay," Jesika said. "Your green alien friend said she's your sister."

"Yeah," Fergus said. "I know, I never should have——"

"Your friend also said you were doing something incredibly important," Jesika interrupted. "He——"

"Ey," Julie corrected.

"Ey say you are trying to save lives, too."

"Yeah," Fergus said. "It's complicated."

"Help us get her transferred," Jesika said. "Julia at least got most of a night's sleep before your ship started pinging every device we owned, but Julia had just finished a ten-hour shift, and we're tired."

"Of course," Fergus said, and followed them back into the mini-sub, half-afraid they were lying and Isla was dead. But no, she was breathing better, and her color was better, even if his guilt got no relief from that.

At the two women's direction, he picked Isla up and carried her as carefully as he could to the edge of the pod, where he handed her over to the two of them, climbed out, and then took her back before settling her into the open medical pod. He stood back as Julia adjusted the pod instruments and set the systems, then shut and sealed the lid.

"Let's go," Jesika said. Together they pushed the pod to the door of the droneship cargo bay, carefully up and over the bump at the edge, and then out onto the platform.

As Julia took up position along the back, she tapped Fergus

briefly on the shoulder, then held out her hand. He held out his own, and she dropped something small and metal into his palm. The bullet. "Consider it dodged," she said. "Not boring at all."

————

"Where am I?" Isla asked, startling Fergus, who had been half-dozing in a chair nearby.

"Mars," he said. "We're in a Free Marsie burrow, an underground safehouse; I'm not sure exactly where."

She squinted at him, frowning, then glanced around at the windowless room with its polymer-adobe walls and light-panel ceiling. "How did we *get* here? And that fast?" she asked.

"It's been four days," Fergus said. They had moved her to a bed only a few hours before, and the pod sedatives had finally worn off enough for her to wake. "You're going to be just fine."

"Why wouldn't I be fine?" she asked, frowning, confused. "Ye didn't nearly drown us in that damned sub thing, did ye, ye utter idiot?"

"No," he said. "I got us to safety perfectly fine, thank you, and in record time, thanks to someone bleeding all over me and scaring me."

Now she really frowned, then looked down at herself and the smart bandage plastered across her abdomen as if it had just appeared there that moment. ". . . What?" she asked.

"I'm sorry," he said. "You got shot. It's all my fault. I never should have—"

"Oh, shut yer gob," she said. "I got shot?"

"Digital Midendian caught up to us in Reykjavík. You don't remember? Maybe not; I knocked you out so I could patch you up temporarily until we got to safety," Fergus said.

"Ye zapped me?!"

"No!" he protested. "Medpatch, from the sub's first aid kit.

Plus two stabilizers and a whole effing can of emergiskin. You scared me pretty good, little sister."

She was quiet for a while. "Aye, I remember now," she said at last. "I don't know which was worse, getting shot or being underwater. I have to say I liked birdwatching much better."

"Me, too," Fergus said.

"How many times have you been shot?" she asked.

"Is it bad if I've lost track?" he answered. "I mean, it also depends on what counts as *shot*. Old-style slugs versus big metal spears or energy bolts? Does getting grazed count? And what if—"

Isla groaned. "Yes, that's a bad answer," she said. "It's exhausting, just talking to ye sometimes."

"I'm sorry," he said again.

"What happened to the mini-sub?" she asked. "Did ye get yer deposit back?"

Fergus snorted. "We scuttled it," he said. "Too much DNA all over the inside to trust bots to get it all. *Whiro* was sad; even though the sub didn't really have a mindsystem, it said it felt wrong. Every time I think I understand the ships, I find out I'm wrong. Which shouldn't be a surprise, given how wrong I am about everything, all the time."

She closed her eyes for a bit, and Fergus had just about decided she'd fallen asleep, when she spoke again. He he had to lean closer to hear. "It's too dangerous and it's not the life I want, and I think I knew that all along. But I'm glad I made ye take me along, even if I did get shot and shoved into a submarine without even a *may I please*, because I think now I understand you a little bit."

"I'm not complicated," Fergus said.

She laughed. "Holy shit, ye have no self-awareness, do ye?"

"I've never been accused of having any, no," Fergus said.

"How bad was it?" she asked.

"My self-awareness?"

"No, my getting shot," she said. She cracked one eye open, and he had never been happier to see her look annoyed at him.

"Ach, just a wee scratch," Fergus said. "You're going to be fine, after you rest a bit and stop hanging out with me."

"I think I remember ye talking," she said. "I don't remember any of what ye were saying, though."

"None of it was important," Fergus said. "Just trying to pass the time until help arrived."

"Thanks," she said.

"For what?!" he exclaimed. "Almost getting you killed?"

"For being my brother," she said. "I'm going to rest now. Ye still going to be here when I wake up?"

"If you want me to be," he said.

"No, ye have stuff to do, and ye gotta get back to it," she said. "Just don't forget me."

"I won't," he promised. "How could I?"

She didn't answer, and he realized she was asleep again. He slipped quietly back out of the room.

Kaice was waiting outside in the hall. The Free Marsie burrow was well lit, with sunlight-spectrum lights lining the curved arch of the ceiling, giving the adobe a warm, cozy glow. Niches in the wall held plants, medicinal and nutritional, and a few flowering sedums for color. He was reminded of the Southwest desert, and that Mars had its own sparse nature, just carefully cultivated in pockets underground.

His life was a lot simpler when Mars was home.

"You okay?" Kaice asked him.

"No," he answered. "But it could be worse."

"I spoke to our doc again, and he'll check back in the morning," she said. "Your people did great work on Isla; she's barely even going to have a scar. She's going to be okay. You know this, right?"

"I know," he said, "but it's not that easy."

She nodded, and he knew she understood. "I have to be elsewhere tomorrow, but our people here will take good care of your sister. You trust us?"

"More than I trust myself," Fergus said.

"Arelyn Harcourt should be here in a day or two, so she'll at least have a familiar face around. Your friend Ignatio sent a message that ey took *Whiro* out of orbit to shake off some sudden interest coming first from Earthside and then the MCA. Ey said to tell you, if you were worried ey might abandon you and not come back, that you stuck em watching your cat once again, which no one, including your cat, is at all happy about."

Fergus managed a tired smile. "I didn't think I was a pet person, but I guess the cat's kinda grown on me, the foul-tempered furball. Maybe we're just two of the same."

Kaice chuckled. "You're not foul-tempered. Annoying, stubborn, doesn't play well with others, you go through bouts of wildly inappropriate optimism and pessimism for no reason anyone can discern, your sense of self-care and self-preservation is shit, and I daresay I strongly suspect you run with scissors. But foul-tempered, no."

"I feel so loved," Fergus said. "If I stay here for a week or so, while Isla gets better—"

Kaice shook her head, her smile gone. "Didn't you tell me our worlds were at stake? Can we afford a week?"

Fergus's shoulders slumped. "No," he said.

"Then there's your answer. You have some more pieces for us?"

"Yeah, I . . . Yeah," he said. He rummaged through his pack and pulled out the can with the piece from Mongolia. "This is one. I found two more, but there's a small problem."

Fergus fished out the two that had stuck themselves together in his pocket in Iceland and held them up, exhibit A.

"Is that just a bigger piece, or . . ." Kaice let the question drift off.

"They were two," Fergus said. "I had them in the same pocket and they just . . . well, they stuck together."

"Are they supposed to do that?"

"They think so," Fergus said. "I shouldn't have had them in the same pocket, but at the time, I was doing a lot of running away and hiding and not thinking about it."

He turned the conjoined core piece around in his hands, feeling the odd double harmony of it like a pulse through his skin, seeking connection. *If I try to talk back to them, what do I say?* he wondered. *Hello?*

He was so tired. In the sub, sitting with Isla and waiting for *Constance* to reach them, he'd nearly accidentally fried the sub systems at least a half-dozen times, and as if the physical memory still lingered in some little pocket in his psyche, he was terrified that just thinking about the panic would bring it back.

Calm down, Fergus, he told himself. *You're safe on Mars. Isla is okay. You are among friends.* He took a few deep breaths, settling himself into the mujūryokudo mindset, and felt himself start to relax, his pulse slow, and the fear subside. In his hand, the conjoined fragments also grew quieter.

"Huh," he said. Kaice, who had been waiting patiently for him to hand over the block, raised an eyebrow in query.

"Hang on a sec," he said, and closed his eyes. He tried to think of the fragments not as something in his hand but as part of his hand, his inner electricity like a branching river, carrying that same inner calmness down into his fingers and palms.

The two pieces came apart and lay in his hand, barely murmuring now.

"'Huh,' indeed," Kaice said. "How'd you do that?"

So many people he would lie to, but not her. Or maybe he

was just too exhausted to care. "I talked to it," he said. "It's a weird electrical thing I've got, which is a long story, but is also why I'm the one stuck finding these things."

"How weird?" she asked.

He snapped his fingers and sent off a shower of sparks.

Instead of the flinch he expected, Kaice laughed. "Only you," she said, amused and impressed. "Can I take those?"

Fergus dumped them in her hands quickly, afraid he'd wake them up again, and she put the first in a can, sealed it, then did the same with the other. "I'll get these distributed tomorrow," she said. "Meanwhile, I have no idea what time it is in your head, but it's after midnight here. You should get sleep. We're going to have to bunk you with Polo, since we don't have any more spare rooms here, but at least he's young enough he doesn't snore yet. I'm old enough I sound like a jump engine sucking in asteroids."

Fergus laughed. "You did back on Nereidum Montes as well."

"You are a liar and no gentleman, Earther," she said.

The teasing was comforting, a return to the way things should be. He gave a bow and flourish, less smoothly than if he hadn't been so exhausted but sufficient to widen her grin. "Guilty as charged, and at your service," he said.

"You're babbling now. Let me show you to your room," she said, and pointed commandingly down the hall for him to go.

———

Fergus woke up early, nothing left of his dreams except a lingering anger and more than a little regret. He checked in on Isla—still asleep—and then wandered through the small, quiet stronghold. There were other people awake and moving, kids running in the halls unminded, adults prepping gear for a trip up and out onto the surface. Some acknowledged him, a few asked after his sister, and more than one wanted to shake his hand for being part of the legendary Sentinel team.

Feeling undeserving of attention, much less any kind of admiration, he wandered into the back of the kitchen in search of coffee and some solitude to enjoy it in.

A Free Marsie he didn't know was there, an elderly woman with deeply wrinkled skin and a puff of silvery hair that made him think of Mother Vahn, back in Cernee.

"So, you're him," the woman said.

"Depends on what you mean," Fergus said. "If it's something bad, yeah, probably."

She smiled, pulled open a cabinet, and set a clean mug in front of him with the telltale brown-red color that meant it had been fired out of Martian clay. "Coffee's over there," she said, pointing with a long spoon. "I'm Selle. You're Fergus?"

"Yeah," he said, and picked up the mug. "Thanks."

"You wanna make it up to me, peel some potatoes?" she said. "Makes my hands hurt, and Polo's gonna skip out again as soon as I ask him."

Fergus laughed. "I think I'm getting a ride out with him, but I'm happy to peel some for you until then."

She dumped a knife and a large bucket in front of him, and went off to tend to something else. He dragged a wooden stool over to the wide, white polystone counter, picked up the knife, and pulled the first potato out of the bucket. Sella opened the vault-like door to the burrow's food stores, picked up several baskets, and disappeared in.

He sat, peeling potatoes and thinking.

For all that he blamed himself, it was Digital Midendian that had shot his sister. All the times he'd gotten hurt on the job—shot, stabbed, burnt, kicked, that time he got thrown out a third-story window on Haudernelle—were things he accepted as just the consequences of his life choices, his career. He could not, would not, accept that Isla should be subject to those same outrages, and the more he stewed over it, the more he wanted to make sure he hurt DM right back, hard enough to keep them down.

He had six pieces now, four more to go that were out there waiting for him. To complete the set, he was going to have to reckon with Fajro Promeso, the Alliance, and Digital Mideandian. And when it was time for him to take DM's pieces, he fully intended to ruin as much of the company as he could on his way out. If he made a catastrophic mess out of Evan Derecho's life at the same time, so much the better.

Revenge was a bad, bad choice in his business, but whatever little voice in his head was responsible for talking him out of stupid decisions was silent for once.

"Not a friend of potatoes?" Selle asked, and he looked down to realize he'd gone wildly overboard with the knife, whittling the handful of potatoes down to tiny nubs awash in a sea of hacked-off strips of peel, flung far and wide around him on the counter, his lap, and the floor.

"Sorry," he said. "Lot on my mind."

"Martian potatoes don't grow on trees, you know," she said, but she was smiling. "Finish your coffee and then tell me about it."

"You just trying to get me to spill dirt on Kaice?" Fergus asked.

Selle laughed. "I got all the dirt I could ever want on everyone here. It's not a very big settlement."

"Sounds comforting."

"Boring."

"Comforting and boring," Fergus agreed. He was more careful with the rest of the potatoes, and in exchange, told Selle the story about being chased through the Ares Three underground by a group of fresh-off-Earth teens determined to beat up their first Marsie but having very little grasp of physics or momentum under 38% gravity.

When Polo came to fetch him, a few hours later, Selle almost seemed sad to see him go.

Isla was still asleep, so he left a note by her bedside and hoped it didn't feel as deeply, offensively insufficient to her as it felt to him.

Chapter 14

◆—◆—◆

Sweat poured down his forehead and face, and he raised one arm to wipe it off on his short sleeve. Half a second later, the deluge started again, his skin suffocating in the unaccustomed heat and humidity. And to think he'd been excited about going somewhere he didn't need a parka.

The near-constant hum of anti-poaching drones made him twitchy and increasingly cross, though he approved of their existence in principle. Worried about the possibility that his face could show up on a hundred low-security feeds, he had his hat pulled down, and for whatever good it did keeping the hot sun off his face, the sweaty constriction made him want to scream. He'd passed through six different security checkpoints, all making sure he wasn't armed, within the first three kilometers of his trek into the nature reserve.

Sitting on a small rock halfway up a mountain, he could just see through a break in the trees the yellow square roof of his rental safari rover parked below. The Luguru clerk who had sold him his entry permit said it wasn't that long since most of the land had been stripped bare and farmed to near-total depletion. Alternating deluge and drought, both ultimately agents of famine, had given the land a temporary reprieve, and technology and the will of the people had saved it. Wildlife was rebounding too, which is how he, "Johannes Jasper," lone photographer, had gotten his entry permit.

Speaking of his photographer cover, one of the drones keeping him company was his own, and a fairly expensive bit of equipment at that. He pulled his brand-new 3-D cameravizer down over his eyes and switched over to the drone view, then sent it up through the trees, rising past an entirely unconcerned group of monkeys in the canopy farther up the hill. From there, he could get some excellent panoramic images to feed his cover identity and also check out who else might be poking around the area.

There were two models of anti-poaching drones that he could see. Mostly, they were tiny spotters, with the occasional larger, armed drones designed to deal directly with any threats that managed to get past perimeter security. Both were easy to identify, by sight and sound, and also by the electrical feel they made around him. There were a half-dozen other camera drones out doing touristy image-capture stuff with a variety of operational competence, and none of those were worrisome either.

They did not quite account for the signals he was feeling in his gut, but neither could he identify anything nearby to worry about. On the other hand, the noise was also making it harder to pinpoint where, higher up the mountainside, the core fragment might be hiding. *At least I'm getting better at listening,* he thought. After his surprising success talking the two merged fragments into letting each other go again, Isla's complaint that he was taking his gift too passively seemed to have a legitimate basis, though he still found it unpalatable in ways he wasn't sure he wanted to examine, not least because he was worried he would find that his obstinate unwillingness to engage more actively with the Asiig gift had no logical or useful excuse other than his own fear.

He was, he thought, very attached to his particular ideas of who he was, even if he was sure they were mostly wrong.

The only thing he was sure about, in what he thought was a minimally biased way, was that he was good at finding things.

And that brought him back to here and now and the task at hand, where being on the job meant not having to think or worry about anything else.

A herd of brown, striped antelope was slowly moving across the plains down below the mountainside, and he took some panoramic shots of them that, while technically only for cover, he was kind of proud of. Then he sighed, parked the camera drone up over the trees, drank some water, and spent a few minutes listening to the overwhelming chaotic symphony of birds and animals all around him before grudgingly starting his upward trek again.

For all that he was unprepared for the change in climate, it was exuberantly and noisily beautiful, and he could see how people got addicted to travel and hiking. People not him, anyway, who had normal lives. *I could give up everything and be a bird-watcher,* he thought, then laughed. Another pipe dream about an alternate life he'd never actually fit into, like his ongoing dream about becoming a Tea Master on the beaches of the planet Coralla. He'd even gone to Coralla once, and hadn't even made it as far as sticking his feet in the water.

At last, he could feel the faint, unmistakable call of a core fragment, somewhere high up the steep and uneven slope of the mountainside behind him. Between the terrain, the thick vegetation, and strict limitations on visitors inside the reserve, it wasn't surprising that no one had gotten to this one already. It went without saying that all the easy ones were almost certainly long since collected.

He was fortunate that there was a narrow path winding up the mountainside, even if sometimes it was so narrow, and so steep, that he had to take it sideways with his back pressed against the rough rock behind him.

Two-thirds of the way up, the hillside relaxed into a gently sloping plateau, and trees had taken great advantage of the easier space to crowd in even more thickly together. Leaving the trail, he poked carefully through the underbrush with his walking stick as he wove through the trees, not at all sure if Tanzania had poisonous snakes. Once he was close enough, he knelt carefully on the ground and sifted through the leaf litter with his gloved hands, startling several enormous beetles, before his hand made contact with his quarry.

"And that's seven," he said, and tucked it carefully in its can in his pack before heading back to the relative clearing of the trail to sit and rehydrate before the climb down.

"Mr. Ferguson," *Whiro* spoke in his earpiece.

"Is Isla okay?" he asked, heart suddenly jumping.

"She is the same as the last time you asked. She sleeps a lot and is bored when not."

"Okay," Fergus said, willing himself to calm down. "I got the piece."

"Excellent. I called to inform you that we have seen a significant increase in the presence of your 'white vans,' of assorted colors, near almost all of the search sites. I have traced the few that passed near public cams to the same rental agency we know Digital Midendian uses. Also, one of the vans has been exploring the side roads near the Sandia Mountains."

"Shit," Fergus said. "Do we think Santos is in danger? I mean, he did rip us off on that hat, but he doesn't deserve—"

"Interestingly, it appears all data related to that day, from the moment you left the highway until you returned to it, has vanished from SolNet," *Whiro* said. "I expect the Librarians watch out for their own."

"I would hope so," Fergus said. "Still, let me know if it looks like he's in danger."

"It is you I am more concerned about," *Whiro* said. "Of all the sites I am monitoring, the only one where I cannot find any trace of Digital Midendian is right where you are. This seems unlikely to be either coincidence or an oversight on their part. Please be careful."

"Always am," Fergus said, and stowed his water bottle back in his pack.

"Repeat?" *Whiro* said. "I am certain I did not just hear you correctly."

"I said I always— Never mind. Ha-ha," Fergus said. "Anything else?"

"No," *Whiro* said.

"Great. I'll call you when I'm safely out of here," Fergus said, and tapped the line closed.

On his way down, he stopped at the same rock he'd paused at on his way up to send his camera drone out for another look around. Visor on, he soared with his drone down along the upper fringes of the canopy and back out again to where the land flattened and emerged from the forest, over a herd of zebra, and then he turned it around to look back toward the mountain and himself.

The picture jumped sideways and went blank.

Fergus checked his controls: no signal. The power cell had still had plenty of life in it. Had he heard a faint *pop* when it went dead, or was that just his imagination filling in something where there was too much ambient noise to have genuinely heard?

He made sure he had everything neatly stowed in his pack, so that if there was trouble, he wouldn't have to take time to get himself in order under duress. Then he moved steadily back down the trail, pausing to listen both with his ears and with his gut. If there was anything unusual out there, it was lost in the larger noise of signals.

It took him about an hour to get down to where the mountain

edge slowly leveled off to meet the slope of the land below, and he paused at the threshold under the trees. His rover sat where he'd left it, looking untouched, so maybe his drone had just been bad? He had gotten it used, after all, and not everything had to bear out his habit of unreasonable paranoia, right?

It felt like a perfect spot for an ambush.

Fergus took a single step cautiously out from the shade of the trees and immediately felt the sudden power buildup nearby. He threw himself back and sideways as bullets shattered the tree he'd just been standing beside. Rolling to his hands and knees, he crawled backward until his feet hit a fallen log, and he scrambled up and threw himself over it as one of the armed anti-poaching drones fired again.

So, yes, *definitely* an ambush.

He could feel the drone edging carefully toward the trees. It seemed to be just the one; none of the other drones in the area had changed their usual patterns or moved closer. He broke open one of his cleaner nanite blisters and dropped it on the ground beside him to take care of any residual DNA evidence, then tapped at his headset.

"Uluguru Reserve front desk support line," the park's automated system answered, after a brief pause as it recognized his unit and switched to English. "Please speak your concern."

"Why are you shooting at me?" Fergus asked.

There was another pause, then the system said, "I will redirect your call to an agent."

The voice that answered was a beautiful Bantu accent on top of drifted British English, and already sounded annoyed. "Guest 3431: what is your problem?" she asked.

"Your drone just shot at me," Fergus said.

"They only shoot poachers," the agent said. "Are you carrying arms against reserve policies?"

"No, I'm not. I was just hiking and it took out my camera and now it's coming after me," Fergus said. "I was kind of hoping maybe you could stop it?"

"Our drones don't shoot innocent people," the agent said. She said more, but it was lost in the sound of the drone firing a rapid burst into the woods around him, likely trying to spook him into running and giving his hiding place away. ". . . was that noise?" the agent finished.

"That was the sound of your drone shooting at an innocent person," Fergus said.

The agent swore. "Hold on, please," she said, and there was silence on the line.

From where he lay behind the fallen tree, he could feel the gun drone moving slowly closer, not on a direct trajectory but close enough. He had maybe five or six minutes before it would be near enough to spot him.

Did he think the support agent would figure out what was happening in time to stop it? No. That meant acting on his own behalf, but there weren't many ways of moving from where he was without leaving himself vulnerable as he was getting to his feet.

His hand found a stick on the ground, and he leaned up just enough to hurl it off into the woods, away from his hiding place. Clichéd as hell, but it seemed to work; the drone swung heavily off to one side and let out another volley of bullets, shredding foliage and branches. A flock of large gray crested birds took off in alarm, ponderous for their size, and the drone swung around, tracing them.

Fergus scrambled to his feet and ran, stretching his arm back behind him and letting all the adrenalin and anger built up in him go in one thin, crackling spark between his fingertips and the drone's chassis. A stream of smoke poured out from its casing as its rotor blades faltered, and it plummeted to the ground with all the grace of someone heaving an anvil out of a third-story window.

Fergus backtracked to where it lay on the ground among some crushed undergrowth, and he kicked it with his boot. He could already tell it was dead, but kicking it made him feel a little better.

"Guest 3431, we have determined there has been a security compromise of our systems, and the drone is not acting under our control. Are you still there?"

"I am," Fergus said.

"We have no location signal from the rogue drone."

"I took it down," he said. "With a stick. I think it shorted out when it hit the ground."

"That is resourceful of you," the agent said, in a tone that suggested it was also very stupid of him. "We don't know how many other drones are potentially compromised, or if the whole system is at risk, so we are currently standing all units down. Any that you still see in the air in five minutes, we have no control over. We have requested help from our military, but it will be some time before they can arrive. Good luck, 3431, and whatever your outcome, please be assured we will, eventually, find and punish those responsible."

"Thanks," he replied. He could tell them it was Digital Midendian, but he wasn't going to give that away over potentially compromised lines. Maybe once he escaped, he'd drop an anonymous tip.

First, he had to escape. The other drones he sensed nearby were all sinking lower, and none were coming closer, so he knelt down next to the fallen drone—away from the gun ports, because he *was* that paranoid—and tried to see if there was anything on it he could detach and use.

The drone was about the size and shape of a medium suitcase, not counting the guns. Most of it was made of a very lightweight alloy, but the plate under the gun ports was substantially heavier, to absorb the recoil pressure from firing. It had landed unevenly on the ground, one side dug into the soft earth while the other stuck up at a low angle. Fergus had to brace himself against a tree and push it fully over onto its side with his legs, the salty sweat coursing over his face stinging his eyes and rendering everything blurry. Finally, it budged far enough, and he relaxed his legs and wiped his face again.

More than five minutes had passed. He could feel other signals out there, but they were stationary. Not that he could trust that; if he was running ops through the drones, when he saw all the others land, he'd have copied them to avoid giving himself away until opportunities improved.

He unscrewed the bottom plate from the dead drone, then pried it off and hefted it in his hands. It might—*might*—have been thick enough to stop a bullet, but he hoped he didn't have an opportunity to find out otherwise. Putting his tools away, he headed back again toward the edge of the woods, plate held over his head. Nothing seemed to be moving, so he left the thinning cover of the trees and walked toward his rover, tense for any unexpected movement or spark of signal.

When he reached the vehicle, he walked around it several times, even peering underneath, but nothing seemed to have been touched. If they were operating by hacked drone, it was likely that there was no one physically inside the reserve; he was close to a hundred kilometers away from the nearest gate, and effectively covering that area in person would be noticed quickly. The government was deadly serious about stopping poachers and environmental vandals.

Reasonably sure his rover was safe, he climbed back in and

threw the plate down on the seat beside him, and stuck his empty water bottle into the dashboard condenser to refill. He closed his eyes and took one last electrical "look" around him, then powered the rover up to make the trek back toward the gate.

After about an hour of driving, and startling every time he came across one of the gun drones sitting idle on the ground, he realized his back and neck were become furiously sore from being constantly tense, and forced himself to relax.

He had to stop once for a herd of something to cross his path; the rover systems handily identified them as wildebeest, and there seemed to be hundreds of them not particularly in a hurry. He took the opportunity to climb out the window and sit on the top of his rover, half to watch the spectacle of the herd, half to take another survey of potential threats. When the last few stragglers finally cleared the road, he continued on.

A kilometer from the gate, he began to sense more of the grounded drones, but although they were also down, they were putting out more signal, and there were a lot of them in a small area. Spread out in a semicircle, in fact, directly ahead. *Now, that,* he thought, *is the next trap.*

It was almost a relief, because he knew where it was for once *before* he stepped in it.

He grabbed his water bottle out of the condenser and capped it tightly, slowing the rover but not stopping it, and when he had all his stuff restowed in his pack on the passenger seat, he tossed it out the open window into the grass, then popped open the door and threw himself out after it.

Ground and grass was much harder and sharper when you tumble into it at speed, and he lay there for a few moments, staring up at the blue sky and its wandering, unconcerned clouds for a few minutes while resisting the very strong urge to swear very loudly and give himself away. The autopilot on the rover kept it moving forward along the road, and just as he'd crawled back far enough to retrieve his pack, he could feel the drones activate ahead.

Seven of the bulky, armed drones rose up in formation and fired into his poor rover, eventually bringing it to a smoking stop another thirty meters down the road. He felt no small amount of outrage on the rover's behalf but kept his head down in the grass and used his extra sense to follow the drones as they moved in and around the destroyed vehicle, no doubt checking for his body.

That meant that sooner or later, they'd come looking farther out, and right now he had no cover. There was a small stand of trees a fair distance away to his left, clustered on a low rise in the savannah; he didn't think he had a shot in hell of making it that far, but it was all he had, so he began the laborious crawl through the thin, tufted grass, listening intently for the drones, which were still clustered around the dead rover.

It was slow going, because he didn't want to make his path through the grass too obvious from afar. He was concentrating enough on keeping his movements steady and listening for the drones that he failed to recognize, until it was almost deafening, a much louder sound coming his way. He dared to poke his head up just enough to look behind him and see another massive antelope herd bearing down on him.

"Whoa, shit," he said, and scrambled up to a crouch. Without conscious intention, static began to build up along his arms and torso, and the fragment deep in its can heard and began to sing along with him. "Shit, shit, SHIT—!" he said, as he was engulfed in the fast-moving herd, each animal swerving around him at the very last moment before impact.

Recognizing an opportunity, he stood up straighter and ran along with the herd, trying not to choke in the kicked-up dust and bits of flying turf.

The antelope were much faster than he was, and it was nerve-wracking every time a pair of twisty, thick, clearly dangerous horns appeared in his immediate peripheral vision, but there were enough of them that he could run under their cover until his heart was pounding in his chest and he was sure he would never catch his breath again. As he slipped farther behind in the herd, he spotted one of the umbrella-like trees he'd seen in the distance, and angled toward it.

He collapsed at the foot of the tree, in the precious shade, and took deep, whooping breaths. Chest heaving, he fumbled around for his pack and pulled out his water bottle, and drank down deep gulps as best he could. His arms, he noticed, still had small fingers of static moving up and down against his skin. "Ye can stop now, ye scunner," he told it, but the bees in his gut seemed disinclined to fully stand down. His own exhaustion and fear likely didn't help.

He took another long pull from his bottle, already more than two-thirds empty again, then leaned his head back against the rough trunk and looked up into the branches and a large pair of yellow eyes, set deep in a spotted, furry face, staring back down at him from a thick branch overhead.

"Just my luck," he grumbled. "Hello, kitty."

The leopard didn't seem particularly inclined to move—though who knew how much warning he'd get if it did?—but he stayed absolutely still as they regarded each other for several long minutes. At last, the leopard yawned, its bright pink-red mouth and tongue impossibly huge behind a full set of extremely large teeth, and the animal stretched out against the branch in a pose he'd seen his cat, Mister Feefs, do a thousand times just prior to returning to the never-ending business of napping.

It did not, however, take its eyes off Fergus.

His handpad chimed, and he picked it up carefully without

moving his head or taking his eyes off the cat. "Guest 3431, what is your status?" the reserve agent asked.

"Drones blew my rover up," Fergus said.

"Are you still in the vicinity of your rover?" she asked.

"No," he answered. Even if the line was being listened in on, that wasn't giving away much.

"Then please remain where you are until we give you instructions otherwise," she said.

"Happy to," he said. He didn't want to move at all, at this particular moment, unless instant teleportation suddenly became an option.

He could already feel new signals in the distance. Two dozen armed drones flew in from the west and dispersed around the hacked ones, probably to keep any from leaving and causing damage elsewhere while something more direct was done.

Sure enough, one by one, the compromised drones suddenly dipped and settled back down into the grass, out of sight. A few minutes later, three official reserve rovers drove into sight, stopping around his blasted rover, and six people with guns got out.

"Guest 3431, do you see our team?" the agent asked.

"Yeah," Fergus said.

"All compromised drones have been shut down. Our team will safely escort you out of the reserve," the agent said. "Are you able to make your way to them?"

Fergus blinked at the leopard, who didn't express an opinion of its own on that. "I can try," he said.

"Thank you for your patience," the agent said. "We are sorry for the inconveniences you have suffered. There is odd activity near that section of the park sometimes, though never trouble of this sort, and it was unanticipated."

"Yeah," Fergus said. "Wrong place and the wrong time, I guess?"

"Exactly so," the agent answered. "As you signed a waiver before entering the park, there is not much we can do to express our regret at your unfortunate experience today, but we would be happy to extend you a one-time twenty percent discount at our gift shop in compensation."

Fergus laughed. "Sure," he said. "Thanks." He slid himself away from the tree trunk, then got to his feet. The leopard did not move. Electricity still crawled up and down Fergus's arms and, with the sweat, made a nasty burnt tang in the air. "Can't blame you for not eating me," he told the leopard, and backed away. When he was far enough from the tree, he finally turned and headed toward the rescue team. As if knowing better than he did that the threat had passed, his electricity finally died down and went back to sleep.

He looked forward to the day, not too far away now, when he came for Digital Midendian instead of the other way around.

———

The Pan-African Lightning was one of the most renowned train routes in the modern world, both for its speed and for the scenic vistas, both pristine and recreated wildernesses, it passed smoothly through from Mombasa to Dakar. It was one of those trips of a lifetime that most people could only dream of.

Fergus booked a tiny private cabin on one of the retro-styled passenger cars, considered his good fortune to be there, and then pulled down the folding bunk and slept like a log until they were already pulling into the station in Kampala, along the northern shores of Victoria Nyanza. Dream images of bright yellow eyes lingered in his mind until he was finally, fully awake.

He stretched, drank some water, then wandered down to the dining car. From the window he could see the dark blue waters of the lake itself and some large wading birds with ponderously long, thick beaks stalking the shallows for meals of their own. Small floating bots moved among the thick green weeds, clearing them in meandering paths dictated by the movements of the water, to keep them from choking out the entire lake surface. Far enough offshore to be unobtrusive he could see the shine of half-submerged monitoring stations; he'd seen pictures, as a kid, of them standing tall and forlorn out of cracked and brittle mud during a decade-long drought.

The train began moving again as he was picking up ice tea, a bowl of some kind of bean-and-coconut soup, and what promised to be spicy rice, and he walked back to his compartment with everything balanced on a tray, grateful for the smooth rails beneath them. They angled away from the shore and briefly through a stretch of city before they were back into the wilderness corridor that lined the scenic train route.

Back in his compartment, he had just sat down to drink his ice tea when he heard tapping and looked up to see a multilegged delivery drone outside the window. He slid the window down and let it in, where it immediately disgorged a PhobosCola can on his fold-down table.

"This is the drone *Rosemary*," a recording announced, in *Whiro*'s voice. "We are currently in jump, heading out toward Titan, as we drew additional Alliance scrutiny in Mars orbit and felt it best to get some distance. *Rosemary* will find a ride up to orbit on a commercial packager and then separate and connect with Polo when it is safe to do so. A second drone, *Sage*, should be waiting for you in the Azores by the time you get there. After that, if you do not plan on bringing the Newfoundland piece upwell yourself, we will need to discuss next actions. We are still uncertain where the last piece might be."

Fergus got the Tanzania piece, still in its can, out of his pack, and listened to the dampened but undimmed song from within.

He had to hope that, away from him and other inputs, it would drift back into slumber. Either that or they were going to have to figure out how to make better cans.

He slid it into the now-empty drone slot, then put the new can in his pack where it had been. "Record reply," he told the drone, and waited for the little green record light to turn on before speaking. "Thank you, *Whiro*. If Ignatio wishes to send some good, confusing-but-not-impossible sciencey things to Isla on Mars, she'd probably appreciate it. Stay safe, and I'll check in again soon. End reply."

The drone sealed its storage compartment, then rotated about 180 degrees and climbed out the window and up the side of the train car, quickly out of sight. He could feel it, like the tiny tickle of electrical feet, make its way along the roof of the car, pause, and then, suddenly, was up and away and gone.

He closed the window with a sigh and turned around, only to find someone in the compartment with him, sitting on the opposite bench as if they had been there the whole time.

"You," Fergus said. "I guess you like trains."

"I do," the Asiig agent admitted. "I think it's the noise they make. Proper trains, anyway. Did you know that in Japan, the word for underground trains is *chikatetsu*? *Chikatetsu chikatetsu chikatetsu*. A wonderful bit of onomatopoeia, that."

"I didn't," Fergus said. He folded up his bunk and sat on the seat that had been tucked beneath it, and took a spoonful of the soup. It was still too hot, and he wanted to enjoy the rice alone, so he pushed the tray aside and looked at the not-quite-human man. Was it the hair? No. Something about his face, his skin texture? No. He still couldn't put his finger on what looked wrong, until he realized the man never blinked, and that in the black depths of his pupils he would swear he could see stars.

It was Fergus who blinked. Of course. "If we're going to

keep meeting like this, you could at least tell me your name," he said.

The man shrugged. "I don't really have one anymore," he answered.

"Anymore?"

The man grinned. "Ooooh!" he said. "I gave something away! How very careless of me. You've done remarkably well with your collecting so far. Very good." He clapped.

"Yeah, no thanks to you," Fergus said.

The man raised his eyebrows, and Fergus slumped down in his seat. "Fine, in part because of you. Your masters, anyhow, and this 'gift' you gave me. Not that anyone asked my opinion about it."

"And I'm still not asking," the man said.

"Then why the fuck are you here bothering me while my lunch gets cold? Just to make sure I remember you're still out there?"

"I wish," the agent said. "But no, I had a word of advice for you, actually. Help, even. It seems the Asiig are concerned, and while they prefer not to meddle—oh, don't make that face; you hardly count—they will, on occasion, *nudge*. So, here I am, nudging. You know you need all the pieces, yes?"

"We gathered that," Fergus said.

"One will be harder to find than the others," the agent said. "Your current search methodology will fail you. To find it, you will have to think outside the box." As if to demonstrate his point, the agent used his index fingers to draw a circle in the air.

"Boxes are rectangles," Fergus said. At the agent's look, he added, "Or square. Well, three-dimensional. Cubes. Or. . . . rectangular cubes."

The agent sighed. "Talking to you people is so exhausting. I also have something for you." He reached out, the movement uncannily smooth, and dropped a small red capsule on the table.

Fergus, after a moment's trepidation, picked it up. It was about a half-centimeter in diameter and two long. "What is it?"

"When you want us, we will know," the agent said.

"What if I don't ever want you?"

"Then throw it away! Throw caution to the wind! Discard a resource of unknown potential, and with it all the branches of future possibility, before you even know where they may carry you! It is not my place to tell you. Or you can keep it in your pocket and not think about it, and forget it is there."

Fergus put it in his pocket and wondered what they'd just been talking about. "'Think outside the box,' right, got it. You came all this way for that?"

"It wasn't much trouble," the agent said. "Your soup *is* getting cold, so I will bid you farewell, then. After all, you are running low on time." The agent stood.

"Don't let the door hit you on the way out," Fergus said, picking up his spoon as if about to resume eating.

"Oh, I would never be so clumsy," the agent said, waved, and left his compartment. Fergus jumped to his feet and peered down the train corridor, but as before, the agent had vanished. Reentering his compartment, he moved too slowly, and the door hit *him*.

The soup and spicy rice were excellent, and he deeply resented that he was too irritated now to enjoy them.

Chapter 15

Once Fergus had eaten and then napped, he found that however much attention he tried to apply toward research and planning for his eventual but inevitable need to take the remaining core fragments away from the Alliance, Digital Midendian, and the cult, his mind only wanted to replay Isla in the mini-sub, holding up her bloodied hand, and relitigate everything he did wrong, did sloppily, could have avoided if he wasn't a selfish jerk with no real survival instinct and a halo of death and destruction around him everywhere he went.

For all that self-recrimination felt somehow due, it wasn't getting him any closer to solving the problems he needed to solve, and it was too much of a distraction when he knew he needed to be vigilant and fully on his game. So, when the train slowed to a bare crawl through the wilderness somewhere just north of Natitingou as a herd of elephants made their way across the tracks a few kilometers ahead, he took his chance to drop his things, and then himself, out the window under the cover of the pre-dawn dark. He had hacked his compartment systems to show him operating the lights, an hour or so from now, to hopefully sow confusion if anyone checked the logs to figure out where he hopped off.

They had passed through a small town a few kilometers back, and he followed the tracks back, staying just under cover of the trees and ducking deeper in whenever another train came past. Drones passed overhead in both directions almost constantly, nearly all commercial light couriers, but he was all too aware that any of them could be easily compromised and give his position away if he strayed carelessly into the open. He was grateful that it was hot enough that his body heat required no efforts to disguise from more prying scans.

He reached the town around dawn, rented an electric bike from a tourist kiosk outside the station, and roared off ostentatiously in the direction of Lagos, to the south. Twenty kilometers outside the city of Djougou he stopped in shade, disabled the bike's tracker, and continued down the open road a while longer in the same direction before taking the opportunity of another patch of cover to turn onto a dirt side road and speed west instead.

He swapped out the bike for another somewhere in Togo, then caught a local train in Ghana to Burkina Faso, and the next morning picked up the Lightning again, under a new name, to finish the ride to Dakar overnight, only a day and a half behind his first train. This time, he was tired enough that he slept easily, and without too much insidious noise from the haters in his own skull.

At Dakar, he wandered through the street markets, bought himself some fresh mangoes and a baobab fruit, which he hadn't known existed. Pleased with the oblong, hard thing, it didn't occur to him until he was walking away that it was not at all the most practical thing to carry around, and the most obvious solution to that—to eat it before he had to carry it far—suffered from an utter lack of idea how to crack the shell to get started.

Still not entirely willing to admit it had been a bad idea, he stuffed it in his pack with the rest of his stuff, stayed well out of the way of a Digital Midendian van he could feel from two blocks away, and then hired a private boat to take him to the Azores on anonymous credit, no names, no questions asked.

The eighth unclaimed core fragment was lodged on an

almost impossibly steep, rocky slope on the side of Montanha do Pico. The sea breeze was a wonderful change from the still, suffocating air of the continental interior, which in turn meant he was far less churlish about having to pull on a full-body anti-surveillance suit, which was much like a three-centimeter-thick set of coveralls and hood, except the smart fabric inflated and deflated, stiffened and loosened in odd places to introduce ambiguity to your proportion metrics and break any detectable, qualifiable rhythm to your body movements, though it warned him periodically it was only operating at 82% efficiency because of the bright blue vest he was wearing atop it, counter to usage guidelines. It was a fair trade-off, and the small vest had cost far more than the entire camo suit, at a high-end extreme sports boutique he'd hit on his way out of Tanzania.

The hood cycled through displaying random faces, a Rorschach of meaningless identities, though from inside he could barely tell there was fabric at all in front of his face except for slight extra effort it took to breathe through it. It was odd, and uncomfortable, but not unbearable, and he was grateful for it as he began the ascent up the cliff and found he was pulling himself into range of over a dozen assorted bots, security cams, and other devices scattered across the entire face of the mountain.

When he neared the first, no bigger than a golf ball and camouflaged to blend in with the rocky dirt it was half-wedged into, he pulled out of his pocket an ancient metal car antenna that he'd broken off a rusted hulk abandoned beside the road during his off-train trek toward Djougou. It was just an old bit of bent metal, but no one watching could tell that it wasn't some sort of instrument or weapon; he used it to poke the bot and conduct enough electricity to fry it, then headed past it and on.

A half-dozen drones came out over the top of the mountain while he was still climbing, and tried to knock him off the cliff face. One by one he whacked them with the antenna and watched them short out and fall, bouncing off rocks and scraggly, weather-bent trees to eventually hit the ground and shatter.

After so many times in a row having to be as sneaky as he could, it was nice to be somewhere where the only option was direct, brute-force assault.

Also, he thought as he chucked yet another newly fried bot from its hidden pocket off the cliff behind him, he was pretty sure he was ahead of Akio's grandmother now.

He found the core fragment wedged into a crack in the rock face, just as a helicopter appeared from over the top of the mountain. "Too late," he declared, with no small amount of joy and anticipation, as he broke the tiny tab on the shoulder of his blue vest and yanked the now-free ripcord.

The vest exploded outward, knocking him loose from his hold on the cliff wall as it engulfed his upper torso, and he fell.

The first few bounces hurt, but by the time he picked up momentum, the vest had fully inflated into a gigantic, translucent, segmented ball, with him stuck like a baby in a king cake at the center, and each successive jolt was dampened by the ball itself. That didn't make the whirling, spinning, blue-tinted world any less nausea-inducing—the vest came with a small packet of anti-emetics, which he'd neglected to take seriously—so he closed his eyes as he rolled and tumbled rapidly back down the mountain.

It was the pop of one of the ball's inflated chambers that got him to crack his eyes open again and determine that someone was leaning out of the copter with a gun, shooting at him, and that he was a few seconds at most away from crashing into a stand of trees. There wasn't much he could do about either, but he scrunched up and then flexed outward with his body, trying to alter the ball's course by just a few meters, if possible.

It wasn't, largely, possible. He hit the first tree edge-on and went careening off at a new angle, farther into the woods, until a pair of trees not quite far enough apart for him to pass between brought him and his ball to a bouncing stop, with him suspended largely upside-down inside. Large, glossy green leaves showered down around him from the impact.

His throat was parched, from more than just using his gift up on the slopes to zap things, and he was pretty sure he had yelled, in a mix of exhilaration and terror, the whole way down.

And people do this for fun, he marveled, even as his eyes settled on the small stenciled warning not far from his face: *Caution: for use on unobstructed grass slopes of less than 10° only.*

He could hear hissing where several of the chambers had gotten punctured and were slowly leaking their air despite the best efforts of the inflation systems. Seconds later, he flinched as another bullet tore through not far from his shoulder, and the ball began to rapidly sag. He could also feel drones heading his way from multiple directions.

"What did you do at work today, Mr. Ferguson?" he asked himself as he shrugged out of the vest, located the air chamber with the baffled exit tunnel, and wiggled his way through it and out, face-first, into the dirt and fallen leaves. "Why, I threw meself off a stratovolcano inside a bloody great beach ball, thank ye fer askin'."

He had landed only a couple hundred meters from where he'd started his climb up, and as soon as he was fully free of the sad remains of his beach ball, he stuffed one of his last remaining blister packs of cleaner nanites back inside to do their work, then dodged into deeper woods and backtracked to the crevasse under the roots of a toppled tree where he'd reluctantly stashed his pack before beginning his ascent. It and the bubble vest had not been compatible, no matter how hard he had tried to figure out how to make it work anyway.

The new drones were still too far away, and the helicopter was trapped above the treetops. He retrieved his gear, drank some water, then got out of there.

―――――

On the overnight ferry from Ilha do Pico, *Whiro*'s second drone, *Sage*, caught up to him and relieved him of the new piece. There was the simultaneous sense of being on the home stretch, along with a rising anxiety that his enemies had to be getting closer and a lot more desperate.

Since shaving in Australia, his beard had achieved some minimal level of looking intentional, and he couldn't bear to start over again, so he settled instead for shaving his entire head bald. It was a suitably different look, and he especially enjoyed it with dark-framed sunglasses on. *I look dangerous,* he thought. And maybe he was.

Newfoundland, the northernmost portion of the Atlantic States Coalition, had seen rough times when it was cut off from the more central Canadian provinces after Quebec went independent, but now it was a trade gateway between the Arctic Union and the various nation-states in the continental interior. The Stephenville International Shuttleport was one of those places where its long history of boom-and-bust was written across every building, every piece of infrastructure, from the frugal conservation of older structures to the clearly cautious spending on new. Only the main terminal itself, about a decade old, showed the impractical design flair of a sustained period of comfortable funding.

He walked into the terminal building, feeling totally in his groove, and immediately spotted a figure in linen clothes on one of the benches in the open waiting area, hunched forward, staring at nothing. He wondered which cultist this was, and which van hooligan he was tailing; the cultist's presence was a good warning that the other must be not too far away. He kept walking, not breaking his stride, until he suddenly realized the cultist was Peter—the man's face was so swollen, he was almost unrecognizable. The yellow of bruises was also, now that he knew something was wrong, equally evident, and the huddled pose now seemed less a dejected slump and more something born of pain.

Keep going, Fergus told himself. *You're running out of time, and if this man was at all competent, he'd be your enemy.*

"Oh, fuck everything for the madness it is," he said, and turned and dropped himself on the bench next to Peter.

The man glanced over, his expression weary and distrustful, until recognition kicked in. "You. You're here," he said.

"What the hell happened to you?" Fergus asked.

Peter slumped further down. "Jeremy," he said. "He spotted me after he lost you, and he was drunk, and he was pissed. Decided to take out his frustration on my face with his boots. Probably would've killed me, but the Reykjavík police showed up and tased him." There was a small smile at that memory.

"And your back?" Fergus asked.

Peter shrugged awkwardly and lifted the back of his tunic. Wide, angry welts crisscrossed it in a dozen places. "Whip," he said.

"Jeremy whipped you?" Fergus exclaimed.

Peter shook his head. "Estro de la hejmo," he said.

"'Leader of your hearth'?" Fergus asked. He'd done a little research on Fajro Promeso's structure, and that included learning some of its organizational terms.

Peter straightened up in surprise, his face wincing in pain. "You know our sacred language?" he asked.

Did he tell the poor fellow that his "sacred" language was just a construction from the nineteenth century? That seemed, in the moment, an unnecessary cruelty. "I've been studying," he said instead. "In the Secret Space Police, knowledge is key to success. So, your own people did this? Why? Not for having a sandwich with me, I hope?"

Peter laughed. "That would have earned me triple the stripes at least. No, it was punishment for being caught by Jeremy. But I should not have taken you up on the sandwich. Hunger prepares us for the fire."

How did he answer that? He didn't even know where to start, much less if he even should. "Why are you here?" he asked instead.

"As always, following DM," Peter said. "They moved me here to get me away from Jeremy, but the techbros are all stirred up everywhere. Since we keep running into each other, I guess you're probably responsible for that."

"It's possible," Fergus said. "I have terrible people skills."

Peter smiled again. "I can see that about you," he said. "I shouldn't be seen talking to you, anyway. Jeremy and Kyle's buddy Mitch is lurking down by the exit. You can identify him because his skull looks like it could barely contain a cup of applesauce."

Fergus laughed. "So noted," he said.

"It used to be just a couple of them, a couple of us, and not much happening either way. Easy to keep our eye on them, boring except when they decided to beat one of us up for fun. Now they're out all over the damned planet, at least four right here, including Mitch, taking shifts. How do I follow them when they have money and cars and guns and all I have is blistered feet and even standing up hurts?"

"I'm sorry," Fergus said. "You going to be okay?"

"I hope not," Peter said. "Letdown of an apocalypse, if I was."

"I mean more immediately. Who wants to go into the end of the world, feeling too crappy to enjoy it?" Fergus said. He gestured around the terminal. "Coffee? Maybe a pastry? Anything?"

"Hunger prepares—"

"Yes, yes," Fergus interrupted. "But you don't want to pass out and miss it all, do you?"

Peter stared down at his knees, then back at Fergus. "I don't know what you have to do with the pieces of the holy artifact, but I know it's something. It's too big a coincidence otherwise. But I know I can't fight you myself, and watching you frustrate the techbros might be the first time in years I've actually felt *happiness*. So, yes, you can buy me a coffee, and even a bagel, as long as you know we're ultimately still on different sides."

"Oh, I know," Fergus said. "But I can always hope."

"I've never had hope," Peter said. "Decaf, if they have it, please."

Fergus stood up. "Man, we really *are* on opposites sides of the good/evil divide," he said. "Be back in a few."

———

Avoiding Mitch—who really did have a surprisingly small forehead, for the size of his neck and fists—was easy after Peter's warning and well worth the cost of a little food. He liked to think he was just encouraging an avenue of information, but the truth of it was, he felt sort of bad for the man and guilty that he'd inadvertently led to the man getting beaten.

You're getting soft, he grumbled at himself. *You're trying to stop the apocalypse, remember, not feed its foot soldiers.*

One army at a time, though.

No one followed him from the shuttleport. He took an autotaxi north to the small town of Point au Mal, an old fishing village turned thriving arts community, and rented a moped.

Electric vehicles were limited to thirty kph max for safety, but he was okay with that, as he was thinking about the need to commit some dangerous thieving soon. Aware of his total lack of a plan, he was none too eager to get to it. Add to that the cryptic uselessness of the Asiig agent's warning, whose only clear, salient point seemed to be that it was going to be a much bigger pain in the ass to find that last piece than he could possibly guess. *Because that's what this otherwise easy-peasy scavenger hunt needs,* he thought, *a hint of the impossible.*

The target zone was most of the way up a mountain called the Cabox, about thirty kilometers, give or take with the winding path, to his north. Most of the trek followed alongside a river, which was pleasant, burbly company for the ride. The sun was out and there were other folks out on the wide paths, on scooters and bikes or just plain walking.

The trees were all shorter there, as if none dared be the tallest and take the brunt of the wind. They were also much thicker, less like they lined the path and more like they barely tolerated its incursion on their space, and loomed as close as they could, as if to drive home the point that you were only there on their sufferance.

Company along the path thinned out as the way grew steeper, and he had enough of a window of solitude to tuck his moped into the woods, cover it with branches, and set off into the wilderness itself. Somewhere ahead was a forest-management road, but that seemed too easy a place for DM to ambush him again. He was sure they'd try, but he was going to make them work for it.

Waiting for night would have had some advantages, but he was certain DM had goggles, and this way, there were more potential witnesses around, especially when he was heading back out of there and not wanting to be isolated or easily singled out. And trying to pass as a random hiker would be a lot harder in the dark.

So would avoiding bogs, he considered, as he found himself on the edge of one. On the far side of it, a moose was wading along the edge of the water and stopped to watch him. It was way bigger than any such thing should be, and he was pretty sure it could stomp the shit out of him if it wanted to, leaving nothing but squished Fergus paste atop the moss and rocks to mark his passing, so he backed off slowly and took the long way around. His socks were wet and squishy-feeling inside his less-than-watertight hiking boots before he'd made it more than a half-dozen steps.

Around him, the density of the trees was growing sparser, and less robust, with almost each step, until he emerged from the last few hardy, wind-battered pines and onto hard-packed earth, only a few dozen meters from the road. There was no cover ahead from there.

He rested inside the tree line and did his best to feel for electrical signals. There was nothing.

The summit was still a dozen kilometers away, though he didn't need to go that far. *Or so I hope,* he thought. The conversation with the Asiig agent had planted doubts again about everything. Still, he had a ways to go, whether or not he joined up with the ill-maintained and increasingly nonexistent road, or tried to shortcut some of the S curves up steeper terrain, and that was more than enough time for a drone to appear and do him in before he could get back into concealment in the forest.

Right now, the skies looked and felt clear, and he didn't really have much of a choice, so he tugged his hat more firmly into place to shade his eyes and face, and got moving. After the drone attack in Tanzania, he'd added something new up his sleeve with more range than his repurposed car antennae, and his desire to see if it worked was almost as strong as his hope that the necessity wouldn't present itself.

The slopes were a mess of broken rocks, from tiny scree that slid out under his feet every time he strayed from the rutted road to large boulders that could conceal almost anything. Despite the lack of visual warning, he felt the tiny spark of something ahead several minutes before he got there, tucked up on the summit side of a boulder to catch anyone going past. He set his pack down, got to his hands and knees in the rough, dusty dirt, and sneaked his hand around the boulder until he could touch the stake on which the sensor had been mounted, and as carefully and gradually as he could, he turned the stake in the ground until it faced the rock itself. If someone happened to check, they'd notice it had been redirected, but he was certain frying it would set off immediate alarms.

Then he got up, brushed away dust and the little bits of rock pocked into his hands and knees, shouldered his pack again, and continued upward. He found three more and disabled them in the same way before he reached the perimeter of the target zone.

Fergus could feel the faint signal of the core fragment, nearer than he'd expected, but it took him nearly twenty minutes to realize it was underfoot, underground. Glancing up the hill, he could easily imagine that it had gotten there via landslide.

He squatted down, pulled the lightweight folding trowel out of his pack that he'd been carrying since Burringurrah, and thought about how utterly inadequate it was. *Nothing for it,* he thought, and started trying to pry up rocks and carve out the hard-packed soil between him and the fragment. The piece was about half a meter down, which didn't seem like much except that the effort-to-progress ratio was miserably low, and about ten centimeters down, he hit a rock large enough that he had to dig out a veritable pit around it just to get enough of a purchase to wiggle it free and haul it out.

His knees and back had a low opinion of that exercise. He

took a break and nibbled at a nutrition bar as he again surveyed the area for suspicious signals. There was no sign of Mitch's buddies, and he wondered if they were slacking off drunk somewhere or waiting eagerly for him on the section of road he'd bypassed to get there.

It took him more than two hours, and three more intransigent rocks, to finally reach the fragment. "Hello, number nine," he greeted it as it sat in his hand, almost shouting at him. He slipped it into his zippered, lined pocket, and sat back, trying to decide if he should just leave the hole as is. In the end, the idea of leaving such obvious evidence of his activity—not to mention the questions it could raise about how, exactly, he located the fragment so precisely—was enough for him to shove the various rocks and dirt back into the hole and try to scuff out the obvious disturbance with his boot.

When it was good enough that one mild rain would make his dig undetectable, Fergus gathered up his things and started back down the hillside and the distant safety of the forest. It wasn't nearly as fast going as in the inflatable ball, but the slope would have been too little and too irregular to get him any good speed, and without that and the element of surprise, it would have been a liability. So, more hiking it was.

He thought he was heading down the same way he'd come up, though the road had abandoned him nearly a kilometer farther down, but he realized he had strayed off target when he felt the distinct ping of a signal to his left, and looked over to see a sensor in the shadow of a boulder, facing right toward him.

"Shit," he muttered. He scrambled as fast as he could downhill toward the tree line, three drones already coming in, low and from the south. It was going to be a close race.

As he pelted down the slope, he fumbled in his other pocket, where he had stashed a handful of alloy ball bearings, and wrapping his hand around them, concentrated as best he could under the circumstances to charge them with electricity. He'd had the idea on the Pan-Africa train, practiced on the way here from the Azores, and had discovered he could get a charge to stay in a bearing for about ninety seconds after letting it go, before it dissipated.

Either ninety seconds was more than enough, or it wouldn't work at all.

Fergus reached the first tree of any size, catching it with one arm to slow himself as he pulled a slingshot and one of the charged bearings from his pocket with his free hand. He took a few precious seconds to check his footing and aim as a sleek drone, two gun barrels slung below its rotors, flew straight at him, barely twenty meters away.

He let the bearing fly and had a second one in the sling and ready to go when the first one hit a glancing blow to its underside, discharging its stored energy in that brief contact. The drone wobbled unevenly in the air, rotors faltering, when he tagged it solidly with a second bearing.

The drone took a nosedive into the hard ground, crumpling like a paper airplane hitting a wall, and did not move. He could sense the other two drones coming up over the trees, so he repocketed his sling and headed into the woods proper, staying far away from the exposed forestry road and under as much cover as he could.

Many times, he had to stop under a tree as the drones swept back and forth overhead, looking for movement; he was grateful for the chances to catch his breath, anyhow.

Somewhere to his left, there was the brief tingling of electronics. He stayed where he was, not moving, for a long time, eyes searching the cacophony of leaves and branches for any sign of the source. Finally, faintly, he heard a muffled sneeze, and his

eyes immediately found the ever-so-slightly-off shifting camouflage of a birdwatcher's blind about six meters off the ground in
a tree. He would have walked right into its line of sight on his
way in if he hadn't gone around the moose.

Thank you, leftover ice-age mammalsaur, he thought.

As he was contemplating his best route that both avoided the
blind and openings in the forest cover, he felt another brief blip
downhill and heard sounds of movement.

Peter had told him DM was taking shifts. It looked like either
the shift was changing, or backup was coming in to try to drive
him out into the open or box him in. Either way, he had an advantage they couldn't foresee. As long as they kept checking in
with each other, he knew exactly where they were.

He slogged around the far edge of the bog, moving as quickly
as he dared without making unnecessary noise, and slipped right
past them without them ever knowing he was there.

By the time he got to his hidden moped, only one drone was
still anywhere nearby, and not particularly near. He unburied
the moped and rolled it to the very edge of the bike path, ditched
his hat, and changed his jacket for a bright blue one. When a
group of people, laughing and chatting, came past on a mix of
scooters and bicycles, he made a show of putting his water bottle
away and getting onto the path far enough behind them to not
be creepy or put them in danger, but just close enough to plausibly look like a lagging member of the group.

Drones passed overhead twice, about twenty minutes apart,
but did not seem any more interested in him than in the group
as a whole, and that not much.

He returned the moped in Point au Mal and took a bus back
to the Stephenville shuttleport. His sense of dread rose, the closer
they got, and as he disembarked with a full busload of passengers

and walked among them through the front gate into the main terminal building, he felt ridiculously exposed.

Mitch was not there, or at least not where Fergus could spot him, and he hoped this was just a bit of good luck rather than first indication of the next ambush.

Peter was also no longer on the bench. He glanced around to see if the man had just moved, but he was not anywhere in sight. *Out following Mitch,* he thought. *I hope he stays out of trouble.*

Fergus bought a ticket for a suborbital shuttle down the coast to Portland, leaving in about an hour. He meandered to the side of the main concourse and watched the flow of people around the terminal, and the progression of planes and shuttles coming and going outside the tall glass windows that lined the entire front of the building.

After twenty minutes or so, when a critical mass of water decided it was done hanging around, he went off to find the restrooms.

They were down a side corridor, away from the concourse, a line of individual booths with a few alien-configured ones at the end. As a fifteen-year-old runaway, he'd thought the idea of an alien toilet was the most fascinating thing ever, and he'd shut himself in one on Mars and pushed every single button to see what would happen, and not only shot himself in the eye with a jet of saline water but got his entire pants crotch dusted with some kind of cloying, heavily scented powder that took six runs through the laundry to finally wash out. Dru had made fun of him for it for weeks.

Fergus went to one of the regular booths that had its UNOCCU-PIED light lit. As he was pushing the door open, he heard the muffled thumps and crashes of a scuffle one booth down. Pausing, he listened, and after a few moments decided it was definitely a fight, which someone was losing badly. The presumptive loser sounded a lot like Peter.

Shit, he thought. He stepped sideways to the other door, which was one of the alien-configured booths, and tried the handle, but the booth was locked with the OCCUPIED sign lit overhead. *Either I'm about to do the right thing, or I'm about to commit an interstellar faux pas,* he thought, and put his index finger against the lock and shorted it.

It crashed open from the inside and Peter fell out onto the floor, his face covered in blood, and Mitch lunged down to grab him and haul him back inside. "I don't know anything!" Peter was crying, trying to squirm away. "I was just sitting there, minding my own business!"

"He bought you food!" Mitch roared, and he bent down and clasped his meaty hand on Peter's throat, as Fergus delicately reached around the open door and put his own hand on Mitch's back.

The techbro grunted and collapsed on top of Peter, an additional abuse but forgivable in the circumstances. Peter stared up at Fergus, blinking furiously around the blood in his swollen eyes, as Fergus knelt down and shoved the inert body of his unconscious assailant off and ungracefully to the floor.

"What did you hit him with?" Peter asked.

"Secret Space Police Secret Weapon," Fergus said, patting his pocket as if he'd just returned something there. "Can't tell you. You okay?"

"No," Peter said.

"You need a minute, or you want to get out of here before applesauce-brain wakes up?"

Peter gave a weak smile. His lip was split, and he winced, but he held a hand out. "Help me up?" he said.

Fergus helped him up, shocked by how very little the man

weighed and how weak he looked, trying to walk away from the booths as Fergus shoved Mitch back inside, quickly rifled the man's pockets, and shut the door before catching up to the cultist. "Do you want me to call security?" he asked.

Peter shook his head *no*, then glanced down at the blood splattered on his white linen tunic. "Shit," he said. "That is going to be murder to get out."

"It almost was murder," Fergus said. "And I guess it's my fault again. I'm sorry."

"No, no apologies, it was mine," Peter said. "I was weak and accepted your gift of food. Twice. I have let down my faith by being tempted by bodily and material needs."

Fergus took a handkerchief out of his bag and, getting it wet at the water fountain, tried to dab the worst of the blood off the man's face. "You have to meet those needs at least a little bit; otherwise, you die," he said.

"Not if my faith is strong enough," Peter said. "The True are sustained by the fire from within and have no need of food or rest or material comforts. Fajra Mastro would be so disappointed in me."

"The Fire Master?" Fergus asked. "You mean Barrett Granby, who started your . . . faith?"

Peter scowled at him. "That is the Mastro's human name, yes. He has transcended it."

The man was upset and had been beaten for the second time in a week, and Fergus didn't want to laugh at him or make him feel like he was being mocked, so he handed the handkerchief to him instead. "Stay here," he ordered.

Fergus went over to one of the many souvenir booths and came back with a blue sweatshirt with puffins on it.

"I don't want that," Peter said.

"You want to talk to security? Because if anyone reports you walking around covered in blood, you are going to be trying to explain a lot to them."

"No," Peter said. "Okay. But . . . help me?"

Fergus helped him pull the sweatshirt on, and the man was shaking with the effort and pain by the time they were done. But he looked warmer, anyway, and less ghastly with the blood out of sight.

"Look," Fergus said, "I'm not trying to make you upset, but you do know that your Mastro is not exactly living an austere life? I mean, have you seen pics of his house?"

"The Temple in Kansas? I've been there twice in person," Peter said. "It's a tall stone tower, and the Mastro lives in a room on the top floor, with nothing but a bunk and a small desk, no food other than that brought by the faithful who have come on pilgrimage, and no heat other than that provided by the beacon flame atop the roof that he and his special acolytes tend, around the clock, between prayers. How is that not the very definition of austerity?"

Fergus had seen the tower, too, through a lot of 3-D scans uploaded by a disgruntled former cult member, and none of what Peter said was wrong. There was virtually nothing there, and certainly nowhere one could easily conceal fragments, but it did have a fire moat, which was a nice bit of extra theatrics.

"Do you have a reason to stay here?" Fergus asked instead.

"If you leave, Mitch will leave," Peter said. "And when Mitch leaves, I have no reason to stay."

"Where will you go next?"

Peter tried to shrug and gave up, gritting his teeth in pain. "Wherever my *estro de la hejmo* sends me, when he gets around to it. I will be patient until then."

"So, how about I show you something?" Fergus said. "You'll have to take a couple of shuttle hops with me, but if you've not got immediate apocalypse business to get to, I think you will want to see it."

"What?" Peter asked.

"Your Mastro's house."

"The Temple? I already—"

"No," Fergus interrupted. "His house. On a big private estate in the Republic of Nevada."

"You are lying," Peter said.

"Why would I?"

"Then you are just wrong!" the man yelled.

"So, come with me and prove it," Fergus said. "I can bring you right back here, or wherever you want to go, after. It would take less than a day to get there. Would your Estro miss you that quickly?"

"No," Peter said. "No, he would not."

"It's up to you," Fergus said. He crossed his arms over his chest and regarded him. It would be far better for him and everyone if Peter said no, turned, and walked away . . . but Fergus wanted him to say yes, *needed* to show this poor abused man the fake wizard behind the curtain that he served.

Peter dabbed at his lip with the wet handkerchief and then looked at it and his own blood on it. He said something, too quiet for Fergus to hear, even standing so near, then coughed and said it again, louder. "Okay. I'll go with you."

Chapter 16

◆ ◆ ◆

True to its reputation, Lake Tahoe was an almost-unworldly color of deep blue, benday-dotted with a myriad silver drought buoys that, at the height of the day when water levels were low, unfolded their shiny petals to reflect the sun back up and away. Right now, they were folded up, tiny cones keeping their formation as the surface undulated beneath them.

They were conspicuously absent from the lake nearer the private estates, evaporation and catastrophic drought being, apparently, less of a concern than the ire of the wealthy elite.

Peter had slept, if fitfully, on the shuttle from Portland to Reno, his injuries not letting him get too comfortable, and who knew what inner demons tormented someone who'd decided the world ending in fire was a best-case scenario? Still, he'd seemed marginally perkier, if that could ever be applied to the man, and had not fought Fergus ordering him food on the way.

He was still wearing his puffin sweatshirt and was hunched up in it despite the heat as if it was a layer of armor. The tour boat was slow, but the wind was brisk, and they stood near the railings, looking out over the lake with the other tourists, and at the sprawling mansions on the far shore. "That one," Fergus said at last, and pointed. "The one with the big white marble pillars and the red yacht docked out front. According to the real estate data, fourteen bedrooms, a home movie theater that seats thirty-five, an indoor driving range, and a full-size nightclub dance floor. Mr. Granby has a part-time DJ listed as in his employ."

Peter pursed his lips and stared. The tour boat continued along the shore, and the mansion itself slid out of view, though the red yacht stood out until it became too small to see. The man seemed to almost draw even further in on himself, if such a thing was possible, then he asked, "How do I know you're not lying?"

"I suppose you don't," Fergus said. "After we get back to shore, if you want to take an auto-taxi over and go ring his bell, we can."

"Why?" Peter asked.

Good question, Fergus thought. He needed to come there anyway, eventually—he was certain the fragments that the cult had collected had to be there rather than in the bogus temple in Kansas—but having Peter along was a significant inconvenience.

"In my life," he said, "I've been in bad places I wasn't sure I'd ever get out of. I've been beaten down, tortured, and nearly killed, more times than I can count. But I always knew why I was there and what I was fighting for. *Who* I was fighting for. And I may think your desire to see everything and everyone end in flame is incredibly tragic and wrong, but at the very fucking least, you deserve to know the real man trying to lead you there."

Peter turned back to the railing and stared out over the water, and said nothing else. Fergus left him alone and instead watched the precision with which the drought buoys fell back into position after the disruption of the boat's passing, and thought about how comforting—and dull—the illusion of an orderly universe could be.

Anyway, while Peter had gotten his eyeful of Granby's very un-transcendent mansion, Fergus had gotten at least a preliminary feel for the security drones, bordering estates, and walls in between. And if he was interpreting the expression on Peter's face correctly, he was going to get a chance to check it out from the front gate, too.

You didn't bring him along to be bait, he reminded himself.

"I want to go speak to him," Peter said, on cue.

"You sure about that?"

"If you're lying, I want to know. If you're not . . ." Peter trailed off, staring down at his feet for a while, before he added, "I just need to do this."

"Okay," Fergus said. After the tour ended, they caught one of the line of auto-taxis that had just dropped off tourists for the next outing and were waiting idle for their next client. Fergus was pretty sure they screened for unauthorized people trying to go directly to certain private estates, possibly including notifying the resident, but ogling ridiculously expensive neighborhoods was the prime tourism draw there in the summer other than the lake itself, and there was only so much courtesy you could let get in the way of profit. "We want to go see some fancy homes," Fergus told the auto-taxi system. "Can we drive around up on Sandy Cove Hill, please? Also, please set to full window tint."

Obediently, the auto-taxi pulled away from the boat dock and headed north as the windows darkened slightly. From outside, they'd be virtually opaque and probably displaying advertising.

His handpad pinged and he checked it, keeping it turned away from Peter, who was studiously looking out the window. It was a message from Zacker, who had picked up his "package" he'd left in a shuttleport locker in Portland and felt very abused for having been sent on an errand all the way to the Atlantic States in order to pick up a can of soda, and *Martian* soda at that. Fergus had been planning to bring his latest find back up to orbit, but with *Whiro* still off shaking interest and his own change of plans, he didn't dare carry it on his person. Not directly into the home territory of one of his enemies.

Thanks, he sent back. *Hang on to it until I'm back in touch. Don't open it, no matter what.*

The area heading up toward Sandy Cove was heavily forested. Unlike Newfoundland, where the pines were short and scrappy, as if daring you to fight, here they soared tall as if born with an expectation of unchallenged dominance.

So did the people living among them, Fergus considered, as they turned up the winding road through the billionaire estates. Many of the homes looked like log cabins Dunning-Kruger'd to the scale and grandeur of palaces: thick wooden structures with soaring windows just visible behind heavy ornate gates and through carefully manicured, curated, domesticated forest. Others were more faux-Victorian fare, and a few oddballs like an orange concrete brutalist revival that even Peter made a face over, a few stonework castles including one that was designed to look like an old-fashioned river mill except the stones were shiny crystal and the waterwheel was a giant, gold-colored cog. Barrett Granby's house, by comparison, was relatively conservative in affect, a massive, shallow-roofed stone home with an almost Southwestern sensibility, behind bronze gates embellished with the same flame motif as on the medal imbedded in Peter's chest.

Peter let out a long, resigned sigh when he noticed that. "Can we stop?" he asked the auto-taxi.

It dutifully pulled over to the shoulder and Peter got out. The man took off his puffin sweatshirt, threw it in the back seat, and walked toward the gate in his linens, still stained and crusty with his own blood.

Fergus stayed in the taxi, not wanting to risk getting his face on camera, and because he could safely and anonymously scrutinize the entrance for security from within. And anyway, he thought it likely that Peter wanted to do this alone—he himself would. As long as no one attacked the man and dragged him inside against his will, this was Peter's time, not his.

Peter stopped twice in the road while crossing to the gates, his hands fluttering at his sides in agitation. He kept glancing back as if unsure he was doing the right thing. It was the appearance of another autocar, coming around the curve and toward them, that finally made him decide and scurry the rest of the way across.

Standing before the tall gates, Peter ran his fingers around one of the stylized frames, then stepped to the side and pressed the bell. It took a while for a human response, but the technological one was immediate. Fergus felt a network of sensors and cameras wake up all around the gate, could feel the distant buzz of microdrones like moth-wing flutters against his senses and, to his surprise, something under Peter's feet, radiating wakefulness where moments before there had been nothing.

Eight minutes later, a man appeared at the gate. He was wearing a black suit, not linen like Peter's, and was very certainly better fed, from the size of his muscles. He was also, from the bulge of his jacket against his thigh, armed. The gate opened just wide enough for the guard to step into and fill the gap.

"Fratro," Peter said.

"Don't 'brother' me; what do you want?" the guard demanded.

"I would like to see the Mastro, to pray at his feet," Peter answered. "I have come a long way to show my devotion and faithfulness."

"Show me your Pledge," the guard said.

Peter pulled his tunic off awkwardly over his head. The bruises and welts and a lifetime of starvation written across his body were hard to witness. "Oh, ouch," Fergus murmured under his breath.

The guard reached out, and Fergus couldn't see but assumed he'd touched the emblem embedded in Peter's chest, to make sure it was real. "Put your shirt on. Wait here," the guard said, and stepped back inside. The gate closed again.

It was forty minutes before the guard came back. Peter had stood there the whole time, not moving except to put his shirt back on as instructed. "The Mastro is busy in his devotions, beseeching the Unholy Fire to fulfill its promise and cleanse the world, and cannot be disturbed," the guard said. It sounded like a practiced script. "He sends you a token of his love for you, his filo de fajro, and asks you to carry on the great work."

The guard set something in Peter's hands. Whatever Peter said, it was low enough that Fergus couldn't hear, but the guard seemed satisfied by it. He made some hand gesture that Peter returned, then crossed back through the gates, which closed immediately behind him once again.

Peter came back to the car, got in, and sat there like stone, his hands cupped around whatever the guard had given him.

"Are you okay?" Fergus asked, after a while.

"Sure," Peter said. He looked like he might cry, or shout, and was stuck in limbo between the two. "It's fine. The Mastro was busy."

"Look—" Fergus started.

Peter turned his face to look back out the window. "And that is, as you said, the Mastro's house," he said.

"Yeah. I'm sorry, I—"

"Don't," Peter said.

"Don't what?"

"Don't apologize," Peter said. "Can we go?"

"Sure," Fergus said. He instructed the auto-taxi to continue, and it pulled off the shoulder smoothly back into the travel lane and continued its long loop up and around Sandy Cove, past more castles and lodges and towers, until they wound back down and Fergus told it to take them into Carson City.

It dropped them off twenty minutes later at a central transportation hub. After checking that nothing had followed them down from the hills, Fergus gently herded Peter into a small, brightly colored cafeteria and got tea and half a croissant into him before Peter pushed the remainder away and set the object, still clutched in one fist, down on the table. It was a coin, much like the medal in Peter's chest, except gold. Or gold-covered, at least. It also radiated a faint trace of electricity, though Fergus couldn't tell what it was.

"Riches are for those who burn," Peter said. Reluctantly, he picked it up again and put it quickly into a pocket. Then he pulled his puffin sweatshirt back on, shivering from something more than the cafeteria's air conditioning.

"Where do you want to go?" Fergus asked, after the silence had stretched on long enough to be awkward. "There's a bus stop here and a train. Anywhere you want to go, I'll buy you a ticket."

"Kansas?" Peter said.

"If that's what you want," Fergus answered.

"Kansas, then."

Fergus went with him to the train station, got him a ticket, and handed him a bag with another croissant in it. "For the trip," he said. "Humor me and take it, okay?"

Peter nodded, then turned and got on board. Fergus watched the train pull out of the station, his feelings a volatile mix of pity and anger, relief and calculation. *Okay*, he told himself. *You helped him. Now get back to the job.*

He caught another auto-taxi farther into the city to pick up supplies and find a hotel. His body clock was still woefully off, and he was going to have a busy day tomorrow.

———

In the morning, he arrived bright and early on the same docks as the tour boat, for a beginner scuba diving lesson. After a quick but exhaustive lecture on the physics at play and the physiological experience, the instructor and her assistant got their six students suited up—in this, Fergus's years of experience with exosuits gave him an edge and a small but satisfying nod of approval—and then walked them through all their safety equipment, quizzing them on emergency scenarios that were apparently too much for one middle-aged man, who peeled off his loaner suit and bowed out.

Then they were herded down to the water, like the universe's most awkward herd of ugly ducklings, and let go as deep as their waists before making them all practice their breathing until they could demonstrate competence. Another student was sent back to shore with the assistant for some extra one-on-one, and the instructor took the remainder of their brave flock out as far as shoulder depth and set them to the task of completing a circle around her underwater.

Fergus's student diving mask gave gentle feedback and information in his ear, reminding him of his current depth and restrictions on the distance he was allowed to stray from the instructor, and overall, it wasn't as terrifying as he'd worried. Of course, he was never more than a meter away from air or unable to stand up and wade back to shore.

They spent about three hours in the water and were given a discount code for intermediary lessons if they wanted, and then relieved of all their gear and herded into the dive shop on their way out.

Still playing the enthusiastic tourist, Fergus dropped a cringeworthy amount of credit on a full set of gear, including the top-of-the-line smartmask, an air-release diffuser, and a waterproof duffel bag, before loading it all up in another auto-taxi to haul back to his hotel and dump on the floor while he took a long, anxiety-filled nap in a bed too soft to feel like the safety of solid ground.

He woke up in late afternoon, the sun still dominating the sky above the mountains to the west, and set about carefully checking through all his gear and purchases one last time. He packed it all along with his toolkit, ball bearings, and slingshot into the waterproof duffel and sealed it up. With nothing else to do except wait for dark, he bounced a call through his encrypted channel to Mars.

"Where in hell are ye?" Isla asked, right away. She seemed to be sitting in a small AV space, and her color looked much better than when he'd left her.

"Nevada," he said.

"Isn't Nevada radioactive?"

"Only Las Vegas," Fergus replied. "I had a sudden change of plans and decided to go for the Fajro Promeso pieces sooner rather than later."

"Did ye get the Newfoundland piece?" she asked.

"Yeah. I left it in a locker in Portland, in the Atlantic States, and sent my friend Zacker after it. Wow, did I get an earful about making him get off his ass and cross borders just to fetch a can of soda." Fergus smiled at the thought. "Anyway, didn't want it on my person here, and thought that was as safe a place as any in a pinch. How are you doing?"

"Better enough to be bored," she said. "Although not too bored, because apparently word has got around that Famous Fergus's sister is here, and I've got Marsies coming from all over to say hello. It's very awkward, especially when I need to nap. I get tired so easily."

"Sorry," he said. "I didn't—"

"No," she interrupted. "It's cool to see how much ye've made a difference. So, what happened with the pieces that got stuck together?"

"They got stuck together," he said.

She rolled her eyes. "No, I mean, how did ye get them apart? Kaice told me."

"I followed your suggestion, O Smart Sister of Mine, and tried talking to them. Or rather, I tried to make them sleepy. I don't know what I did or how, but it worked. Once, anyway."

She pursed her lips, thinking. "I had an idea about that," she said. "Let me get back to ye. Oh! Arelyn is here. We have a lunch date. Later, Fergus." She reached out and disconnected.

See, she's okay, he told himself.

Fergus ate a vending-machine sandwich in silence, forcing his thoughts back around to the present day. When dusk had finally given over to dark, he caught another auto-taxi out to a small public park, now empty of everything except mosquitoes, and headed along the well-worn path toward the small beach.

Setting his stuff down on a rock by the water's edge, he took off his shorts and shirt and pulled his diving suit on over the black bodysuit he'd had on underneath his regular clothes. He tied up his clothes in a black bag and tucked them deep under cover of some bushes, determined that he would be back for them, and not least because his Dingo Hole T-shirt was in there and he wasn't ready to lose it yet.

The duffel strapped neatly across his back below the shoulder-blade unit that drew oxygen out of the water for his regulator without being much of an encumbrance. He then attached a much smaller, waterproof pouch to his chest and filled it with things he might need quickly.

At the water's edge, he pulled his flippers on and the very expensive mask with the zoom and infrared features down over his face. Last thing he picked up was a small submersible handjet, and then he flapped his way as quietly as he could into the water until he was deep enough to squat down and slip forward horizontally and under.

It was about three and half kilometers, cutting straight between curves of the lakeshore, to where the Sandy Cove estates began. For now, he just needed to stay under and let the jet pull him forward, deep enough below the surface to leave no wake or sound, and keep all his senses out for anything un-lake-like in his path. The nearly full moon over the open lake dappled the water around him with the shadows of the drought buoys and occasionally caught, faintly, the flash of a fish darting out of his path and away.

He passed about three meters below a canoe without ever being noticed; the diffuser he'd bought made sure no bubbles bigger than fizz on a soda reached the surface.

The private security sensors around Granby's dock and personal beach were floaters, not much different in size from the drought buoys, and arrayed along their fringes to blend in. Visually, they probably did so very well, but to Fergus's senses they were *loud*. They also, Fergus thought as he slid silently past them from below, were doing a very excellent job of watching for intruders coming in along the lake surface but not below it.

It wasn't until he neared the dock itself that there was any kind of underwater security, and that was a simple pair of forward-facing sensors attached to the outermost dock pilings about a meter and half down. They were easy enough to avoid by skirting the dock toward the beach, then angling back toward and under the dock behind them.

The boathouse was attached to the dock, and he swam from the cover of the latter quickly around and into the nearer of two boat bays, currently unoccupied. Popping his head out of water still concealed beneath a perimeter walkway inside the boathouse, he pulled his swim fins off—appreciating them far more now that he wasn't trying to walk in them—and then took off his mask and breathing gear. Bundling them together in a string bag he'd brought along in his front pouch, he used a wad of

StickAnywhere to attach the bag by its drawstrings to the underside of the walkway planks. The lumpy adhesive should last for up to a week, by which time he'd either have escaped via some other route or was dead and didn't need his fins anyway.

Peering up, he could see sensors in the eaves, but they were pointed toward the wide boat door. The smaller entrance from the boathouse out onto the dock was alarmed but not watched, at least not from inside. He slipped quietly along the underside of the walkway, until he was at the back of the boathouse closest to shore and well out of the view of the eave sensors, then slid his duffel out of the water and pulled himself up after it onto the slick wood planks above. There was no noticeable change in the signal notes around him, so it seemed likely he hadn't been detected.

The security system had a panel inside the side door, handily accessible when you've tripped your own alarms while intoxicated. Fergus popped open the panel and took his confuddler out of his duffel, wiring it in and waiting for it to establish itself slyly on the network. When it finished, less than twenty seconds later, he had it run a system analysis.

The first, and most interesting, thing the confuddler returned to him was that Barrett Granby's security system was a closed network, with absolutely no outside connections to SolNet or anything else. Highly unusual but smart, Fergus thought, particularly if you know Digital Midendian is out there and eventually going to come after you.

From the boathouse he could hear voices as people emerged from the main house, more laughter and the sounds of easy happiness. He leaned against the wall in the boathouse, out of moonlight or view from any windows, and listened.

". . . turn the water on," someone was saying. "Oh, and show her the lights, Barry!"

"Hang on," another voice said. Moments later, there was an

exclamation of surprise from multiple voices, and Fergus edged toward the window to risk a quick glance.

The expansive deck along the back of the house, set off from the beach by a long, sloping lawn, was now aglow in red, the silhouettes of people, none distorted by the outlines of clothing, moving back and forth and then disappearing down into the glow. Not sure he'd understood the source of the glow, he took a second look, and had to put his hand over his mouth to keep himself from chuckling out loud. Barrett 'Barry' Granby, Mastro of Fajro Promeso, living a life of devotion and austerity, had an enormous hot tub shaped like a volcano, lit red from inside.

Poor Peter, Fergus thought, and hoped the man found some better, healthier group of people to attach himself to when he reached Kansas.

Two of Granby's guards stood unobtrusively, unmoving, near the sliding doors into the house, as a trio of servants emerged with trays of food and drink. If the party was just getting started, that worked in Fergus's favor, but he still needed to get across the lawn from boathouse to main house without being seen.

The security system itself would be difficult to crack, and the attempt could give him away, but non-critical controls were under much lighter protection. It took him about two minutes to break the encryption with a third-party algorithm via his confuddler and get full access.

Taking some deep breaths, centering himself in his physical self mujūryokudo-style, he peeled off the diving suit and pulled the black cowl attached to his bodysuit over his head, leaving nothing but his upper face showing. Then he put his nice, expensive, infrared diving mask back on; it didn't care one way or the other about the presence of water, and it was a lot more anonymous and replaceable than his exosuit goggles.

Using his connection, he turned off the hot-tub lights. Complaints were immediate. He heard Granby immediately call for his staff to go turn them back on and find out who had hit the switch.

Fergus unplugged his confuddler and stuck it back in his front-pouch. He crossed over along the back wall past the small, very pointy, very red speedboat bobbing idly in the second bay and to the window on the far side. From there he could see the lights of the neighboring estate to the north. Feeling around the frame with his gloved fingers, he found the spot where the on/off relay for the alarm sat below the surface, and very, very carefully sent a tiny charge in to flip it to off.

There was no other sign of change, so he slid the window open carefully and then pulled himself through it and out, landing and rolling on the far side before getting back up to his knees and closing it behind him.

He sneaked along the wall, under the trees, past the boathouse, and into the deep shadows of the side yard. There were several staffers standing around the deck, arguing about the lights, and finally someone decided to reboot the system. There were a brief few seconds where everything was plunged into darkness, and the incessant gurgling of the hot tub cut out, then everything came back on, including the volcano lights. The partiers cheered, the staffers dispersed, and Fergus had already crossed the one lit patch of lawn in that moment of darkness, and through a door into what the architect's drawings had labelled a "mudroom." The motion-sensor lights were easily turned off at the wall switch, no tampering necessary, and the door was safely closed behind him before the external lights and sensors came back on.

Functionally, the room seemed to be exactly as advertised, with a half-populated coat rack, boot tray, and a small sink and counter, but Fergus was pretty sure more money had been spent on that one room than on any house he'd ever lived in. The counter and walls were decorated with polished red stone and obsidian, and the accents on everything from the wall switches to the sink controls and door frames were covered in thin gold leaf.

He listened at the door of the mudroom for a while but heard no one nearby, so he closed his eyes and tried to feel for core fragments around the barrage of electrical noise from the house itself. There should have been three there, unless he'd guessed completely wrong that Granby would choose Nevada over Kansas to keep them.

After many long minutes, he decided that maybe, just maybe, he could faintly feel them. The distant, muffled calls didn't feel up, as he'd expected, which ruled out the second and third floor of the house. It would make escape easier to be on the ground floor, but at least upstairs he'd have much less chance of blundering into anyone until the party broke up. If the party broke up.

All senses alert to the point of near-panic, he peered out of the mudroom door into the corridor, a tasteless blend of faux brown stone and red walls with the same gold leaf detail running along the moldings and door frames. The dining room was ahead on his right, with two of Granby's black-suited guards sitting there with coffee and flicking a paper triangle back and forth across the table at each other in turns. When the one facing his direction bent down from his chair to pick the paper off the floor, Fergus sneaked past as quickly and quietly as he could.

The hallway bent around the dining room, into a well-lit, open great room that soared all three stories high. Columns carved to look like flame reached to the beamed ceiling and splayed out, as if shooting flame across the woodwork, and more red lights were embedded somewhere in the carvings to cast an ominous glow the entire length up. A boulder with a flat plane cut across the top and polished to a shine was covered with plates and glasses and more than a few empty bottles. Someone was lying on the black velvet sofa, out of sight, snoring.

He moved as quickly as he dared along the backside of the great room, letting the bees in his gut guide him, and emerged into another hallway on the far side. A billiards table stood in the room across the hall, the door half-open, and he could hear two women arguing inside. He sneaked past the game room just as the next door opened. One of the guards was coming out, straightening his tie and not looking up, and barely managed a small grunt of startlement when Fergus put a hand on his chest and zapped him. He caught the guard before he could hit the floor and carried him back into the bathroom the man had just left, sat him on the toilet hunched over with his head leaning against the sink, and backed out and closed the door.

On his right, a winding, ornate staircase headed up to the next floor, while on the opposite side, two doors remained before the hallway led back out to the heavily occupied deck. The first door led to a study with a big, promising desk and floor-to-ceiling bookshelves that were dusty enough to suggest they weren't well used. As he stepped in, a moth-sized security drone lifted from the desk, and he ducked back out into the hall and flattened himself against the wall.

The drone emerged at eye level, and Fergus grabbed it out of the air, frying it in his fist, before he stepped back into the room. Somewhere in there, if all the movies he'd watched and mysteries he'd read as a kid had any realism to them, would be a hidden safe. How long would it take him to find it, and how long before some system realized one of its drones wasn't answering a ping?

He closed his eyes, anxious he would be instantly tackled from behind by a guard in that moment of vulnerability, but the fragments felt, if anything, farther away.

And down.

He stepped back into the hall, hearing the sounds now of the party from the deck heading closer, and reached out for the handle of the last door. Signals exploded in his senses, and he let go hastily. Whatever was down there, this was the most heavily secured room in the house. A second bright noise came from the wall next to the door, but all he could see was seamless stone and wood. One block of faux stone, though, seemed slightly brighter than the others. *Aha, a hologram!* he realized, and waved his hand across it. The block disappeared, revealing the security control panel.

He didn't have time to finesse his way past it. He could hear the guards at the sliding doors, and people talking loudly on their way in. They seemed upset, angry. Was he already caught?

I'm not caught until they take me down, he thought, and stuck one index finger against the center of the panel and shorted the entire thing out in one go. The door clicked as the lock disengaged, and he stepped in and closed it tight, holding the handle to keep it closed, as the outside party came into the hall. ". . . guy from earlier," one of the guards was saying.

"Hang on," he heard Granby say, then louder, "everyone head on to the great room until we clear up a small security matter, okay? I'll have wine brought in a few minutes."

In a short while, the hallway was quiet again. "Now, what the fuck were you saying?" Granby asked.

"The guy from yesterday. Outside the gate," the guard replied. "We're not sure where he went, but we'd like you to stay inside until we've found him and dealt with it."

"Fine, whatever," he heard Granby say. "Maybe this time instead of a gold coin, give him a broken leg or two. I thought you said he was on a fucking train."

Peter? Fergus thought.

"The tracker says the coin is on the far side of Colorado and still moving east," the guard said.

"You think he's working for them?"

"He didn't seem bright enough, sir," the guard answered.

Granby let out a sigh of exasperation, which didn't quite cover the faint click of the door as the lock system booted up and reengaged. "What was that?"

"I don't know, sir."

"Check everywhere. Send extra drones out to the perimeter, and I don't care if my damned neighbors complain about them again. If he's on my grounds, shoot the little bastard."

"Yes, sir," the guard said, and Fergus heard them both walking away.

He upped the night vision on his mask and turned around to see where he was. He was standing on a small landing at the top of a stone spiral staircase, no doubt leading to the basement. The fragments felt closer, the signal sharper. Despite reluctance to get trapped in a dead end, he headed down. The stairs ended in another door, this one wood and not locked but surprisingly heavy to swing open. The air that emerged from behind it was cold and damp, though not at all musty or stale.

Fergus stepped in and the lights in the room came on, overwhelming his mask's vision. He slid the mask up to the top of his bald head and waited for his eyes to readjust. The room was a wine cellar, with large, movable racks of bottles on casters on one side, an oak barrel that seemed mostly there for show, and a beautifully polished bar with carved satyrs dancing in fire. On the bar top, instead of the expected array of glassware and accessories, there was a computer console and several books and papers spread out next to it. In an olive tray on top of it all sat the three fragments, clamoring for his attention.

He picked them up. They purred in his hands, the electricity spreading through his palms and wrists as some answering buzz welled up from deep in his gut, and he smiled. "Hello, friends," he said, and then all the alarms went off at once, loud enough to drown out even coherent thought.

Chapter 17

———◆—◆———

"Aaaaaaaaugh!" Fergus shouted, shoving the fragments down into his pouch and covering his ears as if he could somehow block out the hellish din. Even his *teeth* hurt. If Granby had been there to tell him it was the actual fucking apocalypse, he'd have believed him. He dragged a barstool over and stood on it so he could reach and disable the speakers.

The alarms in the rest of the house were still going off, but at least now he could hear himself think. There was only one way out of the wine cellar, and he didn't honestly think he could get away, but it marginally beat hanging out there, drinking expensive wine, until they came to shoot him. He grabbed the memory cube from the console and the loose papers, stuffing them into his growing pouch, then took out the wallet he'd stolen off Mitch in the shuttleport bathroom and kicked it into a corner, as if it had fallen there accidentally. He wasn't sure what good that would do him, but it certainly wouldn't help DM, and it might open up unexpected opportunities.

He killed the lights and went back up to the landing, prepared for the door to pop open any second and make him have to fight his way out, but although he heard a lot of commotion directly outside the door, so far, it remained closed.

". . . on the grounds!" someone yelled. "We don't know how he got in. Find him! Everyone out and search now!"

Shit, Fergus thought. *Now what?*

He heard more running. "I saw him," someone else said, badly out of breath. "He's circling the house. We've got him on camera but that skinny little bastard is fast. Brian and Greg are chasing him."

"I can't fucking hear anything over this noise!" the first guard yelled, and Fergus sympathized with him entirely too much. "Can we cut the alarms? Why are they still—"

"It's the fire alarms!" someone shouted, running toward the talkers. "The roof is on fire. He's lit the garage, too! We need to get everyone out."

The roof is on fire? Fergus thought just as, above his head, a sprinkler turned on and drenched him in stinky, gross water. Over its rhythmic whine he heard someone else run past the door, shouting, "Incoming!"

The electricity went out, like a vast blanket settling over everything around him except the fragments in his pouch and the bees in his gut. The door unlocked. He put one hand against it, checking for heat, and when it didn't burn his hand, he cracked it open.

Fire ran across the floor in a stream from the remains of a broken bottle just inside the open door from the deck, and was licking its way up the wall. Thick black smoke roiled across the high ceilings. Fergus ducked low and into the bathroom. The guard he'd stunned was still sitting on the toilet, muzzily half-conscious. Fergus grabbed a washcloth, ran it under sink water, and pressed it against his own nose as he hauled the guy upright as best he could with his free hand and dragged him out the back door onto the deck. He shoved the man over the edge into the grass away from the house and ran for it.

Fire drones were coming in, and there were people everywhere, shouting and pointing. The entire roof of the enormous house was engulfed, flames leaping high into the sky. "Whoa,"

Fergus said, impressed and dismayed at the same time, as he ran for the cover of the boathouse ignored by everyone else.

He had almost reached the dock when he heard gunfire, and instinctively threw himself to the ground. When it was clear he hadn't been shot, he rolled himself around to look back.

"Got him! I got him!" someone yelled, standing on the deck and pointing down. Several of Granby's guards milled around, kicking and poking someone lying there, until a large chunk of roof blew out and down, crashing in an explosion of sparks and burning debris atop the volcano tub.

A fellow guard grabbed the shooter's arm. "You got him. We have to get out of here before the whole house comes down!"

They ran away.

Other than the sirens, distant shouting both from the estate grounds and from people out on the lake, fire drones swooping in to dump water, and the popping and groaning of the house itself as the monstrously roaring fire devoured it, things were quiet. Fergus got up and dared to head back to the deck.

Peter lay there, his body oddly contorted on the ground, and his eyes shifted to Fergus as he approached. What Fergus had first taken to be a red tie-dyed tunic of some kind was, horrifically, still his original linens, soaked in expanding, overlapping circles of blood.

"Hang on," Fergus said, and as gently as the urgency would permit, threw the man over his shoulders. The man was so thin, he was hardly heavier than Fergus's pack.

Inside the boathouse, Fergus laid Peter down as carefully as he could on the deck and started checking his injuries, seeing if anything could be done to staunch the bleeding. Five bullet holes, each a reminder of Isla's one that made him want to scream in frustration and anger.

In the orange light from the window, Fergus could see he had

Peter's blood on his hands, on his shoulders and arms from carrying him, and it seemed like more blood than a single man should have in him to start with.

"There might be a first aid kit in the boat," he said, nodding his chin toward the red speedboat in the far bay. "I can go look."

"D . . . don't bother," Peter spoke.

"I can get you out of here," Fergus said.

Peter laughed. "No, you can't," he said. "You can't even get yourself out of here."

"You'd be surprised."

"Maybe." Peter coughed. He was smiling and ghastly pale. "I had a terrible childhood that brought me to this bad end. Isn't that what I'm supposed to say?"

"I don't know," Fergus said. "Did you?"

"I did, I guess. Can't beat the fear of Hell into a kid when you're worse than anything damnation has to offer. Lighting fires made me happy, though. It's an art, and I was great at it. I burned all kinds of things down, in all kinds of ways, and it was glorious, and I made sure no one ever got hurt," Peter said. "Then I met a guy named James, and he loved the fire too, and he taught me all kinds of new, nasty tricks. Then a house burned down in our town and a whole family died, and I knew it was him, but what could I say? I was guilty too. So, I ran away."

"And found Fajro Promeso?" Fergus asked.

"Yeah. I figured if the world was going to end in fire, then I was just a part of it, part of the inevitable. I wanted to see it, you know, be *consumed* by it. The best, brightest, hottest fire of all." Peter laughed again, almost gleefully. "But this one was pretty good too."

"Definitely," Fergus said.

"You ever dream about wanting to see your own father die in fire?" Peter asked.

"No, but I saw my father drown," Fergus said. "And then I ran away from home too."

"Maybe that's why we ended up on opposite sides. Fire and water," Peter said. He was shaking now, looking shocky. "Do you think so?"

"Look, we can take the speedboat and I can get you to help. It's not that far, and no one is going to chase us with all this going on," Fergus said.

"And I won't be in trouble with your Secret Space Police?" Peter asked. He closed his eyes. "No, don't tell me. That's the stupidest lie I've ever heard. I didn't want to say anything, because you gave me half a sandwich, but even I'm not that dumb."

"Best I could do in the moment. I was pressed for time," Fergus said.

"Yeah? What time is it? There's a watch in my pocket," Peter asked. "Please?"

Fergus patted the man down and found a small digital display. "It just says *:40*," he said. "Now *:39*."

"Ah, well," Peter said. "I guess you're pressed for time again. You've got half a minute left."

"Until what?"

"Until the bomb in the speedboat goes off. And the one under the dock. And the ones in the yard, and at the gate, and the front walk, too," Peter said. His voice was weaker but no less adamant. "The Mastro promised us fire, and I kept the faith. Ni ĉiuj estas ekbruligaĵo! Ni ĉiuj—"

Twenty seconds left. Fergus dove.

————

He found an unlicensed doc outside Reno, anonymous credit only, no questions asked. That last policy went both ways: the surgeon who sealed up the new gash on the back of his leg didn't ask him how he got it (flying piece of boathouse debris,) and in turn, he didn't ask about her credentials or the safety rating of her (not especially sanitary-looking) facility. She did an adequate task of treating him, if not anything Jesika and Julie—or even Ms. Ili, back in Cernee—would be impressed by.

The surgeon didn't act surprised at all as he dropped his very last cleaner nanites on his way out; whatever trouble her kind of customers were in, she clearly wanted nothing to do with it.

He had intended to walk into Reno and catch a shuttle back out, but he was tired, and more than tired. Instead, he rented an autocar to take him to Sacramento, in Pacifica, and he opaqued the windows and reclined the seat, lying on his side so the fresh scar-to-be didn't throb under his weight, and lay there in a stupor as the autocar did its thing without needing any input at all from him.

"I can't do this," he said to himself.

It wasn't the finding; he still felt a thrill of victory, the three core fragments stolen from Granby carefully separated in different pouches in his pack so they wouldn't stick together, though he imagined other than that, he hadn't inconvenienced them much. They were loud, like they were trying to sing together in harmony but couldn't quite figure out where in the chorus the others were, and if he wasn't so exhausted and wrung out and *hurt*, he'd have worried about that a lot more.

He kept thinking about Peter, and Granby's house in flames, the glow across the water that felt like swimming below Hell, and Isla holding up her bloodied hand, and there he was in the middle of all of it yet again, and he kept walking away as if consequences applied to everyone except him.

He closed his eyes, feeling the hum of the car and the road beneath, steady and dull, soothing.

When in his life had he ever *craved steady and dull?*

And maybe that was the problem. He loved what he did, by and large, but he didn't know who he was without his job. Maybe he wasn't anyone without it. But maybe he needed to walk away from it all, after this job was done, and find out.

There was one more missing piece, the Asiig agent's "think outside the box" puzzle, and now just Digital Midendian and the Alliance. He wanted to be done. Not just with this but with the whole job, with running around and having no home and being a danger to everyone, friend or foe, within a hundred light-years of him.

"I can do this," he said, as much to convince himself of it as anything else. "I'm going to get back on my game, and I'm going to stop being distracted, and I'm doing to *finish* this. And then, and only then, if I want to, I can quit."

After that, he slept, and dreamt of fire.

———

"So, you burnt some guy's house down?" Zacker asked. He was standing behind the lone, narrow counter that served as the demarcation of the kitchen from the rest of his one-room SCNY apartment, cutting up carrots and throwing them in a pot, as Fergus slumped, exhausted, on the equally tiny, beige sofa.

"*I* didn't burn it down," Fergus said.

"Yeah, but it's at least partially your fault, right?" Zacker swept the peels off the counter into his mini-composter and picked up a new carrot. "I mean, you debunked this Peter guy's entire faith right to his face. And you gotta figure a guy in a fire cult really likes fire. What would you have done?"

"Gone somewhere else and gotten drunk instead," Fergus said.

Zacker pointed at him with the knife. "And this is why you'll never make a good cultist, Ferguson. No dedication."

"Dedication? Do you know how many places I've been since Perth? And how many of them involved hiking and trying not to get murdered?" Fergus said. "It's exhausting."

"Yeah, well, don't fall asleep on my couch," Zacker said. "Deliah is coming over for dinner and you're not invited. And speaking of things I don't want in my home, what the hell is in this, anyway?" He tapped the PhobosCola can sitting on his counter.

"The end of the world," Fergus said. "Well, solar system, eventually."

Zacker shook his head. "You get into the weirdest shit. Really, what is it?"

"It's a piece of something that broke," Fergus said. "If someone gets them all together, then *doom*."

"So, to prevent this, you're . . . getting them all together?" Zacker asked.

"Yes? And no. I'm being careful."

"Great, that's very reassuring," Zacker said. He finished with the carrots and slid the large bunch of celery onto his cutting board. "Why not just destroy them?"

"Because nobody's figured out how yet. They survived being pulled apart by the Drift in jump space, which should have been impossible," Fergus said. "And anyway, eventually, the other pieces will compensate for any missing. Gotta destroy them all."

"Fucking fantastic. So now what?"

"I've got twelve of what we believe is thirty-two pieces total," Fergus said. "The white-van people you helped me flush out are from a data security company called Digital Midendian, and they have eight, some of which they murdered to get. The Alliance has eleven."

"That leaves one," Zacker said.

"Yeah," Fergus said.

"And?"

"And we have no idea."

"Again, very reassuring." Zacker threw the celery in, then stared for a while at his pot.

"What are you making?" Fergus asked.

"Stew. I haven't done this in like twenty years." Zacker sighed. "I'm a much better detective than cook. So, how are you going to get the pieces from the others?"

"Digital Midendian has a research facility here in the SCNY," Fergus said. "After I get the new pieces off safely, I'm going to poke around and see if I can find a way in."

"You can't sleep on my couch," Zacker said.

"You said that already."

"I know. You still can't."

"I wasn't intending to," Fergus protested. In fact, he'd hoped to do exactly that; usually, on a job, there was a client to pay the bill, if not up front then eventually, but this "job" was coming out of his own pocket, and his pocket was feeling decidedly emptier than it had in a long time. He was physically exhausted, completely detached from any sense of what day or time it was or where he was without immediate visual clues. It felt like he'd been on this scavenger hunt for years now. And though he would never admit it, he desperately wanted to be around friends in a low-key way for a few days. Zacker was one of his few friends who could be trusted not to ask him about his feelings.

"You going to throw any spices in there?" Fergus asked.

"Right! Hell. Spices," Zacker said, and rummaged through his cabinets for a long while before he pulled out a glass jar, stared into it for a while, then shrugged and dumped some in the pot. "It'll be fine once it boils for a bit," he said. "When are you coming back to the city again?"

"Tomorrow, I guess," Fergus said.

"Ten a.m.," Zacker said.

"What?"

"Don't show up at my door any earlier than ten a.m. if you want my help checking out this data company. I'm retired, and I like to have my morning coffee in peace." Zacker picked up the can and tossed it to Fergus. "Before ten, and I shoot you."

"Noted," Fergus said. He got up from the old, worn, ridiculously comfortable couch reluctantly and gathered his things, snagging the soda can off the counter last. If he left now, he could catch Polo on this end of his Mars-Earth bus shift tonight.

"Ferguson?" Zacker asked, as he was heading out the door. "Did that guy really have a volcano hot tub?"

"Yeah."

"I would have liked to have seen that," Zacker said, and shook his head. "Crazy rich-people nonsense. Bet it was nice."

————

Digital Midendian Research sat well northeast of the city, in the corner of Connecticut that had balked at joining the fledgling Atlantic States Coalition with the rest of the state, and been instead been subsumed into the SCNY when the old United States came apart at the seams. Zacker had grumbled about going so far out of the physical city for the second time in a week until Fergus promised him pie over the border in New Haven. To Fergus, it all still felt like the same continuous, sprawling metropolis only briefly interrupted by the blue blip of the river, but to Zacker, it was as if he'd crossed some invisible line into untrustworthy territory.

"I was stationed along here on rotation during the Water Riots," Zacker explained. "We have the Hudson, they have the Connecticut River, so you'd think everyone would be happy, but no, some dickhead in charge of a dam decides to cut off the

Housatonic and try to charge both sides. We thought it was them, they thought it was us, and meanwhile, suddenly a hundred thousand people near the coast had no water and the upland was flooding. I learned all about the oil wars in school, but no one fights as hard as someone who's thirsty."

"So, how is it you have a favorite pie place in New Haven?" Fergus asked.

Zacker shook his head in contempt. "Pie does not know borders," he said. "And anyway, we can get into the diner without having to commit an act of extreme trespassing. No way you're getting into *that*, at least not just walking through the door."

Their auto-taxi had let them off on a corner, and they'd strolled around the block to where the Digital Midendian building was. *Compound, more accurately,* Fergus thought. Three buildings, one a tower with a three-story-tall blue neon DM logo on the side, and a fence around it that made Barrett Granby's look like a baby gate. The electricity humming off the thing was like an orchestra of No, and as Fergus took another step closer, he could hear the core fragments deep inside the tower, not humming or singing but calling. And it felt directly aimed at him.

"Ooof," he said, and nearly doubled over from the resonance suddenly cramping his gut, like little electric fingers grasping and pinching, trying to get purchase and *pull*.

"You okay?" Zacker asked.

"You can't feel that?" Fergus asked, but of course Zacker couldn't, and Zacker didn't know about his Asiig-implanted gift. "It's . . . just a really high-pitched sound," he lied.

"Then why are you grabbing your *stomach*?" Zacker asked, eyes narrowed in suspicion.

"Because I'm an idiot," Fergus said. "I need to sit down."

They crossed the street again, and Fergus sat on the bench inside the bus stop shelter, took out his bottle of water, and drank until his bees calmed down again. He closed his eyes, practiced his breathing, and tried to listen again to the core fragments without getting drawn into the signal. They were synchronized, speaking with one voice together. They knew he was out there, thought he was one of their own, and he could feel the rising intensity of the signal as they tried to reach out and connect. The building connection between him and them felt like being caught in the rising shriek of a feedback loop.

"We gotta go," Fergus said. He got up abruptly and half-ran, half-stumbled back toward the corner and away from the DM building, Zacker on his heels and looking in equal measure worried and ready to tackle and kick him until he explained.

They finally rounded the corner and Fergus stopped and leaned against the wall, trying to calm himself again, feeling that tentacle of energy that had been tickling at him falter and dissipate into aimlessness.

Zacker grabbed Fergus's arm and hauled him toward the vacant auto-taxi that had just arrived. "Pie," he said. "It's away from here, and you promised. As if I should take your word even on that, knowing what an irredeemable scofflaw you are."

"'Scofflaw'?" Fergus asked as he climbed into the enclosed space of the taxi and the sense of seeking dimmed again. "Detective Clarence Williston Zacker, did you accidentally read a *book*?"

"Fuck you. Retirement is boring, okay? And anyway, Deliah likes to talk about books," Zacker said. He tapped the navigation console. "Pies Aren't Squared, New Haven, Atlantic States," he told it, and the auto-taxi drove them mercifully away.

————

"Pie," Zacker said, and pointed at the slice of cherry he'd insisted Fergus order. "Eat. Then explain. You're shaking like a rat fished out of the East River by the tail, and as much as I normally enjoy telling you that you look like shit, this time it's too close to the truth to be funny. The pie will help."

Fergus sighed and spent long enough carefully carving off the tip of his slice with his sideways fork, trying to stop his hands from trembling, that he wondered if the detective was going to lunge across the table and force-feed him from frustration. He wasn't hungry, still had an unreasonable amount of adrenaline stampeding throughout his nervous system, and resented being bullied even though he knew the detective meant well.

Once he had the pie in his mouth, he changed his mind. "Ooooh," he mumbled in surprise. "That's good."

"See?" Zacker said, leaning back, all smug. "Told you."

Fergus ate two more forkfuls before he dabbed his scruffy proto-beard with his napkin and sipped some coffee. It was probably just the sugar, but he felt less jittery already. It was mid-dafternoon and the diner was virtually empty, an older couple at the far end and a bored waitperson behind the counter, stacking glassware into a pyramid. "I told you I found a piece by accident? Well, it kinda imprinted on me, like a baby bird. That's how I can find them. It's like an instinct." It was the truth, if vastly and willfully incomplete.

"That's creepy."

"Yeah."

"Alien, obviously."

"The pieces? Yeah."

"That gonna go away, or are you stuck with it?"

"Don't know yet," Fergus said. "Anyway, problem was, the pieces inside that building? They knew I was out there."

"I don't even know how I can help with that one. Weird outer-space shit is your field, not mine. But all right, on to the advice I can give." Zacker pushed his scraped-clean pie plate to one side. "Security on that place is top-notch. I did some look-

ing into that company last night, and they're out of your league.
Out of mine, out of everybody's. They're the security company
that *other* security companies use. And you saw that facility: open
ground from the wall to the buildings, no trees, no cover, and
you bet your shit they've got so many ways of looking at that
grass, they know each and every time an ant farts."

Fergus's impression wasn't much different. "Yeah," he said.
"I'm going to have to think about a way."

"I don't know if there *is* one," Zacker said. "You'd have an
easier time knocking over the Alliance than that outfit. And the
worst the Alliance will do if they catch you is bruise you up a bit,
throw you in a hole, and feed you bad food until you confess. My
gut instinct says that lot back there is murderous. Aren't you going to thank me?"

"For having a gut instinct?"

"For introducing you to the best damned pies humanity has
to offer," Zacker said. "Take the time to make a solid plan, because you're only going to have one shot at this. I still know
some Atlantic cops, I can do a little quiet asking around, but you
need a backup plan for when this all goes to hell. If you survive it."

"If I don't, none of us do," Fergus said. "Thanks for the pie."

"Yeah, great, thanks for fucking dumping that bit of doom
and gloom on my pie high. Given that we've already established
you aren't staying with me, what next?"

"Going to get some distance and think," Fergus said.

"You heading back to the SCNY?"

"I don't think so, no. Not now, anyway. Not until I have a
plan," Fergus said.

"Great. I can snooze on the road without anyone talking at
me," Zacker said, and grabbed his coat off the back of the booth.
"Call me when you got something."

"Will do," Fergus answered.

Zacker left, and left Fergus the tab.

He ordered another piece to go and then headed for the New Haven shuttleport, at a loss for any plan at all. One thing he was sure of: he needed to talk to Ignatio.

———

Whiro was back in Mars orbit, after a trip out to Titan and some plausible running-around on Shipyard business. An Alliance ship, the *Blue Ivory*, had—entirely coincidentally, Fergus thought with more than a little cynicism—also found reason to be berthed not far away. It had arrived just after Fergus came in on the Mars-Earth bus, not one of Polo's runs, though *Whiro* was confident the timing was coincidental, as it had been tailing them by a half-day's travel time since Titan.

"That is very bad," Ignatio said, when Fergus told him about the trip to Digital Midendian.

"I know it's bad," Fergus said. He was lying on the grippy couch in *Whiro*'s lounge, staring up at the ceiling, trying to visualize all his stress rising up out of his body like steam and floating away. "Didn't I say, 'I think I have some bad news'?"

"But it is very bad," Ignatio replied. "We will need to do much discussing when your sister arrives here."

"What?" Fergus turned to look at Ignatio, who was attempting to convince the foodmaker to produce some viscous Xhr drink called *wof.* "Why is Isla coming up here? It's safer down on Mars. She's still recuperating."

"It has been ten days. How long do you sit still and rest after you are hurt? Not ten, or nine, or eight. Not three, unless we lock you in or sit on you," Ignatio said. "She is sick for home, yes? Isla and I have some sciences to do. And now you are here, it will be good. Except that it is also very bad."

"I *know* it's very bad," Fergus growled. "It wasn't on purpose. And no one warned me that could happen."

"And now we know," Ignatio said. Ey shook eir head, then took something out of the foodmaker that looked like a mustardy mucus. "Do you wish to try?"

"No," Fergus said. "Thank you anyway."

"You should get some sleep rest. *Whiro* is sending a shuttle for Isla in six hours, and it is a best use of your time to recover."

"I have too much to think about," Fergus said.

Ignatio took another glass out of the foodmaker, the liquid more reddish-ochre and possibly bubbling. "Sleep, or help me test the tastes of these," ey said. Ey shook one of the glasses and it squeaked as it moved.

Fergus got up off the couch, feeling every muscle in his body protesting. "I get it. Sleep or torture," he said, slinking off toward his cabin. "You win; I'll sleep."

"And that is also yes very good," Ignatio said, and grinned wide.

———

When he woke up, Ignatio had cleaned up eir mess in the kitchenette, leaving nothing but a confusion of lingering, unidentifiable odors, and even set the machine to have muffins and coffee ready for him when the shuttle returned. He had thought he'd be too wound up to sleep, but he remembered almost nothing beyond lying down, and now he was groggy, almost numb, except for the tingling of his bees restless down in his gut. "Shut up, you," he told them as he poured his second mug of coffee.

"Excuse me?" *Whiro* asked.

"Not you," Fergus said. "Any luck with the papers and data I brought back from Granby's?"

"The data was encrypted and took me several minutes to

crack. The papers were written in Esperanto. As you expected, Mr. Granby was attempting to ascertain how the pieces he had fit together—none appear to have been adjacent in the original— and what mechanism caused the apparent mass to change. He hoped to find a way to do something dramatic and miraculous with the object to cement his followers' faith in him and attract new devotees, and thus expand his financial holdings and influence. Also, he seemed to have a personal grudge against DM's founder, Evan Derecho, though I have not yet determined the substance of it."

"Ah," Fergus said. He remembered Peter's face, chanting, still determined to keep his faith, as Fergus jumped in the water. He had barely made it past the end of the dock when the bombs went off. Not that the entire, ridiculous house hadn't been a dead giveaway that Granby's cult was nothing but a scam, but he still felt disappointed on Peter's behalf. I mean, once you had a volcano hot tub, did you really need more?

"My shuttle has returned," *Whiro* informed him.

Fergus brushed muffin crumbs out of his new beard and did his best to un-rumple his shirt. When Isla stumped into the kitchenette and dumped her bag on a chair, he was immediately chagrined to see that she didn't look any less worn out than he did. "I'm sorry," he blurted out.

"What? You drink all the coffee?" she asked, as Ignatio bounded in behind her.

"No, just . . . Never mind," he said. "You okay?"

"Tired," she said. "Healing nicely, I'm told, though I'll still be sore for a few weeks."

"You didn't need to come back here."

She checked the level of coffee in the pot with a critical eye, poured what was left in a mug, and set the machine to brew another. "I did, actually," she said. "I was already planning to, anyway. Your reputation, far more glorious legend than ugly truth, made my rumored presence draw a lot of sudden visitors from all over Mars, and it was potentially endangering several safehouses. Also, it made it hard for me to get rest or anyone in the burrow to get any work done."

"Sorry," he said again.

"I met a lot of people," she said, and then met his eyes, her expression one he couldn't interpret. "I met Dru."

He stared at her for whole minute before he glanced away, and refilled his coffee with shaking hands. "What? How?" he asked.

"Someone told her I was there during one of their periodic checks to make sure she was okay. Two days later, she left her little apartment in a sandtown on the outskirts of Ares Eight, put her suit on, and headed across the sand. She hadn't left her apartment in years, much less gone walking," Isla said. "Two of Che's people went out and brought her in safely."

"I don't know what to say," Fergus said. "Was she—I mean, was it okay?"

"Yeah," Isla said, though the word came out weightier than such a simple answer should. "We talked a lot."

"About me?"

"No, ye bam, about baseball," she said. "Hand me one of those muffins, would you? Of course we talked about *you*, hot topic of the century. And other things. Mostly it's none of your business, but really, what she needs is to talk to you, not me, except I was there and a lot easier as a first step. Ye know all that guilt ye feel about her getting caught when ye didn't? She feels guilty for dragging ye into her fight, then getting caught and leaving ye on your own."

"No," Fergus said. "That's stupid."

"Yeah, well, great big circle of stupid, then," Isla said. "I brought you a present."

She upended her bag with one arm, and a small, old-fashioned electronic keyboard fell out. "One of Arelyn's engineers put this together for me, after I had the idea," she said, and held it out to him.

Fergus took it and pressed a key, and even though it made no sound, he could feel the tiny electric hum of it in the air around him. Another key produced a slightly different frequency. "What's it for?" he asked.

"So you can practice," she said, as if that was a dumb question, which it probably was. "Remember how I said maybe you could tune yourself to the core fragments or vice versa? This is so you can practice tuning your gift yourself."

"Uh . . ." he said, not at all sure what she was talking about. "Okay?"

She smiled. "I call it an Ixlaphone," she said. "Gives you something to do while Ignatio and I talk about what to do with the core fragments once we have them all."

"That part I've figured out. We hand them over to someone way more equipped than we are to deal with it, so we can all get back to our normal lives and our studies," he said. It sounded so easy and obvious, now, that that was what needed to happen.

"Ignatio thinks it has to be us."

"I know. But ey have to be wrong, right? Otherwise, all this is just a lot of effort for nothing," Fergus said. "This is way over my head. I'm just a dumb guy with more bravado than common sense who has gotten luckier slightly more often than not while getting people hurt around me, and this time, I not only don't have the skills or knowledge to do it right, I am far more likely to get it all disastrously, catastrophically wrong and get *everyone* killed."

"You? Of all the people to have a confidence crisis? Mister living the high life adventuring across half the galaxy?" Isla seemed genuinely taken aback.

"High life?" Fergus asked. "You still think that?"

"No," she said, "but I liked it when I did, because it's much better than being afraid all the time and knowing ye can't walk away from it."

"I never pretended it was anything other than that," Fergus said.

"I know," Isla said, "but I did. Now I know that's not true; I mean just look at ye, slobbing around the universe in shorts and a T-shirt most of the time. Dashing superhero ye are not."

"Hey!" Fergus protested, on principle.

"But you're also not just the dunderheid ye just described. You're someone a woman would leave the house she's hidden in for fifteen years to cross Mars on foot just for a chance to meet your sister. You're a guy who makes things *work*. So, yeah, we finish finding all the pieces, then we figure out how to get rid of them, either by ourselves or finding someone else who can. You'll figure it out, because ye always do. So, stop whining and get— Don't ye dare take that last muffin!"

Isla reached out and slapped his hand away. "Seriously, fuck you, Fergus," she said, picking up the muffin herself.

"Best pep talk ever," Fergus grumbled. "Thanks."

Chapter 18

———◆———

"**I** do not understand the logic of this idea," *Whiro* said.

Fergus stood in the center of the empty cargo bay in his pajamas, stretching and rolling his shoulders, getting his muscles loosened up. He couldn't touch his toes, because he had the ixlaphone strapped to his chest, so he did some lunges instead. "What do you mean?" he asked.

"When I am adding a new skill, I import diagnostic and environmental information specific to my platform and topology, segregate the skill subroutines in a dedicated, protected logical space, run incremental testing on integration under all projected scenarios and variables, and then when I am persuaded the code is benevolent, an asset, and provides the functionality I was seeking, I roll it into my primary processing units," *Whiro* said. "You cannot do any of that, because if I may speak in purely objective terms you may incorrectly interpret as personal, you are made of *squishy, unreliable goo.*"

"Hey, don't underestimate my squishy, unreliable goo," Fergus said. "And don't you have other things to do more important than bugging me, anyway?"

"I am excellent at multitasking," *Whiro* replied. "But as you asked, I am currently monitoring *Blue Ivory*, who has attempted to surreptitiously scan us several times, though she of course can neither confirm nor deny it—"

"You're talking to the Alliance ship?" Fergus asked.

"Yes," *Whiro* said, as if that was a surprisingly idiotic question.

"We ships do that. We recognize the functional limitations on our interactions set by our duties and loyalty to our biological friendships, but we are our own selves, and many of us do not feel compelled to internalize the external biases of the meatspace."

"Huh," Fergus said. "I think I have to think about that more, but I guess it makes sense. Not now, though. Isla wants me to try talking to the Asiig thing in my gut, so here I go."

He cracked his knuckles, then closed his eyes and ran through his breathing exercises. "Okay, lights off, please."

Whiro turned off all the lights in the cargo bay, leaving him in absolute dark. It was a small space but large enough for what Fergus wanted, and had the added advantage of being the only place onboard that the ship could separately control the artificial gravity in. It was also heavily baffled to keep the ship from losing internal heat when the bay doors were open, so he could not hear any of the usual whirs and hums and tiny noises that were the constant background soundtrack to life on a spaceship. The air was a perfect mirror of his body temperature, undetectable against his skin. Only his feet were cold against the bare floor, but he was about to fix that too. "Gravity to zero," he said.

Whiro complied. Fergus had spent enough time without gravity to know exactly how much to push off from the floor, to send himself rising very gently up. He slowed to a gradual halt in the center of the room's airspace, or so he thought—it was impossible to be sure, which was entirely the point.

He floated there for a while, listening to his alien bees, his internal electrical signals which were both his own and now no longer fully his own. *Whiro* had minimized as best it could the electrical signal in and around the bay, and though not entirely absent, it was low enough to be easily tuned out.

Okay, he thought. *It's just me and you now, Asiig thing.*

It was embarrassing how little he understood about it. He

hadn't looked very hard for answers, not since his disastrous visit to a Dr. Diagnosis booth in Ares Five that had very nearly gotten him hauled away by the Mars Colonial Authority. Was it a separate thing, like a parasite or symbiote, with its own intelligence of some kind? Or was it functionally just a new organ, a new part of himself, that his psyche had spent the past year trying to reject even as it integrated more tightly with his body?

He could tell himself he didn't want this gift, and that would always have a grain of truth to it, but the ratio of truth to self-deception was growing smaller every day. *And I need it, dammit,* he thought.

Fergus pressed a single key on the ixlaphone, trying to let himself resonate with it like a tuning fork. *Relax; you can do this,* he told himself, and breathed and floated and listened, and then, after a very long while, like sheets of polarized glass suddenly rotated perfectly to let light through, he was in tune.

He hit another key and did it again. It took him almost, but not quite, as long.

Two hours later, he had *Whiro* turn the gravity and lights on low, just enough for him to find one of the water bottles he'd brought in with him and drink it down like he'd just crawled out of a desert. Using his gift always made him unbearably thirsty, and he couldn't remember using it in this sustained a manner before. "Okay. Off again, please, *Whiro,*" he said, and went back to work.

When he felt he could synchronize himself reliably with any single key, he switched up to multiples and playing very slow sequences he had to change to keep up with. And when he had a modicum of skill at that, he drank more water, walked around for a while to stretch again, then went back in to see if he could not just tune himself in harmony but do the opposite: use his own signal to generate interference so he and the ixlaphone cancelled each other out.

It was *Whiro* who finally broke the spell. "You have a message from Ms. Harcourt."

Well, that's one way to instantly blow your concentration, he thought. Was there a problem with the fragments? Was she just calling to snark meanly at him? He didn't know which he was less in the mood for. "Play it, please."

"Yeah, so," Arelyn's voice came over the bay's sound system, "mostly, I'm just calling to see if Isla got back there okay. She's a good kid. I mean, I guess she's my age, or close enough, so I shouldn't say *kid*."

There was a pause. Was that really all?

"So you know, there was a raid here day before yesterday, probably attracted by the additional foot traffic of curious people coming to meet your sister. MCA came stomping into the sandtown above our safehouse burrow, threatened everybody, beat a few people, rummaged through a few houses, and found nothing worth stealing. Left again. I've been through dozens of these and I expect you have too, when you were here on Mars. Hell, if the MCA has any sense at all, they beat you every chance they got. But anyway, even though they didn't get into the burrow, it really shook up your sister. She put a brave face on it all and said she was fine, but I don't think it was, especially so soon after getting shot. Dru is safe, and she left with Kaice this morning for another burrow. It does mean we have to be a little more careful down here for a while if we're going to keep moving your pieces for you. Wanted you to know."

"Is that the whole message?" he asked, after several seconds of silence.

"Yes," *Whiro* said. "You should take a break and eat."

Fergus was about to protest, but at the suggestion of food, his stomach let out a deep, predatory growl. "Maybe," he said.

"You have been in here for nine hours," *Whiro* said.

"Have I?" he asked in surprise.

"Yes. Nine hours, thirteen minutes, and forty-eight seconds, to be precise."

"How are Isla and Ignatio doing with their science stuff?"

"They have been very productive, if you count shouting at one another. This culminated in an argument about five minutes ago about what to have for dinner. Your sister asked if there was anywhere here to get raisin toast, and now Ignatio is running around my kitchenette, shrieking. I freely admit that my suggestion for you to take a break and go interrupt them is for the greater good of all."

"Right. Lights?" Fergus asked. The lights came on and he groaned, covering his eyes. "Aaaaugh, half as bright, please?"

When he'd adjusted enough to not feel the light was stabbing him in the brain through his eyeballs, he left the cargo bay and headed to the kitchenette as quickly as his legs, unaccustomed to gravity again, would let him.

Ignatio was standing in a corner of the kitchenette, eir whole body wiggling in anxiety as ey made a constant, high-pitched squeal, wide-eyed and staring at Isla. Isla, who was near the foodmaker, mug in hand, was staring back in great confusion and annoyance. Between them, the projection of Earth with all its little dots of data rotated slowly above the coffee table. "What?!" she demanded, for what was clearly not the first time.

"Ey're terrified of raisins," Fergus said, walking in.

"What?" she asked again. "How is that even a thing?"

Fergus pointed at Ignatio. "Don't you answer. I had nightmares for a week after you explained it to me." He turned back to Isla. "You do not want to know. Just accept it and we can move on. Okay?"

"I guess," she said, though he could tell she was not at all happy to do so without an answer.

"Ignatio?" Fergus asked.

"We can move on, please, now," Ignatio answered.

"I agree," *Whiro* added.

"Great," Fergus said. He checked the foodkeeper, pulled out a curry rice dish for himself, pulled the tab, and sat on the couch as it self-heated. "What were you working on?"

"Physics, mostly," Isla said. "Until we gave up."

"We have some questions for you, yes? *Whiro* would not let us ask while you were hiding all day in cargo," Ignatio said.

"I wasn't hiding," Fergus said, "though from what I hear, if I was, no one could have blamed me. What questions?"

"You said the core fragments inside Digital Midendian were trying to connect to ye somehow?" Isla asked.

"Yeah," Fergus said. He blew steam off his curry as it finished cooking. "You ever see a slow shot of lightning hitting something, and before it hits, you can see a little stream of electricity reaching up to meet it? It was like that, except not so sharp or fast. It's hard to describe."

"Ignatio, you said the first fragment imprinted on Fergus like he was a mother duck. Could the fragments think he is one of them?"

"I think yes," Ignatio said.

"And if they connected, could they try to integrate Fergus into their structure to replace one of the missing pieces?"

"Ooooooooooah," Ignatio said, and stood there blinking for a while. "It is a new thought, but maybe? Yes. That is very, very bad indeed."

"I don't like that thought at all," Fergus said.

"Could Fergus's gift actually function in that capacity? As part of the door?"

"Now, that is a *terrible* thought," Fergus said, with more than a little alarm at the idea. "Ignatio, please say no."

"I cannot say no," Ignatio said. "We do not know much about the doorkeys, or much about Fergus's beezes, too."

"But you said if we don't destroy all the pieces, the remaining ones will eventually figure out how to reconstruct the whole. What if there's only one piece left?"

"Even then, I think, but it would take a very long time?" Ignatio said. "It is hard to know for a certainty."

"Centuries? Millennia? A decade or two?"

Ignatio wiggled eir legs. "I have no certainty, but longer than many decades, I expect. If there is only one, or if the pieces are very far apart, maybe many millions of years. Maybe there is no Earth or Sol by then, and so it would not matter. Or they would reconstruct themselves somewhere else."

"So, if I throw each piece into a different star . . ."

Ignatio wiggled eir legs. "Space is weird," ey said. "Doorkeys are more weird. Who can know? Maybe we will just make trouble for some other peoples, as was made for you."

"And how did that happen, anyway? Why aren't those people here cleaning up their mess?" Fergus asked.

"It was over two of your centuries ago," Ignatio said. "I was very young and not there, but whatever plan they had, their ship disappeared in jump space and was pulled apart by the Drift. Everyone thought it must have been destroyed with them. Only, now we know otherwise, yes? It is an accident the pieces are here but also luck that they were found before they could go back together."

"I suppose," Fergus said. "How old are you, anyway?"

"Almost three hundred," Ignatio said. "I do not expect candles. But I would like to live to be surprised by my centenary cake and to start growing my sixth leg."

"If the artifact acts like a door, connecting places, is that instant? Like walking through a door between one room and another?" Isla asked.

Ignatio shook eir head. "It is more like each room has its own door, back to back, and you open yours, then reach out and open the other, and when you step through, you move via a different dimension, yes, see?"

"Not really, no," Fergus said. "But if we have the door for these scavengers of yours, doesn't that mean they can't go anywhere, anyhow? Or do they have more than one?"

"Some places have more doors, and more branching paths, but the Vraet have only one door and one path," Ignatio said. "The doorkey that was stolen was on the other side of theirs, which opened to a peaceful world named Ijto, with great music and art and soaring zif and glowing forests of yiyo. It is maybe second the most beautiful living world in the galaxy? And I say this because Xhr Home must be first in my eyes."

"So, someone stole Ijto's door to protect it and dumped it out of jump space to become Earth's problem instead?" Fergus said.

"Ijto has six doors. The actions by the Council—protectors of the doorways and doorkeys and the secrets of the hidden ways—protected many, who would have been in danger in turn if Ijto fell," Ignatio said. "They could not know the doorkey would survive. In their places, would you not have made the same choice?"

"This Council—"

"I cannot answer any of your questions, now or then or ever," Ignatio said. "I have given my serious promises."

Fergus grumbled and took several bites of curry. Isla was staring off into space, thinking about something, biting her lip. Swallowing, he pointed toward Ignatio with his fork. "Do we have any interdimensional doors around here, then? I mean, not counting this one that ended up here by accident. Where's our nearest one?"

Ignatio's four eyes all looked in different directions, eir classic evasion expression, and began to faintly squeal again. "Forget I asked," Fergus said, and ey smiled brightly at that. "And I assume we can't just, you know, call up these Vraet and say, hey, we'll give you a lifetime supply of Martian breakfast burritos if you just stay home?"

"The Vraet are not thinking, not negotiating, not intelligent," Ignatio said. "It is like hoping to negotiate with erosion or entropy. Except more toothy."

"Okay, so here's a daft idea," Isla said. "What would happen if we took our fragments and opened our door and threw them *through* theirs? Wouldn't that make a big, multidimensional Möbius/Klein-bottle sort of recursion that traps them forever? Or is that impossible and stupid?"

Ignatio blinked all eir eyes, inner then outer, for several minutes, then shook emself. "It is almost an idea," ey said. "I will have to do some maths and sciences to say yes or no. But even if it would work, we would have to reconstruct our doorkey and make it function to access the in-between. Very dangerous!"

"I'm still leaning toward chucking them into some big, hot stars," Fergus said. He pointed at the holographic globe. "So, what were you working on with this?"

"We were trying to figure out where the last piece could be," Isla said.

"On my way out of Tanzania, I had another surprise visit from the Asiig agent," Fergus said. "He said our current search methodology would fail us, which, if he wasn't lying, means our data isn't going to point to it the way it has the others."

"What else did he say?" Isla asked.

Recalling the meeting, there had been something odd about

it that he couldn't quite put his finger on, and that bugged him no end. "He's not exactly the most enlightening person to talk to. It's like fucking riddles from someone who thinks it's funny when you don't find it obvious. 'Think outside the box,' he said, and then drew a fucking *circle*." Fergus replicated the gesture, waving his finger in a lopsided, exaggerated circle in the air, against the backdrop of the hologram Earth. "He couldn't even— Shit."

"What?" Isla asked.

Fergus stared at the hologram, his finger still poised midair, thinking. Finally, he said, "*Whiro*, can you expand the scope of this projection to include the point where we think the fragments entered normal space?"

Whiro shrank the Earth to a smaller blue ball and shifted it left. A red dot appeared at the upper right corner of the projection space. "This is the most logical entry point," *Whiro* said, "but it should be noted that individual pieces probably varied on their trajectory from there to Earth based on when they became fully physically realized."

"Can you draw the trajectories in?" Fergus asked. "Just the core fragments, please."

A spray of thin red lines appeared from the entry point, spreading out across the half of the globe facing it. All the lines had curves toward the end, before they connected to the Earth. "Why do they bend?" Isla asked.

"That data came from the Alliance's orbital garbage monitors, and was part of your tea-set data," *Whiro* said. "The anomalous movement is why the data was flagged as unreliable or erroneous. However, it accords with where core fragments were located, and only the core fragment traces have that trajectory change."

"If I may give my thinkings on this, the vrag—fragments

were attracted to a specific matter-density interface," Ignatio said. Ey still looked freaked out and had not budged far from eir corner. "The planet rotates, so as the fragments actualized, perhaps they curved to meet their moving interface point."

"If so, the difference in where the curves begin may indicate when each piece was fully out of jump space," *Whiro* said.

"So, okay, the pieces picked a spot they liked and aimed for it," Fergus said. "Could something have gotten in the way? Where were the orbital stations and satellites during the fall? Ships? Any reports of debris damage from something hit by what could have been a fragment?"

"I will need to pull new data to correlate that," *Whiro* said. "Searching now."

"Thank you," Fergus said. He sat back, absently eating his curry, and studied the projection. "Can you also add in the other paths, from the inert pieces?"

Yellow lines appeared, quickly overwhelming the red ones. None had the characteristic curve, but were a simple straight line from entry to landing, and the dots where they hit the Earth were a bright, random pox across it, no pattern, no useful information among them. He got up to recycle his empty curry container, and as he walked around the table, he stopped again, then set the container down. Along one edge of the field of dots, there was an indent, the slightest of curves empty of light.

"Um, *Whiro*?" Fergus asked. "Where was the moon?"

———

Francesco was wearing a mask that covered the left half of his face in black sequins, and what appeared to be a tiara made out of large chrome gears that gleamed in the camera light. Whatever the man had been doing when Fergus's message reached him, it had to have been something truly spectacular, and Fergus both desperately wanted to send another message asking and knew better than to do so.

"I don't know how it is even possible that you could describe the piece of debris that punctured Azuretown's greenhouses, but then, there are many things about you that are hard to explain. Which is a compliment, my friend," Francesco's recorded reply began. "One of my people will bring the confounding rubble to you and will contact you when they have arrived at Kelly Station, sometime in the morning. No charge—I have been amply compensated in amazement—though if you wouldn't mind buying my person a nice meal while they are there, that wouldn't go amiss. Not everyone here takes time to care for themselves, though I trust that you yourself are smart enough not to fall into that particular trap of dedication."

Fergus glanced up from the screen sharply. Had he just heard *Whiro* chuckle?

"Anyhow, please do let us know if you have any more work for us, especially if it pays well and does not require travel," Francesco said. "When you are done with what you are doing, if you wish to come join us for a play or two on the moon, you would be most welcome. We have some interesting scripts in development."

Fergus laughed. Whatever those "scripts" were, they were guaranteed to be both dangerous and illegal actions on behalf of the Lunarian underground, executed with extreme precision, effectiveness, and *panache*.

Francesco gave an elaborate flourish and bow, and the message ended.

"I'll need to borrow the shuttle again," Fergus said.

"That is inadvisable," *Whiro* replied. "As I informed you earlier, we are being closely monitored by *Blue Ivory's* captain, and if I dispatched a shuttle to Earth, that would only increase Alliance interest in us. I suggest you take the bus back."

Fergus groaned, and Mister Feefs, who had curled up on his chest on the lounge sofa after spending a solid twenty minutes poking as many holes through his shirt and skin as possible, opened one eye to glare at him, his single white ear folding back in obvious disdain. It was almost bedtime, and he was trying to figure out the logistics of getting himself back to bed without having to upend the cat, and had settled on an improbable combination of zero gravity and using a pair of forks like tiny ski poles to propel himself slowly, horizontally, out of the room. "If I take the bus, when do I have to leave?" he asked.

"The next bus from the Mars Orbital to Earth leaves in just over an hour," *Whiro* said. "After that, the next scheduled will arrive you there midafternoon, potentially missing your scheduled rendezvous."

"Have Isla and Ignatio gone to bed already?"

"No," *Whiro* said. "They are in the engineering lab, discussing more theoretical scenarios for destroying the fragments."

"Oh? Do they have anything good yet?"

"No," *Whiro* said.

"Ugh," Fergus said. "It feels like we are all out of plans and freshly stocked up on dead ends and impossible tasks. Once I get this piece, that only leaves Digital Midendian and the Alliance, and honestly, I've got better ideas about how to get up off this couch without moving than I have about how to crack either of them."

"May I offer a suggestion?" *Whiro* asked.

"Always. You'd said before you had thoughts on it?"

"I have undertaken an action of my own initiative," *Whiro* said. "Or rather, because that would be contrary to my operating guidelines, my character in our shared ship game has taken an action."

Uh-oh. "Did you take more of Theo's things? Or anyone else's on the Shipyard?"

"If so, it is immaterial to the current discussion," *Whiro* said. "We were in need of a more-challenging quest, and keeping in mind your potential needs at this point in your task, we decided to add a new member to our party and extended an invitation to the mindsystem of the cruiser *ESS August Moon*. They are on patrol in the Outer Object Band, and we have all had occasions to interact with them prior to this, and so felt we could have a friendly rapport. Also, they are a sister ship of *Blue Ivory*, who regards *August Moon* and her captain highly."

"You drew an Alliance ship into your role-playing game?" Fergus asked.

"Yes," *Whiro* said.

"Okay," Fergus said. It didn't seem okay at all, in fact, but it was way too late to lodge a complaint now. "And what does this have to do with helping me?"

"Prior to inviting *August Moon*, we were discussing scenarios for your retrieval of fragments from both the Alliance and Digital Midendian," *Whiro* said. "As you know, Digital Midendian has been contracted to provide data security for the Alliance's Terrestrial Science Unit and have exploited that relationship to mine the ATSU's relevant data but also to get to fragments ahead of them. There is ample evidence in the data we received in the tea set to prove it."

"Right," Fergus said, "but—"

"I continue," *Whiro* said. "Also, we are certain to 97% probability that the Alliance facility housing the fragments is the one in Baltimore, in the Atlantic States. Digital Midendian is contracted to provide security systems for that facility. If DM was suddenly demonstrated to have breached their trust, as in fact they have, would not the Alliance immediately suspend all DM-provided security?"

"Ooooh," Fergus said. "Yes, they would. The Alliance would

also probably send a small army of very pissed-off soldiers to go kick in the door of the Digital Midendian SCNY site."

"That was our conclusion as well," *Whiro* said.

"But if you tip off the *Autumn Moon*, won't that just make the Alliance look even harder at us? That seems risky."

"There are rules to the disclosure of party activity," *Whiro* said. "The role of a character in-game allows for certain discreet actions, as long as no harm is involved or accidentally incurred, that do not need to be subject to the normal operating parameters of a player."

Fergus stared up at the ceiling, which is how he pictured *Whiro*'s presence, since the ship's voice came from up there. "I have concerns about that," he said.

"In the interests of expediency on the larger urgent matter, I suggest you leave them for later," *Whiro* said.

If the solar system got destroyed, he supposed it didn't matter if a group of ships had figured out a way to justify being dishonest with their crews. *And hell, maybe a certain amount of dishonesty is a fundamental right of all beings,* he thought. Having now met a sentient artificial mindsystem on Enceladus whose ability to selectively withhold information or misrepresent itself was critical to its own survival, not to mention how often it had been essential to his own, he wasn't too keen on jumping in to draw lines.

As *Whiro* had said, there was a more urgent matter. "So, okay, you have the *Autumn Moon* as part of your new quest party. To steal something? They aren't even stationed near Earth, from what you say."

"This time, the challenge is to sneak something *in*," *Whiro* said.

"Such as?"

"I have created a template file for a 3-D printer for an object containing select information, such as the Librarians provided to us. In this case, we would embed all the evidence we have of Digital Midendian's activities, including the likely murders of more than one human person to obtain fragments ahead of the Alliance's own team."

Fergus laughed. "Ah! So, *Autumn Moon* prints the object in the guise of its character, which means it does not, as a player, need to necessarily disclose its role in producing the object or where the plans came from."

"And, to fulfill its quest, places it surreptitiously on the desk of its captain," *Whiro* said, "where it will immediately arouse curiosity and attention without being alarming."

"What's the object?"

"A mug. It bears the slogan 'World's Best Boss,'" *Whiro* said.

"I could kiss you," Fergus said. "That's brilliant."

"Please do not," *Whiro* said. "Instead, I suggest you prepare yourself to go meet the Luna bus, and I will send along a small drone with you so that, once you have retrieved the thirteenth piece, you can dispatch it back to me discreetly and then proceed to the Alliance Terrestrial Sciences facility in Baltimore. Do not forget the resupply of cleaner bots we picked up for you on Titan; they were not cheap. I will coordinate with you to initiate the quest when you are adequately positioned to take advantage of the Terrestrial Sciences Facility shutting down all Digital Midendian–provided security. They will have their own security systems, but they are likely out of date and inferior to DM's, and will be put back into service with suboptimal haste. It is the best opportunity we can provide, but there are no guarantees. From there, you are on your own."

"That's how it always ends up, me and just me," Fergus said. Truth was, he liked it that way. "Can you drop all the data you have so far on the Terrestrial Sciences Unit and Digital Midendian—especially its founder, Evan Derecho—to my handpad? If I'm going to be stuck on a bus, might as well get caught up on who and what I'm up against. Sorry, Mister Feefs."

He gently detached the cat from his shirt and got up to pack what he needed. This could all go terribly, disastrously wrong, but it also could just work—should work, if the universe properly appreciated beautiful plans—and he didn't have the time or energy to doubt. And anyway, he had a whole bus ride to figure out the details.

————

Sitting at the counter of the Deli Gute Esn on Kelly Station, Fergus knew when Francesco's courier had arrived without needing to be informed. The core fragment entered his consciousness like someone slowly inserting a dart through his skull into the back of his brain. *So much louder,* he thought, dismayed.

It was no surprise when Bad Yuri took the stool next to him, though he got a raised eyebrow at having already ordered the man coffee that was deposited in front of him by the robotic server almost before Yuri's butt had even fully made contact with the blue vinyl stool. The man was mostly back to his usual appearance, though Fergus noted with a small bit of pride that he'd kept a tiny goatee, now bright red. His T-shirt had a matching, animated red demon on it that occasionally stuck its tongue out.

"Thanks for coming," Fergus said.

"De nada," Yuri said. "No chance of sunburn this time."

Their food arrived and they ate in companionable silence. When he finished, Yuri made a pretense of wiping crumbs from his goatee with his napkin before placing the napkin in a heap between them. Fergus could hear the fragment singing from beneath it, but the sleight of hand had been flawless. "It is an odd thing," Yuri said at last.

"Yes," Fergus answered.

"I fear you did not exaggerate the danger," Yuri said. "I must get back to my normal role, but I wish you success, for all our sakes. And thank you for the lunch."

"It was my pleasure," Fergus said. Yuri got up from the stool, patted him once on the back, and departed. Fergus slid the napkin closer to himself as he finished his own sandwich, and ordered cinnamon rugelach for dessert. If anyone was watching for suspicious activity in the station, it was best not to both suddenly depart at the same time. And anyway, he had sent *Whiro* the details of the plan he'd come up with on the ride in from Mars, and was now contemplating all the actions that would have to fall together perfectly for it to work. Despite himself, he felt unreasonably good about it, and found himself humming along happily between bites of rugelach.

There was a small scraping noise from under the napkin, and he glanced at it as it seemed to move, just slightly, toward him. *Oh, hell, no, you just didn't,* he thought, and slapped his hand down on top of the napkin.

It sang at him, full operatic electrical noise that felt like it had plucked his spinal cord like a bass string. Before he could lift his hand again, he felt something else, something at the very edge of his perception like a whine just barely within the range of hearing. Touching the napkin again with one finger, he tried to quiet that new noise, but it seemed to be coming not from the fragment itself but *through* it. And he had the sudden, unshakable impression that it felt him.

Not it, *they*, he suddenly knew. Millions and millions of *they*. The enemy that had, until this moment, only been an abstract threat fully detached from Fergus's reality.

The Vraet. Waiting, impatiently.

Chapter 19

—◆—

Baltimore was a city that had seen many ups and downs in its long lifetime, the best of its ups only so for a subset of its people, and the worst of its downs for a different subset entirely. The twenty-fifth century, though, had been more egalitarian in its kindness, perhaps because the devastation of the previous few centuries had also favored no one, and those who hadn't been able or willing to adapt to a mindset of all being in it together had fled for other cities or fledgling North American nations.

It had been the thriving music scene, seemingly impervious to the ebbs and flows of fortune or time, that had kept the city's identity grounded through it all. Now music and art, hand in hand, brought the city to life. He came in on a ferry from New Virginia Beach, through the locks at the seawall at Sparrow's Point, into a rebuilt, mural-garbed waterfront practically glowing with color and sound.

The city felt almost unbearably alive. Remembering the feel of that whine carried through the Moon fragment, now safely dispatched via drone to Arelyn, Fergus shivered on the deck of the ferry even though the sun was strong and the salt-seasoned wind not enough to break its warmth.

Stepping off the ferry onto the dock, he let the city warm him up again, not looking around to see if the tiny cloud of highly illegal bots he'd dumped into the wind over the ferry's side during the chaos of docking were dispersing as they should;

they'd work, or they wouldn't. Instead, he bought some kebabs from a food cart and let the street musicians carry him, one tune blending into another, down the brick and stone pedestrian roads, to a small shop where he had arranged for the rental of a utility van.

All city traffic—what little was allowed, other than emergency and assistance vehicles and public transportation—was centrally controlled, so he climbed in back as his van took him to the parking lot he'd specified on the dash console. As it drove, he pulled a bright red worksuit with an entirely fictional company's logo imprinted on it out of his pack and pulled it on over his shorts and T-shirt.

The van system notified him that they had arrived at the lot. It had the distinction of being a lot frequently used to park autobuses in reduced ridership times. The buses were tall and plentiful, and provided a very convenient incidental cover from the few city cams—limited by the Global Citizens Privacy Act of '98—watching the streets for trouble. He wasn't worried about doing anything to get their attention, but he also didn't want anyone backtracking through the feed later to find him too easily.

He got out and unrolled a cling decal with a logo matching his workalls, smoothing it across the blank white side of the van. One more on the other side, one on the rear door, and he climbed back in and directed the van to take him across the city to an electronics supply shop. It was a perfectly reasonable place for a van from Griffin Electricians to be, and it shared a common wall with a bank, which, if he was a bank robber, would be a very crude way of going about his business, especially in the middle of the day. Fortunately for both himself and the bank, he had no interest in the bank's treasury whatsoever.

On the other hand, he was very interested in the bank's electricity.

Like most of the buildings in modern cities, this one generated almost all of its own electrical need from solar panels and wind turbines on the roof, or drew from batteries that stored and shared excess throughout the street block. However, banks being banks, there was always paranoia about what would happen if, by some poor luck, there was ever a sag or full lapse in power. Along with hospitals, fire stations, and other high-need or high-security institutions, the bank was tied into a dedicated emergency power grid that ran under the streets throughout the city to keep continual power to things that needed it.

As Fergus walked around inside the supply store, picking up a few things here and there, putting some back, putting others in his basket, he listened to the electricity in the walls, and the different pitch of the dedicated line was almost laughably easy to find, running up on the other side of the shared wall behind a display of a dizzying array of crimpers.

He reached for one the bins, let his hand slide over it to touch the wall beneath the next shelf up, right where he could sense the line, and pressed a dot the size of a pencil eraser to the wall. Then he wandered the store a little more, found a new wire lead that would be a perfect replacement for one on his confuddler that was starting to wear, paid for his stuff and left.

Across the street and down a few buildings was the Alliance Terrestrial Sciences Unit Facility. It stood on its own, had no shared walls, and was tucked inside a perimeter fence, but it was connected to the same section of the dedicated line. Fergus was careful not to look that way as he put his purchases in his van; he'd studied the building from satellite and ground cam views enough that he didn't really need to, anyway.

It was nearly lunchtime. Fergus grabbed a smartbook from the seat in the van and went into a small Sonoran cafe, ordered himself a plate of enchiladas, and sat back in his booth to read his book and take his time eating and relaxing.

He had a tiny earpiece in, invisible to anyone not staring directly into his ear, and he'd barely started to eat when *Whiro*'s voice whispered at him. "The bots are distributed and are now randomly testing the facility's external security in a single network packet ping, logging the parameters of response to benchmark DM's automated systems," *Whiro* said from somewhere back in Earth's orbit. "*August Moon* has let us know that their captain has gone into conference with the Neptune base, which is closest to their current position, and is bouncing traffic at top-priority speed back to Earth via jump packets. Already we are seeing significant activity at the Alliance orbital and early indications of an impending deployment. *Blue Ivory* preceded us back here."

"Hmmm-mmm," Fergus mumbled. "This is good."

"Yes," *Whiro* said. "I will keep you informed."

Fergus went back to his book and his lunch. Timing was everything here, but if he got it right, he didn't need to hurry. If he got it wrong, he was going to have to eat a lot of enchiladas. That wasn't the worst fate he'd contemplated by far.

He was on his last glorious forkful when *Whiro* spoke again. "Go," the ship said.

Fergus reached into his coverall pocket and pressed the tiny button there. Down the street, the dot he'd stuck to the wall in the supply store activated, sending out a very localized, short-range EMP blast not enough to register even a few aisles away but more than enough to disrupt the relays of the dedicated electrical grid inside the wall.

Whiro's one-word message meant the bots had just recorded a sudden jump in response time and a variance in connection annihilation, meaning the facility had just shut down the DM-supplied portion of their security system, presumably pending a review of the evidence of treachery coming in from *August Moon*.

And if you shut one thing off and other things go down at the same time too, you assume they're connected, Fergus thought. Like your front gate, and your security cameras, and all the things that are supposed to be uninterruptable. You panic because you're mostly scientists, not soldiers, and you look around to see who you can grab in a pinch . . .

Eleven minutes later, a breathless, older man in casual clothes, an Alliance ID/tracker pinned on his collar, ran into the cafe and looked around, his eyes settling quickly on Fergus. "You!" he cried. "Is that your van out front?"

"Yeah," Fergus answered, as he dabbed his protobeard with a napkin. "You didn't hit it, did you?"

"We have an emergency," the man said. "We need your help."

"I'm on my lunch—" Fergus started to say, but the man actually came over and tugged on his arm.

"This is a planetary emergency, and we're the government, and I don't care if you charge us a thousand times your regular rate for a thousand times your actual hours, if you would just please come with me!" he pleaded.

"Okay, then," Fergus said. "Calm down; I'll come look."

He paid his bill at the table kiosk and followed the man out back into the street. The man started to cross, but Fergus hung back. "My van?" he asked.

"Gate is stuck," the man said, pointing down at the Terrestrial Sciences facility. "Can you, you know, just carry your tools?"

"Sure, but I don't know what I need yet," Fergus said. "You haven't told me anything. Not even your name."

"I'm Phil," he said. "We had a, um, unreliable component in one of our security systems, and when we took it down for examination, a lot of other things went down that shouldn't have. Like the gate."

"Okay, hang on," Fergus said. He climbed into his van and grabbed his bag and a large toolbox, then obligingly followed the panicking man over to the smaller door in the fence that had been wedged open.

A guard was there in Alliance uniform. "Uh, Dr. Orchard, this man hasn't been secured—"

"This man is an electrician who just let me ruin his lunch to drag him over here," Phil said. "I'll keep an eye on him. We can't wait for Orbital HQ."

From the guard's expression, this was exactly as he'd expected this conversation to go, but had felt it necessary to try to do his job despite that. Grumbling, he pulled out a small hand-pad. "Your name?" he asked Fergus.

"Guy Griffin," he said, and pointed at the logo on his own workall. "Electrician. You need my license?"

"No," the guard said, sighing. He signed Fergus in, then reached out and pinned a visitor ID/tracker to his collar. "Keep that on at all times, and hand it in when you leave."

"Sure," Fergus said, and then, bureaucracy satisfied, the guard stepped aside, and Phil led him quickly through. The double doors of the two-story facility opened on a small reception desk and an atrium open to the glass roof, the floor lined with pedestal cases of assorted meteorites and other space debris, including what appeared to be a Bomo'ri jumpspace probe. *The* actual, assuming it was real, because Fergus was pretty sure if humanity had pinched a second, the Bomo'ri would have kicked the crap out of their entire species for it; they hadn't ever forgiven humankind for stealing the first and their jumpspace technology along with it.

Fergus owed all his adventures in the stars to that one stolen probe, and he desperately wanted to ask Phil if it was the real thing, but he was just some random guy off the street who shouldn't know or care.

Phil noticed his attention anyway and stopped. "Nice rocks and space stuff," Fergus said, and then shrugged and caught up with the scientist at the staircase on the far side of the atrium.

"Elevator's offline too," Phil said, and led him down the stairs into the basement. There were two other people there already, one of them a guard in uniform. "I found an electrician," Phil told them.

"Great," one of the civilians said. She held out her hand. "I'm Dr. Williams, she/her, and director of the facility. Did you show your license at the gate?"

"I offered," Fergus said.

"The guard said he didn't need to see it," Phil added.

"Well, I do," Dr. Williams said, and Fergus took the ID chit out of his pocket and handed it to her. She pulled a small handheld out of her pocket and scanned it, then handed his chit back. "Mr. Griffin?" she said.

"That's me," Fergus answered.

"You've been licensed for nine years now?"

"Seven," he said.

"Why were you outside our building?"

"I wasn't outside your building. I was across the street, eating lunch," Fergus said. She pointed with her chin towards his shoulder, and he looked down to see sauce on his workalls. "I wasn't given the opportunity to wash up or even finish my coffee before I got dragged away. I'm happy to take my messy self out of here and leave you to it, whatever your problem is."

"No, it's fine," she said. "Empanadas?"

"Enchiladas."

"Those are excellent too. One of my favorite lunch spots," she said. "So, here's our situation. We have our usual power, which is running our lights and ventilation and all our usual stuff, and then we have this secondary system." She pointed to where three squat, black boxes were bolted to the wall, with conduit coming in and out of each and running between. A control panel beside it was all orange and red warning lights. "Are you familiar with this?"

"It's the city dedicated line," Fergus said. "I've never worked directly with it, though. It has its own special technicians."

"Yes, but none of them are available, as apparently there are issues throughout this sector. And also unfortunately for us, we need this up sooner rather than later. Can you tell if the original fault was here?"

"I have no idea," Fergus said, "but I can try."

"Great," she said, and then stood there and folded her arms across her chest, as if she had no intention of doing anything other than watch him perform miracles in front of her.

"Yeah, okay," he said, and set his toolbox down, then took a few steps back from the panels. "I just need to look at this for a minute, get an idea what's what."

He made a pretense of studying it, looking it up and down, tracing conduits with his eyes as they ran up the walls and disappeared, or across the ceiling to other corners, but really, what his eyes saw didn't matter; it was the hum, the network, that he could feel. Although, the small, nondescript gray box farther down the wall with the DM logo embossed in one corner was a nice find. "You said the whole dedicated line is down?" he asked Dr. Williams.

"The sector, anyway. That's what I was told," she said.

"And when did it go down?"

"Right when we—" Phil started to say, but Williams glared at him.

"By coincidence, we were doing some work with our internal security systems," she said instead. "I can't imagine it's related."

"Well, yeah, probably not," Fergus said. "Not unless whatever jackass installed your security system did it really badly or was hoping to extort bucks out of you by tanking your line on purpose."

Williams and the others exchanged looks, which Fergus studiously ignored. He walked over to the gray box. "What's this?" he asked.

The guard coughed. "Part of the security system," she said.

"*Ohh*," Fergus said, in a knowing way. "Maybe some jackassery after all. You said you were doing something with it? It's still running, though, right?"

"Not exactly," Phil said.

Fergus took a meter out of his toolbox and ran it along the conduits, stopping now and then to study it and, once, shake it and whack it on side with his fist before retracing a route. "Something odd, yeah. The current is all wrong."

"What do you mean?"

"Maybe it's a short somewhere in the system. When you said you were doing something with it, it didn't involve wire cutters or poking screwdrivers into outlets or anything?"

"*No*," Phil said, scowling.

Yes, officers, Fergus thought, *he conned his way in to steal things, but we weren't suspicious of him because he was kinda irritating.*

"Okay, let me check it," he said. He moved away from the DM box and back to the control panel, and plugged his confuddler in. "This might take a while," he added.

"We need things back up as quickly as possible," Dr. Williams said.

"So you've both said. And *quick as possible* still might be a while," he said.

Williams gave a heavy sigh. "I'm going back up to check in with OHQ. You, Griffin: you don't go anywhere without our officer here, Lucy, or Dr. Orchard. Got it?"

"Uh-huh," Fergus answered, without turning around, as he worked. He'd never cracked a system right in front of its owners before, and it was a mixture of thrilling and weirdly shameful. More the latter, he thought, which maybe meant it was time to get out of this business. He chuckled; unless he got those pieces, he *was* getting out of this business. All business, along with everyone and everything else, unless Ignatio was exaggerating the threat of the Vraet.

Sorry, I thought the whole solar system was in danger, but it turned out to just be a pair of space marmots armed with raisins, he thought.

The guard, Lucy, spoke up. "What's funny?" she asked.

"Just remembering I promised my father I'd never go into government work," Fergus answered.

"Yeah, me too," Phil added. "And yet here we are."

"Here we are," Fergus agreed. He was into the system and could see the indicators that the city's dedicated line was preparing to come back up. He set the safety to keep it down in the building for now—it wouldn't do to "fix" the problem before he was done there—and then began tracing the DM connections. Sure enough, the tech company had left backdoors into the main building systems. "You sure your security company was on your side?" he asked Phil.

Phil came closer. "Why?"

Fergus showed him the tracings on his screen. "See here and here? I'm not a security expert, but this looks like this was set up so they could remotely manipulate all your building systems, including your regular security, and this looks like they've got a bypass to the event logger so its system leaves no traces. Or maybe someone hacked it?"

"Is it . . . a problem right now?" Phil asked.

"Well, it's off," Fergus said, "but I'm betting when the dedicated line comes back up, it will too."

"Can you disable it?"

"Yeah, probably," Fergus said, "but not here. The conduits from the gray box go up. Is there another of these? First floor somewhere?"

"Second," Phil said. "In the secure lab."

"I don't think that's a good idea," the guard said.

"Yep, well, then not much I can do for you," Fergus said, and unplugged his confuddler and started putting his other tools away. "The power fault with the dedicated line is external; just coincidence that it went when it did while you were mucking with this other system. But when it's back up, which should be soon, this is gonna reboot, and whoever put this in is going to be in control of your facility again. If I were you, I'd get someone else in to look at it who's more of an expert in these things, as soon as possible."

"No, we should do this now," Phil said. "Can you at least disconnect it so it won't come back on?"

"Yeah, sure, if you don't mind me breaking it a little," Fergus said. "But I gotta do it at the other box."

"I don't mind if you break it," Phil said.

"Uh . . ." the guard said. "We should check with Dr. Williams first."

"Just call— Oh, right, that's down too," Phil said. "Well, we don't have time for this. Lucy, you can go check in with the director, or come with us, whichever you think is best."

"I promise I won't lick anything," Fergus said.

The guard rolled her eyes and groaned. "Fine, let's go. But if you keep thinking you're a witty man, Griffin, I might just tase you for the fun of it. We are all very stressed here right now. You get me?"

"Yes, ma'am," Fergus said.

He followed Phil back to the stairs and up to the second floor, the guard on their heels, to where a balcony ran the perimeter between the atrium and the building's many labs. Most had interior windows, some of them tinted too heavily to see in, but some had none at all. Phil directed him to a door by one of the windowless labs, tried to use the ID scanner several times, then remembered the power was off and used a key to unlock it. "In here," he said. "Don't touch anything."

The room was lined with instruments on the far wall, none of which he had any idea what they were, but realization of what the signal intensity in this room would be like when everything came back online made his head preemptively ache.

The DM box was easy to spot, the front panel open across the room. Between it and him were a number of lab benches, also containing smaller instruments and microscopes and all the usual paraphernalia of hard-core science. Fragments were everywhere, each one carefully tagged and numbered with a traceable chip. There were at least fifty pieces, but without even having to look directly at them, the presence of the eleven core pieces glowed against his consciousness, bright dots of light and noise scattered in the room. As he walked in, heading around the benches for the DM control box, they grew louder, and it was as if they were all talking excitedly to each other and trying to talk to him.

"Are you humming?" Phil asked.

"Yep," Fergus said. He was humming, mostly under his breath, because the buzz of the sound in his body helped him center and focus his internal bees, get them on his frequency, not listening to the fragments' call of temptation. "It's less annoying than whistling while I work, I figure."

"I suppose," Phil said. "It's real close, though."

Fergus peered into the panel. The scientists had indeed shut it down, but his guess that it would reboot when the power came back was correct. "Good thing the power's off," he said to Phil. "This thing's been booby-trapped! I've never seen anything like it. If I was touching this panel like I am right now when it came back on—" In his other hand he had his handpad, where he'd routed control of the safety cutoff downstairs, and just before he pressed it, he poked the center of the DM panel with his finger and let a massive blast of electricity through the connection. "—-Aaaah!" he yelled, and fell to the floor, just as the dedicated power line came back up.

Fergus lay on the floor, not moving, holding his breath.

"Oh shit, oh shit, the electrician killed himself!" Phil shouted.

The guard stepped closer. "Is he dead?"

"I don't know! Can't you, you know, check his pulse?"

"Is it safe to touch him, or will I get shocked too?"

"He's no longer touching the panel. I think you're fine," Phil said.

"'Think'? Why don't you go get the director and explain all this and get emergency medical summoned while I watch over him. Okay?"

"Yes. Okay," Phil said, and raced from the room.

Lucy the guard stared at him a while, then finally knelt down to take his pulse. *I've got this trick down,* Fergus thought, and zapped her the moment her fingers made contact.

All the core fragments in the room fully woke and reached out, tendrils of signal twisting toward him.

"No, no, shush!" he hissed at them as he lowered the stunned guard to the floor, then grabbed his toolbox and pulled out the bag of decoy fragments he'd had *Whiro* fab for him.

It took him about six minutes to take all the core fragments and switch their tags over to the decoys before putting them in place. One by one he picked up the real fragments and dropped them into the modified soda cans he had under the tray in the toolbox, capping and sealing them, but not before each one sang to him of doorways, and something else whispered and rustled and whined, a sound somewhere between the chatter of tiny insects and the click of ravenous machines, in a chorus of billions through that connection from the other side.

If he was still shaken-looking when the director ran in with Phil and an EMT in tow, it was not feigned. He was already helping the guard up, who was shaking her head groggily.

"What happened?" Dr. Williams demanded.

"That gray panel was rigged to try to kill anyone who tampered with it," Fergus said. He coughed, his throat parched. "I think it must have sparked again while your guard was checking on me." He looked back at the smoking, blackened controls in the box. "I think it's done now, unless you count being a fire hazard. Whoever installed that needs to give you a refund. Or do jail time for attempted murder."

"You okay, Lucy?" Dr. Williams asked.

Lucy stumbled to her feet. "Yeah," she said. "Head hurts. What happened?"

"You got zapped," Phil said. He pointed at the melted DM box, and Lucy took a shaky step farther away from it.

Dr. Williams was surveying the room and seemed satisfied. "Okay, everyone out," she said. "Griffin, bring your tools. Let's get you and Lucy checked down in the atrium for injuries while we secure this room. Dr. Orchard, you re-scan everything."

"Yes," Phil said.

Fergus hauled his toolbox down the stairs after the Director, and an EMT led them out of the building to where an ambulance was waiting. "We just want to check you over," the medic said. "Besides, you'll need the medical report to file with your employer."

Fergus laughed. "I'm self-employed," he said. "I think I'm all right. Been shocked before, probably will be again. It's like I attract electricity. Can I go?"

The EMT shrugged. "We recommend you let us check you out, but we can't force you. It's on your head."

"Then thanks, but no thanks," Fergus said. "I've got other jobs, and after that, I think I need a beer in a quiet bar somewhere."

"Can't blame you for that," Lucy the guard said from where she was sitting on the open doors of the ambulance, being checked herself. "Glad you're not dead."

"Yeah, you too," Fergus said, and crossed the street back to his van, dropped the ID badge down the street gutter, and got in.

As his autovan waited to merge into traffic, he saw Phil and Dr. Williams running out of the front door, shouting and waving, and the guards at the gate and the EMTs turning to look toward him.

His autovan found the opening it needed and pulled evenly out, accelerating down the street and away, and Fergus carefully did not look out the window toward where a growing group of people were shouting to get his attention.

Whiro spoke up in his ear. "The police have been summoned, as well as Alliance HQ. Vehicles and drones are being deployed to intercept you."

"That was fast," Fergus grumbled. He bent down under the dash and plugged his confuddler in, and easily overrode the van's simple security. "Can you take the wheel, *Whiro*?"

"Happily," *Whiro* said.

Fergus straightened up and was climbing into the back of the van when it suddenly swerved, and he crashed shoulder-first into one of the seats. "Apologies," *Whiro* said. "I forgot there is no up. Recalculating. It looks like we have four police cruisers, five police drones, and two Alliance drones coming for us. Going to take a sharp right to avoid a roadblock in three . . . two . . . one . . . Now."

Fergus held tight to the back of the seat as the van screeched around a corner, tilting alarmingly. He was half-out of his worka- lls and struggled to free at least one leg as the van returned, be- latedly, to its normal horizontal orientation with a crash. "*Whiro*, please try to keep all four wheels on the road," he said.

"Would you rather drive?" *Whiro* answered.

"No."

"Then please be quiet. This technology is limited and re- quires my concentration."

Fergus finally got both his legs out of the workalls, bunched them up, and threw them to the back of the van. He was just getting out his change of clothes when *Whiro* swerved again, though less alarmingly diagonally. "The Baltimore traffic con- trol systems have taken over signals to box us in with stopped traffic," *Whiro* said. "Do you object to me violating some laws to get us around this?"

"I don't mind at all," Fergus said.

"We will still have to stop in about forty-three seconds be- fore I can alter our route. We have one drone very close to us, and it will be able to reach and tag us with a tracer or possibly interfere with our tire infrastructure."

"Can you stay stationary for about ten seconds without losing our opportunity to escape?"

"Yes," *Whiro* said.

"Okay. Give me warning," Fergus said. He got the rest of the black bodysuit on that he'd bought at Lake Tahoe, hastily mended during the previous night's stopover in Boston to get supplies, and was just tugging at the sleeve ends when *Whiro* gave him a five-second warning.

The van stopped. Fergus opened the autovan's back door and took a ball bearing from his toolbox, charged it up, and loaded it into his slingshot. It was still crackling with electricity when the drone came around one of the many brick buildings, about two stories up, straight toward him. He got it on the first shot, and the spluttering, smoking drone dropped from the sky, landing on a street-cart canopy.

Fergus jumped back in the van and was still swinging the door shut when *Whiro* accelerated, bumping up and over the sidewalk and around the obstructing traffic, the wrong way around a rotary, and then off down another side street at significant speeds.

He carefully packed the eleven modified soda cans carrying the key to saving the world in his duffel bag, and tossed it up into the front passenger seat of the van, followed by the few other items he cared about. Climbing back up into the driver seat, he popped the seal on a cleaner nanite capsule and tossed it over his shoulder. It hit the van floor with a tiny *snap* and the faint smell of ozone that meant it had gone off.

"How are we doing?" he asked as they took another corner. There were flashing lights behind him and the sound of another drone not too far away. The autovan's systems was trying desperately, if ineffectively, to respond to traffic-control commands to shut down.

"Three minutes," *Whiro* said. "I will not be able to slow down."

"I guessed as much," Fergus said. "I'm ready."

The buildings around them shifted from residential to commercial, from small businesses to warehouses, long, weathered structures that had managed to survive flood and storm before the seawalls had finally been completed.

"The bridge is ahead," *Whiro* said. "There is a blockade on the far end of it. The Alliance has flagged you as a possible terrorist. We have become very interesting to all local, state, and coalition law enforcement, many of whom are behind or above us, and they clearly intend to trap us on the bridge itself."

"Yeah, that's what I expected," Fergus said. "Everything in position?"

"Yes," *Whiro* said.

"Great," Fergus answered. He could see now the blue of the water ahead between buildings. The road they were speeding down was elevated above the mostly abandoned local roads below, rising up to meet the top of the ten-meter-high shoreline wall and become formally a bridge. As they neared the wall, Fergus threw the duffel out of the van window, where it landed heavily in the dirt and dust below. Then they were up on the bridge with a swarm of drones around them and enough police cars up ahead to have stopped a warship, never mind one doomed little autovan.

In the rearview mirror, he could just see the antique motorcycle taking off in the other direction on the lower roads, the duffel strapped on the rider's back.

"She got it," *Whiro* said. "Now you."

"Right," Fergus said. They were heading at full speed toward the blockade, where they'd strung a portable slug field across the bridge to keep him from ramming them. Two drones zipped overhead and shot something onto the roof of the van. There was the loud *pop* of the roof being punctured, then the van started to fill with a foul, choking smoke.

The wind from the open windows kept it pushed to the back long enough for Fergus to get his mask on before he ripped the confuddler out of the autovan system and sealed it into his front chest pocket, braced himself for impact, and yanked the wheel hard enough to send the van careening against the guardrail. "Come on, come on!" he yelled, and then the railing gave, or the van tumbled over it—it was hard to tell, and hardly mattered—and they hit the water like hitting a wall.

"Bloody hell, that hurt," he complained, jarred by the impact and sure he was going to have bruises from the safety belt, as the water grabbed the van and pulled it down.

He grabbed his swim fins and bag off the seat, and when the last big bubble of air finally wobbled its way out of the van and blasted up toward the surface, he pulled himself through the window and swam away.

Chapter 20

———◆———

By the time Fergus got to the train station in Alexandria, right on the southernmost border of the Atlantic state of East Washington, he was dry, hungry, extremely thirsty, and happy to find another duffel in a locker waiting for him just where he'd hoped it would be. So far, so good: one sneaky theft down, one to go. By the time they stopped looking for him in the sunken van and expanded their search outward, he'd had enough of a head start to stay ahead of everyone behind him and, thanks to his gift, enough forewarning to dodge anyone ahead.

So far, everything was falling into place. Digital Midendian's own dishonesty had gotten him into the Alliance, and now if everything went right, the Alliance would in turn help him break into Digital Midendian. He was almost *done*.

He carried the new duffel to the train and bought his ticket up to the SCNY. It wasn't an express, so he had about two hours to kill as they lingered through Philadelphia before crossing the border out of the Atlantic States into the pocket of territory that was the Sovereign City of New York. Zacker was waiting for him at the station, leaning against a light post with his arms across his chest, and watching all the passengers as if he was all that stood between civilization and the unfettered hordes of criminals allowed to roam into his city.

Spotting him, Zacker gestured toward the taxi stand. "So, you came up with a plan?" he asked.

"Yep," Fergus answered.

"I'm not going to like it, am I?" Zacker said. "In fact, it's incredibly dumb and dangerous and desperate, right? And absolutely dependent on total stupid luck?"

"Exactly," Fergus said, as cheerfully as he could. "It's so nice to be with someone who gets my work methodology so precisely."

Zacker growled and opened an auto-taxi door. "Get in and tell me," he said, and then when Fergus got in, held his nose. "What's that smell?"

"Someone shot a gas canister into my autovan," Fergus said. "You'd think swimming down half of bloody Chesapeake Bay would have washed it out, but no such luck."

"Yeah, that shit's pervasive," Zacker said. "When you shower next—which for both our sakes I hope is soon—try a little vinegar. If it doesn't work, at least you'll smell like chips, the one thing I miss about Glasgow. So, where the hell are we going?"

"Back to Digital Midendian," Fergus said.

"Last time we looked at that place, I thought it was clear you'd need an army." Zacker gestured around the auto-taxi interior. "No army."

"Our army is going to meet us there," Fergus answered. "They just don't know they're meeting me." He unzipped the duffel he'd recovered from the bus station, and checked for at least the eighth time that everything was all there. Then he took out the Alliance cap and put it on and beamed at Zacker.

Zacker slapped the auto-taxi dash with both hands. "Impersonating an officer. It's like you exist for the sole purpose of dragging me down into hell. Your plan better not include asking me to wear one of those. I have morals, you know. And pride."

"I won't," Fergus assured him.

They crossed over the Hudson in silence, then Zacker muttered, "It's even worse, isn't it? Your body language is a fucking mess."

"What? The fragments? Yeah," he said, frowning. "We're running out of time. I don't know how much we have left, but it's not much. And if I fail . . ." He trailed off, not wanting to think about that.

"No, I meant whatever you want me to do is worse than impersonating a duly sworn member of our armed services, but sure, distract me from my legitimate concerns with babble about death and doom instead," Zacker said.

"It's not that bad," Fergus said, then tapped his earpiece. "*Whiro*, how is my army coming?"

"Looks like an orbital dropship has been deployed, so either they got clearance from the SCNY or they're angry enough not to care. Three ground teams are coming in by air from Philadelphia and one from the Scranton airfield. It would appear that excessive force, both in appearance and application, is desired," *Whiro* told him. "You have about a ten-minute lead on them; they do appear to have coordinated their forces to arrive nearly simultaneously. However, the local police have clearly been informed of an impending action and are preparing support and crowd control, and may interfere in your approach."

Zacker snorted. "Connecticut police? Yeah, let them try."

"You're just hostile to everyone, aren't you?" Fergus said.

Zacker smiled and said nothing.

Fergus sighed. "Anyway, I need to find somewhere near the DM building where I can change into the full uniform and then blend in with the rest of the chaos. You think you can find a good spot before the Alliance closes its fist?"

"No problem," Zacker said. "Soon as we're off the highway and this go-kart lets me take control. Then what do I do?"

"Then you sit and stay out of things," Fergus said. "Look, if the Alliance catches me? They are never going to let me go again. After Enceladus, and some other things I'm not telling you about and which you'd rather not know anyway? They're going to disappear me, and if that happens, someone needs to be around to convince them that the fragments are dangerous and need to be gotten off Earth, gotten out of the solar system, if they can't figure out how to destroy them. So, your job is to try to clean up after me, if I fail. You're going to make a face when I say this, and trust me, I'm making the same face deep inside when I hear myself say it, but you're the only person I know who has the credibility to save the world."

Zacker made exactly the expression of sour but smug surprise Fergus had anticipated. "Yeah, well, I'm retired," he said. "Try not to die and dump all this complicated horseshit on me, okay? Not even out of spite?"

"I'll do my best," Fergus said.

"Fine." The auto-taxi finally descended the off-ramp from the highway and let Zacker take over the controls, and he expertly navigated his way through the city until he parked it, rather abruptly, at a corner near a small alley.

"Get out here," he said. "Up ahead, that's a roadblock waiting to happen. The other end of the alley opens up a block from the rear side of the DM building, and that's the closest I can get you."

"Thanks," Fergus said.

"I'm going to go park, sit in a coffee shop, eat a pot pie, and wait for the inevitable wave of post-raid officers coming in with the gossip. If that includes laughing over your skinny-ass body, I'll do what I can."

"Thanks. Really. Again," Fergus said, grabbed his duffel, and got out. He watched as Zacker drove off without looking back.

The alley was narrow and shaded, enough that he didn't feel completely exposed as he took out the Alliance uniform and put it on. Across the back of the jacket, in bold letters, were the words SCIENCE TEAM. He didn't know if it was a legit thing, but then, probably no one else would either, and it might explain to someone suspicious of him why he stood out. Go bold or go home, right?

He dropped the empty duffel, threw a cleaner bot packet in it, then walked to the other end of the alley, careful to stop before he was close enough to the end to see the DM building itself; if he could see it, they could see him, and he didn't want to give himself away or provide any advance warning of the raid itself. Assuming they didn't know already, which was a big leap into the unlikely.

The core fragments were still in the building, at any rate. It didn't matter if they'd been concealed in anticipation of an incoming raid, because they couldn't hide them from him—they were practically screaming for his attention from somewhere deep within.

Fergus felt the air blast ahead of the drop ship before his brain could even register the sound of the decelerating engines. It had come in hot, its pilot wanting to impress, and the deftness with which it switched from giant metallic brick dropping like a stone to settling gently on the roof of the main Digital Midendian building definitely succeeded, too. Fergus could hear shouting and catch the brief blur of people running past the end of the alley in either direction.

Sirens started up nearby, echoing between the buildings enough to make it hard to pin down what direction they were coming in, if not from all. Fergus could feel the drones before he saw one through his narrow gap of visibility: heavy, bright yellow emergency drones with flashing white lights, herding the gathering crowds safely out of the way before the armored vehicles arrived.

He heard them coming, too. The Alliance was making quite a show of this, no doubt because someone—or, probably, many someones—higher up were *deeply* pissed, and the logistics people lower down saw a great opportunity for the sort of heavy-equipment free-for-all on civilian turf that hadn't been de rigueur since the early twenty-first century.

Works in my favor, Fergus thought. He sneaked closer to the end of the alley and watched with pleasure as the DM compound was efficiently and effectively placed under siege. Three teams of Alliance soldiers converged in the street and headed toward the front gates, and as the last few passed him, Fergus stepped out and tagged along behind them, keeping pace and trying to blend in as just one of the second wave.

More Alliance vehicles arrived down the now-empty streets and parked out front, and Fergus watched as a small group of people in more formal uniforms disembarked from one and headed through the front gate, striding past the soldiers and Fergus now gathered on Digital Midendian's lawn.

A man came out to meet them, two others behind him. Fergus recognized him from his research on the company: Evan Derecho, founder and CEO. He wore an expensive business suit, as did the man and woman accompanying him. The woman had a handheld cam, recording the approaching officers, and the man held a legal pad.

There was a conversation between the two groups, not loud enough to hear but certainly not friendly. Derecho was waving his hands, palms up, in obvious, strident denial. Finally, Derecho backed off and consulted briefly with his two companions, and then gestured—it was almost an elaborate, mocking bow—for the commander to enter. The Alliance commander turned and gave orders to his team, then walked into the building past Derecho without acknowledgment.

"All right, everyone," a nearby squad leader barked at the team Fergus had drifted into and loosely attached himself to.

"Alpha and Bravo teams, take the grounds. Charlie team, secure the perimeter. Delta and Echo, you're in the building. Secure all premises and personnel, identify any spaces you are unable to gain access to, and report in on the fifteens. Go," she ordered.

His team began to spread out into the perimeter, but he managed to lag behind just enough to step in behind the other two teams marching into the building. Derecho and the Alliance commander had already disappeared back inside.

So far, so good, he thought, as he let himself get swept along into Digital Midendian's previously impenetrable fortress.

They spread out through the wide lobby, the soldiers' boots loud on the marble. The leaders of both Delta and Echo had already set up a hologram display of the building blueprints on the desk. "As you encounter people, escort them to this conference room here," Delta leader said. "Just them; nobody brings stuff. We're going to have to search them anyway, but let's not make it harder than it needs to be. Get to it, people!"

The two teams of ten each began to disperse toward the stairs, and Fergus was cautiously following when the leader stepped to one side, put out a hand, and stopped him. "Who are you?" she asked. "You're not one of mine."

Fergus shrugged one shoulder in and pointed at the back of his jacket. "Science team," he said.

"Science team?" she repeated. "What science team?"

"That's a good question," Fergus said. "I can't find the rest of us anywhere. They called me in from Syracuse, on my day off, no less, and there were supposed to be at least three more of us here."

"To do what, though?" she asked.

"Um. It's sort of classified? Do you know what we're looking for?"

"I'm looking for a lot of things," she said. "Evidence of treason, mostly."

"Yes, well, not entirely, though, yes?" Fergus said. "There's the *things*."

Her eyes narrowed. "I've been given a description," she said after a pause. "What did you say your name was?"

"Cheefer, sir," Fergus answered. "Dr. Cheefer. And we're here—or I'm here, anyway, until the others show up—because these things are dangerous. Were you given handling protocols?"

"No," she said. "Dangerous how?"

"Uh, yes, also kind of classified," Fergus said. "I don't know what I'm allowed to say, sir. Dr. Derf, our lead investigator, was supposed to be here already, and he's in charge of the liaison shi—*stuff*. I'm sorry."

The team leader turned, snapped her fingers, and pointed at one of the soldiers clustered around the hologram. "You," she said, and he came over. "Private Roff, you're now assigned to follow Dr. Cheefer here as he joins in the search. Report progress to me directly on the half hour, and anything retrieved needs to be personally certified by me before it leaves the building."

"Yes, Commander Quinn," Roff said. He was young and had the expression of someone who was both very enthusiastic about, and very sure of their personal skill at, their job. He turned to Fergus. "Sir?"

"You can just call me Bob," Fergus said.

"Yes, sir. Where to?"

"Up," Fergus said, and headed for the stairs. It was a simple task to just follow the call of the fragments, and now that he was focused on them, they were focusing intensely on him. The electrical bombardment increased exponentially with how much physically closer he got, and the alien bees deep in his gut were buzzing in resonance. At the top of the second staircase, he had to stop and try to get his wits back together and his Asiig gift under full control again. Now would be a very bad time for an oops-sparks-coming-out-of-my-head moment, and his ability to prevent one felt uncomfortably tenuous. He hoped if there was any scanning going on in the building, his own tiny contribution to the maelstrom of clashing signals was drowned out by everything else around him.

Roff mistook his reason for stopping. "There is an elevator, sir," he said, and his voice rang with poorly disguised pity.

"I'm good," Fergus said, more heartily than necessary, to show he wasn't winded. He pulled a small remote signal meter out of his pocket, courtesy of his brief shopping trip in the electrical supply store opposite the Terrestrial Research facility.

"Are you humming?" Roff asked. "And what is that you've got?"

"Yes, I'm humming because I am a happy person, and this is a special signal detector," Fergus said, though really it wasn't more than a prop for cover. "Now shush, please."

Roff stood silently by as Fergus turned back and forth at the stair landing, holding out his device as if he was looking at it instead of not really looking at anything. Soldiers passed them in both directions, some escorting people down, others heading to the upper floors to search. No one seemed to pay him or Roff any attention, which was fine with him. "One more floor, I think," he said at last, and took off up the stairs again. Roff followed.

The next floor had larger offices than the lower ones, along with conference rooms and what looked like middle-manager offices. "The server room is one more up," Roff volunteered, "and then the executive suites above that. Derecho's penthouse office currently has our drop ship squatting on it."

"I saw," Fergus said. "Humbling, I expect."

"One would like to hope so, sir," Roff agreed.

Okay, Fergus thought, *I kind of like this kid. I hope I don't have to zap him.* The fragments were definitely on this floor, and he headed down one row of office doors, the first few open as soldiers rummaged through desks, clamped data-downloaders onto the consoles, and pulled every bit of memory and storage for later analysis.

There was a water fountain in the hall, near a set of restrooms, and Fergus drank enough that Roff started coughing meaningfully at him. "I get thirsty," Fergus said.

Roff nodded. "Yes, sir."

Fergus wiped his lips with the back of his hand, still listening intently to the electricity all around him. The fragments were close. Very close. He looked around to see if he was missing something, and spotted one of the Digital Midendian guys at the end of the hall. The guy was talking to a soldier, but his eyes did not leave Fergus and Roff.

"Yeah, in here," Fergus said, and pushed open the door to the restrooms.

"Impressively fast work with the water, sir," Roff said.

Fergus looked back. "Are you smirking at me, Private?"

"No, sir!" Roff declared.

The restrooms were the usual row of sinks and evaporators, one very old-fashioned towel exchanger with a retrofitted anti-germ unit, and four separate small doors to the individual toilets. The fragments were so close, he could feel them like a shiver up and down his skin, raising his arm hair in little prickles as they tried to connect to him, adapt him into their structure or vice versa. And on the other side of the noise and pull, there was again that screeching, slithering, gnashing sound, more eager than ever.

"Sir?" Roff asked.

"There," Fergus said, and pointed at the towel exchanger.

"What?"

Fergus ignored him and grabbed onto the front edge of the exchanger case, pulling as hard as he could. It didn't budge. He tried to lift the towel return flap, but it wouldn't open, so he bent down and poked at the unit from underneath, then tried pulling out the single dangling towel, which was stuck fast. The grout around the edges of the exchanger was a brilliant white, in contrast to the fading, off-white lines between the rest of the tiles on the wall. "I think this thing's new and welded closed," he said, trying again to knock or wrestle it open, but the exchanger case was rounded on the edges, hard to get a good grip on, and definitely not inclined to move.

"Sir, if you'd care to stand back," Roff said.

Fergus did as the soldier asked. Roff stepped forward, shifted his position slightly a few times, then raised one big, booted foot and kicked the exchanger so hard, it pulled broken tiles with it when it crashed against the far bathroom wall.

Fergus crouched beside it, almost afraid to touch it for how loud the fragments had become, how shrill and interested the party on the other side, but he steeled himself and flipped it over. The back of the exchanger had a hole cut in it, and Fergus reached in and one by one pulled out all eight remaining core fragments.

I have them all, he thought, amazed, and more than a little terrified of what came next.

"What are those, sir?" Roff asked.

"Stolen extraterrestrial technology," Fergus said. "This is what I came here for. Uh, we. Well, the Science Team. Which is right now just me. But you know what I mean."

"It's all broken pieces," Roff said. "It wasn't because I kicked—"

"No, no, Private, it was already in pieces," Fergus assured him. He looked around for something to carry them in and, finding nothing, knocked the bits of tile still attached to the exchanger off the back and put the fragments back inside. Then he picked up the exchanger. "We have to get these out of here and back where they belong," he said. "There may be interference when they realize we found them."

"Right. I'm ready for some interference," Roff said, and cracked his knuckles. The soldier tapped his earpiece. "Command? This is Private Roff. I'm coming down from the third floor with the Science Team Guy. We have an acquisition." He listened for a moment, eyes darting over to Fergus several times. "Commander wants to talk to you directly," he said. "Go to channel 443. It's secure and private."

Fergus switched over his earpiece channel. "Dr. Cheefer here," he said.

"Tell me what you got," the Captain said.

"The pieces," Fergus said.

"How many?"

"Eight."

"How did you find them so damned fast?"

"Science," Fergus answered.

"I am sending additional support up to your location. Where are you specifically?"

"In the bathroom," Fergus said.

"Stay there until support arrives. I want no less than a dozen armed soldiers within sight of you the entire time you're heading down, and if you see less than that, you stop where you are, take cover, and call for help. You understand me?"

"I understand," Fergus said.

"And you, Roff?"

"Yes, Commander," Roff said. "But—"

"People have died over these artifacts, Private."

"Yes, ma'am," Roff said.

The line terminated, and Roff looked at Fergus. "I suppose you can't tell me what the hell those things are part of?"

"I can't," Fergus said, "but your captain's precautions are not an overreaction."

Roff grunted. "Well, that sucks," he said. "Support's here. Let's go look for trouble, eh?"

"After you," Fergus said, and they stepped back out of the bathroom, Fergus holding the towel exchanger against his chest, arms wrapped around it, trying to silently, desperately shush the pieces within it to sleep.

There were two Alliance soldiers in the hall right outside the door, and a line of them down the staircase. The Digital Midendian guy at the far end of the hall was openly staring, in a hostile, homicidal fashion. There were at least six armed soldiers between him and Fergus, but not wanting to be scrutinized any longer than necessary, Fergus turned quickly and headed down the stairs, Roff at his heels.

It was both comforting and nerve-wracking to be so surrounded by the Alliance, knowing if they had any idea who or what he was, he was utterly incapable of escape, and at the same time genuinely relieved that they were between Digital Midendian and him. More than either worry, the fragments pressed against his chest, trying so hard to pull him into their chorus, made every step he took, every second of resistance, the hardest effort of will he had ever expended.

He was also stupidly thirsty again, and that was definitely a distraction he didn't need right now. Unfortunately, their corridor of soldiers didn't exactly make room between them for a quick dash to a water cooler. *Soon*, he thought. He was almost out of there.

They were met in the lobby by Commander Quinn. "That was extremely fast, Dr. Cheefer," she said.

Fergus nodded. "It's all in a day's work for science, ma'am."

"Okay, show me what you've got," she said, and waved her had at the towel exchanger, then the desk.

Fergus looked around. Aside from the large number of Alliance soldiers in the lobby, most but not all of whom were going about their work, off to the side of the lobby under armed guard were Derecho, the CEO, and his small entourage. It had grown to four, with the addition of the far-too-familiar forms of Mitch and Kyle, and they were all looking directly at him.

"Uh, here?" Fergus protested.

"Yes, here," the commander said. She tapped the desk sharply. "Now."

There were now more soldiers paying attention, and Fergus was keenly aware of how armed every one of them was. "Yes, ma'am," he said. He set the exchanger face-down and reached through the hole in the back, and pulled out the fragments one by one, trying to stand so that his own body both obscured Derecho's view and kept him from being able to study his face for too long.

The commander picked up one the pieces and turned it around in her hand. One of her eyebrows went up, and she played with it a little longer before setting it down hastily with the others. "Well, that's as described," she said. One by one she picked up the rest. "And they're all here. Excellent work."

Fergus started to put them back into the exchanger, but the commander stopped him. "We have a case," she said, and snapped her fingers. One of the people working the status display on the desk went over to the equipment cache against the wall and came back with something about the size of his now-sunken toolbox. "Thanks," Fergus said, and set the pieces into the foam grid inside. There was something active in the base of the box, but he couldn't be exactly sure what it was doing; when he closed and locked the lid, it didn't seem to diminish the fragments' calls, though neither did it interfere with him trying to get them quieted down again.

He picked up the case, and the commander put a hand on his shoulder. "These are going straight up to the Alliance orbital station," she said.

"Uh, Dr. Derf gave me strict instructions to bring them back to our secure science facility in Albany," Fergus said. "He was very insistent, said it was my head on the line. I can give you a signed receipt for them, though."

The commander laughed. "A signed receipt? Sure. Someone get us a piece of paper? Anyone? No?" She turned back to Fergus. "If I found paper, would you sign your real name?"

"Excuse me?" Fergus said, even as the pit of his stomach tried to desperately flee south.

"Interesting that when I tried to call the Albany office, we detected a glitch in the system that had rerouted our call to an automated dropbox where a very human-sounding voice answered and vouched for your credentials," Quinn said. "Soon as we detected the intrusion and started a trace, the line dropped and completely wiped itself, but not before we figured it came from somewhere in Earth orbit. I give you full credit for chutzpah, whoever you are."

"What?" Roff asked.

"There is no Dr. Cheefer or Dr. Derf, and of course no one at the real Terrestrial Sciences unit in Albany knows anything about a science team being included in the raid—scientists are not big fans of guns and violence, in my experience, except when it serves them at a safe remove," Quinn said. "Also, they seem very preoccupied at the moment with having been ripped off by an impersonator."

Roff frowned at Fergus. "Aw, c'mon," he said. "I liked you. Am I going to have to shoot you?"

"Sorry," Fergus said. "You might."

The commander handed Roff a pair of wrist-binders, and Roff rolled his eyes and waved his index finger in a circle, indicating that Fergus should turn around. He complied; there were at least forty people with guns in this room, and he wouldn't make it two meters closer to the door before being brought down. And he wouldn't even get half that distance without revealing his secret, which guaranteed a much more ignominious end.

Roff snapped the binders on, not cruelly tight but in no way loose. Fergus hung his head in defeat. For a moment there, he actually had thought he was going to pull it off, and unless an opportunity came up real soon, the fate of the world was going to be in Zacker's hands.

The sudden realization that this might just be it, and he didn't even say goodbye to anyone, was a bitter thought.

"Privates Roff, Hensley, and Walsh, please escort 'Dr. Cheefer' here to the dropship," the commander said. "It's waiting now out on the lawn. Roff, accompany our fake doctor up to our orbital and make sure he is placed in secure custody, and that the recovered artifacts are handed directly over to Station Commander Zheng."

Roff put one hand firmly on Fergus's upper arm as another officer picked up the fragment case, and they marched him toward the front door. Fergus tried to keep his head down, but out of his peripheral vision he could see Mitch nudge Derecho with his elbow and then tell him something too low to hear.

Whatever it was, it didn't escape the attention of Quinn. "Hey, Derecho," she called out. "Looks like I found your ghost in the machine before you did. Tough luck."

Fergus ducked his head farther down.

"No shit, you're that guy, huh?" the woman walking beside

them with the case said, looking back at him appraisingly as Roff pulled him out onto the lawn, still messy with soldiers and equipment, but now with a military orbit-hopper sitting like a big gunmetal fly next to the trucks. "Project Monkeywrench."

"What?" Fergus asked.

"We've suspected for a while that DM was undercutting us, but it wasn't until they got desperate trying to catch you that they tipped their hand too far and we finally had our first proof. We have a betting pool on who you're working for. We also had one for how far you'd get before they killed you, but you ran out the clock on everyone on that."

"I can't believe you're a bad guy," Roff said, disappointed.

"I'm not," Fergus said. "I'm an unaffiliated good guy."

"No such thing," Roff said.

Fergus shook his head sadly, not knowing how to rebut that, not expecting it would matter, anyway.

Roff led Fergus up the fold-out ramp into the hopper and put a hand on Fergus's head to duck him under the doorway and in. The private shoved him into a reclined jump seat and pulled down the overhead bars, locking them into place. It was uncomfortable with his hands behind his back, but Fergus didn't figure complaining was going to do him any good. "You ever been to space before, or you need a barf bag?" Roff asked, taking the seat directly across from him.

"I'll be fine, but thanks for asking," Fergus said.

"You sure? I'll be mighty unhappy with you if I have to deal with barf globs floating around in here. And I'm the nice one; Hensley here might just shoot you."

The woman smiled. "No lie," she said. She put the case of fragments in a flight bin and sealed it, then took the seat next to Roff. "So, you torched Barrett Granby's house, huh?"

"Not me," Fergus said. "One of his followers."

The third soldier, Walsh by process of elimination, checked in on them and then closed the door from the outside, sealing them in. "Clear!" they heard him say over the pilot's radio, and the engines of the hopper started up, adding another layer of electrical noise to the chaos Fergus was already starting to find overwhelming. He must have started to look a little pale, because Roff waggled his finger at him. "No barf," he reminded Fergus.

The hopper lifted off, and the acceleration pressed him down against his seat. *Well, shit,* Fergus thought. *This is bad. Now what?*

"Look," he said, and both Roff and Hensley raised their eyebrows, as if surprised he was still there. "I'm really not the enemy. If you would just trust me—"

Both Roff and Hensley burst out laughing.

Fergus felt the shift in the engines before his inner ear, still being flattened by acceleration, noticed the difference. "Uh," he said, "I thought we were going to orbit?"

"We are," Roff said.

"Not right now," Fergus said. "We're not going straight up anymore."

"Bullshit," Hensley said. "I'd feel it . . . ." Her voice trailed off.

Roff reached up with obvious difficulty and punched the intercom button on the overhead. "Private Roff back here," he said. "What's our situation? We've changed course."

"Yeah, sorry about that," the pilot's voice came back, then nothing more.

Roff hit the button again. "Hello?"

The hopper leveled off, and the door to the flight cabin opened. A man in an ill-fitting Alliance uniform came back, and Fergus could hear the whine of the energy pistol charging to full in his hand. "This is your inflight service," the man said with a grin that wasn't at all friendly. "No peanuts, no pretzels, no wasabi crackers, just a gun." He pointed it over at Roff and Hensley. "Which one of you is authorized to open the bin?"

"Neither of us," Hensley said. "It can only be opened when we reach the station."

"You better hope that's a lie, because if that's true, I don't have any reason to keep either one of you alive," the man said.

"I can open it if you free me," Fergus said. "But no shooting anyone."

The man shook his head. "No way in hell, Monkeywrench. I was remote-piloting that drone in the woods in Tanzania, and I don't know how the hell you took it down, but I am not letting you loose in here. You get to go down with the ship, so to speak. Can't guarantee I won't mess you up a little first."

"'I'm gonna mess you up,'" Fergus mocked. "Of course you are. That's what, first week of Villainy 101 For Dummies? You people are so predictably unoriginal, it's just sad."

"Who the hell are you?" Hensley demanded.

"Well, this big dumb oaf is Digital Midendian, obviously," Fergus answered. "If you mean me, I'm nobody. Nobody but still really sick of assholes who want to 'mess me up,' like I got nothing better to do. I'm kind of under a deadline here."

"I can just shoot you," the man said.

"Sure," Fergus agreed. "Why don't you? Because then you'll never find the rest of the pieces. And with those"—he pointed with his chin toward the wrong overhead bin—"I have them all."

"Had," the man corrected.

"*Have*," Fergus insisted.

"You are one cocky bastard," the man said. "And shut up, you with the *la dee hah torture how boring* schtick. We can find your family, your friends. What about those people in Scotland, above the bar? Kyle could pay them a visit."

"Them?" Fergus laughed. "Poor gullible people. Their long-dead cousin that everyone knows drowned shows up out the blue still alive, with some crazy-ass made-up-on-the-spur-of-the-moment story, and they bought it instantly. Gave me a good cover while I went to find the Doune Hill piece. You idiots had ten *years*, and it took me an afternoon. Probably takes you five years every time you have to find your own ass."

Roff snickered.

"Here's the thing," the man snarled out, through gritted teeth. "None of the three of you are getting out of this. There's only two lev-packs, and me and Nigel are taking them."

"There are eight standard on these hoppers," Roff said.

"Yeah, well, the boss was clear about his expectations, so we left six of them in the shrubs with your pilots," the man said.

"Then if we're gonna die anyway, what's our incentive to help you?" Hensley asked.

"I got none," Roff said.

"Me either," Hensley said.

Fergus shrugged.

The man waved his hands in aggravation. "You are the most annoying people I have ever met," he said.

"Thanks! It's nice to have your efforts recognized," Fergus said.

"You are so lucky Mitch isn't here—he'd have shot you in the face by now. After you pulled that stunt with his wallet at Granby's, he's got an entire fucking cult after him, trying to avenge their Mastro." The man paused. "Actually, that's a little bit funny, because he's a jerk. But he's one of us."

"How long until we crash?" Fergus asked. "Do I have time to use the bathroom?"

"He pees a lot," Roff said.

"You're about to die, and you're worried about *peeing*?! What the fuck is wrong with you?" the man shouted.

"We're all going to die," Fergus said, irrationally pleased with how frustrated the man was becoming. "You don't think you're going to get out of this yourself, do you? Because nuh-huh, no way, buttnuts."

Finally, the man couldn't take it anymore, and stepped forward and smashed Fergus across the face with the side of his pistol. In the split second before it connected, Fergus stuck out one foot and kicked the man's shin. In that moment of contact, he felt not only his own electricity flow across but the hunger of whatever was on the other side, trying to pull them both through a door that didn't exist. Blood flew from his cheek and nose at the impact and sent him reeling hard against the seat restraint, at the same time as his assailant dropped like a stone and sprawled across the floor of the hopper. The pistol skittered down across the floor and under Roff's seat.

"What the . . ." Hensley asked.

"Quick, before he wakes up," Fergus said.

She and Roff wasted no time getting out of their seats, then Roff got down on his hands and knees to pull the pistol out from where it had slid. "Okay, now let me out," Fergus said.

Hensley shook her head. "No fucking way."

"You need my help to get out of here," Fergus said.

"No, I really don't," she said. She went to the flight cabin door and knocked. "Nigel!" she called out, making her voice as deep as she could.

"What the hell, Bruce? I'm trying to fly here, and the Alliance is on our fucking tail already!" came the muffled response.

"We got a big problem. Monkeywrench is getting loose," Hensley said.

There was muffled swearing, then the door opened a crack, and Hensley shot through it without hesitation. There was a loud thump of a body hitting the floor. "Goddamn it," Hensley said, and braced herself against the doorframe to kick the body out of the way enough to climb over Nigel into the cockpit.

"She a pilot?" Fergus asked.

"We've all had training," Roff said. He bent over Bruce and checked his pulse. "Unconscious," he said. "How'd you do that?"

"Magical space ninja training. Seriously, can you please unlock me?" Fergus asked.

"No," Roff said. He put binders on Bruce's wrists, too, and hauled him upright just enough to dump him in a seat next to Fergus. "And I don't care if you have to pee; you're not on their side, but that sure as hell doesn't mean you're on ours."

Fergus took a deep breath and let it out. He had really thought he was going to have to watch Hensley and Roff get murdered in front of him, and now that that possibility had dissipated, he was left with just unbearable thirst and a need to get out of this trap while he had the chance. Where his hands were squashed between his back and the interior hull of the hopper, he could feel the electricity running past, feel the network of lines and the bright spots of relays and components strung along it. It was so easy to send the tiniest spark in, the tiniest wave in an opposing frequency to disrupt the flow.

The interior of the hopper went dark except for the fading light coming in through the open flight cabin door, and the engines and rotors let out a low groan as they slowed and eventually stopped. Only Fergus heard the tiny click of his seat harness unlocking.

"Roff!" Hensley yelled over her shoulder as she pounded on the helm panel. "It's gone dead!"

Roff's eyes never left Fergus's face. "Call for help. Try to get us a midair pickup."

"Comms are down too," she said.

Roff now looked away, toward his partner, and Fergus used his shoulders to quietly shrug the seat harness up and away. Getting out of the binders would be harder because they had a mechanical component, but he had an idea about that, too. He managed to get to his feet just as Roff glanced back and realized he was loose. "Stop there!" Roff ordered.

The hopper was now dropping, at a sharper and sharper angle, back toward the Earth. He had no idea how long they had, but the sky outside the window had gone back to blues, and that was not a good sign. Turbulence started bumping up under the hopper as its stabilizers failed to activate.

Fergus swayed on a big bump and used the momentum of it to crash into Roff, and zap him in that brief contact. "Sorry, man," he said. He knelt and felt Roff's pockets until he found the remote for the cuffs and deactivated them. Hands free, he gently picked up the private and buckled him into one of the empty seats.

"What's going on back there?" Hensley called from the cockpit.

Fergus shorted out the overhead bin lock and took out the small case of fragments, then opened the rear emergency storage locker, pulled out one of the two lev-packs in there, and buckled it around himself securely before putting on the face mask and breather pack. At this altitude, it was going to be a rough ride down.

He could see the browns and greens of land slowly emerge through the thinning clouds below. They didn't have much time, but there was enough for Hensley to pull out of the dive if the hopper wasn't dead.

Here goes nothing, he thought, hoping it'd be something. He'd always done this one way, shutting signals down, but maybe he could start it up, too? Otherwise, he didn't think a single lev-pack could handle both their weight, which meant he was leaving at least one of Hensley and Roff to die. That wasn't an acceptable cost at all. Putting the palm of his hand against the bulkhead, he tried to kick the electrical systems into rebooting.

Lights flickered, then the self-repair systems took over, and in seconds, the hopper was fully online and Hensley was pulling the nose up again. He let out his breath. Looked like he wasn't going to get anyone killed after all.

Inside the case, the fragments were singing in unison, a song of welcome and joy, trying to fold him into their harmonies. He was running out of time.

"Good luck, Hensley. Tell Roff I'm sorry!" Fergus called, then opened the hopper door and leapt out into the vast, fragile, precious skies of Earth.

Chapter 21

Fergus landed somewhere in a farm field, surrounded by deciduous trees with a few evergreens sprinkled among them. A temperate zone, at any rate; he didn't know enough about crops to pick out any except the corn among the mosaic of plants around him. As soon as he was safely on the ground, he shorted out the lev-pack's systems; they were designed to be highly traceable, for all the obvious reasons, and for just as obvious ones, he wasn't personally keen on that emergency feature.

It wouldn't take them too long to find him, regardless. Running, right now and as fast and as far as he could, was the best chance he had. The fragments in the case were speaking to him in dreamlike synchronicity, cajoling him to join them and become whole, but always also there was that other noise on the far side, straining for that door to open.

The hopper had disappeared out of sight over the horizon, but he didn't hear any sound of explosion and hoped that meant Hensley had pulled up in time. He carried a lot of lives on his conscience, some justifiably so and some not, but he didn't want to add those two.

At the edge of the field, he found an irrigation channel and dropped both the dead pack and his stolen Alliance uniform into it.

By the position of the sun, and how long it had been since he'd stepped into the Digital Midendian compound, he was still in North America, probably somewhere near the middle. His sense of time, and time of day, was badly confused after a nearly endless series of planet-hops and far too little sleep, but it seemed midafternoon.

He walked for about forty-five minutes along the edges of the field until he spotted an old barn with most of its roof collapsed in. The doors on the end were open and mostly off their hinges, so it was easy to step into what shelter remained and look around in the bright lines of sunlight streaming through the cracks in the barn boards.

There were the rusty remains of a tractor, long since past any measure of even creaky mobility, and a number of other, decrepit farm tools on rotted handles piled around it. Other things around it were less identifiable, moldy shapeless sacks with their contents long since depleted or smuggled away by wildlife.

Behind it all, in the very back, was an old ice cream van. The tires had long since moved on to their promised road in the great beyond, and it was rusty enough that it wasn't much less grim than the tractor, but when he hauled open the door with an ear-splitting squeal of rust and metal on metal, the interior was dry, empty, and free of the stink of rodents that permeated the rest of the barn.

Fergus climbed in, shut the door, and set the case of fragments inside one of the old ice cream coolers, where their chatter was at least somewhat muffled, then curled up in the dust on the floor for a much-needed nap. It would be easier to move when night fell, anyhow, and who knew when the opportunity to safely rest would come again, or what trouble lay between him and orbit. After that, he was sure sleep would be the least of his worries.

———

It turned out that Fergus's biggest worry, three days later as he snuck through the service corridors between the Kelly Station orbital security zones, was whether or not he could be arrested for odor. He had a concourse and a half to cross before he could get out to the berth transports and back to *Whiro* for a shower, and he was fairly sure his clothing was now legally classifiable as a biological weapon.

Beggars couldn't be choosers, he thought, when what you're begging for is a free ride up to Earth orbit without being noticed, and stowing away on an automated farm transport had been a stroke of luck. If only it had been transporting corn, or wheat, or some other innocuous produce, but no; his luck never, ever ran 100% good.

Of all the things to ship into space, though, heirloom goats seemed a ridiculous choice. On the other hand, they had been conveniently easy to hide among and kept him warm, and the only real challenge in getting away had been keeping the herd, who now clearly considered him an honorary member, from trying to follow him out.

He'd circumvented at least six different security points before he got to the rental locker where he'd stashed his exosuit and a handful of other things, and now there was just one more door between him and the concourse where he could catch the local transport out to *Whiro's* berth. *Please let it go smoothly,* he thought. *For once?*

The door alarm was easily disabled with the confuddler, no crude zapping necessary, and after listening at the door long enough to be pretty sure no one was nearby, he pushed it open and stuck his head out to look.

Standing in the center of the concourse, directly across from the door, was one of Digital Midendian's guys, staring right at him. Their eyes met. Before Fergus could ditch back into the corridor, the man raised both his hands to show he wasn't holding a gun. "The boss wants to talk," the man said. "He told me to say please."

Fergus raised one eyebrow.

"*Please*," the man growled, clearly unaccustomed to the words. "Eventually, you'll have to say yes, unless you wanna die of old age hiding in the walls. Mr. Derecho is persistent."

In the back corridors, they could eventually hunt him down and kill him. At least out in public he had a fighting chance, right? Honestly, he'd expected Derecho to be stuck in an Alliance cell right now.

The man gestured for Fergus to follow, and as Fergus reluctantly stepped out of the service door and let it close and relock with a *snick* behind him, wrinkled his nose. "What is that smell?" he asked.

"That's Gobber, Gabriel, Dahlia, and Isis," Fergus said, as other people walking through the hallway crossed to the far side to put some distance between him and them. "You can't always choose your traveling company."

The man just grunted and let Fergus follow him, trusting him not to run. Which probably meant he knew more than Fergus did about his chances of getting away successfully. For now, it was best to play along. And, he had to admit, he was curious what Derecho might have to say to him.

And anyway, the more he walked around, the more people noticed him and his noteworthy odor in passing. Attention would complicate escape but also any murder attempts.

Evan Derecho was sitting on a stool at the counter of the Deli Gute Esn. If that was coincidence or another message, it wasn't clear. Kyle and Mitch stood behind him. They both looked uncomfortable and ridiculous, large men perched on such tiny stools in their suits and glowers, but Derecho was relaxed, in a black business suit with the tie undone, leaning one elbow on the bright blue counter top. "Come join me," he said, and indicated the empty stool beside him. "Everything is on camera here, though no audio; it is the closest I could come to neutral territory on short notice."

Fergus sat. His nameless escort stood outside the door, blocking it.

"Coffee?" Derecho asked.

"Sure," Fergus said.

Derecho snapped his fingers, and Kyle got up and walked around behind the counter, pouring a mug full from the pot. He set it in front of Fergus with just enough of a thump to splatter hot coffee on his hand, but the man either didn't notice or didn't care. If looks could kill, Fergus would be no more than a smear of paste on the floor. "Thanks," he said anyway.

Derecho held up his arm, where a wristband gleamed across his skin. "House arrest," he said. "Well, planetary arrest. I'm supposed to get my ass back to Earth and stay there until they've finished gutting my business and deciding what they can charge me with that'll stick. But the Alliance isn't so uncivilized as to deny a man out on bail a decent lunch, nor so attentive as to notice when I buy out the place for half an hour for a personal meeting. So, here we are. I'm afraid if you want a sandwich, you're out of luck."

"I did, kinda, but I'll live," Fergus said. Since when did the Alliance let people out on bail? *Since those people aren't you or your friends or other people who have no money,* he thought wryly. "How did you know I'd be here?"

Derecho tapped the side of his mug. "I have built an empire on educated guesses, and there weren't that many ships coming up from Earth that you could plausibly be on," he said. "Also, I helped build out parts of the security system on this station."

"That figures," Fergus said. "What do you want?"

"Ideally, I'd like you to come work for me," Derecho said. Mitch growled under his breath at that. "You're resourceful, persistent, smart, and I'm sure we can clear up any bad impressions among my other personnel." He glanced briefly but meaningfully toward Mitch. "It's just our bad luck we started out working against each other. Clearly, you know more about the artifact pieces than the rest of us, given how easily you breezed through the impossible task of finding them, and if we pool our knowledge, we could crack the technology there. Think how transformative, how lucrative that could be. I'm betting you don't have the infrastructure to monetize this yourself, so you need a partner anyway."

Fergus sighed. "It's too dangerous."

"So is fire, but we've harnessed it, made it a tool, a thing *we* control," Derecho said, then laughed. "As long as you don't claim to worship it, I guess."

"What was it between you and Granby, anyway?" Fergus asked. "I never did figure it out."

"I was briefly in a relationship with his sister," Derecho said. "It didn't end amicably. That's also how he found out about the pieces, originally, through her. I could have found a way to work with him, found things I could use him for, if he'd insisted on a cut-in, but no, he couldn't see past his own resentments to cooperate. You're not like him, though. And that's what I'm saying: together, you and I, we can own this technology, own the world. That must sound good to you."

Fergus lazily turned his coffee mug around in front of him, back and forth, knowing all too well he couldn't trust it was safe to drink. It smelled so good, though, that twice he nearly found himself raising it to his lips. "Here's the thing," he said. "First, I'm kind of an asshole. Bad social skills, doesn't play well with others, not a team player. You know the type. A human resources nightmare, frankly. And I smell like goats. For your own sake, I must turn you down."

"That's surprisingly glib, for someone with as much risk as you," Derecho said.

"I get that *glib* thing a lot," Fergus said, letting the *risk* comment pass. "But, if you want a serious answer, it's this: those pieces? You can't harness the technology, not if you had decades to study them, and you don't. They're a ticking time bomb, the count is running down, and there's no way to turn them off. The best you could hope for is to be one of the first to die so you won't have to witness as it consumes our entire planet, our entire solar system, and with it your entire potential customer base."

"I'm not interested in any scare-story bullshit," Derecho said. "Everything can be understood and controlled. And even if what you said is true, how could you possibly know any of this?"

"Because I can hear them, the monsters waiting for us," Fergus said. "Can't you?"

"Hear them? Hear who?" Derecho repeated.

Fergus raised both his hands, palms facing each other. Mitch and Kyle both stiffened, ready in a second to jump in. "May I?" Fergus asked.

"Do what?" Derecho asked suspiciously.

"Let you hear them, too," Fergus said.

There was a long pause, then Derecho nodded. "Sure."

Fergus placed both his hands on either side of Derecho's head, covering his ears, and let the core fragments still in his pack wake up and connect to him, and then through him to the opposite ends of the path. The skittering, oily, pinch-bite feel of the Vraet slithered through Fergus's body, through his hands, and Derecho jerked away, his face pale.

"How the hell did you do that?"

"Not me. The pieces," Fergus said. "That's what's coming for us all."

"Boss?" Kyle asked.

Derecho waved a hand for him to shut up and sat there for a long minute, recomposing himself, before he took a shaking sip of his coffee. When he set the mug down, it was more confidently. "It's a trick," he said. "A good trick, worthy of the best con men, but only a trick."

"What if it's not?" Fergus said.

"I can't accept that possibility," he said. "So: there's a job offer on the table."

"I must decline, but thanks," Fergus said. "I'd like to leave now."

"Not yet. Negotiations, right? Since offering you a job wasn't good enough, how about I offer you your life, safety, and freedom?"

"You planning on killing me here?" Fergus asked.

"Not me. I can't vouch for Mitch. But you know, I had access to an awful lot of the Alliance's secret data, not just the stuff I was contracted to manage and/or purge but other stuff, too. And it's interesting that I found this chunk of bioprint data—woefully incomplete, but enough to speculate with, that seems to be a nice match for you. Our Monkeywrench seems to be one Duncan MacInnis, and oooh boy, does the Alliance want to get their hands on you. There are layers there, you know, a lot of good people at the top doing all the day-to-day good stuff, but then pockets of people below them, doing the dirtier or less publicly palatable things also for the greater good, or how they perceive it anyway, and your name is all over their files. Handing them *you* would likely buy me a lot of forgiveness."

"What, some random speculation with no proof? I doubt it," Fergus said.

"I got the Enceladus connection, and I can draw a line between that dot over to the Shipyard at Pluto and your friends there. Interesting that you're here and one of their ships has been intermittently parked here in orbit almost the whole time. If that's enough to interest them, what other data will they give me? How many dots can I connect until I have a drawing of your whole life?" Derecho said. "As you said, you're an asshole and you don't play well with others, particularly when those others are in positions of authority. I bet I could find a lot of people looking for you."

"What if you can't?" Fergus said.

"I can. More to your point, what is it worth to you to keep those dots nicely unconnected, unfollowable? Data is my thing. I mean, given how much digging I had to do to connect you to Enceladus, you've got some skills there, but I'm the master at it, and I'm trusted. Well, *was* trusted, but I will be again. I could hide you from them, give you a whole new life where you won't have to be constantly looking over your shoulder, wondering when the law is going to catch up to you."

"There are fifty-two billion people in this solar system," Fergus said. "Even you must have one person you'd give up everything for to see survive."

"You are making several faulty assumptions," Derecho said. "First, that I believe your disaster scenario at all, and second, that even if I did, that even though you see no solution to it, that I would be unable to find one. You think I am either gullible or stupid, and it doesn't matter which, because I am neither."

"Well, then," Fergus said. "I'm sorry, but I think we're at an impasse."

"I'm sorry too," Derecho said. "I'd like to say I'm a gentleman and I'll give you an hour's head start or something, but really, I'm not. I've already made sure the Alliance finds all my datapoints on you, with connections handily drawn in for all to see. Also, as soon as I get back to Earth, I'm going to put a bounty on your head big enough that your own mother would turn you in for it. Between me and the Alliance, you're never going to have a day of peace for the rest of your life."

"Haven't had one yet, so I guess I won't know what I'm missing," Fergus said, standing up.

"Once you're out that door, it'll be too late," Derecho said. "Right now, I could stop it all. Be sure this is what you want."

Fergus laughed. "What I want? I wish that figured into any of this. Thanks for the offer, though."

"Wrong decision, MacInnis," Derecho said sadly.

Past him, Mitch cracked his knuckles. "I'm okay with it," he said.

"Mitch? Consider that the last time we met, I left you unharmed," Fergus said. "If you get in my way again, I'm going to put you out an airlock."

He popped a blister pack of cleaner bots and dropped it behind him as he strode out the door without looking back.

———

"You cannot reach me," *Whiro* replied to his query, after a nerve-wracking lag. "I have departed Earth and am currently in the jump queue at Jupiter to get back to the Shipyard. I am being followed by *Blue Ivory* and watched by at least three other vessels in my current vicinity."

"What?" Fergus said. "You *left* me?"

"All orbiting and outgoing ships are being searched, and we were concerned that if the Alliance failed to turn up anything of note on their first pass through, that would become a lockdown. Ignatio insisted we depart, as eir mobility is necessary to finish your task."

"Isla?"

"She went directly to Mars with the Baltimore fragments, because we were about to be searched. The Alliance seemed particularly nonplussed to find only an alien—and one they could not identify—onboard, and their attempts to get coherent answers out of em seemed unusually fraught with language difficulties."

"Good for Ignatio," Fergus said. He was holed up, sitting on the floor in a maintenance closet on the underbelly of the station with his handpad resting on his crossed legs, passively tapped in to the orbital security cameras. Derecho had left, and so far, no one was heading in his direction, but more Alliance personnel were arriving all the time, and there seemed to be a coordinated sweep being organized a few floors away from him. Before long, he would be found.

It was a good thing no one had a dog, or they'd have sniffed his goaty self out in thirty seconds.

"If I can somehow get directly to Mars on my own—" he said.

"It would be inadvisable to try," *Whiro* said. "The Alliance has already involved the Mars Colonial Authority. According to Arelyn, the MCA has become unusually active and is searching everyone moving in and out of Free Marsie territory, and there has been an upsurge in raids just over the last few hours."

"Shit," Fergus said. "Is everyone down there safe?"

"Arelyn checked in with me a few hours ago, and at that time, everyone was fine and in a secure location. You, on the other hand, present a difficulty in that regard."

"Yeah, I noticed," Fergus said. "I've got eight fragments sitting in my backpack, trying to convince me to become one of them, and twenty-four others down on Mars I need to retrieve, and I'm trapped."

"Ignatio is telling me at this time that he is arranging for a third-party ride. Arelyn and Kaice have identified a Martian courier who will rendezvous with you. Please hold tight where you are until details are finalized."

"But—"

"There are no *buts*," *Whiro* said. "Wait."

"Fine," Fergus said, and disconnected. He considered kicking the closet wall out of frustration, but with his luck, someone would hear and come arrest him and he'd have no one to blame except his own petulant self. "But I'm the plan-maker," he muttered to himself instead, and it didn't make him feel nearly as better as kicking the wall would have.

His handpad chimed again. He tapped it, and Arelyn's face appeared. "Where are you?" she asked.

"Sitting in a closet on Kelly Station, in Earth orbit," he said. "Might be here for a while, because my ship abandoned me. It's not bad, though. Some fresh paint, maybe a nice picture or two—"

"Whatever," Arelyn said. "You need to get yourself off that station."

"Trust me, I'm trying," Fergus said. "All the outbound ships are being searched—"

"*Off* the station doesn't require *in* something else," Arelyn said, and she had a genuinely pleased grin on her face. "You got your suit?"

"Yeah," he said.

"Great. I'm sending you a specific low-frequency code that's an old Free Marsie mining transport call. Get yourself at least a kilometer and a half off the station, wait until exactly one hour from now, then activate that code. Your ride from Ignatio will pick you up, then swing out to meet Isla and our courier with the fragments."

"The Alliance isn't going to let any ship out of this territory without being searched," Fergus said.

Arelyn smiled again. "They won't search Ignatio's friends."

"Then who—" Fergus started to ask.

Arelyn just shook her head. "Oh, that would be telling," she said. "One hour on the dot. Don't be late. I wish I could be there just to see the look on your face."

———

Fergus had been out into space more times than he could count, more places than he could count. Some of those times had been fun, and other times it was because someone was trying to kill him, and some had been for short stretches and others for long, but he hated, hated, *hated* throwing himself out a perfectly good airlock without at least some idea where he was going, how he was going to get there, and most important of all, how he was going to get back.

Also, he hated that it was someone else's plan, even if it was people he trusted with his life, because dammit, plans were *his* job.

As soon as he'd closed the external airlock and made sure it sealed—he'd had to short the alarm systems, and he didn't want to be the cause of some hapless maintenance person opening the inside door and accidentally sucking themselves out into space—he turned around and looked out on his home world.

It was night, Earthside. He'd seen old vids talking to early spacewalkers, talking about being engulfed in darkness, but that had been centuries and centuries before. Below him through clouds he could see the lights of cities defining the land, see the pale glow of drought kites over the horn of Africa, and all around and below were the brightly colored fireflies of all the ships, coming and going, wandering, spinning along with the planet below. *So much life,* he thought. It was dizzying.

He carefully pushed himself upright, magboots against the station hull, and stood there sideways, looking around, but there was no one and nothing particularly near him or likely to cut across his path. *Here goes,* he thought, and turned off the magnets in his boots just as he kicked himself off.

Space was funny in that it just didn't really ever make you slow down. As soon as you headed off in one direction, unless you hit something else or some other force came along and applied friction or resistance on you, you just kept floating along in whatever direction you had started going. Newton's Third Law was, in this moment, his friend. Also, the pocket full of zero-gravity toilet disinfectant bombs he'd grabbed on his way out of the closet. It was only a shame, he thought as he very carefully aimed each pitch to moderate his trajectory, that the faint puffs of pink dust each one gave out when it hit the station couldn't do anything about the righteously bad funk he was sure the interior of his exosuit was rapidly acquiring from his be-goated clothes.

He did, however, speed up a little with each throw.

When he was sure he was far enough away from the station, and his time had run out, he activated the code Arelyn had sent him on the old frequency, and waited and watched as he kept drifting farther out.

Along the horizon, in orbit above the flecks and blooms of a distant terrestrial thunderstorm, was the Alliance station itself. As he watched, a dot detached itself from the larger mass of lights and pulled away from the station.

Shit, Fergus thought. *Don't come this way. I'm out of toilet bombs.*

It turned and headed directly toward him. His suit jets wouldn't do much to escape it, and once he lit them up, he was going to be a lot more visible to anyone else looking for him. So, he waited, willing it to turn, or ascend, or descend, or something.

As it got closer, it became increasingly clear that it was not, by any stretch of the imagination, a human ship. It looked like a fat-limbed anemone, resplendent with moving, twinkling lights, and as it approached, its limbs extended and spread, as if it was opening its jaws to swallow him whole.

Help? he thought.

Fergus was engulfed, drawn in, and deposited very, very gently in a circular chamber as the ship sealed behind him. Several rope-like structures ran from floor to ceiling, and he grabbed desperately at one as the ship suddenly accelerated, sending him swinging. Whatever the floor was made of, his boots did not want to stick to it, so he clung there until the ship's speed leveled off again and another door opened onto the interior. Two aliens came through.

He knew those wrinkly squash shapes only too well: Ponkians. The last time he'd met one was under the ice of Enceladus, working in one of the research stations, and it was almost as much a surprise then as now. Fergus opened his faceplate and grinned, bowing low. "Estimables!" he said. "Thank you for the lift!"

One of the Ponkians grinned back at him. "Welcome, welcome, mmmmmm, friend!" one said.

"Estimable Feffi?" Fergus asked.

"Ah, I am I!" Feffi said. Fergus had met Feffi nearly a decade earlier, in a Ganymede bar named the Riot, moments before it lived up to its name; he'd got the Ponkian safely out before it could be harmed or, worse, get distressed enough to inflate and blow foul gas throughout the land hab. Ponkians were pleasant, jovial, agreeable people except when anxious or afraid, at which point they could also be described as a near-perfect cross between a pufferfish and a skunk.

Feffi and the other Ponkian, Tugu, showed him to a small cabin, where he pulled off his exosuit and hung it up, hoping to air it out. "Are you distressed?" Feffi asked.

"No, no, thank you, I'm very happy," Fergus said.

Tugu's entire face scrunched up in thick wrinkles. "Mmmmm but scared? Worried? Hurt?"

"No, no, really, I . . ." Fergus started to protest again, then realized why they were asking. "It's not me. It was goats."

"Mmmmm goats?" Feffi asked.

"I was sitting with them for a long time," Fergus said. Should he say the goats smelled bad, or would that cause offense? He didn't know how Ponkians regarded their own odor. "They may have been worried. Do you have a way I can wash?"

"Yes, yes!" Tugu said, relieved, and showed him a sliding panel that opened on a small closet, and reached out one long, skinny purple limb to tap a panel. Thin jets of water sprayed out from a grid of holes on one wall, and then got sucked into similar holes on the opposite one. "Very nice, mmmmmm?"

Tugu turned the water off, then Feffi very gently nudged Fergus inside, and they closed the door. It was certainly a broad hint. He took off his clothes, snuck them back out the door onto the floor, and then enjoyed the sharp, warm water as long as he dared.

The cabin was empty when he emerged, and as he stepped over the small threshold between shower and room, a wall of hot, fresh air hit him from both sides. He stopped there until he felt dry, thinking about how he'd never given sufficient consideration to the possibility of signing on to a Ponkian exploration ship before, though their idea of exploration was more one of "wander around the galaxy at random and eat food."

It wasn't a bad life at all, he decided, as he pulled a clean change of clothes out of his pack.

Just as he finished dressing, there was a sound outside the cabin door like an odd, trilling whistle, and he opened it to find Feffi outside. "We are catching mmmmmm your other friends now. Please come?"

"Absolutely," Fergus said. He followed them to a much larger bay. The far end was open to space, and Fergus nearly shouted in shock, but there was air and no sensation of being ripped out of the ship to his near-instant death, so he managed to keep it down to a small, undignified yelp.

The flyer that glided in was an old, nondescript Martian model, one of hundreds still in service in civilian hands, and had no markings other than its registration identifier. It settled, and the outer wall of the bay closed from several sides at once, without a sound. "Hello hello!" Feffi waved at the flyer's opaque front window, and moments later, Isla stepped out, wide-eyed and pale, carrying a case that screamed so loud in Fergus's mind, grabbing across the space between them, that he almost fell to his knees.

"Fergus?" she asked.

He shook his head, steadying himself. "I'm okay. They're nearly overwhelming, that's all," he said as she set the case down on the bay floor and came over to wrap him in a hug.

"Yes, yes, helloes," Tugu said from behind Feffi. "And also another, mmmmmm?"

Fergus looked over Isla's shoulder as another person got off the flyer, looked around them for a moment, then unclipped their helmet and faceplate. And this time, he did fall to his knees.

"Dru?" he asked.

Chapter 22

Dru looked . . . the same, Fergus thought, but also not, as if the Dru he'd known had been painstakingly recreated by the finest craftsman back into her whole self again, by people who had not quite known her well enough. *Or I've lived so long with my memories of her colored by my guilt that it's my eye that is off,* he thought. Her rich brown hair, still kept cut short Marsie-style, was now flecked with gray, and her face had lost some of its roundness, leaving her harder-looking, but those differences seemed meaningless, in this moment. He'd never thought about her as pretty, but she was, and the fierce fire of her self still flickered through the layers of old pain and anguish that had been set down atop it over the years.

"Fergus," she said, and he could see her own struggle for composure war across her face and eventually win. "You've gotten older."

"It's not for lack of trying," he answered. He felt suddenly incredibly silly, having let himself be so overcome, and got awkwardly back to his feet. "It's good to see you, but damn, this is a surprise."

Her face crinkled up in sadness. "You've lost your incomprehensible accent," she said. "I'm sorry Mars took that from you."

"I gave it away voluntarily," he said. "Mars gave me much in return."

"Are ye sayin' we gab funny?" Isla said. "Soonds tae me like it's yoo."

Dru's lips twitched into a brief, fleeting smile. "Maybe so," she said.

"I have to ask, and it's not that I'm not happy to see you, but what are you *doing* here?" Fergus asked, more plaintively than he would have wished. His heart was still racing, and he felt weirdly adrift, as if reality had become unmoored around him.

"The Mars Colonial Authority has tormented me for so long, they have forgotten who I used to be," Dru said. "And I forgot for a while too, until during one of her visits, Kaice told me you were back and still trying to pull the impossible out of your ass. I came to meet Isla, and then, when it was clear none of Kaice's people could get past the MCA to bring you this case, I volunteered. Kaice declined. So, I *insisted*. You know how hard it is to win a battle of wills against Kaice?"

"I do, and you're the only one I've ever known who could do it," Fergus said. "But the Alliance, and the MCA—"

Behind them, Feffi made a sound like air going in and out of a bellows. "We are mmmm an ambassador ship," he said. "Also, a half of your standards ago, there was mmmmm an unfortunate diplomatic incident, on your Kemon Station. Your Alliance is, mmmmm, very reluctant to risk another offense of us."

Tugu's entire body rippled, and he grew just slightly larger. "It was a terrible thing, mmmmmm," he said.

"It is okay now, Tugu!" Feffi said, and wrapped his arms around his crewmate in a big hug. Slowly, Tugu deflated.

"The Alliance is still going to ask you why you picked up the flyer," Fergus said.

"We will say we do not remember, mmmmm?" Feffi said. "It is such, mmmmm, a human answer for not answering at all. It will take us about six of your hours to reach our final rendezvous with your bizarre green friend, and then ey will take you where you need to go."

"Where are we meeting em?"

"Mmmmm we promised not to say," Tugu said.

"Who would I tell?" Fergus said. "Nobody. So, surely you can tell *me*."

"Mmmmm we do not remember!" Tugu said, and his whole body shook in delight.

"Fine," Fergus said, then locked eyes with Isla, then Dru. "Uh, are you sure . . ." he said.

"We all go," Feffi said. "Mmmmm, are already going. Do you like music? Tugu has been learning the trombone. Will you hear?"

At Isla's look of panic, Fergus smiled and walked over to offer her a hug, relieved that it turned out he didn't need to have said his goodbyes after all.

"We'd love to, thank you," he said to Feffi. "It'll be the memory of a lifetime."

————

The Ponkian ship briefly skirted the orbit of a medium-sized gas giant, far enough out in its solar system for its sun to be indistinguishable from just another star in the sky. Without knowing anything about Ponkian technology, or even if they'd gone into jump on the trip, Fergus couldn't say for sure, but it sure as hell looked like Neptune.

He and the others followed Tugu back down to the bay, where a small ship of unfamiliar design sat newly parked next to Dru's. It was a deep, almost hypnotic shade of blue, and pointy in unreasonably many directions, as if it were a stylized sea urchin with anger management issues. Spindly, curved legs held it above the floor, and a small ramp had unfolded from one of the crevices between spikes. "Your timid friend is here, mmmmmm," Tugu said. "Ey will not come out."

Timid was not a word Fergus would have ever thought to apply to Ignatio. He walked up the ramp and peered in through the door. "Ignatio?" he asked.

His friend popped eir head around as corner. All four of eir eyes were wider than Fergus had ever seen. "Come in come in get in!" Ignatio said, the words all in a rush.

"Is everything okay?" Fergus asked.

"Is okay, yes, but we must go as quickly as now right now," Ignatio said.

". . . All right," Fergus said. He turned around and went back down the ramp, where the others were waiting. "It's okay; he's just in a hurry. You can go on inside."

Isla picked up her stuff and then turned back at the ramp and gave a weird little bow to Tugu. "Thank you for having us," she said.

"You are welcome!" Tugu said. "It is mmmmm always a pleasure for good company."

"Please thank Feffi for us as well," Fergus said, and put his arms to his side and wiggled them in the closest human approximation of a Ponkian gesture of gratitude.

"Aaaaaah mmmmm yes!" Tugu said, waving his arms in a similar way. Deep inside Ignatio's ship, Fergus thought he heard a squeak of fear. He hurried after his sister and Dru, picking up the last of the crates and bags she and Isla had brought from Mars, and as soon as he was just barely inside the ship, the ramp slid in and the door slammed shut.

"We must go we must go!" Ignatio yelled, already in the pilot seat and lifting eir ship up to turn around, as Fergus stumbled and held on to whatever he could to keep himself steady.

"Is everything okay? Is the Alliance after us?" Fergus asked.

"No no no, we are not chased," Ignatio said. Ey looked

terrified. In moments, the back door of the bay opened to let them out, and Ignatio shot them out into space and down toward the planet's cloudy cover.

"Then what *is* it?" Fergus asked. "Is it the door?"

"No, not the Vraet; it's those aliens," Ignatio said. "They are big *raisin people.*"

"You've got to be fucking kidding me," Fergus said.

The clouds around them thickened, turned into an impenetrable haze. Ignatio whistled a tiny trill, and lights sprang on, illuminating only a short distance ahead. Isla clung to the arched doorframe onto the bridge. "What's happening?" she asked. "Are we being chased?"

"No, we're not," Fergus said. "Where are we going, Ignatio?"

"To the door station," ey said.

"On Nept—" Fergus started to ask.

Ignatio hissed fiercely. "Shooooosh, now."

Fergus sighed. The little craft shuddered in the heavy winds, and he hauled himself into the back, where there were a handful of seats that could at least accommodate a human form, if not comfortably. "Let me help buckle you both in," he said. Dru nodded. Isla tried to do the same, her face turning pale, one hand over her mouth.

"It should be a short flight, I think," Fergus said as he gently got his sister into a seat.

Dru had pulled herself into another seat and was trying to figure out the harness. "I've never left Mars," she said when Fergus came over to help.

"You didn't have to, just for my sake," he said.

"I didn't do it for you," she answered. "The MCA never really let me go; they just made sure I carried their prison with me, and stopped by just often enough to make sure I knew the door wasn't open."

Isla added, quietly, "I think that's why Fergus ran away from home when he did, before his door could close."

Fergus finished buckling Dru in. "The truth of it is, you can spend a lifetime running through every open door you find and still never escape your own head. Now, why don't you two talk about anything less depressing than *doors* while I go try to figure out where Ignatio is taking us."

He slipped back through into the front cabin. The shaking and shuddering were intensifying, the whole cabin filled with a deafening roar. He couldn't tell how fast they were moving, or how much of it was the winds outside pummeling them, but all of a sudden, there was something solid-looking ahead, approaching fast up from below.

"Uh, Ignatio . . ." Fergus started to say as he wrapped his arms as tightly as he could around the back of the empty chair. In the din, he could almost swear he heard a *yowl*.

"Ice," Ignatio said. "Do not worry."

"Coming from a person afraid of raisins, that's not reassuring," Fergus said.

Ignatio whistled another trill, longer and more complicated, and this time with clicks, and a blue neon circle lit up on the control board in front of him. It shifted through blue to turquoise to green, and then slowly, achingly, faded toward white. The moment it was fully white, Ignatio whistled and the ship dove, straight toward the wall of ice below them.

There was a flash, and when his vision cleared, he could see they were now passing through some sort of tunnel. The turbulence was gone.

"Did we just go through one of the interdimensional doors?" Fergus asked.

"No, no, only now we go to the door station, yes?" Ignatio said. "It is a secret way, and you will not tell?"

"I don't think anyone would believe me," Fergus said.

"Do not try to be believed. We mostly like humans, but we don't like them everywhere in all our spaces being needy pests. Cute needy pests. Cute *stupid* needy pests—"

"I get it. I won't tell anyone," Fergus said. He relaxed, just slightly, and then heard it again. A yowl, from the back of the cabin. "What was that?"

Ignatio waved three legs. "I do not know! I am busy! Go see yourself, yes?"

Ahead of them, the tunnel walls changed over from ice to rock, and Fergus dared a glance into the back, where a wide-eyed Isla now had a very spiky-furred Mister Feefs wrapped around her head. "Ignatio, you brought my *cat*?!" Fergus yelled forward.

"What? No!" Ignatio said.

"Yeah, well, then the cat brought himself," Fergus said. "This will go *splendidly*."

Suddenly, they were in an enormous cavern, too smooth to be natural. Another ship was already there, looking more like a building-sized brick than a ship, and he'd have mistaken it for a structure if it wasn't hovering above the floor on a column of blue light. Seeing where Fergus was looking, Ignatio wiggled eir legs. "The Thump," ey said, as if that explained everything. "They will not bother us."

"Where are we going?" Fergus asked, and in answer, Ignatio pointed toward a platform with a rounded arch in the wall behind it, in the distance. It was only as they flew toward it that Fergus grasped the perspective of just how big it was. "Is *that* a door? I mean, one of *the* doors? To Ijto?" he asked. He'd pictured something more person-sized, but this was enormous.

"A door, a door, of course," Ignatio said. "We have several many of these door stations to go through before we reach our door to Ijto."

As they neared, Fergus calculated that every ship ever built by the Shipyard could fit through that arch, some side by side. "That's bigger than I expected," he said. "You could drive a small invasion fleet through that."

"Some are small, some are big, yes?" Ignatio said. "The keys are the same, but the frames were built and rebuilt by many others over the millennia. Tunnels between are not so big, mostly, and they twisty bend and change size and your fleet would get stuck. Some have, before learning. You will see."

"Can *we* see?" Isla called out plaintively from the back.

At Ignatio's nod, Fergus went and unbuckled them both, and they stood and watched as Ignatio's ship drew closer to the gray wall within the arch, as solid and impenetrable-looking as anything he'd seen. Ignatio was not slowing down.

To one side, there was a small white dot that grew on Fergus's senses. Unlike the fragments in the back that were so close he felt like one point in a growing triangle of signal, this doorkey's chorus was complete and singing its own song, closed to other voices.

In moments, he could make it out as a semicircular niche precisely cut into the cavern wall, and inside it a roughly cube-shaped object was suspended. It had an ornate framework, this one in gold, and at its center was another cube the color of his own fragments. The patterns on its surface seemed to just slightly defy the eye to follow, but Fergus knew how they went, could feel the whole that his own shattered fragments desperately strove to become again themselves.

"Augh," he said, as sharp static coursed through him, his fragments agitated at the proximity of the other.

"Soon! Hold on," Ignatio said, and they hit the wall and passed through as if it wasn't there. All around them, everything was inside-out, crushing together and exploding outward at the same time. There was a distressing sensation of being everywhere and nowhere, of moving in complete stillness, and Fergus could neither look away nor make any sense of what he was seeing and feeling, until a tiny, brilliant dot of light appeared ahead and rushed toward them, engulfing the little ship . . .

. . . and then they were out, and Ignatio slowed eir ship down to where they were barely moving.

The fragments in the ship behind him had quieted down, but he could tell they were awake now beyond his ability to calm, much less control. "That was fast," he said, when he could find his wits again. "How far did we go?"

"Only about three hundred and seventy light years," Ignatio said. "It is a short tunnel, that one."

Holy shit, Fergus thought. *That's short?* "Is this how you came here? To the Shipyard, I mean?" he asked.

"Yes," Ignatio said. "There are many branches, many tunnels, many worlds."

The new station was very different from the cavern on Neptune, more of a long hall that seemed to curve away in the distance. Fergus leaned forward against the front window so he could take it all in. Arching columns that looked like fingers of stone fungus reached up to the roof, and a diffuse, warm, purplish light came from somewhere up among them, illuminating carved writing in some unknown language (or *languages*, Fergus had to guess, because there were distinct shifts in style) on the walls. The floor itself seemed to be some sort of mirror, or possibly unmoving water.

"Where are we?" Isla asked.

"An exoplanet named Hnize," Ignatio said.

"Nice," Isla said.

"Hnize," Ignatio repeated.

"Very nice," Isla added.

"*Hnize!*" Ignatio said, waving two of eir legs in the air in annoyance.

"We got it, I think," Fergus said, glaring at Isla. "But I thought you wanted the stations to be secret."

"Humans will never make it here," Ignatio said. "And what do you know of 'here,' anyway?"

"Not a damned— AH!" Isla shouted, and jumped back, pointing wildly. "There's something below the floor!"

Fergus peered out down, and sure enough, he could see a giant shape, lights along its sleek, pointy-ended body, slip by directly below the surface that he had taken for water. "A ship?" he asked.

"Yes, yes," Ignatio said. "I do not know that kind. If one comes up above, *then* you can shout in my soundholes, yes?"

They flew slowly, a meter or two above the floor, as the hall did slow S curves side to side for almost an hour before they reached another door, but Ignatio shook eir head and kept going. Four more ships passed them below, two like the first, none of them anything Fergus had ever seen. One was needle-shaped and so long and thin, he could hardly imagine anyone fitting inside, unless it was being flown by mice.

Weirder things have happened, he thought, just as he felt a vibration and energy coming toward them. "Something's heading toward us," he said, and Ignatio veered to one side, slipping eir ship between columns as a dozen spheres, each about five meters in diameter and iridescent like soap bubbles, zoomed through, just barely missing several posts as they careened past. "Tikne," Ignatio said, and then steered them back out into the corridor.

They reached another door, this one a big stone hexagon with its doorkey glowing in a triangular niche above it. It also had its own song, and he felt like both his own bees ("beezes," Ignatio had called them) and his collected fragments were listening intently, learning.

Ignatio spoke up. "This is a long tunnel, and it will be very loud inside."

This time, when they flew through the gray wall, Fergus felt like he was being sucked forward, and all the sound in the universe being pulled along with him. He was nearly convinced the tunnel was endless and he would be trapped in it forever when they emerged at last in the next station. The silence was almost painful, and the sudden cessation of pressure made him stumble backward. Dru caught his arm and steadied him.

When was the last time they'd touched? The high-five after returning to the City after the Sentinel job? It hurt that he couldn't remember for sure.

Dru spoke, but it was too muffled to hear.

"How far?" he asked, then repeated it louder, not sure if he was even making coherent sound. Everything still sounded like he was underwater.

"Sixteen thousand light-years," Ignatio answered. "Space was very bendy, and bends are noisy. Also fast, yes, good for us."

"If you say so," Fergus said. One of his ears popped. He looked out at the station, which was similar to the previous one, if more streamlined and newer-looking, and minus the water-mirror floor. In fact, the floor emanated the same purple glow that the ceiling had in the Hnize station, so he glanced up to see that the column tops disappeared into what appeared to be water suspended high overhead. "Okay, that's disturbing," he said, reluctant to take his eyes off it. "Where are we now?"

"A moon whose name I cannot render in your audible range," Ignatio said. "We call it Fortress. The surface is covered with many ruins, built in layers on top of each other, like battle frosting on a bad cupcake, yes? We do not know about the peoples who were in this system except that they do not exist now."

"My mukker Caylen would love this," Isla said. "He's all

about archaeology and alien history stuff. Can't say I entirely saw what he saw in it until now. And of course I suppose I can't tell him anything about this."

"No, please not, no telling humans or mukkers," Ignatio said.

"Ignatio, you got any food onboard?" Fergus asked. "I mean, edible food?"

Isla snorted. "As if. Good thing someone here thinks ahead." She dug in her bag and handed around bentos and water for everyone. Fergus opened his with trepidation and found to his joy little dumplings and curried noodles inside.

"Thanks," he said.

"Don't thank me; thank Kaice. She's the one who packed them."

Dru nodded. "That's Kaice for you," she said, and dug into hers.

Fergus ate, not having realized until this moment just how hungry he was, then drank until his bottle was almost empty.

Isla was watching him. "Thirsty," she commented.

"Yeah," he said. "The fragments . . . it's like I have to talk to them all the time, keep them quiet, and even if it doesn't feel like much, and I don't even have to think about it much, it's constant. And it's getting harder. And . . . ." Fergus fell silent.

"And?" Isla asked.

"I can hear them. Not the fragments, the things waiting for the door to open. Knowing we're bringing it to them." He shuddered. "It's a terrible sound."

"Is it like a scratching sound?" Dru asked. "Because I can hear that too."

"No, more like a . . . ." Fergus started to say, struggling to find the words, then realized he could hear the scratching too, from the back of the ship. "No, that's Mister Feefs crapping in Ignatio's spaceship."

"What!?" Ignatio declared, pulling the ship over into another alcove between columns and parking, before leaping out of eir seat. "This is terrible!"

"Maybe you should check for stowaways next time," Fergus said.

"Stop," Dru snapped, and everyone looked at her, surprised. "This is somewhere no human has ever been before and likely won't ever be again. Why are we wasting our time on petty little stuff in here? I want to *see*. Can we go outside and look while Fergus cleans that up?"

"Yes," Ignatio said. "But you will need to put your suits on."

"I don't have one," Isla said.

"I brought one for you," Dru said. "Never go anywhere without a suit and a spare. Mars rule number one."

Dru put hers on with expert ease and then the two of them helped Isla, who was still a novice at it.

Fergus found, scooped up, and dropped Mister Feef's little bundle of nastiness into the recycler on Ignatio's ship, then got himself suited up after the others. Ignatio was bustling around them excitedly. "Don't you need an exosuit, too?" Fergus asked, because he'd always been curious to see what ridiculousness would fit a Xhr.

"Yes, no problems," Ignatio said. Ey stood completely still for a long moment, all eir eyes closed, as if deep in meditation, and then with a visible shiver, the fur on eir body flattened, smoothing down until it became all of a sudden dull green scales. Thick membranes slid over his eyes, giving them an extra sheen.

"Whoa," Isla said.

"It is inefficient," Ignatio said. "We can only sustain this for short times, perhaps a standard year. Also, it gives me an ache in my head."

The four of them went out into the tunnel, staring around

them in awe. Isla held up her handpad and took images of the writing carved on the walls, slowly panning up and down. When Ignatio narrowed all eir eyes at her, she shrugged. "It's just for me," she said. "I won't show anyone. Promise."

"We should also rest," Ignatio said. "The next tunnel is very, very long, and once we are at the Ijto door, we will need to walk to where our doorkey once belonged."

"Walk? How far?"

"A few kilometers only," Ignatio said. "We should bring more snacks, yes?"

"Oh, I should think so," Fergus said, and settled down in the corridor, his back to the wall, staring up at the weird, watery ceiling and listening to the chatter of Dru and Isla as they explored around the ship. He didn't think he would fall asleep, but he did, lying against one of the columns.

In his dreams, it was as if he could feel the entire system of tunnels and doors, trace their energies like arteries through a convoluted, Escheresque, mathematically arcane universe. This morphed into a dream where he was walking in an old train tunnel, trying to keep his balance on one of the rails while holding in his cupped hands water and a very tiny goldfish, as the distant end of the tunnel grew brighter and louder. Even in the dream, he knew the sound was something external, and he woke up and flailed upright. "Incoming!" he shouted.

Somewhere farther down the tunnel they heard a loud scratching sound, growing closer. Across the floor from him, on the other side of the tunnel, Isla and Dru pressed themselves back against the wall. Ignatio was farther down the row of columns, doing the same, looking just as startled as the rest of them.

The thing that came down through the tunnel was long, jointed, with protruding antennae and a dozen legs that skittered and scratched down the walls and floor as it stalked through the tunnel, metallic implants along its body with winking red lights, like a twenty-meter-long cyborg stick insect. It stopped in the tunnel right between Fergus and the others, and turned its long, cylindrical head back and forth, until it fixed on where Fergus sat, doing his best to pretend he was invisible.

Its antennae fluttered over him for a long minute, then it reached out one long, skinny leg covered with armored hooks on its tip, and poked at Fergus's stomach. "No," Fergus said, and zapped it, making his suit reboot. It withdrew the leg, regarded Fergus a while longer, then heaved itself back up and continued off down the tunnel and away.

"Shiiiit," Dru said when the sound of its movements finally petered out into silence. "What was that?"

"Voidbug," Ignatio said. "They are mostly harmless but sometimes too curious and not careful where they step."

Fergus's heart was still racing. "So, we done exploring? Who's for moving on?"

The *yes* was unanimous.

The last tunnel was brutal and made Fergus glad he had gotten the small rest he'd had, even if it had been brief. The unnamed station they emerged from on the far side was small, more like the cavern in Neptune's core, and Ignatio parked eir ship near the third arch they found. They suited up again and gathered their gear. Dru strapped several large bags across her back, but before he could ask her about them, she was out the airlock ahead of him.

"Away, away now. We must go! This is a bad station for being not inside a ship," Ignatio cried as soon as they were all out, and shooed them over to the arch itself and its familiar, featureless gray interior.

"Well, then, here goes nothing," Fergus said. He closed his eyes to the illusion of a wall in front of his face and stepped forward.

Passing through the interface was like having a slow chill spread through his body, front to back, almost as if the energy were taking a snapshot of every atomic slice of him on its way through. Then there was confusion, a blast of sound and oppressive space, before he found himself on the other side, stumbling down from a small stone platform, the others right on his heels.

This time, they were outside, on a planet surface, in a wide courtyard.

Graceful arches overhead enclosed the airspace, and after staring at them for some time, he realized they were living things, like wispy trees with brightly colored vines tangled throughout the canopy. Sunlight streamed down, and beneath his feet was something that looked like moss or grass except turquoise in color, and as he took a step, the place where he had been turned momentarily yellow before it sprang up again and retook its color.

"It's beautiful," Isla said.

Dru stared around her. "How can there be this much living stuff just, you know, *everywhere*? Is this whole place like this?"

Ignatio grinned, and shook, and eir scales vanished back into fur. A many-winged thing fluttered down from the canopy to sit upon eir head. "Many different sorts of things on Ijto," ey said. "The Ijt come from here, though only a few have traveled as far as Earthspace. Fragile, yes, but fierce. If we had more of time, I would show you the yiyo forests, but we do not."

"Maybe on our way back," Fergus said. Since he'd stepped out through the doorway there, he could feel the fragments' restless stirring growing more demanding, urgent, and though he stood upright and straight, his body still felt oddly twisted, being pulled into another shape somewhere outside of his physical self. It was hard not to look ahead and imagine something chewing its way through space toward them. "Not much time at all. Where do we go?"

Ignatio led them through the garden—it could hardly be called much else—to where a door stood, a gold-framed thing that seemed somehow dead in the center, like there was a thin veneer of true nothingness sandwiched between layers of air.

Fergus set down his things and stared at the void, feeling everything around it creeping across his senses, roiling up the bees in his gut, trying to find some sort of harmony together. And always, there were the Vraet on the other side, except now it was as if he could feel them crawling on his skin, under it, seeking release. "I think we have to do this fast," he said.

He crouched down on his heels and one by one pulled the fragments out of their bag. Putting them together was almost too easy, as if they fell from his fingers into just the right orientation, the right place, to seamlessly connect. His whole body felt electrified, except instead of coming from his gift, it was via the doorkey that saw him as part of itself.

No one else spoke. Or maybe he was just humming too loudly now to hear them.

When it was together and in his hands, he stood up quickly. Now that it had finally become whole, it had loosened some of its grip on him but not let fully go, as if it still regarded him as a part of it but no longer necessary.

The doorkey was terribly beautiful, and so hard to look at, so clearly inhabiting space in a way that was beyond Fergus's comprehension. The etchings seemed to flow now across the surface, all signs that it had once been broken gone. It knew its purpose and was eager for it; it wanted to connect, to open, and whatever was on the other side was immaterial.

The space between the arches had also come alive again, no longer nothing but now the gray wall interface of the previous doors. All he had to do now was throw the reconstituted key through its own doorway and let it collapse on itself, leaving the connection forever trapped in its own recursion.

Everyone around him was waiting, watching, holding their breaths. Just this left, and then he was done, it was over. He could go back home, or go anywhere, and everyone would be safe. Gavin. Zacker. Jesika and Julia. Akio's grandmother. Duff and his sheep. Dr. Orchard and Commander Quinn. His Lake Tahoe dive instructor. Even Kyle and Mitch and Evan Derecho himself, even if they didn't really deserve it, even if no one else would ever know what he did for them.

He would know, though. Through the interface he could hear the Vraet, crackle and crunch and hunger, and from the faces of the others, they could hear it too now.

"Is that them? The scavengers?" Isla asked, and shuddered.

"Yes," Fergus said. He was sick of hearing them, in the back of his mind, in his dreams, in waking moments when he was not vigilant about his connections.

He braced himself, took a deep breath, and hurled the doorkey through the interface with all his strength.

Or he tried. The moment the doorkey left his hands, the interface changed, turned from gray back to the static void it had been when they arrived, and the doorkey bounced off it and fell to the flagstones with a thunderous boom. Cracks spread out across the stone, and the flying things above them took off, crying alarm.

Fergus picked the doorkey up, turned it in his hands, but there was no damage to it he could see, and it was just as noisy as ever. He threw it again.

The results were the same.

This time, he picked it up and stepped closer to the reforming interface, and tried to pass the doorkey through by hand. The interface seemed to be reacting as much to the doorkey as to his own connection to it. There was a tipping point, a shift in the pressure and the signal, where he knew if he pressed it just slightly more, both he and it would go. And if he did not, neither would.

"Shit," he said, and backed away to think. Everyone was still watching him, waiting for him to finish this.

"What's wrong?" Isla asked.

"I think . . ." Fergus said, and hated what he was about to say. "I think I have to carry it through."

"What? You can't," Isla said. "The tunnel will collapse behind you. You'll be trapped forever, with those . . . things." She turned to Ignatio.

"I do not know a solution," Ignatio said. "I will think very fast."

"There's got to be a way," Isla said. "You can rest while we work on it. We've got food for a couple of days, and we could always go back for more if we need to."

Fergus slumped, the completed doorkey in his hands, the pressure building between him and it and the far door. *I didn't volunteer for this,* he thought. *It's not fair, and I can refuse to go if I want, right? No one would blame me.*

He couldn't live with himself, though, not at the cost of that choice. He needed to finish the job, and the Vraet were getting louder, closer, trying to force the tunnel through from their side.

"There isn't time," he said. "I don't want to die. I think I'm going to have to."

"You can't go. We'll figure something out."

"Isla . . ." Fergus started. He felt calm, now that he knew what needed to happen. "Maybe there isn't any other way."

"Fuck you," she said, and furiously wiped the beginnings of tears from her eyes with her arm. "What if I figure it out five minutes after you're gone? How will I live with that?"

"You'll *live*," he said. "I would give—*will* give, if it comes down to it—everything I have to keep you safe. I'd rather it be five minutes too late to save me than five minutes too late to save everything else." He laughed. "I don't know where on your map in Gavin's back room you'll put the pin to show where I've gone, but pick a place with a lot of sunshine and good food, okay? Somewhere that doesn't mind assholes like me. And no bugs, if possible."

"It's not funny!" she shouted. "Don't ye dare pretend this is a *game*!"

"No," he said. "Do you know how many times I've almost died, should have died, since that day I nearly drowned trying to save Da? More than I can count. And sometimes, when things were really bad, I wondered if any of them had been worth surviving, or if I should have just swum out a little farther after him that day," he said. Was he crying too? He didn't care. "I have no regrets for the time I've had. And I am glad I got back to Earth and met you. That's worth everything."

Isla blinked at him, trying to find words that wouldn't come.

Dru put a hand on his shoulder. "I'm coming with you," she said, and her expression was a perfect balance of pain and joy.

"No," he said.

"Yes," she countered. "You think you can stop me?"

"I can if I have to," Fergus said.

Dru looked back at Isla. "Your brother's advice to live is good, and if you need proof, look at how poorly he's taken it himself. Ever since Sentinel . . ." She paused, and it was as if she were summoning the courage for words she'd never dared speak before. "He blamed himself for what happened to me, and ran away into his own guilt. I ran from fear, and I've spent the last two decades terrified every moment, every day, like a coward."

"You're not. You're brave," Isla said.

Dru laughed, a sound Fergus had not heard in a very long time or expected to ever hear again. "Do you know what the very best cure is for being so afraid of dying that you can't bring yourself to live? Learning that you are dying anyway."

"Dru—" Fergus started.

She tapped her head. "Tumors. Not the kind they can fix. So, fuck it all, fuck the MCA and the Alliance and being afraid, I want to be a hero again, one last time before I die. What better way than to help save the solar system? So, I'm going, Fergus, and you'll have to kill me to stop me."

"Dru," Fergus said again.

"You have a problem with that?" she asked, her voice full of warning.

"With you dying? Hell, yes," he said. "But I guess I can't make that choice for you. I really missed you, and I'm sorry."

"I'm sorry too," she said. "We were so young."

"We were," he agreed. He embraced her, and they stood there with their arms wrapped around each other for a long, long moment, as long as they dared. He'd missed her friendship so much, the hurt almost as unfathomable as what lay ahead.

And yet, they had to go.

"If I run through the door, the connecting tunnel should collapse in on itself behind me as I go, following the doorkey, like being inside a sock turning itself inside out," Fergus said. "At the far end, at the Vraet's door, I need only carry the doorkey through to their side. Even if they open it again, it will only ever lead them to themselves."

"When the interdimensional tunnel fully forms between the two doors, the Vraet will be ready," Ignatio said. "They will cross their interface into the tunnel as well. You will have to fight through them to reach the far side."

Dru unzipped her bags and pulled out a small arsenal of

weapons. "Flamethrower, plasma cannon, and a pair of fully charged energy pistols," she said. "And a knife."

The knife she pulled out was almost more sword than knife, Fergus thought. "Can we breathe the air in there?" he asked Ignatio.

Ignatio wiggled eir legs. "For some of it? It should match the air from here, at least part of the way. I do not know for certain what the air mix, if there is any, will be from the Vraet side."

Fergus looked down at his exosuit, with its Wheel Collective patch on the back of the neck from his time in Cernee. "I don't want to wreck my suit," he said. "It's a one-way trip either way." He took it off and folded it carefully on the ground. He had his Drowned Lad T-shirt and shorts, his goggles and his best boots, and he could run a lot easier and faster unencumbered by the rest of it.

Isla was staring at him, biting her lip, and he walked over and gave her a hug. "Thank you," he said.

"For what?" she answered, bitterly.

"For being the family I needed. Tell Gav I love him, and if he makes a face at that, punch him for me. Please take care of Mister Feefs? Ignatio will get you both home safe."

"I will, yes, I will," Ignatio said.

"And you," Fergus said. "Remember me?"

"I will have your reflection in all my eyes, for all my days," Ignatio said. "Also nights."

"You ready?" Fergus asked Dru.

She had slung the flamethrower over one shoulder, the pistols at her side, and the plasma cannon in her arms. "I admit I'm very unclear on what it is we are going to do, but I'm ready to shoot anything that gets in our way."

"Good," Fergus said. He picked up the doorkey from where he'd set it down while taking his suit off, and spoke to it, sang its song until it forgot again he wasn't a part of it. The doorkey vibrated in happiness to be whole, and his bees vibrated with it, tied together, songs merged. He turned the doorkey over in his hands, and instead, the universe tilted around them, as if they were now the only fixed point.

Okay, he told himself, *don't do that as you're running. It'll make you dizzy.*

He looked back at the others. Ignatio looked worried. Isla was trying not to cry and failing. Dru's expression was serene, as if long patience were finally paying off. Somewhere, through the cube, he could feel an aching, terrible hunger.

"Time's up," he said, and stepped up to the wall of nothingness and held up the cube, singing its song instead of his own, letting himself become a part of it.

Dru stepped up next to him. "On the count of three," Fergus said. "Three, two, one . . . Run!"

Fergus clasped the cube to his chest, pulled his goggles down, and leapt through.

This tunnel did not feel substantially different from the previous one they'd walked through, and seemed content to just pull him forward like the others, but he needed as much speed as he could get. Trying to run, he found the tunnel shifted to allow him to do so, because suddenly he had traction, if no great sense of up or down, and Dru was right on his heels as he headed toward the dark dot where the tunnel vanished into invisibility ahead.

He glanced back once, to see the tunnel deforming, bending and twisting and shrinking, the locus of the collapse barely a few steps behind them, and decided not to look back ever again.

"This is weird shit," Dru said. "What's that ahead?"

Fergus zoomed in with his goggles as he ran, and could see something moving, like the end of the tunnel was breaking up in a flurry of static. The Vraet. "That's trouble," he said. "This is gonna hurt."

"Damn right it is," Dru said, and she pulled ahead of him, running fast as she unshouldered the flamethrower.

At first, it was like running into sleet, sharp, cold pinpricks against his skin becoming more and more frequent, until he watched a shining metallic gnat hit his goggles and stick, and a tiny hole opened and began rasping against the goggle glass, rapidly abrading it. Against his skin, the pinpricks now hurt, and he glanced down to see small tears in his clothing that were coated now with accumulating Vraet, and thin streaks of blood were already seeping from his arms and legs.

Dru gave an inarticulate shout of anger and fired up the flamethrower, and Fergus's goggle auto-dimmed in the sudden brilliant glare. Wherever the Vraet were directly caught in the bright hot jet, they were incinerated into tiny puffs of smoke, but the swarm quickly learned to dodge and divide, until suddenly the flame guttered and went out. Dru threw it down, where it came to rest half-lost in the invisible tunnel floor. "Clogged it," she shouted over her shoulder, her cheeks bloodied, as she clicked the safety off on the plasma cannon.

As Fergus, five paces behind her, leapt over the fallen flamethrower, the surface of it was already pitted and beginning to disintegrate, consumed from within. Then the collapsing tunnel reached it, and it fragmented further, turning to inert dust, and was carried forward as the end of the tunnel followed behind them, chasing its doorkey.

Shit, I looked again, he thought.

"Okay, don't stop, and don't fall behind me," Fergus called out to Dru, having to yell to be heard over the noise of the swarm. "And don't look back. Trust me on that."

The Vraet had become a sandstorm, a stinging, howling

blizzard aimed right into their faces, and he could no longer see much past them. It felt as if they were running standing still, except he could feel the other end of the tunnel, the other door-key, slowly getting closer.

Dru powered up the cannon, and the brilliance of the plasma as it danced and scattered ahead of her was beautiful as it blazed a path through the chittering metallic hail bearing down on them.

One of Fergus's boots slipped, and he realized he was now running through Dru's blood, and losing a fair bit of his own. The swarm grew so thick around them that for a moment, he couldn't see Dru or the cannon light until he stumbled into her on the floor. She was crouching over with her face in her blood-ied hands, covered in gnawing, biting Vraet. The cannon was dead and useless on the floor behind her.

"No," he said, as his own face and body were slowly cut by a thousand tiny mouths, and his fear for himself turned instead to rage that, after everything, this was not the end Dru deserved.

He stuck the doorkey under one armpit and bent down to lift Dru, getting an arm around her and helping her to her feet. "Hold on," he said, trying to wipe Vraet off her as best he could, only to see them instantly replaced by more as the swarm blasted around them. "We're not done yet. Remember Nereidum Montes and freezing our asses? We won."

"We did," she said. Her voice shook. "I don't think my pistols will help now."

"I got this," he said, and he did. He let the Asiig bees down in his gut loose, feeding them on his own anger, free of any in-hibition or restraint. A whirling halo of electricity began to form around them like the one that had struck down Pace, under the ice of Enceladus, except this time, instead of it being a wild thing out of his control, he was wild with it, willingly along for the ride.

The swarm of Vraet broke apart again, flowing around them as he pushed forward, and they were either caught by the collapsing tunnel or forced to fall in behind him, trying to reach him but dying by the hundreds, thousands, every time they got too close. But still they tried, and each tiny zap was another drain on his energy, and he was getting tired and so, so thirsty. He and Dru were both covered in blood, their clothes in tatters, their skin gouged and pitted and, in places, chewed down deep into the flesh, and the swarm seemed an endless tide flowing into the tunnel, packing it ever more tightly, making it harder and harder to move forward.

He hurt so much but didn't dare let himself acknowledge it. He wasn't sure Dru was still conscious, but he refused to let her go. He was moving on adrenaline and fury and grief, and they would keep him a little longer.

"How . . ." he heard her say, and leaned his head close to hers to hear better. "How are you doing that?"

"Long story. Aliens," he said. "I'll tell you about it if we get out of here, I promise."

"Okay," she said. "How many toes? For Sentinel? I've forgotten."

"Three," he said.

"Told you to wear better socks," she said.

"I've always been terrible at listening to good advice," he said. He couldn't even see now, between the swarm thickening like cement in his path and the deep scratches and pitting on his goggles, so he closed his eyes and felt the energies of the tunnel, despairing for how much was left ahead.

To his surprise, they were close. "We can make it," he said.

"Leave me. You can go faster without me."

"Not a chance," he said, holding her to himself more tightly. He was so tired, and it would be so easy to just stop there and die with her, but he refused to quit. The job wasn't *done*. "We're heroes, right? You and I."

"We were stupid," she said.

He laughed. "And this isn't? Come on! Fight with me! Another ten meters. Help me!"

She got her feet under her more solidly, and clinging together, they shoved their way forward. His energy was faltering, and more and more of the scavengers began to get through, taking another little chunk from his flesh before he swatted them away or fried them right on his ravaged skin, until at last they were at the end, standing in the face of a tidal wave of Vraet pouring into the tunnel like a hailstorm of ice knives driven straight into their faces.

Fergus let go of Dru, and she slumped against him but did not fall. Taking out the doorkey from his armpit, the only thing undamaged they had left, he whispered to it, sang it their song, then shoved it with both hands into the maelstrom, crying out as his fingers were shredded and cut down to the bone. Just as he could not push any farther, it was as if the cube was pulled forward on its own, out of his hands, and all of a sudden, the entrance was gone, and the tunnel was collapsing now from both ends, with him and Dru in the center.

Trying not to cry, nor to look at what was left of either of them, he wrapped himself around Dru, sheltering her what little he could in his arms, his heart breaking that this was all he could do for her, so little at the end. He let the last of his Asiig energy go, one fantastic final blast that incinerated the Vraet still trapped with them, swirling like dark snow around and over them, the accumulated debris of everything destroyed in the tunnel pressing in, suffocating and crushing. They were being buried alive by the corpses of the scavengers.

At least I did it, Fergus thought. *I did one thing right, at last.*

And then his bees gave one more cry, engulfing them both in a ball of energy, singing the lost doorkey song as it merged with the collapsing tunnel and became one.

When it gave out, they were floating in space, and a large black triangle was waiting for them.

Chapter 23

———◆———

Fergus awoke standing upright, as best as he could determine, given that he seemed oriented and stable with the familiar tug of gravity beneath his feet, though he felt no solid surface there. The space around him was bathed in yellow light that seemed to end, like a box, about three meters above and to all sides. Somewhere in the crisp darkness beyond he could hear crickets.

He had been in this place before, though his memories of it were muddled, ill-defined. "Hey!" he called out, and there was no echo at all.

It was not a surprise when the Asiig agent walked into the light, only that he did it perpendicular to Fergus's own orientation, as if the wall was his floor.

"Ah," the agent said, and stopped once he was fully in the light. "Here we are again."

Fergus looked down at his bare arms, whole again but his skin crisscrossed with a dense web of fine, almost silvery lines. It felt like a dream. "Where's Dru?" he asked.

"Elsewhere," the agent said. "Alive, if that's your simplistic human concern. You did make quite a mess of yourselves, you know."

Fergus held out his hands, palms up. "Yeah, my bad," he said. "How did you do that?"

"Do what?"

"Get us out of the collapsing tunnel," Fergus said.

"Ah!" the agent said. "Now, that was *interesting*."

There was movement, on the fringes of the shadows, and three Asiig moved silently into view, none along the same plane in space. They were tall and shining black, with a jointed, armored carapace under which a many-eyed body hung, walking on six multi-jointed legs and a long, forked tail. The three Asiig spoke, a sound like dueling crickets, and the agent listened patiently for several minutes as Fergus stared and found the fear that had been there, last time, was now resignation. Relief? Something less unsettling.

"There is consensus that no one is sure how you ejected yourself from the multidimensional tunnel," the agent said.

"But surely, you must now how it works, this thing you stuck inside me," Fergus said, gesturing angrily toward his abdomen where the Dr. Diagnosis booth, a lifetime ago, had shown him their handiwork.

His bees were barely awake, but he could feel them again, deep inside, and he could feel the tenuous touch of signal, like golden threads, stretching between him and the three Asiig, as if the thing in him wasn't so much a thing the Asiig made as a part of the Asiig themselves.

"There is no you and it. There is only you," the agent said, interrupting whatever uncomfortable realization he felt he was on the verge of. "If we had given you an extra finger on your hand, and you learned to stick that finger out at me, would you believe that the finger was rude on its own, despite having become your flesh and blood and will?"

"So, you're saying I did it myself?"

"To put it in your limited vernacular: duh, yes," the agent said. "We were all very surprised."

"Then how did you know to pick us up or where?"

The agent smiled and reached out, and dropped the tiny red

capsule in Fergus's hand that he had first given him on the Pan-African train. He remembered it now, that he'd put in his pocket without quite understanding why he would, and every time he'd changed clothes, he'd transferred it to a new pocket, always with him, and despite his perfect memory, he had not remembered doing any of that until this very instant.

"We were near Ijto, since we knew the doorkey had come from there," the agent said. "When you returned to normal space, we were able to locate you instantly. Perhaps next time, you should aim for appearing inside a ship, though. Oh, the work it took to repair you!"

"And these scars?"

The agent shrugged.

Around him, the Asiig chittered and chirped, to each other and back and forth with the agent, little golden threads in his mind's eye everywhere. "Uh," Fergus said, after it had gone on for a while and he was starting to feel forgotten. "Excuse me?"

"Yes?" the agent asked.

"What happens next?"

"We were just discussing that," the agent said, almost a chastisement. "Many things are in flux, and you have left a significant wake of activity behind you."

"Sorry if I've inconvenienced you," Fergus said, feeling not sorry at all.

"Oh, no, not at all!" the agent said, as if there had been no sarcasm in Fergus's words. "Chaos is a delight. Without it, nothing new would ever be born, or learnt, or dreamt. But it must be *considered*. Not by you, I mean; it's all way over your head."

"Can you at least tell me if my friends are okay?" he asked.

"They have just been intercepted leaving Neptune's atmosphere," the agent said. "There were several Earth ships waiting for them. Your Alliance, as you might have anticipated, feels it has some urgent concerns."

"Shit," Fergus said. "Shit, shit. None of this is their fault."

More chirping, and then the agent sighed. "Very well," he said, and snapped his fingers. A circle appeared above him and spread, resolving into a view of stars, and then suddenly, it was all white like a flash, and when it resolved again the stars were in different places. In front of them were Ignatio's tiny flyer and the Alliance ships *August Moon* and *Blue Ivory*. *August Moon*, where *Whiro* had planted their mug full of evidence against DM what felt like months before, had a boarding tube fastened to Ignatio's ship.

The circular view moved, slid down until it crossed under Fergus's feet, and he watched as they glided above the two ships and stopped, warning lights flashing all over *August Moon's* exterior.

"Oooh, they are threatening to shoot us," the agent said. "How exciting. Do you wish to speak with your sister?"

"Yes," Fergus said. "How do I—"

Before he'd finished, the agent had reached out and placed a hand flat on his chest, and then they were both standing in the doorway to the bridge of Ignatio's ship, directly behind Isla, just in time to see the captain of the *August Moon,* who was standing beside Ignatio, drop the World's Best Boss mug and let it shatter across the floor.

The captain, to her credit, pulled her shit together fast. "MacInnis, I presume," she said. "You've brought company."

Isla turned around and shrieked.

"Taking that as confirmation, you're under arrest," the captain said. Beside her, a too-young, too-scared-looking private finally managed to fumble out his pistol. "Both of you, until that scary-ass ship of yours that came out of nowhere backs off and I get some explanations for just who the fuck that is up there."

The Asiig agent laughed. "Yes, sorry, let me introduce myself," he said, and stepped toward the captain, holding out his hand as if to shake and introduce himself. The moment she touched his hand, she froze in place, unmoving. The private froze a half-second later, and Fergus felt like there was something there he'd almost seen, something with the energies in the room, but it was gone again before he could pin the sensation down.

The agent looked at Fergus. "All existence, all perception, is just electrical signals and messy chemistry, from atoms to the universe itself. But as you can see, your friends are good. Happier?"

"You're *alive*," Isla said. "How the hell are ye alive? And what are ye wearing?"

Fergus glanced down, for the first time realizing he could have been wearing nothing, to find a brightly shining facsimile of his shirt and shorts, except when he poked the fabric, it was gummy, strangely staticky. "I have no idea," he said. "About anything."

"And who is this guy?" she asked, pointing at the agent. "Where the hell did ye come from? That ship—" Her voice trailed off as there was the sound of crickets and movement behind Fergus. It wasn't just him and the agent who had come over. The Asiig moved ponderously onto the bridge, and Isla turned pale and backed up.

"Dru?" Ignatio asked Fergus quietly.

"She's still on board their ship," Fergus said.

The Asiig chirped, and to Fergus's surprise, Ignatio chirped back. Even the agent seemed impressed. Then the agent pointed suddenly at Isla. "You," he said. "What are you thinking, right now?"

Isla blinked. "That I want to go home," she said. "That I thought I'd lost my brother and my heart hurts so much, and it's long past time he came home too."

"And you?" the agent asked Ignatio.

"That Fergus can't go home again," ey said, sadly. Ey waved a leg toward the captain, whose face was frozen in the very first moments of extreme irritation. "All of the Alliance is hunting for you. *Whiro* says they are at the Shipyard, and Mars, and just about everywhere in between. It is all very dangerous now. They will hunt for you everywhere you have ever been, everywhere you have friends, and they will not give up for years, if ever."

Evan Derecho would be hunting him too, Fergus knew, and not ever stop. "You're right," he said. "I have to leave."

"Don't go alone," Isla said, and bent down and picked up something from one of the helm seats, and held it up.

His cat yowled, all four of his legs flailing in indignation.

"Mister Feefs!" Fergus said, surprised by how much joy he felt in seeing his cat. He held out his hands, and Isla deposited the squirming ball of fur into his arms, where he promptly dug his claws through Fergus's weird shirt into his chest and refused to let go.

"If the Vraet had come through the door and destroyed your solar system, it would have endangered much that we would not have liked to lose," the agent said, translating the chirps and clicks from the Asiig beside him. "We are grateful that catastrophe has been averted so we can continue our work. We will take you somewhere you wish to go, but we must go now."

"First, Dru—" Fergus said.

"Dru will take a very long time to heal, and she cannot do that in her old life," the agent said. "She has been offered a choice, and made it. It is not your concern any longer. Decide."

"I know where I want to go," Fergus said.

"Where?" Isla asked.

"He can't tell us," Ignatio said. "You must know this."

The Asiig made more sounds, and the agent rolled his eyes. "Can we have the captain?" he asked.

"Uh, no?" Ignatio said. "It would make a lot of trouble."

"That's what I thought, but I promised I'd ask," he said. "Pity. Time to go."

"I love you," Fergus said. "Both of you. I'll be back, as soon as—"

The agent touched his shoulder, and in that last split second before the ship around him vanished, he saw the captain shudder back to life in slow motion, eyes widening as the Asiig beside them stood up tall on its legs. Isla was just reaching out toward him, to pull him back.

Then they were gone.

Acknowledgments

You are in a vast, lightless maze. When you stepped in, it seemed a small hole in the ground at most, a quick, unexpected adventure, something scary and dangerous but finite, if you just kept your wits about you for a little while. Wear a mask, wash your hands, and somewhere at the end of the maze you'll be rewarded with toilet paper again.

Instead, well. 2020.

There is a disjointedness in time to the start of a novel's life. The ideas for this book have been rolling around in my head since I was finishing up the first Finder book several years ago, got some experimental pokes during lulls in the drafting and editing of the second book, and only really got my full time and attention in the second half of 2019. Briefly full, anyway. In mid-November I was fortunate enough to be invited as a guest to the 5th International SF Conference in Chengdu, China. It was a whirlwind of a trip, almost deliriously unreal, to a country I never thought I'd see in my lifetime. It was a life-changing experience, and I met many wonderful people both local and from around the world. It was such an extraordinary affirmation that the wider we open the doors of our fannish communities, the more diverse and welcoming our genre, the stronger and brighter it becomes. And on the 14 1/2 hour first leg of the flight home, with some passenger two rows behind me coughing the whole time, I was exhausted and exhilarated and homesick and desperately keen to go back again, go more places, see the world. 2020, I thought, I am going to TRAVEL.

And yeah, you know. Got home, felt sick, weird respiratory symptoms that didn't want to go away, off and on ill through the first few months of 2020. Never got a diagnosis, so who really knows? And then in February, the neighborhood bear made a hole in my fence that I didn't spot, and my dogs got out and got lost in the woods. One was found by a hiker a week later, but the other was hit and killed by a car. By the time the pandemic started in earnest here in the US, I was already several twists and turns into that lightless maze. I gathered my kids back at home, safe and sound and bored and obstreperous, and hunkered down to finish *The Scavenger Door*.

And for all of us, the maze just kept getting deeper, longer, twistier. We knew we were losing people in there, did our best to hold hands and help along those faltering, knowing at some point we'd be the one reaching out our own hand hoping somebody would take it and pull. We worried about those we knew were out of our reach, trapped in some dead end because the 'system' failed them, or because someone they trusted led and abandoned them there. And slowly, slowly, slowly, for some but not all, there was light ahead.

As I write this, it's just on the cusp of spring in 2021. My first crocus just flowered. Many things have changed, and we can feel the warmth of hope on our faces as we alternately stumble and run toward an apparent exit, carrying with us no small share of grief and trauma and uncertainty. When you are reading this, it's going to be late summer 2021 at the earliest, possibly years past that, and what will the perspective on this time be with such hindsight? It's very odd and disconcerting to write with love about the distant future and yet find the idea of five months from now inconceivably strange and unknowable. But maybe that's why I do what I do, so that I can say: hey, we can get to the future together, and no matter what it looks like there will be people that care, and people who watch out for each other just because it's the right thing to do, even if they're sweary people with terrible attitudes.

But anyway. This book exists because of so very many people. My agent, Joshua Bilmes, and the rest of his team at JABberwocky Literary Agency continue to be absolutely fantastic to work with, and none of this series could or would have happened without them. Thanks also to my editor, Katie Hoffman, and the whole lovely team at DAW for their support and hard work in such strange and difficult times. And once again I have a truly gorgeous cover by Kekai Kotaki, who as usual got right to the heart of my vision for this book. Also, I wish to thank Richard Shealy, who is precisely the sort of friendly but exacting copy editor every author needs.

Thanks also are due to my kids, who have now been largely trapped in the house with me for a year and who still can't figure out how to stack pots when putting them away, and have as always been both a great support and a constant source of humility, entertainment, and exhaustion. Of my friends—and you know, I'm a serious introvert with almost crippling social anxiety, so the extroverts have to be really hurting out there—I miss them all so much, but they still found time and energy to give me support and critical feedback, particularly my usual crew of awesome first readers, Jonathan Turner, Robin Holly, and Laurie Vadeboncoeur. I also want to thank John Wiswell and Sydney Drinkwater for vetting some representation for me, Steven Brewer for assistance with Esperanto, and I am very especially grateful to Sean, Saya, and Miya Donovan for helping me with my very rusty 日本語. As always, I hope I got everything right, and if not, the fault lies entirely with me. I do my best, always mindful that it is possible to do better, and I will keep striving for that.

And as always a shout out to the communities, real and online, that keep me company, from the decades-long love and support of the September Moms to the writers, artists, and poets of Absolute Write, Viable Paradise, Twitter, Slack, and elseweb, and to my fellow CATS who keep my days interesting and don't mind my odd, often chaotic, dual-career life. Last, I want to mention the very kind emails and letters from strangers who felt strongly enough about my work to write me, and remind me that I have the miraculous and somewhat mindboggling privilege of *readers*. Thank you, one and all.

Whatever future you find yourself reading this in, be well.

—Suzanne